THE BEST OF
O. HENRY

INDIALOG PUBLICATIONS PVT. LTD.

THE BEST OF
O. HENRY

Selected Short Stories

INDIALOG PUBLICATIONS PVT. LTD.

Published in November 2003

Indialog Publications Pvt. Ltd.
O - 22, Lajpat Nagar II
New Delhi - 110024
Telefax: 91-11-29830504/29835221
www.indialog.co.in

10 9 8 7 6

Printed at Brijbasi Art Press Ltd.

ISBN 81-87981-17-2

CONTENTS

A BIRD OF BAGDAD   7

A LITTLE LOCAL COLOR   14

A NEWSPAPER STORY   19

A TECHNICAL ERROR   23

AFTER TWENTY YEARS   29

AN UNFINISHED STORY   32

BESTSELLER   38

BLIND MAN'S HOLIDAY   48

CALLOWAY'S CODE   65

CUPID À LA CARTE   72

GIRL   87

MEMOIRS OF A YELLOW DOG   92

NEMESIS AND THE CANDYMAN   97

NO STORY   102

PSYCHE AND THE PSKYSCRAPER   111

SCHOOLS AND SCHOOLS   117

THE ADVENTURES OF SHAMROCK JOLNES   127

THE COP AND THE ANTHEM   132

THE DETECTIVE DETECTOR   138

THE DIAMOND OF KALI   143

THE DUEL   149

THE FURNISHED ROOM   154

THE GIFT OF THE MAGI   160

THE HANDBOOK OF HYMEN   165

THE HYPOTHESIS OF FAILURE   175

THE LAST LEAF   186

THE MARRY MONTH OF MAY   192

THE POET AND THE PEASANT   197

THE MOMENT OF VICTORY   203

THE PRINCESS AND THE PUMA   214

THE SKYLIGHT ROOM   220

THE SLEUTHS   226

THE SNOW MAN   232

THE SPARROWS IN MADISON SQUARE   246

THE WHIRLIGIG OF LIFE   250

TICTOCQ: THE GREAT FRENCH DETECTIVE, IN AUSTIN   256

TO HIM WHO WAITS   263

A BIRD OF BAGDAD

WITHOUT A DOUBT much of the spirit and genius of the Caliph Harun Al Rashid descended to the Margrave August Michael von Paulsen Quigg.

Quigg's restaurant is in Fourth Avenue – that street that the city seems to have forgotten in its growth. Fourth Avenue – born and bred in the Bowery – staggers northward full of good resolutions.

Where it crosses Fourteenth Street it struts for a brief moment proudly in the glare of the museums and cheap theatres. It may yet become a fit mate for its high-born sister boulevard to the west, or its roaring, polyglot, broad-waisted cousin to the east. It passes Union Square; and here the hoofs of the dray horses seem to thunder in unison, recalling the tread of marching hosts – Hooray! But now come the silent and terrible mountains – buildings square as forts, high as the clouds, shutting out the sky, where thousands of slaves bend over desks all day. On the ground floors are only little fruit shops and laundries and book shops, where you see copies of "Littell's Living Age" and G. W. M. Reynold's novels in the windows. And next – poor Fourth Avenue! – the street glides into a mediaeval solitude. On each side are shops devoted to "Antiques."

Let us say it is night. Men in rusty armor stand in the windows and menace the hurrying cars with raised, rusty iron gauntlets. Hauberks and helms, blunderbusses, Cromwellian breastplates, matchlocks, creeses, and the swords and daggers of an army of dead-and-gone gallants gleam dully in the ghostly light. Here and there from a corner saloon (lit with Jack-o'-lanterns or phosphorus), stagger forth shuddering, home-bound citizens, nerved by the tankards within to their fearsome journey adown that Eldrich Avenue lined with the bloodstained weapons of the fighting dead. What street could live inclosed by these mortuary relics, and trod by these spectral citizens in whose sunken hearts scarce one good whoop or tra-la-la remained?

Not Fourth Avenue. Not after the tinsel but enlivening glories of the Little Rialto – not after the echoing drum-beats of Union Square. There need be no tears, ladies and gentlemen; 'tis but the suicide of a street. With a shriek and a crash Fourth Avenue dives headlong into the tunnel at Thirty-fourth and is never seen again.

Near the sad scene of the thoroughfare's dissolution stood the modest restaurant of Quigg. It stands there yet if you care to view its crumbling red-brick front, its show window heaped with oranges, tomatoes, layer cakes, pies, canned asparagus – its papier-mache lobster and two Maltese kittens asleep on a bunch of lettuce – if you care to sit at one of the little tables upon whose cloth has been traced in the yellowest of coffee stains the trail of the Japanese advance – to sit there with one eye on your umbrella and the other upon the bogus bottle from which you drop the counterfeit sauce foisted upon us by the cursed charlatan who assumes to be our dear old lord and friend, the "Nobleman in India."

Quigg's title came through his mother. One of her ancestors was a Margravine of Saxony. His father was a Tammany brave. On account of the dilution of his heredity he found that he could neither become a reigning potentate nor get a job in the City Hall. So he opened a restaurant. He was a man full of thought and reading. The business gave him a living, though he gave it little attention. One side of his house bequeathed to him a poetic and romantic adventure. The other gave him the restless spirit that made him seek adventure. By day he was Quigg, the restauranteur. By night he was the Margrave – the Caliph – the Prince of Bohemia – going about the city in search of the odd, the mysterious, the inexplicable, the recondite.

One night at 9, at which hour the restaurant closed, Quigg set forth upon his quest. There was a mingling of the foreign, the military and the artistic in his appearance as he buttoned his coat high up under his short-trimmed brown and gray beard and turned westward toward the more central life conduits of the city. In his pocket he had stored an assortment of cards, written upon, without which he never stirred out of doors. Each of those cards was good at his own restaurant for its face value. Some called simply for a bowl of soup or sandwiches and coffee; others entitled their bearer to one, two, three or more days of full meals; a few were for single regular meals; a very few were, in effect, meal tickets good for a week.

Of riches and power Margrave Quigg had none; but he had a Caliph's heart – it may be forgiven him if his head fell short of the measure of Harun Al Rashid's. Perhaps some of the gold pieces in Bagdad had put less warmth and hope into the complainants among the bazaars than had Quigg's beef stew among the fishermen and one-eyed calenders of Manhattan.

Continuing his progress in search of romance to divert him, or of distress that he might aid, Quigg became aware of a fast-gathering crowd that whooped and fought and eddied at a corner of Broadway and the crosstown street that he was traversing. Hurrying to the spot he beheld a young man of an exceedingly melancholy and preoccupied demeanor engaged in the pastime of casting silver money from his pockets in the middle of the street. With each motion of the generous one's hand the crowd huddled upon the falling largesse with yells of joy. Traffic was suspended. A policeman in the center of the mob stooped often to the ground as he urged the blockaders to move on.

The Margrave saw at a glance that here was food for his hunger after knowledge concerning abnormal working of the human heart. He made his way swiftly to the young man's side and took his arm. "Come with me at once," he said, in the low but commanding voice that his waiters had learned to fear.

"Pinched," remarked the young man, looking up at him with expressionless eyes. "Pinched by a painless dentist. Take me away, flatty, and give me gas. Some lay eggs and some lay none. When is a hen?"

Still deeply seized by some inward grief, but tractable, he allowed Quigg to lead him away and down the street to a little park.

There, seated on a bench, he upon whom a corner of the great Caliph's mantle has descended, spake with kindness and discretion, seeking to know what evil had come upon the other, disturbing his soul and driving him to such ill-considered and ruinous waste of his substance and stores.

"I was doing the Monte Cristo act as adapted by Pompton, N. J., wasn't I ?" asked the young man.

"You were throwing small coins into the street for the people to scramble after," said the Margrave.

"That's it. You buy all the beer you can hold, and then you throw chicken feed to – Oh, curse that word chicken, and hens, feathers, roosters, eggs, and everything connected with it!"

"Young sir," said the Margrave kindly, but with dignity, "though I do not ask your confidence, I invite it. I know the world and I know humanity. Man is my study, though I do not eye him as the scientist eyes a beetle or as the philanthropist gazes at the objects of his bounty – through a veil of theory and ignorance. It is my pleasure and distraction to interest myself in the peculiar and complicated misfortunes that life in a great city visits upon my fellow-men. You may be familiar with the history of that glorious and immortal ruler, the Caliph Harun Al Rashid, whose wise and beneficent excursions among his people in the city of Bagdad secured him the privilege of relieving so much of their distress. In my humble way I walk in his footsteps. I seek for romance and adventure in city streets – not in ruined castles or in crumbling palaces. To me the greatest marvels of magic are those that take place in men's hearts when acted upon by the furious and diverse forces of a crowded population. In your strange behavior this evening I fancy a story lurks. I read in your act something deeper than the wanton wastefulness of a spendthrift. I observe in your countenance the certain traces of consuming grief or despair. I repeat – I invite your confidence. I am not without some power to alleviate and advise. Will you not trust me?"

"Gee, how you talk!" exclaimed the young man, a gleam of admiration supplanting for a moment the dull sadness of his eyes. "You've got the Astor Library skinned to a synopsis of preceding chapters. I mind that old Turk you speak of. I read 'The Arabian Nights' when I was a kid. He was a kind of Bill Devery and Charlie Schwab rolled into one. But, say, you might wave enchanted dishrags and make copper bottles smoke up coon giants all night without ever touching me. My case won't yield to that kind of treatment."

"If I could hear your story," said the Margrave, with his lofty, serious smile.

"I'll spiel it in about nine words," said the young man, with a deep sigh, "but I don't think you can help me any. Unless you're a peach at guessing it's back to the Bosphorous for you on your magic linoleum."

THE STORY OF THE YOUNG MAN
AND THE HARNESS MAKER'S RIDDLE

"I work in Hildebrant's saddle and harness shop down in Grant Street. I've worked there five years. I get $18 a week. That's enough to marry on, ain't it? Well, I'm not going to get married. Old Hildebrant is one of these funny Dutchmen – you know the kind – always getting off bum jokes. He's got about a million riddles and things that he faked from Rogers Brothers' great-grandfather. Bill Watson works there, too. Me and Bill have to stand for them chestnuts day after day.

Why do we do it? Well, jobs ain't to be picked off every Anheuser bush – And then there's Laura.

"What? The old man's daughter. Comes in the shop every day. About nineteen, and the picture of the blonde that sits on the palisades of the Rhine and charms the clam-diggers into the surf. Hair the color of straw matting, and eyes as black and shiny as the best harness blacking – think of that!"

"Me? well, it's either me or Bill Watson. She treats us both equal. Bill is all to the psychopathic about her; and me? – well, you saw me plating the roadbed of the Great Maroon Way with silver tonight. That was on account of Laura. I was spiflicated, Your Highness, and I wot not of what I wouldst."

"How? Why, old Hildebrandt say to me and Bill this afternoon: 'Boys, one riddle have I for you gehabt haben. A young man who cannot riddles antworten, he is not so good by business for ein family to provide – is not that – hein?' And he hands us a riddle – a conundrum, some call it – and he chuckles interiorly and gives both of us till tomorrow morning to work out the answer to it. And he says whichever of us guesses the repartee end of it goes to his house o' Wednesday night to his daughter's birthday party. And it means Laura for whichever of us goes, for she's naturally aching for a husband, and it's either me or Bill Watson, for old Hildebrant likes us both, and wants her to marry somebody that'll carry on the business after he's stitched his last pair of traces."

"The riddle? Why, it was this: 'What kind of a hen lays the longest?' Think of that! What kind of a hen lays the longest? Ain't it like a Dutchman to risk a man's happiness on a fool proposition like that? Now, what's the use? What I don't know about hens would fill several incubators. You say you're giving imitations of the old Arab guy that gave away – libraries in Bagdad. Well, now, can you whistle up a fairy that'll solve this hen query, or not?"

When the young man ceased the Margrave arose and paced to and fro by the park bench for several minutes. Finally he sat again, and said, in grave and impressive tones:

"I must confess, sir, that during the eight years that I have spent in search of adventure and in relieving distress I have never encountered a more interesting or a more perplexing case. I fear that I have overlooked hens in my researches and observations. As to their habits, their times and manner of laying, their many varieties and cross-breedings, their span of life, their –"

"Oh, don't make an Ibsen drama of it!" interrupted the young man, flippantly. "Riddles – especially old Hildebrant's riddles – don't have to be worked out seriously. They are light themes such as Sim Ford and Harry Thurston Peck like to handle. But, somehow, I can't strike just the answer. Bill Watson may, and he may not. To-morrow will tell. Well, Your Majesty, I'm glad anyhow that you butted in and whiled the time away. I guess Mr. Al Rashid himself would have bounced back if one of his constituents had conducted him up against this riddle. I'll say good night. Peace fo' yours, and what-you-may-call-its of Allah."

The Margrave, still with a gloomy air, held out his hand. "I cannot exppress my regret," he said, sadly. "Never before have I found myself unable to assist in some way. 'What kind of a hen lays the longest?' It is a baffling problem. There is a hen, I believe, called the Plymouth Rock that –"

"Cut it out," said the young man. "The Caliph trade is a mighty serious one. I don't suppose you'd even see anything funny in a preacher's defense of John D. Rockefeller. Well, good night, Your Nibs."

From habit the Margrave began to fumble in his pockets. He drew forth a card and handed it to the young man.

"Do me the favor to accept this, anyhow," he said. "The time may come when it might be of use to you."

"Thanks!" said the young man, pocketing it carelessly. "My name is Simmons."

***

Shame to him who would hint that the reader's interest shall altogether pursue the Margrave August Michael von Paulsen Quigg. I am indeed astray if my hand fail in keeping the way where my peruser's heart would follow. Then let us, on the morrow, peep quickly in at the door of Hildebrant, harness maker. Hildebrant's 200 pounds reposed on a bench, silverbuckling a raw leather martingale.

Bill Watson came in first.

"Vell," said Hildebrant, shaking all over with the vile conceit of the joke-maker, "haf you guessed him? 'Vat kind of a hen lays der longest?'"

"Er – why, I think so," said Bill, rubbing a servile chin. "I think so, Mr. Hildebrant – the one that lives the longest – Is that right?"

"Nein!" said Hildebrant, shaking his head violently. "You haf not guessed der answer."

Bill passed on and donned a bed-tick apron and bachelorhood.

In came the young man of the Arabian Night's fiasco – pale, melancholy, hopeless.

"Vell," said Hildebrant, "haf you guessed him? 'Vat kind of a hen lays der longest?'"

Simmons regarded him with dull savagery in his eye. Should he curse this mountain of pernicious humor – curse him and die? Why should – But there was Laura.

Dogged, speechless, he thrust his hands into his coat pockets and stood. His hand encountered the strange touch of the Margrave's card. He drew it out and looked at it, as men about to be hanged look at a crawling fly. There was written on it in Quigg's bold, round hand: "Good for one roast chicken to bearer."

Simmons looked up with a flashing eye.

"A dead one!" said he.

"Goot!" roared Hildebrant, rocking the table with giant glee. "Dot is right! You gome at mine house at 8 o'clock to der party."

A LITTLE LOCAL COLOR

I MENTIONED TO Rivington that I was in search of characteristic New York scenes and incidents – something typical, I told him, without necessarily having to spell the first syllable with an "i."

"Oh, for your writing business," said Rivington; "you couldn't have applied to a better shop. What I don't know about little old New York wouldn't make a sonnet to a sunbonnet. I'll put you right in the middle of so much local color that you won't know whether you are a magazine cover or in the erysipelas ward. When do you want to begin?"

Rivington is a young-man-about-town and a New Yorker by birth, preference and incommutability.

I told him that I would be glad to accept his escort and guardianship so that I might take notes of Manhattan's grand, gloomy and peculiar idiosyncrasies, and that the time of so doing would be at his own convenience.

"We'll begin this very evening," said Rivington, himself interested, like a good fellow. "Dine with me at seven, and then I'll steer you up against metropolitan phases so thick you'll have to have a kinetoscope to record 'em."

So I dined with Rivington pleasantly at his club, in Forty-eleventh street, and then we set forth in pursuit of the elusive tincture of affairs.

As we came out of the club there stood two men on the sidewalk near the steps in earnest conversation.

"And by what process of ratiocination," said one of them, "do you arrive at the conclusion that the division of society into producing and non-possessing classes predicates failure when compared with competitive systems that are monopolizing in tendency and result inimically to industrial evolution?"

"Oh, come off your perch!" said the other man, who wore glasses. "Your premises won't come out in the wash. You wind-jammers who apply bandy-legged theories to concrete categorical syllogisms send logical conclusions skally-bootin' into the infinitesimal ragbag. You can't pull my leg with an old sophism with whiskers on it. You quote Marx and Hyndman and Kautsky what are they? – shines! Tolstoi? – his garret is full of rats. I put it to you over the home-plate that the idea of a cooperative commonwealth and an abolishment of competitive systems simply takes the rag off the bush and gives me hyperesthesia of the roopteetoop! The skookum house for yours!"

I stopped a few yards away and took out my little notebook.

"Oh, come ahead," said Rivington, somewhat nervously; "you don't want to listen to that."

"Why man," I whispered, "this is just what I do want to hear. These slang types are among your city's most distinguishing features. Is this the Bowery variety? I really must hear more of it."

"If I follow you," said the man who had spoken first, "you do not believe it possible to reorganize society on the basis of common interest?"

"Shinny on your own side!" said the man with glasses. "You never heard any such music from my foghorn. What I said was that I did not believe it practicable just now. The guys with wads are not in the frame of mind to slack up on the mazuma, and the man with the portable tin banqueting canister isn't exactly ready to join the Bible class. You can bet your variegated socks that the situation is all spifflicated up from the Battery to breakfast! What the country needs is for some bully old bloke like Cobden or some wise guy like old Ben Franklin to sashay up to the front and biff the nigger's head with the baseball. Do you catch my smoke? What?"

Rivington pulled me by the arm impatiently.

"Please come on," he said. "Let's go see something. This isn't what you want."

"Indeed, it is," I said resisting. "This tough talk is the very stuff that counts. There is a picturesqueness about the speech of the lower order of people that is quite unique. Did you say that this is the Bowery variety of slang?"

"Oh, well," said Rivington, giving it up, "I'll tell you straight. That's one of our college professors talking. He ran down for a day or two at the club. It's a sort of fad with him lately to use slang in his conversation. He thinks it improves language. The man he is talking to is one of New York's famous social economists. Now will you come on? You can't use that, you know."

"No," I agreed; "I can't use that. Would you call that typical of New York?"

"Of course not," said Rivington, with a sigh of relief. "I'm glad you see the difference. But if you want to hear the real old tough Bowery slang I'll take you down where you'll get your fill of it."

"I would like it," I said; "that is, if it's the real thing. I've often read it in books, but I never heard it. Do you think it will be dangerous to go unprotected among those characters ?

"Oh, no," said Rivington; "not at this time of night. To tell the truth, I haven't been along the Bowery in a long time, but I know it as well as I do Broadway. We'll look up some of the typical Bowery boys and get them to talk. It'll be worth your while. They talk a peculiar dialect that you won't hear anywhere else on earth."

Rivington and I went east in a Forty-second street car and then south on the Third avenue line.

At Houston street we got off and walked.

"We are now on the famous Bowery," said Rivington; "the Bowery celebrated in song and story."

We passed block after block of "gents'" furnishing stores – the windows full of shirts with prices attached and cuffs inside. In other windows were neckties and no shirts. People walked up and down the sidewalks.

"In some ways," said I, "this reminds me of Kokomono, Ind., during the peach-crating season."

Rivington was nettled.

"Step into one of these saloons or vaudeville shows," said he, "with a large roll of money, and see how quickly the Bowery will sustain its reputation."

"You make impossible conditions," said I, coldly.

By and by Rivington stopped and said we were in the heart of the Bowery. There was a policeman on the corner whom Rivington knew.

"Hallo, Donahue!" said my guide. "How goes it? My friend and I are down this way looking up a bit of local color. He's anxious to meet one of the Bowery types. Can't you put us on to something genuine in that line – something that's got the color, you know?"

Policeman Donahue turned himself about ponderously, his florid face full of good-nature. He pointed with his club down the street.

"Sure!" he said huskily. "Here comes a lad now that was born on the Bowery and knows every inch of it. If he's ever been above Bleecker street he's kept it to himself."

A man about twenty-eight or twenty-nine, with a smooth face, was sauntering toward us with his hands in his coat pockets. Policeman Donahue stopped him with a courteous wave of his club.

"Evening, Kerry," he said. "Here's a couple of gents, friends of mine, that want to hear you spiel something about the Bowery. Can you reel 'em off a few yards?"

"Certainly, Donahue," said the young man, pleasantly. "Good evening, gentlemen," he said to us, with a pleasant smile. Donahue walked off on his beat.

"This is the goods," whispered Rivington, nudging me with his elbow. "Look at his jaw!"

"Say, cull," said Rivington, pushing back his hat, wot's doin'? Me and my friend's taking a look down de old line – see? De copper tipped us off dat you was wise to de bowery. Is dat right?"

I could not help admiring Rivington's power of adapting himself to his surroundings.

"Donahue was right," said the young man, frankly; "I was brought up on the Bowery. I have been newsboy, teamster, pugilist, member of an organized band of 'toughs,' bartender, and a 'sport' in various meanings of the word. The experience certainly warrants the supposition that I have at least a passing acquaintance with a few phases of Bowery life. I will be pleased to place whatever knowledge and experience I have at the service of my friend Donahue's friends."

Rivington seemed ill at ease.

"I say," he said – somewhat entreatingly, "I thought – you're not stringing us, are you? It isn't just the kind of talk we expected. You haven't even said 'Hully gee!' once. Do you really belong on the Bowery?"

"I am afraid," said the Bowery boy, smilingly, "that at some time you have been enticed into one of the dives of literature and had the counterfeit coin of the Bowery passed upon you. The 'argot' to which you doubtless refer was the invention of certain of your literary 'discoverers' who invaded the unknown wilds below Third avenue and put strange sounds into the mouths of the inhabitants. Safe in their homes far to the north and west, the credulous readers who were beguiled by this new 'dialect' perused and believed. Like Marco Polo and Mungo Park – pioneers indeed, but ambitious souls who could not draw the line of demarcation between discovery and invention – the literary bones of these explorers are dotting the trackless wastes of the subway. While it is true that after the publication of the mythical language attributed to the dwellers along the Bowery certain of its pat phrases and apt metaphors were adopted and, to a limited extent, used in this locality, it was because our people are prompt in assimilating whatever is to their commercial advantage. To the tourists who visited our newly discovered clime, and who expected a realization of their literary guide books, they supplied the demands of the market.

"But perhaps I am wandering from the question. In what way can I assist you, gentlemen? I beg you will believe that the hospitality of the street is extended to all. There are, I regret to say, many catchpenny places of entertainment, but I cannot conceive that they would entice you."

I felt Rivington lean somewhat heavily against me. "Say!" he remarked, with uncertain utterance; "come and have a drink with us."

"Thank you, but I never drink. I find that alcohol, even in the smallest quantities, alters the perspective. And I must preserve my perspective, for I am studying, the Bowery. I have lived in it nearly thirty years, and I am just beginning to understand its heartbeats. It is like a great river fed by a hundred alien streams. Each influx brings strange seeds on its flood, strange silt and weeds, and now and then a flower of rare promise. To construe this river requires a man who can build dykes against the overflow, who is a naturalist, a geologist, a humanitarian, a diver and a strong swimmer. I love my Bowery. It was my cradle and is my inspiration. I have published one book. The critics have been kind. I put my heart in it. I am writing another, into which I hope to put both heart and brain. Consider me your guide, gentlemen. Is there anything I can take you to see, any place to which I can conduct you?"

I was afraid to look at Rivington except with one eye.

"Thanks," said Rivington. "We were looking up ... that is ... my friend ... confound it; it's against all precedent, you know ... awfully obliged ... just the same."

"In case," said our friend, "you would like to meet some of our Bowery young men I would be pleased to have you visit the quarters of our East Side Kappa Delta Phi Society, only two blocks east of here."

"Awfully sorry," said Rivington, "but my friend's got me on the jump tonight. He's a terror when he's out after local color. Now, there's nothing I would like better than to drop in at the Kappa Delta Phi, but – some other time!"

We said our farewells and boarded a home-bound car. We had a rabbit on upper Broadway, and then I parted with Rivington on a street corner.

"Well, anyhow," said he, braced and recovered, "it couldn't have happened anywhere but in little old New York."

Which to say the least, was typical of Rivington.

A Newspaper Story

AT 8 A. M. it lay on Giuseppi's news-stand, still damp from the presses. Giuseppi, with the cunning of his ilk, philandered on the opposite corner, leaving his patrons to help themselves, no doubt on a theory related to the hypothesis of the watched pot.

This particular newspaper was, according to its custom and design, an educator, a guide, a monitor, a champion and a household counsellor and *vade mecum*.

From its many excellencies might be selected three editorials. One was in simple and chaste but illuminating language directed to parents and teachers, deprecating corporal punishment for children.

Another was an accusive and significant warning addressed to a notorious labor leader who was on the point of instigating his clients to a troublesome strike.

The third was an eloquent demand that the police force be sustained and aided in everything that tended to increase its efficiency as public guardians and servants.

Besides these more important chidings and requisitions upon the store of good citizenship was a wise prescription or form of procedure laid out by the editor of the heart-to-heart column in the specific case of a young man who had complained of the obduracy of his lady love, teaching him how he might win her.

Again, there was, on the beauty page, a complete answer to a young lady inquirer who desired admonition toward the securing of bright eyes, rosy cheeks and a beautiful countenance.

One other item requiring special cognizance was a brief "personal," running thus:

DEAR JACK: – Forgive me. You were right. Meet me at corner of Madison and –th at 8.30 this morning. We leave at noon.

PENITENT.

At 8 o'clock a young man with a haggard look and the feverish gleam of unrest in his eye dropped a penny and picked up the top paper as he passed Giuseppi's stand. A sleepless night had left him a late riser. There was an office to be reached by nine, and a shave and a hasty cup of coffee to be crowded into the interval.

He visited his barber shop and then hurried on his way. He pocketed his paper, meditating a belated perusal of it at the luncheon hour. At the next corner it fell from his pocket, carrying with it his pair of new gloves. Three blocks he walked, missed the gloves and turned back fuming.

Just on the half-hour he reached the corner where lay the gloves and the paper. But he strangely ignored that which he had come to seek. He was holding two little hands as tightly as ever he could and looking into two penitent brown eyes, while joy rioted in his heart.

"Dear Jack," she said, "I knew you would be here on time."

"I wonder what she means by that," he was saying to himself; "but it's all right, it's all right."

A big wind puffed out of the west, picked up the paper from the sidewalk, opened it out and sent it flying and whirling down a side street. Up that street was driving a skittish bay to a spider-wheel buggy, the young man who had written to the heart-to-heart editor for a recipe that he might win her for whom he sighed.

The wind, with a prankish flurry, flapped the flying newspaper against the face of the skittish bay. There was a lengthened streak of bay mingled with the red of running gear that stretched itself out for four blocks. Then a water-hydrant played its part in the cosmogony, the buggy became matchwood as foreordained, and the driver rested very quietly where he had been flung on the asphalt in front of a certain brownstone mansion.

They came out and had him inside very promptly. And there was one who made herself a pillow for his head, and cared for no curious eyes, bending over and saying, "Oh, it was you; it was you all the time, Bobby! Couldn't you see it? And if you die, why, so must I, and –"

But in all this wind we must hurry to keep in touch with our paper.

Policeman O'Brine arrested it as a character dangerous to traffic. Straightening its dishevelled leaves with his big, slow fingers, he stood a few feet from the family entrance of the Shandon Bells Café. One headline he spelled out ponderously: "The Papers to the Front in a Move to Help the Police."

But, whisht! The voice of Danny, the head bartender, through the crack of the door: "Here's a nip for ye, Mike, ould man."

Behind the widespread, amicable columns of the press Policeman

O'Brine receives swiftly his nip of the real stuff. He moves away, stalwart, refreshed, fortified, to his duties. Might not the editor man view with pride the early, the spiritual, the literal fruit that had blessed his labors.

Policeman O'Brine folded the paper and poked it playfully under the arm of a small boy that was passing. That boy was named Johnny, and he took the paper home with him. His sister was named Gladys, and she had written to the beauty editor of the paper asking for the practicable touchstone of beauty. That was weeks ago, and she had ceased to look for an answer. Gladys was a pale girl, with dull eyes and a discontented expression. She was dressing to go up to the avenue to get some braid. Beneath her skirt she pinned two leaves of the paper Johnny had brought. When she walked the rustling sound was an exact imitation of the real thing.

On the street she met the Brown girl from the flat below and stopped to talk. The Brown girl turned green. Only silk at $5 a yard could make the sound that she heard when Gladys moved. The Brown girl, consumed by jealousy, said something spiteful and went her way, with pinched lips.

Gladys proceeded toward the avenue. Her eyes now sparkled like jagerfonteins. A rosy bloom visited her cheeks; a triumphant, subtle, vivifying smile transfigured her face. She was beautiful. Could the beauty editor have seen her then! There was something in her answer in the paper, I believe, about cultivating kind feelings toward others in order to make plain features attractive.

The labor leader against whom the paper's solemn and weighty editorial injunction was laid was the father of Gladys and Johnny. He picked up the remains of the journal from which Gladys had ravished a cosmetic of silken sounds. The editorial did not come under his eye, but instead it was greeted by one of those ingenious and specious puzzle problems that enthrall alike the simpleton and the sage.

The labor leader tore off half of the page, provided himself with table, pencil and paper and glued himself to his puzzle.

Three hours later, after waiting vainly for him at the appointed place, other more conservative leaders declared and ruled in favor of arbitration, and the strike with its attendant dangers was averted. Subsequent editions of the paper referred, in colored inks, to the clarion tone of its successful denunciation of the labor leader's intended designs.

The remaining leaves of the active journal also went loyally to the proving of its potency.

When Johnny returned from school he sought a secluded spot and removed the missing columns from the inside of his clothing, where they had been artfully distributed so as to successfully defend such areas as are generally attacked during scholastic castigations. Johnny attended a private school and had had trouble with his teacher. As has been said, there was an excellent editorial against corporal punishment in that morning's issue, and no doubt it had its effect. After this can any one doubt the power of the press?

A TECHNICAL ERROR

I NEVER CARED especially for feuds, believing them to be even more overrated products of our country than grapefruit, scrapple, or honeymoons. Nevertheless, if I may be allowed, I will tell you of an Indian Territory feud of which I was press-agent, camp-follower, and inaccessory during the fact.

I was on a visit to Sam Durkee's ranch, where I had a great time falling off unmanicured ponies and waving my bare hand at the lower jaws of wolves about two miles away. Sam was a hardened person of about twenty-five, with a reputation for going home in the dark with perfect equanimity, though often with reluctance.

Over in the Creek Nation was a family bearing the name of Tatum. I was told that the Durkees and Tatums had been feuding for years. Several of each family had bitten the grass, and it was expected that more Nebuchadnezzars would follow. A younger generation of each family was growing up, and the grass was keeping pace with them. But I gathered that they had fought fairly; that they had not lain in cornfields and aimed at the division of their enemies' suspenders in the back – partly, perhaps, because there were no cornfields, and nobody wore more than one suspender. Nor had any woman or child of either house ever been harmed. In those days – and you will find it so yet – their women were safe.

Sam Durkee had a girl. (If it were an all-fiction magazine that I expect to sell this story to, I should say, "Mr. Durkee rejoiced in a fiancée.") Her name was Ella Baynes. They appeared to be devoted to each other, and to have perfect confidence in each other, as all couples do who are and have or aren't and haven't. She was tolerably pretty, with a heavy mass of brown hair that helped her along. He introduced me to her, which seemed not to lessen her preference for him; so I reasoned that they were surely soul-mates.

Miss Baynes lived in Kingfisher, twenty miles from the ranch. Sam lived on a gallop between the two places.

One day there came to Kingfisher a courageous young man, rather small, with smooth face and regular features. He made many inquiries about the business of the town, and especially of the inhabitants cognominally. He said he was from Muscogee, and he looked it, with his yellow shoes and crocheted four-in-hand. I met him once when I rode in for the mail. He said his name was Beverly Travers, which seemed rather improbable.

There were active times on the ranch, just then, and Sam was too busy to go to town often. As an incompetent and generally worthless guest, it devolved upon me to ride in for little things such as post cards, barrels of flour, baking-powder, smoking-tobacco, and – letters from Ella.

One day, when I was messenger for half a gross of cigarette papers and a couple of wagon tires, I saw the alleged Beverly Travers in a yellow-wheeled buggy with Ella Baynes, driving about town as ostentatiously as the black, waxy mud would permit. I knew that this information would bring no balm of Gilead to Sam's soul, so I refrained from including it in the news of the city that I retailed on my return. But on the next afternoon an elongated ex-cowboy of the name of Simmons, an oldtime pal of Sam's, who kept a feed store in Kingfisher, rode out to the ranch and rolled and burned many cigarettes before he would talk. When he did make oration, his words were these:

"Say, Sam, there's been a description of a galoot miscallin' himself Bevel-edged Travels impairing the atmospheric air of Kingfisher for the past two weeks. You know who he was? He was not otherwise than Ben Tatum, from the Creek Nation, son of old Gopher Tatum that your Uncle Newt shot last February. You know what he done this morning? He killed your brother Lester – shot him in the co't-house yard."

I wondered if Sam had heard. He pulled a twig from a mesquite bush, chewed it gravely, and said:

"He did, did he? He killed Lester?"

"The same," said Simmons. "And he did more. He run away with your girl, the same as to say Miss Ella Baynes. I thought you might like to know, so I rode out to impart the information."

"I am much obliged, Jim," said Sam, taking the chewed twig from his mouth. "Yes, I'm glad you rode out. Yes, I'm right glad."

"Well, I'll be ridin' back, I reckon. That boy I left in the feed store don't know hay from oats. He shot Lester in the back."

"Shot him in the back?"

"Yes, while he was hitchin' his hoops."

"I'm much obliged, Jim."

"I kind of thought you'd like to know as soon as you could."

"Come in and have some coffee before you ride back, Jim?"

"Why, no, I reckon not; I must get back to the store."

"And you say –"

"Yes, Sam. Everybody seen 'em drive away together in a buckboard, with a big bundle, like clothes, tied up in the back of it. He was drivin' the team he brought over with him from Muscogee. They'll be hard to overtake right away."

"And which –"

"I was goin' on to tell you. They left on the Guthrie road; but there's no tellin' which forks they'll take – you know that."

"All right, Jim; much obliged."

"You're welcome, Sam."

Simmons rolled a cigarette and stabbed his pony with both heels. Twenty yards away he reined up and called back:

"You don't want no – assistance, as you might say?"

"Not any, thanks."

"I didn't think you would. Well, so long!"

Sam took out and opened a bone-handled pocket-knife and scraped a dried piece of mud from his left boot. I thought at first he was going to swear a vendetta on the blade of it, or recite "The Gipsy's Curse." The few feuds I had ever seen or read about usually opened that way. This one seemed to be presented with a new treatment. Thus offered on the stage, it would have been hissed off, and one of Belasco's thrilling melodramas demanded instead.

"I wonder," said Sam, with a profoundly thoughtful expression, "if the cook has any cold beans left over!"

He called Wash, the Negro cook, and finding that he had some, ordered him to heat up the pot and make some strong coffee. Then we went into Sam's private room, where he slept, and kept his armory, dogs, and the saddles of his favorite mounts. He took three or four six-shooters out of a bookcase and began to look them over, whistling "The Cowboy's Lament" abstractedly. Afterward he ordered the two best horses on the ranch saddled and tied to the hitching-post.

Now, in the feud business, in all sections of the country, I have observed that in one particular there is a delicate but strict etiquette belonging. You must not mention the word or refer to the subject in the presence of a feudist. It would be more reprehensible than commenting upon the mole on the chin of your rich aunt. I found, later on, that there is another unwritten rule, but I think that belongs solely to the West.

It yet lacked two hours to supper-time; but in twenty minutes Sam and I were plunging deep into the reheated beans, hot coffee, and cold beef.

"Nothing like a good meal before a long ride," said Sam. "Eat hearty."

I had a sudden suspicion.

"Why did you have two horses saddled?" I asked.

"One, two – one, two," said Sam. "You can count, can't you?"

His mathematics carried with it a momentary qualm and a lesson. The thought had not occurred to him that the thought could possibly occur to me not to ride at his side on that red road to revenge and justice. It was the higher calculus. I was booked for the trail. I began to eat more beans.

In an hour we set forth at a steady gallop eastward. Our horses were Kentucky-bred, strengthened by the mesquite grass of the west. Ben Tatum's steeds may have been swifter, and he had a good lead; but if he had heard the punctual thuds of the hoofs of those trailers of ours, born in the heart of feudland, he might have felt that retribution was creeping up on the hoof-prints of his dapper nags.

I knew that Ben Tatum's card to play was flight – flight until he came within the safer territory of his own henchmen and supporters. He knew that the man pursuing him would follow the trail to any end where it might lead.

During the ride Sam talked of the prospect for rain, of the price of beef, and of the musical glasses. You would have thought he had never had a brother or a sweetheart or an enemy on earth. There are some subjects too big even for the words in the "Unabridged." Knowing this phase of the feud code, but not having practised it sufficiently, I overdid the thing by telling some slightly funny anecdotes. Sam laughed at exactly the right place – laughed with his mouth. When I caught sight of his mouth, I wished I had been blessed with enough sense of humor to have suppressed those anecdotes.

Our first sight of them we had in Guthrie. Tired and hungry, we stumbled, unwashed, into a little yellow-pine hotel and sat at a table. In the opposite corner we saw the fugitives. They were bent upon their meal, but looked around at times uneasily.

The girl was dressed in brown – one of these smooth, half-shiny, silky-looking affairs with lace collar and cuffs, and what I believe they call an accordion-plaited skirt. She wore a thick brown veil down to her nose, and a broad-brimmed straw hat with some kind of feathers adorning it. The man wore plain, dark clothes, and his hair was trimmed very short. He was such a man as you might see anywhere.

There they were – the murderer and the woman he had stolen. There we were – the rightful avenger, according to the code, and the supernumerary who writes these words.

For one time, at least, in the heart of the supernumerary there rose the killing instinct. For one moment he joined the force of combatants – orally.

"What are you waiting for, Sam?" I said in a whisper. "Let him have it now!"

Sam gave a melancholy sigh.

"You don't understand; but he does," he said. "He knows. Mr. Tenderfoot, there's a rule out here among white men in the Nation that you can't shoot a man when he's with a woman. I never knew it to be broke yet. You can't do it. You've got to get him in a gang of men or by himself. That's why. He knows it, too. We all know. So, that's Mr. Ben Tatum! One of the 'pretty men'! I'll cut him out of the herd before they leave the hotel, and regulate his account!"

After supper the flying pair disappeared quickly. Although Sam haunted lobby and stairway and halls half the night, in some mysterious way the fugitives eluded him; and in the morning the veiled lady in the brown dress with the accordion-plaited skirt and the dapper young man with the close-clipped hair, and the buckboard with the prancing nags, were gone.

It is a monotonous story, that of the ride; so it shall be curtailed. Once again we overtook them on a road. We were about fifty yards behind. They turned in the buckboard and looked at us; then drove on without whipping up their horses. Their safety no longer lay in speed. Ben Tatum knew. He knew that the only rock of safety left to him was the code. There is no doubt that, had he been alone, the matter would have been settled quickly with Sam Durkee in the usual way; but he had something at his side that kept still the trigger-finger of both. It seemed likely that he was no coward.

So, you may perceive that woman, on occasions, may postpone instead of precipitating conflict between man and man. But not willingly or consciously. She is oblivious of codes.

Five miles farther, we came upon the future great Western city of Chandler. The horses of pursuers and pursued were starved and weary. There was one hotel that offered danger to man and entertainment to beast; so the four of us met again in the dining room at the ringing of a bell so resonant and large that it had cracked the welkin long ago. The dining room was not as large as the one at Guthrie.

Just as we were eating apple pie – how Ben Davises and tragedy impinge upon each other! – I noticed Sam looking with keen intentness at our quarry where they were seated at a table across the room. The girl still wore the brown dress with lace collar and cuffs, and the veil drawn down to her nose. The man bent over his plate, with his close cropped head held low.

"There's a code," I heard Sam say, either to me or to himself, "that won't let you shoot a man in the company of a woman; but, by thunder, there ain't one to keep you from killing a woman in the company of a man!"

And, quicker than my mind could follow his argument, he whipped a Colt's automatic from under his left arm and pumped six bullets into the body that the brown dress covered – the brown dress with the lace collar and cuffs and the accordion-plaited skirt.

The young person in the dark sack suit, from whose head and from whose life a woman's glory had been clipped, laid her head on her arms stretched upon the table; while people came running to raise Ben Tatum from the floor in his feminine masquerade that had given Sam the opportunity to set aside, technically, the obligations of the code.

AFTER TWENTY YEARS

THE POLICEMAN ON the beat moved up the avenue impressively.
The impressiveness was habitual and not for show, for spectators were
few. The time was barely 10 o'clock at night, but chilly gusts of wind
with a taste of rain in them had well nigh depeopled the streets.

Trying doors as he went, twirling his club with many intricate and
artful movements, turning now and then to cast his watchful eye down
the pacific thoroughfare, the officer, with his stalwart form and slight
swagger, made a fine picture of a guardian of the peace.

The vicinity was one that kept early hours. Now and then you
might see the lights of a cigar store or of an all-night lunch counter;
but the majority of the doors belonged to business places that had
long since been closed.

When about midway of a certain block the policeman suddenly
slowed his walk. In the doorway of a darkened hardware store a man
leaned, with an unlighted Cigar in his mouth. As the policeman
walked up to him, the man spoke up quickly.

"It's all right, officer," he said, reassuringly. "I'm just waiting for a
friend. It's an appointment made twenty years ago. Sounds a little
funny to you, doesn't it? Well, I'll explain if you'd like to make
certain it's all straight. About that long ago there used to be a
restaurant where this store stands – 'Big Joe' Brady's restaurant."

"Until five years ago," said the policeman. "It was torn down
then."

The man in the doorway struck a match and lit his cigar. The light
showed a pale, square-jawed face with keen eyes, and a little white
scar near his right eyebrow. His scarf-pin was a large diamond, oddly
set.

"Twenty years ago tonight," said the man, "I dined here at 'Big
Joe' Brady's with Jimmy Wells, my best chum, and the finest chap in
the world. He and I were raised here in New York, just like two
brothers, together. I was eighteen and Jimmy was twenty. The next

morning I was to start for the West to make my fortune. You couldn't have dragged Jimmy out of New York; he thought it was the only place on earth. Well, we agreed that night that we would meet here again exactly twenty years from that date and time, no matter what our conditions might be or from what distance we might have to come. We figured that in twenty years each of us ought to have our destiny worked out and our fortunes made, whatever they were going to be."

"It sounds pretty interesting" said the policeman. "Rather a long time between meets, though, it seems to me. Haven't you heard from your friend since you left?"

"Well, yes, for a time we corresponded," said the other. "But after a year or two we lost track of each other. You see, the West is a pretty big proposition, and I kept hustling around over it pretty lively. But I know Jimmy will meet me here if he's alive, for he always was the truest, staunchest old chap in the world. He'll never forget. I came a thousand miles to stand in this door tonight, and it's worth it if my old partner turns up."

The waiting man pulled out a handsome watch, the lids of it set with small diamonds.

"Three minutes to ten," he announced. "It was exactly ten-o'clock when we parted here at the restaurant door."

"Did pretty well out West, didn't you?" asked the policeman.

"You bet! I hope Jimmy has done half as well. He was a kind of plodder, though, good fellow as he was. I've had to compete with some of the sharpest wits going to get my pile. A man gets in a groove in New York. It takes the West to put a razor-edge on him."

The policeman twirled his club and took a step or two.

"I'll be on my way. Hope your friend comes around all right. Going to call time on him sharp?"

"I should say not!" said the other. "I'll give him half an hour at least. If Jimmy is alive on earth he'll be here by that time. So long, officer."

"Good-night, sir," said policeman, passing on along his beat, trying doors as he went.

There was now a fine, cold, drizzle falling, and the wind had risen from its uncertain puffs into a steady blow. The few foot passengers astir in that quarter hurried dismally and silently along with coat collars turned high and pocketed hands. And in the door of the hardware store the man who had come a thousand miles to fill an appointment, uncertain almost to absurdity, with the friend of his youth, smoked his cigar and waited.

About twenty minutes he waited, and then a tall man in a long overcoat, with collar turned up to his ears, hurried across from the opposite side of the street. He went directly to the waiting man.

"Is that you, Bob?" be asked, doubtfully.

"Is that you, Jimmy Wells?" cried the man in the door.

"Bless my heart!" exclaimed the new arrival, grasping both the other's hands with his own. "It's Bob, sure as fate. I was certain I'd find you here if you were still in existence. Well, well, well! Twenty years is a long time. The old restaurant's gone, Bob; I wish it had lasted, so we could have had another dinner there. How has the West treated you, old man?"

"Bully; it has given me everything I asked it for. You've changed lots, Jimmy. I never thought you were so tall by two or three inches."

"Oh, I grew a bit after I was twenty."

"Doing well in New York, Jimmy?"

"Moderately. I have a position in one of the city departments."

"Come on, Bob; we'll go around to a place I know of, and have a good long talk about old times."

The two men started up the street arm in arm. The man from the West, his egotism enlarged by success, was beginning to outline the history of his career. The other, submerged in his over-coat, listened with interest.

At the corner stood a drug store; brillant with electric lights. When they came into this each of them turned simultaneously to gaze upon the other's face.

The man from the West stopped suddenly and released his arm.

"You're not Jimmy Wells," he snapped. "Twenty years is a long time, but not long enough to change a man's nose from a Roman to a pug."

"It sometimes changes a man into a bad one," said the tall man. "You've been under arrest for ten minutes, 'Silky' Bob. Chicago thinks you may have dropped over our way and wires to us she wants to have a chat with you. Going quietly, are you? That's sensible. Now, before we go to the station here's a note I was asked to hand to you. You may read it here at the window. It's from Patrolman Wells."

The man from the West unfolded the little piece of paper handed him. His hand was steady when he began to read, but it trembled a little by the time he had finished. The note was rather short.

Bob: I was at the appointed place on time. When you struck the match to light your cigar I saw it was the face of the man wanted in Chicago. Somehow I couldn't do it myself, So I went around and got a plain clothes man to do the job.
JIMMY

An Unfinished Story

WE NO LONGER groan and heap ashes upon our heads when the flames of Tophet are mentioned. For, even the preachers have begun to tell us that God is radium, or ether or some scientific compound, and that the worst we wicked ones may expect is a chemical reaction. This is a pleasing hypothesis; but there lingers yet some of the old, goodly terror of orthodoxy.

There are but two subjects upon which one may discourse with a free imagination, and without the possibility of being controverted. You may talk of your dreams; and you may tell what you heard a parrot say. Both Morpheus and the bird are incompetent witnesses; and your listener dare not attack your recital. The baseless fabric of a vision, then, shall furnish my theme – chosen with apologies and regrets instead of the more limited field of Pretty Polly's small talk.

I had a dream that was so far removed from the higher criticism that it had to do with the ancient, respectable, and lamented bar-of-judgment theory.

Gabriel had played his trump; and those of us who could not follow suit were arraigned for examination. I noticed at one side a gathering of professional bondsmen in solemn black and collars that buttoned behind; but it seemed there was some trouble about their real estate titles; and they did not appear to be getting any of us out. A fly cop – an angel policeman – flew over to me and took me by the left wing. Near at hand was a group of very prosperous-looking spirits arraigned for judgment.

"Do you belong with that bunch?" the policeman asked.

"Who are they?" was my answer.

"Why," said he, "they are –"

But this irrelevant stuff is taking up space that the story should occupy.

Dulcie worked in a department store. She sold Hamburg edging, or stuffed peppers, or automobiles, or other little trinkets such as they keep in department stores. Of what she earned, Dulcie received six dollars per week. The remainder was credited to her and debited to somebody else's account in the ledger kept by G – Oh, primal energy, you say, Reverend Doctor – Well then, in the Ledger of Primal Energy.

During her first year in the store, Dulcie was paid five dollars per week. It would be instructive to know how she lived on that amount. Don't care? Very well; probably you are interested in larger amounts. Six dollars is a larger amount. I will tell you how she lived on six dollars per week.

One afternoon at six, when Dulcie was sticking her hat-pin within an eighth of an inch of her medulla oblongata, she said to her chum, Sadie – the girl that waits on you with her left side:

"Say, Sade, I made a date for dinner this evening with Piggy."

"You never did!" exclaimed Sadie admiringly. "Well, ain't you the lucky one? Piggy's an awful swell; and he always takes a girl to swell places. He took Blanche up to the Hoffman House one evening, where they have swell music, and you see a lot of swells. You'll have a swell time, Dulcie."

Dulcie hurried off homeward. Her eyes were shining, and her cheeks showed the delicate pink of life's – real life's – approaching dawn. It was Friday; and she had fifty cents of her last week's wages.

The streets were filled with the rush-hour floods of people. The electric lights of Broadway were glowing – calling moths from miles, from leagues, from hundreds of leagues out of darkness around to come in and attend the singeing school. Men in accurate clothes, with faces like those carved on cherry-stones by the old salts in sailors' homes, turned and stared at Dulcie as she sped, unheeding, past them. Manhattan, the night-blooming cereus, was beginning to unfold its dead-white, heavy-odored petals.

Dulcie stopped in a store where goods were cheap and bought an imitation lace collar with her fifty cents. That money was to have been spent otherwise – fifteen cents for supper, ten cents for breakfast, ten cents for lunch. Another dime was to be added to her small store of savings; and five cents was to be squandered for liquorice drops – the kind that made your cheek look like the tooth-ache, and last as long. The liquorice was an extravagance – almost a carouse – but what is life without pleasures?

Dulcie lived in a furnished room. There is this difference between a furnished room and a boarding-house. In a furnished room, other people do not know it when you go hungry.

Dulcie went up to her room – the third floor back in a West Side brownstone-front. She lit the gas. Scientists tell us that the diamond is the hardest substance known. Their mistake. Landladies know of a compound beside which the diamond is as putty. They pack it in the tips of gas-burners; and one may stand on a chair and dig at it in vain until one's fingers are pink and bruised. A hairpin will not remove it; therefore let us call it immovable.

So Dulcie lit the gas. In its one-fourth-candle-power glow we will observe the room.

Couch-bed, dresser, table, washstand, chair – of this much the landlady was guilty. The rest was Dulcie's. On the dresser were her treasures – a gilt china vase presented to her by Sadie, a calendar issued by a pickle works, a book on the divination of dreams, some rice powder in a glass dish, and a cluster of artificial cherries tied with a pink ribbon.

Against the wrinkly mirror stood pictures of General Kitchener, William Muldoon, the Duchess of Marlborough, and Benvenuto Cellini. Against one wall was a plaster of Paris plaque of an O'Callahan in a Roman helmet. Near it was a violent oleograph of a lemon-colored child assaulting an inflammatory butterfly. This was Dulcie's final judgment in art; but it had never been upset. Her rest had never been disturbed by whispers of stolen copes; no critic had elevated his eyebrows at her infantile entomologist. Piggy was to call for her at seven. While she swiftly makes ready, let us discreetly face the other way and gossip.

For the room, Dulcie paid two dollars per week. On weekdays her breakfast cost ten cents; she made coffee and cooked an egg over the gaslight while she was dressing. On Sunday mornings she feasted royally on veal chops and pineapple fritters at "Billy's" restaurant, at a cost of twenty-five cents – and tipped the waitress ten cents. New York presents so many temptations for one to run into extravagance. She had her lunches in the department-store restaurant at a cost of sixty cents for the week; dinners were $1.05. The evening papers – show me a New Yorker going without his daily paper! – came to six cents; and two Sunday papers – one for the personal column and the other to read – were ten cents. The total amounts to $4.76. Now, one has to buy clothes, and – I give it up. I hear of wonderful bargains in fabrics, and of miracles performed with needle and thread; but I am in doubt. I hold my pen poised in vain when I would add to Dulcie's life some of those joys that belong to woman by virtue of all the unwritten, sacred, natural, inactive ordinances of the equity of heaven.

Twice she had been to Coney Island and had ridden the hobby-horses. 'Tis a weary thing to count your pleasures by summers instead of by hours.

Piggy needs but a word. When the girls named him, an undeserving stigma was cast upon the noble family of swine. The words-of-three-letters lesson in the old blue spelling-book begins with Piggy's biography. He was fat; he had the soul of a rat, the habits of a bat, and the magnanimity of a cat. He wore expensive clothes; and was a connoisseur in starvation. He could look at a shop-girl and tell you to an hour how long it had been since she had eaten anything more nourishing than marsh-mallows and tea. He hung about the shopping districts, and prowled around in department stores with his invitations to dinner. Men who escort dogs upon the streets at the end of a string look down upon him. He is a type; I can dwell upon him no longer; my pen is not the kind intended for him; I am no carpenter. At ten minutes to seven Dulcie was ready. She looked at herself in the wrinkly mirror. The reflection was satisfactory. The dark blue dress, fitting without a wrinkle, the hat with its jaunty black feather, the but-slightly-soiled gloves – all representing self-denial, even of food itself were vastly becoming.

Dulcie forgot everything else for a moment except that she was beautiful, and that life was about to lift a corner of its mysterious veil for her to observe its wonders. No gentleman had ever asked her out before. Now she was going for a brief moment into the glitter and exalted show. The girls said that Piggy was a "spender." There would be a grand dinner, and music, and splendidly dressed ladies to look at, and things to eat that strangely twisted the girls' jaws when they tried to tell about them. No doubt she would be asked out again.

There was a blue pongee suit in a window that she knew – by saving twenty cents a week instead of ten, in – let's see – Oh, it would run into years! But there was a second-hand store in Seventh Avenue where – Somebody knocked at the door. Dulcie opened it. The landlady stood there with a spurious smile, sniffing for cooking by stolen gas.

"A gentleman's downstairs to see you," she said. "Name is Mr. Wiggins."

By such epithet was Piggy known to unfortunate ones who had to take him seriously.

Dulcie turned to the dresser to get her handkerchief; then she stopped still, and bit her underlip hard. While looking in her mirror she had seen fairyland and herself, a princess, just awakening from a long slumber. She had forgotten one that was watching her with sad, beautiful, stern eyes – the only one there was to approve or condemn what she did. Straight and slender and tall, with a look of sorrowful reproach on his handsome, melancholy face, General Kitchener fixed his wonderful eyes on her out of his gilt photograph frame on the dresser.

Dulcie turned like an automatic doll to the landlady.

"Tell him I can't go," she said dully. "Tell him I'm sick, or something. Tell him I'm not going out."

After the door was closed and locked, Dulcie fell upon her bed, crushing her black tip, and cried for ten minutes. General Kitchener was her only friend. He was Dulcie's ideal of a gallant knight. He looked as if he might have a secret sorrow, and his wonderful moustache was a dream, and she was a little afraid of that stern yet tender look in his eyes. She used to have little fancies that he would call at the house some time, and ask for her, with his sword clanking against his high boots. Once, when a boy was rattling a piece of chain against a lamp-post she had opened the window and looked out. But there was no use. She knew that General Kitchener was away over in Japan, leading his army against the savage Turks; and he would never step out of his gilt frame for her. Yet one look from him had vanquished Piggy that night. Yes, for that night.

When her cry was over Dulcie got up and took off her best dress, and put on her old blue kimono. She wanted no dinner. She sang two verses of "Sammy." Then she became intensely interested in a little red speck on the side of her nose. And after that was attended to, she drew up a chair to the rickety table, and told her fortune with an old deck of cards.

"The horrid, impudent thing!" she said aloud. "And I never gave him a word or a look to make him think it!"

At nine o'clock Dulcie took a tin box of crackers and a little pot of raspberry jam out of her trunk, and had a feast. She offered General Kitchener some jam on a cracker; but he only looked at her as the Sphinx would have looked at a butterfly – if there are butterflies in the desert.

"Don't eat if you don't want to," said Dulcie. "And don't put on so many airs and scold so with your eyes. I wonder if you'd be so superior and snippy if you had to live on six dollars a week."

It was not a good sign for Dulcie to be rude to General Kitchener. And then she turned Benvenuto Cellini face downward with a severe gesture. But that was not inexcusable; for she had always thought he was Henry VIII, and she did not approve of him. At half-past nine Dulcie took a last look at the pictures on the dresser, turned out the light, and skipped into bed. It's an awful thing to go to bed with a good-night look at General Kitchener, William Muldoon, the Duchess of Marlborough, and Benvenuto Cellini.

This story really doesn't get anywhere at all. The rest of it comes later – some time when Piggy asks Dulcie again to dine with him, and she is feeling lonelier than usual, and General Kitchener happens to be looking the other way; and then –

As I said before, I dreamed that I was standing near a crowd of prosperous-looking angels, and a policeman took me by the wing and asked if I belonged with them.

"Who are they?" I asked.

"Why," said he, "they are the men who hired working-girls, and paid 'em five or six dollars a week to live on. Are you one of the bunch?"

"Not on your immortality," said I. "I'm only the fellow that set fire to an orphan asylum, and murdered a blind man for his pennies."

BESTSELLER

I

ONE DAY LAST summer I went to Pittsburgh – well, I had to go there on business.

My chair-car was profitably well-filled with people of the kind one usually sees on chair-cars. Most of them were ladies in brown-silk dresses cut with square yokes, with lace insertion, and dotted veils, who refused to have the windows raised. Then there was the usual number of men who looked as if they might be in almost any business and going almost anywhere. Some students of human nature can look at a man in a Pullman and tell you where he is from, his occupation and his stations in life, both flag and social; but I never could. The only way I can correctly judge a fellow-traveler is when the train is held up by robbers, or when he reaches at the same time I do for the last towel in the dressing-room of the sleeper.

The porter came and brushed the collection of soot on the window-sill off to the left knee of my trousers. I removed it with an air of apology. The temperature was eighty-eight. One of the dotted-veiled ladies demanded the closing of two more ventilators, and spoke loudly of Interlaken. I leaned back idly in chair No. 7, and looked with the tepidest curiosity at the small, black, bald-spotted head just visible above the back of No. 9.

Suddenly No. 9 hurled a book to the floor between his chair and the window, and, looking, I saw that it was *The Rose-Lady and Trevelyan*, one of the best-selling novels of the present day. And then the critic or Philistine, whichever he was, veered his chair toward the window, and I knew him at once for John A. Pescud, of Pittsburgh, traveling salesman for a plate-glass company – an old acquaintance whom I had not seen in two years.

In two minutes we were faced, had shaken hands, and had finished with such topics as rain, prosperity, health, residence, and destination. Politics might have followed next; but I was not so ill-fated.

I wish you might know John A. Pescud. He is of the stuff that heroes are not often lucky enough to be made of. He is a small man with a wide smile, and an eye that seems to be fixed upon that little red spot on the end of your nose. I never saw him wear but one kind of necktie, and he believes in cuff-holders and button-shoes. He is as hard and true as anything ever turned out by the Cambria Steel Works; and he believes that as soon as Pittsburgh makes smoke-consumers compulsory, St. Peter will come down and sit at the foot of Smithfield Street, and let somebody else attend to the gate up in the branch heaven. He believes that "our" plate-glass is the most important commodity in the world, and that when a man is in his home town he ought to be decent and law-abiding.

During my acquaintance with him in the City of Diurnal Night I had never known his views on life, romance, literature, and ethics. We had browsed, during our meetings, on local topics, and then parted, after Chateau Margaux, Irish stew, flannel-cakes, cottage-pudding, and coffee (hey, there! – with milk separate). Now I was to get more of his ideas. By way of facts, he told me that business had picked up since the party conventions, and that he was going to get off at Coketown.

II

"Say," said Pescud, stirring his discarded book with the toe of his right shoe, "did you ever read one of these best-sellers? I mean the kind where the hero is an American swell – sometimes even from Chicago – who falls in love with a royal princess from Europe who is traveling under an alias, and follows her to her father's kingdom or principality? I guess you have. They're all alike. Sometimes this going-away masher is a Washington newspaper correspondent, and sometimes he is a Van Something from New York, or a Chicago wheat-broker worth fifty millions. But he's always ready to break into the king row of any foreign country that sends over their queens and princesses to try the new plush seats on the Big Four or the B. and O. There doesn't seem to be any other reason in the book for their being here.

"Well, this fellow chases the royal chair-warmer home, as I said, and finds out who she is. He meets here on the corso or the strasse one evening and gives us ten pages of conversation. She reminds him of the difference in their stations, and that gives him a chance to ring in three solid pages about America's uncrowned sovereigns. If you'd take his remarks and set 'em to music, and then take the music away from 'em, they'd sound exactly like one of George Cohan's songs.

"Well, you know how it runs on, if you ve read any of 'em – he slaps the king's Swiss body-guards around like everything whenever they get in his way. He's a great fencer, too. Now, I've known of some Chicago men who were pretty notorious fences, but I never heard of any fencers coming from there. He stands on the first landing of the royal staircase in Castle Schutzenfestenstein with a gleaming rapier in his hand, and makes a Baltimore broil of six platoons of traitors who come to massacre the said king. And then he has to fight duels with a couple of chancellors, and foil a plot by four Austrian archdukes to seize the kingdom for a gasoline-station.

"But the great scene is when his rival for the princess' hand, Count Feodor, attacks him between the portcullis and the ruined chapel, armed with a mitrailleuse, a yataghan, and a couple of Siberian bloodhounds. This scene is what runs the best-seller into the twenty-ninth edition before the publisher has had time to draw a check for the advance royalties.

"The American hero shucks his coat and throws it over the heads of the bloodhounds, gives the mitrailleuse a slap with his mitt, says 'Yah!' to the yataghan, and lands in Kid McCoy's best style on the count's left eye. Of course, we have a neat little prize-fight right then and there. The count – in order to make the go possible – seems to be an expert at the art of self-defence, himself; and here we have the Corbett-Sullivan fight done over into literature. The book ends with the broker and the princess doing a John Cecil Clay cover under the linden-trees on the Gorgonzola Walk. That winds up the love-story plenty good enough. But I notice that the book dodges the final issue. Even a best-seller has sense enough to shy at either leaving a Chicago grain broker on the throne of Lobsterpotsdam or bringing over a real princess to eat fish and potato salad in an Italian chalet on Michigan Avenue. What do you think about 'em?"

"Why," said I, "I hardly know, John. There's a saying: 'Love levels all ranks,' you know."

"Yes," said Pescud, "but these kind of love-stories are rank – on the level. I know something about literature, even if I am in plate-glass. These kind of books are wrong, and yet I never go into a train but what they pile 'em up on me. No good can come out of an international clinch between the Old-World aristocracy and one of us fresh Americans. When people in real life marry, they generally hunt up somebody in their own station. A fellow usually picks out a girl that went to the same high-school and belonged to the same singing-society that he did. When young millionaires fall in love, they always select the chorus-girl that likes the same kind of sauce on the lobster that he does. Washington newspaper correspondents always marry widow ladies ten years older than themselves who keep boarding-houses. No, sir, you can't make a novel sound right to me when it makes one of C. D. Gibson's bright young men go abroad and turn kingdoms upside down just because he's a Taft American and took a course at a gymnasium. And listen how they talk, too!"

Pescud picked up the best-seller and hunted his page.

"Listen at this," said he. "Trevelyan is chinning with the Princess Alwyna at the back end of the tulip-garden. This is how it goes:

'Say not so, dearest and sweetest of earth's fairest flowers. Would I aspire? You are a star set high above me in a royal heaven; I am only – myself. Yet I am a man, and I have a heart to do and dare. I have no title save that of an uncrowned sovereign; but I have an arm and a sword that yet might free Schutzenfestenstein from the plots of traitors.'

"Think of a Chicago man packing a sword, and talking about freeing anything that sounded as much like canned pork as that! He'd be much more likely to fight to have an import duty put on it."

"I think I understand you, John," said I. "You want fiction-writers to be consistent with their scenes and characters. They shouldn't mix Turkish pashas with Vermont farmers, or English dukes with Long Island clam-diggers, or Italian countesses with Montana cowboys, or Cincinnati brewery agents with the rajahs of India."

"Or plain business men with aristocracy high above 'em," added Pescud. "It don't jibe. People are divided into classes, whether we admit it or not, and it's everybody's impulse to stick to their own class. They do it, too. I don't see why people go to work and buy hundreds of thousands of books like that. You don't see or hear of any such didoes and capers in real life."

III

"Well, John," said I, "I haven't read a best-seller in a long time. Maybe I've had notions about them somewhat like yours. But tell me more about yourself. Getting along all right with the company?"

"Bully," said Pescud, brightening at once. "I've had my salary raised twice since I saw you, and I get a commission, too. I've bought a neat slice of real estate out in the East End, and have run up a house on it. Next year the firm is going to sell me some shares of stock. Oh, I'm in on the line of General Prosperity, no matter who's elected!"

"Met your affinity yet, John?" I asked.

"Oh, I didn't tell you about that, did I?" said Pescud with a broader grin.

"O-ho!" I said. "So you've taken time enough off from your plate-glass to have a romance?"

"No, no," said John. "No romance – nothing like that! But I'll tell you about it."

"I was on the south-bound, going to Cincinnati, about eighteen months ago, when I saw, across the aisle, the finest-looking girl I'd ever laid eyes on. Nothing spectacular, you know, but just the sort you want for keeps. Well, I never was up to the flirtation business, either handkerchief, automobile, postage-stamp, or door-step, and she wasn't the kind to start anything. She read a book and minded her business, which was to make the world prettier and better just by residing on it. I kept on looking out of the side doors of my eyes, and finally the proposition got out of the Pullman class into a case of a cottage with a lawn and vines running over the porch. I never thought of speaking to her, but I let the plate-glass business go to smash for a while.

"She changed cars at Cincinnati, and took a sleeper to Louisville over the L. and N. There she bought another ticket, and went on through Shelbyville, Frankfort, and Lexington. Along there I began to have a hard time keeping up with her. The trains came along when they pleased, and didn't seem to be going anywhere in particular, except to keep on the track and the right of way as much as possible. Then they began to stop at junctions instead of towns, and at last they stopped altogether. I'll bet Pinkerton would outbid the plate-glass people for my services any time if they knew how I managed to shadow that young lady. I contrived to keep out of her sight as much as I could, but I never lost track of her.

"The last station she got off at was away down in Virginia, about six in the afternoon. There were about fifty houses and four hundred niggers in sight. The rest was red mud, mules, and speckled hounds."

"A tall old man, with a smooth face and white hair, looking as proud as Julius Caesar and Roscoe Conkling on the same post-card, was there to meet her. His clothes were frazzled, but I didn't notice that till later. He took her little satchel, and they started over the plank-walks and went up a road along the hill. I kept along a piece behind 'em, trying to look like I was hunting a garnet ring in the sand that my sister had lost at a picnic the previous Saturday.

"They went in a gate on top of the hill. It nearly took my breath away when I looked up. Up there in the biggest grove I ever saw was a tremendous house with round white pillars about a thousand feet high, and the yard was so full of rose-bushes and box-bushes and lilacs that you couldn't have seen the house if it hadn't been as big as the Capitol at Washington.

"'Here's where I have to trail,' says I to myself. I thought before that she seemed to be in moderate circumstances, at least. This must be the Governor's mansion, or the Agricultural Building of a new World's Fair, anyhow. I'd better go back to the village and get posted by the postmaster, or drug the druggist for some information.

"In the village I found a pine hotel called the Bay View House. The only excuse for the name was a bay horse grazing in the front yard. I set my sample-case down, and tried to be ostensible. I told the landlord I was taking orders for plate-glass.

"'I don't want no plates,' says he, 'but I do need another glass molasses-pitcher.'

"By-and-by I got him down to local gossip and answering questions.

"'Why,' says he, 'I thought everybody knowed who lived in the big white house on the hill. It's Colonel Allyn, the biggest man and the finest quality in Virginia, or anywhere else. They're the oldest family in the State. That was his daughter that got off the train. She's been up to Illinois to see her aunt, who is sick.'

"I registered at the hotel, and on the third day I caught the young lady walking in the front yard, down next to the paling fence. I stopped and raised my hat – there wasn't any other way.

"'Excuse me,' says I, 'can you tell me where Mr. Hinkle lives?'

"She looks at me as cool as if I was the man come to see about the weeding of the garden, but I thought I saw just a slight twinkle of fun in her eyes.

"'No one of that name lives in Birchton,' says she. 'That is,' she goes on, 'as far as I know. Is the gentleman you are seeking white?'

"Well, that tickled me. 'No kidding,' says I. 'I'm not looking for smoke, even if I do come from Pittsburgh.'

"'You are quite a distance from home,' says she.

"'I'd have gone a thousand miles farther,' says I.

"'Not if you hadn't waked up when the train started in Shelbyville,' says she; and then she turned almost as red as one of the roses on the bushes in the yard. I remembered I had dropped off to sleep on a bench in the Shelbyville station, waiting to see which train she took, and only just managed to wake up in time.

"And then I told her why I had come, as respectful and earnest as I could. And I told her everything about myself, and what I was making, and how that all I asked was just to get acquainted with her and try to get her to like me.

"She smiles a little, and blushes some, but her eyes never get mixed up. They look straight at whatever she's talking to.

"'I never had any one talk like this to me before, Mr. Pescud,' says she. 'What did you say your name is – John?'

"'John A.,' says I.

"'And you came mighty near missing the train at Powhatan Junction, too,' says she, with a laugh that sounded as good as a mileage-book to me.

"'How did you know?' I asked.

"'Men are very clumsy,' said she. 'I knew you were on every train. I thought you were going to speak to me, and I'm glad you didn't.'

"Then we had more talk; and at last a kind of proud, serious look came on her face, and she turned and pointed a finger at the big house.

"'The Allyns,' says she, 'have lived in Elmcroft for a hundred years. We are a proud family. Look at that mansion. It has fifty rooms. See the pillars and porches and balconies. The ceilings in the reception-rooms and the ball-room are twenty-eight feet high. My father is a lineal descendant of belted earls.'

"'I belted one of 'em once in the Duquesne Hotel, in Pittsburgh,' says I, 'and he didn't offer to resent it. He was there dividing his attentions between Monongahela whiskey and heiresses, and he got fresh.'

"'Of course,' she goes on, 'my father wouldn't allow a drummer to set his foot in Elmeroft. If he knew that I was talking to one over the fence he would lock me in my room.'

"'Would you let me come there?' says I. 'Would you talk to me if I was to call? For,' I goes on, 'if you said I might come and see you, the earls might be belted or suspendered, or pinned up with safety-pins, as far as I am concerned.'

"'I must not talk to you,' she says, 'because we have not been introduced. It is not exactly proper. So I will say good-bye, Mr. –'

"'Say the name,' says I. 'You haven't forgotten it.'

"'Pescud,' says she, a little mad.

"'The rest of the name!' I demands, cool as could be.

"'John,' says she.

"'John-what?' I says.

"'John A.,' says she, with her head high. 'Are you through, now?'

"'I'm coming to see the belted earl to-morrow,' I says.

"'He'll feed you to his fox-hounds,' says she, laughing.

"'If he does, it'll improve their running,' says I. 'I'm something of a hunter myself.'

"'I must be going in now,' says she. 'I oughtn't to have spoken to you at all. I hope you'll have a pleasant trip back to Minneapolis – or Pittsburgh, was it? Good-bye!'

"'Good-night,' says I, 'and it wasn't Minneapolis. What's your name, first, please?'

"She hesitated. Then she pulled a leaf off a bush, and said:

"'My name is Jessie,' says she.

"'Good-night, Miss Allyn,' says I.

"The next morning at eleven, sharp, I rang the door-bell of that World's Fair main building. After about three-quarters of an hour an old nigger man about eighty showed up and asked what I wanted. I gave him my business card, and said I wanted to see the colonel. He showed me in.

"Say, did you ever crack open a wormy English walnut? That's what that house was like. There wasn't enough furniture in it to fill an eight-dollar flat. Some old horsehair lounges and three-legged chairs and some framed ancestors on the walls were all that met the eye. But when Colonel Allyn comes in, the place seemed to light up. You could almost hear a band playing, and see a bunch of old-timers in wigs and white stockings dancing a quadrille. It was the style of him, although he had on the same shabby clothes I saw him wear at the station.

"For about nine seconds he had me rattled, and I came mighty near getting cold feet and trying to sell him some plate-glass. But I got my nerve back pretty quick. He asked me to sit down, and I told him everything. I told him how I followed his daughter from Cincinnati, and what I did it for, and all about my salary and prospects, and explained to him my little code of living – to be always decent and right in your home town; and when you're on the road, never take more than four glasses of beer a day or play higher than a twenty-five-cent limit. At first I thought he was going to throw me out of the window, but I kept on talking. Pretty soon I got a chance to tell him that story about the Western Congressman who had lost his pocket-book and the grass widow – you remember that story. Well, that got him to laughing, and I'll bet that was the first laugh those ancestors and horsehair sofas had heard in many a day.

"We talked two hours. I told him everything I knew; and then he began to ask questions, and I told him the rest. All I asked of him was to give me a chance. If I couldn't make a hit with the little lady, I'd clear out, and not bother any more.

"At last he says: 'There was a Sir Courtenay Pescud in the time of Charles I, if I remember rightly.'

"'If there was,' says I, 'he can't claim kin with our bunch. We've always lived in and around Pittsburgh. I've got an uncle in the real-estate business, and one in trouble somewhere out in Kansas. You can inquire about any of the rest of us from anybody in old Smoky Town, and get satisfactory replies. Did you ever run across that story about the captain of the whaler who tried to make a sailor say his prayers?' says I.

"'It occurs to me that I have never been so fortunate,' says the colonel."

"So I told it to him. Laugh! I was wishing to myself that he was a customer. What a bill of glass I'd sell him!

"And then he says:

'The relating of anecdotes and humorous occurrences has always seemed to me, Mr. Pescud, to be a particularly agreeable way of promoting and perpetuating amenities between friends. With your permission, I will relate to you a fox-hunting story with which I was personally connected, and which may furnish you some amusement.'

"So he tells it. It takes forty minutes by the watch. Did I laugh? Well, say! When I got my face straight he calls in old Pete, the super-annuated darky, and sends him down to the hotel to bring up my valise. It was Elmcroft for me while I was in the town.

"Two evenings later I got a chance to speak a word with Miss Jessie alone on the porch while the colonel was thinking up another story.

"'It's going to be a fine evening,' says I."

"'He's coming,' says she. 'He's going to tell you, this time, the story about the old negro and the green watermelons. It always comes after the one about the Yankees and the game rooster. There was another time,' she goes on, 'that you nearly got left – it was at Pulaski City.'

"'Yes,' says I, 'I remember. My foot slipped as I was jumping on the step, and I nearly tumbled off.'

"'I know,' says she. 'And – and I – I was afraid you had, John A. I was afraid you had.'

"And then she skips into the house through one of the big windows."

IV

"Coketown!" droned the porter, making his way through the slowing car.

Pescud gathered his hat and baggage with the leisurely promptness of an old traveller.

"I married her a year ago," said John. "I told you I built a house in the East End. The belted – I mean the colonel – is there, too. I find him waiting at the gate whenever I get back from a trip to hear any new story I might have picked up on the road."

I glanced out of the window. Coketown was nothing more than a ragged hillside dotted with a score of black dismal huts propped up against dreary mounds of slag and clinkers. It rained in slanting torrents, too, and the rills foamed and splashed down through the black mud to the railroad-tracks.

"You won't sell much plate-glass here, John," said I. "Why do you get off at this end-o'-the-world?"

"Why," said Pescud, "the other day I took Jessie for a little trip to Philadelphia, and coming back she thought she saw some petunias in a pot in one of those windows over there just like some she used to raise down in the old Virginia home. So I thought I'd drop off here for the night, and see if I could dig up some of the cuttings or blossoms for her. Here we are. Good-night, old man. I gave you the address. Come out and see us when you have time."

The train moved forward. One of the dotted brown ladies insisted on having windows raised, now that the rain beat against them. The porter came along with his mysterious wand and began to light the car.

I glanced downward and saw the best-seller. I picked it up and set it carefully farther along on the floor of the car, where the rain-drops would not fall upon it. And then, suddenly, I smiled, and seemed to see that life has no geographical metes and bounds.

"Good-luck to you, Trevelyan," I said. "And may you get the petunias for your princess!"

BLIND MAN'S HOLIDAY

ALAS FOR THE man and for the artist with the shifting point of perspective! Life shall be a confusion of ways to the one; the landscape shall rise up and confound the other. Take the case of Lorison. At one time he appeared to himself to be the feeblest of fools; at another he conceived that he followed ideals so fine that the world was not yet ready to accept them. During one mood he cursed his folly; possessed by the other, he bore himself with a serene grandeur akin to greatness: in neither did he attain the perspective.

Generations before, the name had been "Larsen." His race had bequeathed him its finestrung, melancholy temperament, its saving balance of thrift and industry.

From his point of perspective he saw himself an outcast from society, forever to be a shady skulker along the ragged edge of respectability; a denizen des trois-quartz de monde, that pathetic spheroid lying between the haut and the demi, whose inhabitants envy each of their neighbors, and are scorned by both. He was self-condemned to this opinion, as he was self-exiled, through it, to this quaint Southern city a thousand miles from his former home. Here he had dwelt for longer than a year, knowing but few, keeping in a subjective world of shadows which was invaded at times by the perplexing bulks of jarring realities. Then he fell in love with a girl whom he met in a cheap restaurant, and his story begins.

The Rue Chartres, in New Orleans, is a street of ghosts. It lies in the quarter where the Frenchman, in his prime, set up his translated pride and glory; where, also, the arrogant don had swaggered, and dreamed of gold and grants and ladies' gloves. Every flagstone has its grooves worn by footsteps going royally to the wooing and the fighting. Every house has a princely heartbreak; each doorway its untold tale of gallant promise and slow decay.

By night the Rue Chartres is now but a murky fissure, from which the groping wayfarer sees, flung against the sky, the tangled filigree of

Moorish iron balconies. The old houses of monsieur stand yet, indomitable against the century, but their essence is gone. The street is one of ghosts to whosoever can see them.

A faint heartbeat of the street's ancient glory still survives in a corner occupied by the Café Carabine d'Or. Once men gathered there to plot against kings, and to warn presidents. They do so yet, but they are not the same kind of men. A brass button will scatter these; those would have set their faces against an army. Above the door hangs the sign board, upon which has been depicted a vast animal of unfamiliar species. In the act of firing upon this monster is represented an unobtrusive human levelling an obtrusive gun, once the color of bright gold. Now the legend above the picture is faded beyond conjecture; the gun's relation to the title is a matter of faith; the menaced animal, wearied of the long aim of the hunter, has resolved itself into a shapeless blot.

The place is known as "Antonio's," as the name, white upon the red-lit transparency, and gilt upon the windows, attests. There is a promise in "Antonio"; a justifiable expectancy of savory things in oil and pepper and wine, and perhaps an angel's whisper of garlic. But the rest of the name is "O'Riley." Antonio O'Riley!

The Carabine d'Or is an ignominious ghost of the Rue Chartres. The café where Bienville and Conti dined, where a prince has broken bread, is become a "family ristaurant."

Its customers are working men and women, almost to a unit. Occasionally you will see chorus girls from the cheaper theaters, and men who follow avocations subject to quick vicissitudes; but at Antonio's – name rich in Bohemian promise, but tame in fulfillment – manners debonair and gay are toned down to the "family" standard. Should you light a cigarette, mine host will touch you on the "arrum" and remind you that the proprieties are menaced. "Antonio" entices and beguiles from fiery legend without, but "O'Riley" teaches decorum within.

It was at this restaurant that Lorison first saw the girl. A flashy fellow with a predatory eye had followed her in, and had advanced to take the other chair at the little table where she stopped, but Lorison slipped into the seat before him. Their acquaintance began, and grew, and how for two months they had sat at the same table each evening, not meeting by appointment, but as if by a series of fortuitous and happy accidents. After dining, they would take a walk together in one of the little city parks, or among the panoramic markets where exhibits a continuous vaudeville of sights and sounds. Always at eight o'clock their steps led them to a certain street corner, where she prettily but firmly bade him good night and left him. "I do not live far from here," she frequently said, "and you must let me go the rest of the way alone."

But now Lorison had discovered that he wanted to go the rest of the way with her, or happiness would depart, leaving him on a very lonely corner of life. And at the same time that he made the discovery, the secret of his banishment from the society of the good laid its finger in his face and told him it must not be.

Man is too thoroughly an egoist not to be also an egotist; if he loves, the object shall know it. During a lifetime he may conceal it through stress of expediency and honor, but it shall bubble from his dying lips, though it disrupts a neighborhood. It is known, however, that most men do not wait so long to disclose their passion. In the case of Lorison, his particular ethics positively forbade him to declare his sentiments, but he must needs dally with the subject, and woo by innuendo at least.

On this night, after the usual meal at the Carabine d'Or, he strolled with his companion down the dim old street toward the river.

The Rue Chartres perishes in the old Place d'Armes. The ancient Cabildo, where Spanish justice fell like hail, faces it, and the Cathedral, another provincial ghost, overlooks it. Its centre is a little, iron-railed park of flowers and immaculate gravelled walks, where citizens take the air of evenings. Pedestalled high above it, the general sits his cavorting steed, with his face turned stonily down the river toward English Turn, whence come no more Britons to bombard his cotton bales.

Often the two sat in this square, but tonight Lorison guided her past the stone-stepped gate, and still riverward. As they walked, he smiled to himself to think that all he knew of her – except that be loved her – was her name, Norah Greenway, and that she lived with her brother. They had talked about everything except themselves. Perhaps her reticence had been caused by his.

They came, at length, upon the levee, and sat upon a great, prostrate beam. The air was pungent with the dust of commerce. The great river slipped yellowly past. Across it Algiers lay, a longitudinous black bulk against a vibrant electric haze sprinkled with exact stars.

The girl was young and of the piquant order. A certain bright melancholy pervaded her; she possessed an untarnished, pale prettiness doomed to please. Her voice, when she spoke, dwarfed her theme. It was the voice capable of investing little subjects with a large interest. She sat at ease, bestowing her skirts with the little womanly touch, serene as if the begrimed pier were a summer garden. Lorison poked the rotting boards with his cane.

He began by telling her that he was in love with someone to whom he durst not speak of it. "And why not?" she asked, accepting swiftly his fatuous presentation of a third person of straw. "My place in the world," he answered, "is none to ask a woman to share. I am an outcast from honest people; I am wrongly accused of one crime, and am, I believe, guilty of another."

Thence he plunged into the story of his abdication from society. The story, pruned of his moral philosophy, deserves no more than the slightest touch. It is no new tale, that of the gambler's declension. During one night's sitting he lost, and then had imperilled a certain amount of his employer's money, which, by accident, he carried with him. He continued to lose, to the last wager, and then began to gain, leaving the game winner to a somewhat formidable sum. The same night his employer's safe was robbed. A search was had; the winnings of Lorison were found in his room, their total forming an accusative nearness to the sum purloined. He was taken, tried and, through incomplete evidence, released, smutched with the sinister devoirs of a disagreeing jury.

"It is not in the unjust accusation," he said to the girl, "that my burden lies, but in the knowledge that from the moment I staked the first dollar of the firm's money I was a criminal – no matter whether I lost or won. You see why it is impossible for me to speak of love to her."

"It is a sad thing," said Norah, after a little pause "to think what very good people there are in the world."

"Good?" said Lorison.

"I was thinking of this superior person whom you say you love. She must be a very poor sort of creature."

"I do not understand."

"Nearly," she continued, "as poor a sort of creature as yourself."

"You do not understand," said Lorison, removing his hat and sweeping back his fine, light hair. "Suppose she loved me in return, and were willing to marry me. Think, if you can, what would follow. Never a day would pass but she would be reminded of her sacrifice. I would read a condescension in her smile, a pity even in her affection, that would madden me. No. The thing would stand between us forever. Only equals should mate. I could never ask her to come down upon my lower plane."

An arc light faintly shone upon Lorison's face. An illumination from within also pervaded it. The girl saw the rapt, ascetic look; it was the face either of Sir Galahad or Sir Fool.

"Quite starlike," she said, "is this unapproachable angel. Really too high to be grasped."

"By me, yes."

She faced him suddenly. "My dear friend, would you prefer your star fallen?" Lorison made a wide gesture.

"You push me to the bald fact," he declared; "you are not in sympathy with my argument. But I will answer you so. If I could reach my particular star, to drag it down, I would not do it; but if it were fallen, I would pick it up, and thank Heaven for the privilege."

They were silent for some minutes. Norah shivered, and thrust her hands deep into the pockets of her jacket. Lorison uttered a remorseful exclamation.

"I'm not cold," she said. "I was just thinking. I ought to tell you something. You have selected a strange confidante. But you cannot expect a chance acquaintance, picked up in a doubtful restaurant, to be an angel."

"Norah!" cried Lorison.

"Let me go on. You have told me about yourself. We have been such good friends. I must tell you now what I never wanted you to know. I am – worse than you are. I was on the stage ... I sang in the chorus ... I was pretty bad, I guess ... I stole diamonds from the prima donna ... they arrested me ... I gave most of them up, and they let me go ... I drank wine every night ... a great deal ... I was very wicked, but –"

Lorison knelt quickly by her side and took her hands.

"Dear Norah!" he said, exultantly. "It is you, it is you I love! You never guessed it, did you? 'Tis you I meant all the time. Now I can speak. Let me make you forget the past. We have both suffered; let us shut out the world, and live for each other. Norah, do you hear me say I love you?"

"In spite of –"

"Rather say because of it. You have come out of your past noble and good. Your heart is an angel's, Give it to me."

"A little while ago you feared the future too much to even speak."

"But for you; not for myself. Can you love me?"

She cast herself, wildly sobbing, upon his breast.

"Better than life – than truth itself – than everything."

"And my own past," said Lorison, with a note of solicitude – "can you forgive and –"

"I answered you that," she whispered, "when I told you I loved you." She leaned away, and looked thoughtfully at him. "If I had not told you about myself, would you have – would you –"

"No," he interrupted; "I would never have let you know I loved you. I would never have asked you this – Norah, will you be my wife?"

She wept again.

"Oh, believe me; I am good now – I am no longer wicked! I will be the best wife in the world. Don't think I am – bad any more. If you do I shall die, I shall die!"

While he was consoling, her, she brightened up, eager and impetuous. "Will vou marry me tonight?" she said. "Will you prove it that way. I have a reason for wishing it to be tonight. Will you?"

Of one of two things was this exceeding frankness the outcome: either of importunate brazenness or of utter innocence. The lover's perspective contained only the one.

"The sooner," said Lorison, "the happier I shall be."

"What is there to do?" she asked. "What do you have to get? Come! You should know."

Her energy stirred the dreamer to action.

"A city directory first," he cried, gayly, "to find where the man lives who gives licenses to happiness. We will go together and rout him out. Cabs, cars, policemen, telephones and ministers shall aid us."

"Father Rogan shall marry us," said the girl, with ardor. "I will take you to him."

An hour later the two stood at the open doorway of an immense, gloomy brick building in a narrow and lonely street. The license was tight in Norah's hand.

"Wait here a moment," she said, "till I find Father Rogan."

She plunged into the black hallway, and the lover was left standing, as it were, on one leg, outside. His impatience was not greatly taxed. Gazing curiously into what seemed the hallway to Erebus, he was presently reassured by a stream of light that bisected the darkness, far down the passage. Then he heard her call, and fluttered lampward, like the moth. She beckoned him through a doorway into the room whence emanated the light. The room was bare of nearly everything except books, which had subjugated all its space. Here and there little spots of territory had been reconquered. An elderly, bald man, with a superlatively calm, remote eye, stood by a table with a book in his hand, his finger still marking a page. His dress was sombre and appertained to a religious order. His eye denoted an acquaintance with the perspective.

"Father Rogan," said Norah, "this is he."

"The two of ye," said Father Rogan, "want to get married?"

They did not deny it. He married them. The ceremony was quickly done. One who could have witnessed it, and felt its scope, might have trembled at the terrible inadequacy of it to rise to the dignity of its endless chain of results.

Afterward the priest spake briefly, as if by rote, of certain other civil and legal addenda that either might or should, at a later time,to cap the ceremony. Lorison tendered a fee, which was declined, and before the door closed after the departing couple Father Rogan's book popped open again where his finger marked it.

In the dark hall Norah whirled and clung to her companion, tearful.

"Will you never, never be sorry?"

At last she was reassured.

At the first light they reached upon the street, she asked the time, just as she had each night. Lorison looked at his watch. Half-past eight.

Lorison thought it was from habit that she guided their steps toward the corner where they always parted. But, arrived there, she hesitated, and then released his arm. A drug store stood on the corner; its bright, soft light shone upon them.

"Please leave me here as usual tonight," said Norah, sweetly. "I must – I would rather you would. You will not object? At six tomorrow evening I will meet you at Antonio's. I want to sit with you there once more. And then – I will go where you say." She gave him a bewildering, bright smile, and walked swiftly away.

Surely it needed all the strength of her charm to carry off this astounding behavior. It was no discredit to Lorison's strength of mind that his head began to whirl. Pocketing his hands, he rambled vacuously over to the druggist's windows, and began assiduously to spell over the names of the patent medicines therein displayed.

As soon as be had recovered his wits, he proceeded along the street in an aimless fashion. After drifting for two or three squares, he flowed into a somewhat more pretentious thoroughfare, a way much frequented by him in his solitary ramblings. For here was a row of slops devoted to traffic in goods of the widest range of choice – handiworks of art, skill and fancy, products of nature and labour from every zone.

Here, for a time, he loitered among the conspicuous windows, where was set, emphasized by congested floods of light, the cunningest spoil of the interiors. There were few passers, and of this

Lorison was glad. He was not of the world. For a long time he had touched his fellow man only at the gear of a levelled cog-wheel – at right angles, and upon a different axis. He had dropped into a distinctly new orbit. The stroke of ill fortune had acted upon him, in effect, as a blow delivered upon the apex of a certain ingenious toy, the musical top, which – when thus buffeted while spinning, gives forth, with scarcely retarded motion, a complete change of key and chord.

Strolling along the pacific avenue, he experienced singular, supernatural calm, accompanied by an unusual activity of brain. Reflecting upon recent affairs, be assured himself of his happiness in having won for a bride the one he had so greatly desired, yet he wondered mildly at his dearth of active emotion. Her strange behavior in abandoning him without valid excuse on his bridal eve aroused in him only a vague and curious speculation. Again, he found himself contemplating, with complaisant serenity, the incidents of her somewhat lively career. His perspective seemed to have been queerly shifted.

As he stood before a window near a corner, his ears were assailed by a waxing clamor and commotion. He stood close to the window to allow passage to the cause of the hubbub – a procession of human beings, which rounded the corner aid headed in his direction. He perceived a salient hue of blue and a glitter of brass about a central figure of dazzling white and silver, and a ragged wake of black, bobbing figures.

Two ponderous policemen were conducting between them a woman dressed as if for the stage, in a short, white, satiny skirt reaching to the knees, pink stockings, and a sort of sleeveless bodice bright with relucent, armor-like scales. Upon her curly, light hair was perched, at a rollicking angle, a shining tin helmet. The costume was to be instantly recognized as one of those amazing conceptions to which competition has harried the inventors of the spectacular ballet. One of the officers bore a long cloak upon his axm, which, doubtless, had been intended to veil the candid attractions of their effulgent prisoner, but, for some reason, it had not been called into use, to the vociferous delight of the tail of the procession.

Compelled by a sudden and vigorous movement of the woman, the parade halted before the window by which Lorison stood. He saw that she waš young, and, at the first glance, was deceived by a sophistical prettiness of her face, which waned before a more judicious scrutiny. Her look was bold and reckless, and upon her countenance, where yet the contours of youth survived, were the finger-marks of old age's credentialed courier, Late Hours.

The young woman fixed her unshrinking gaze upon Lorison, and called to him in the voice of the wronged heroine in straits:

"Say! You look like a good fellow; come and put up the bail, won't you? I've done nothing to get pinched for. It's all a mistake. See how they're treating me! You won't be sorry, if you'll help me out of this. Think of your sister or your girl being dragged along the streets this way! I say, come along now, like a good fellow."

It may be that Lorison, in spite of the unconvincing bathos of this appeal, showed a sympathetic face, for one of the officers left the woman's side, and went over to him.

"It's all right, Sir," he said, in a husky, confidential tone; "she's the right party. We took her after the first act at the Green Light Theatre, on a wire from the chief of police of Chicago. It's only a square or two to the station. Her rig's pretty bad, but she refused to change clothes – or, rather," added the officer, with a smile, "to put on some. I thought I'd explain matters to you so you wouldn't think she was being imposed upon."

"What is the charge?" asked Lorison.

"Grand larceny. Diamonds. Her husband is a jeweler in Chicago. She cleaned his show case of the sparklers, and skipped with a comic-opera troupe."

The policeman, perceiving that the interest of the entire group of spectators was centred upon himself and Lorison – their conference being regarded as a possible new complication – was fain to prolong the situation – which reflected his own importance – by a little afterpiece of philosophical comment.

"A gentleman like you, Sir," he went on affably, "would never notice it, but it comes in my line to observe what an immense amount of trouble is made by that combination – I mean the stage, diamonds and light-headed women who aren't satisfied with good homes. I tell you, Sir, a man these days and nights wants to know what his women folks are up to."

The policeman smiled a good night, and returned to the side of his charge, who had been intently watching Lorison's face during the conversation, no doubt for some indication of his intention to render succour. Now, at the failure of the sign, and at the movement made to continue the ignominious progress, she abandoned hope, and addressed him thus, pointedly:

"You damn chalk-faced quitter! You was thinking of giving me a hand, but you let the cop talk you out of it the first word. You're a dandy to tie to. Say, if you ever get a girl, she'll have a picnic. Won't she work you to the queen's taste! Oh, my!" She concluded with a taunting, shrill laugh that rasped Lorison like a saw. The policemen urged her forward; the delighted train of gaping followers closed up the rear; and the captive Amazon, accepting her fate, extended the scope of her maledictions so that none in hearing might seem to be slighted.

Then there came upon Lorison an overwhelming revulsion of his perspective. It may be that he had been ripe for it, that the abnormal condition of mind in which he had for so long existed was already about to revert to its balance; however, it is certain that the events of the last few minutes had furnished the channel, if not the impetus, for the change.

The initial determining influence had been so small a thing as the fact and manner of his having been approached by the officer. That agent had, by the style of his accost, restored the loiterer to his former place in society. In an instant he had been transformed from a somewhat rancid prowler along the fishy side streets of gentility into an honest gentleman, with whom even so lordly a guardian of the peace might agreeably exchange the compliments.

This, then, first broke the spell, and set thrilling in him a resurrected longing for the fellowship of his kind, and the rewards of the virtuous. To what end, he vehemently asked himself, was this fanciful self-accusation, this empty renunciation, this moral squeamishness through which he had been led to abandon what was his heritage in life, and not beyond his deserts? Technically, he was uncondemned; his sole guilty spot was in thought rather than deed, and cognizance of it unshared by others. For what good, moral or sentimental, did he slink, retreating like the hedgehog from his own shadow, to and fro in this musty Bohemia that lacked even the picturesque?

But the thing that struck home and set him raging was the part played by the Amazonian prisoner. To the counterpart of that astounding belligerent – identical at least, in the way of experience – to one, by her own confession, thus far fallen, had he, not three hours since, been united in marriage. How desirable and natural it had seemed to him then, and how monstrous it seemed now! How the words of diamond thief number two yet burned in his ears: "If you ever get a girl, she'll have a picnic. What did that mean but that women instinctively knew him for one they could hoodwink? Still again, there reverberated the policeman's sapient contribution to his agony: "A man these days and nights wants to know what his women folks are up to." Oh, yes, he had been a fool; he had looked at things from the wrong standpoint.

But the wildest note in all the clamor was struck by pain's forefinger, jealousy. Now, at least, he felt that keenest sting – a mounting love unworthily bestowed. Whatever she might be, he loved her; he bore in his own breast his doom. A grating, comic flavor to his predicament struck him suddenly, and he laughed creakingly as he swung down the echoing pavement. An impetuous desire to act, to battle with his fate, seized him. He stopped upon his heel, and smote his palms together triumphantly. His wife was – where? But there was a tangible link; an outlet more or less navigable, through which his derelict ship of matrimony might yet be safely towed – the priest!

Like all imaginative men with pliable natures, Lorison was, when thoroughly stirred, apt to become tempestuous. With a high and stubborn indignation upon him, be retraced his steps to the intersecting street by which he had come. Down this he hurried to the corner where he had parted with – an astringent grimace tinctured the thought – his wife. Thence still back he harked, following through an unfamiliar district his stimulated recollections of the way they had come from that preposterous wedding. Many times he went abroad, and nosed his way back to, the trail, furious.

At last, when he reached the dark, calamitous building in which his madness had culminated, and found the black hallway, he dashed down it, perceiving no light or sound. But he raised his voice, hailing loudly; reckless of everything but that he should find the old mischief-maker with the eyes that looked too far away to see the disaster he had wrought. The door opened, and in the stream of light Father Rogan stood, his book in hand, with his finger marking the place.

"Ah!" cried Lorison. "You are the man I want. I had a wife of you a few hours ago. I would not trouble you, but I neglected to note how it was done. Will you oblige me with the information whether the business is beyond remedy?"

"Come inside," said the priest; "there are other lodgers in the house, who might prefer sleep to even a gratified curiosity."

Lorison entered the room and took the chair offered him. The priest's eyes looked a courteous interrogation.

"I must apologize again," said the young man, "for so soon intruding upon you with my marital infelicities, but, as my wife has neglected to furnish me with her address, I am deprived of the legitimate recourse of a family row."

"I am quite a plain man," said Father Rogan, pleasantly; "but I do not see how I am to ask you questions."

"Pardon my indirectness," said Lorison; "I will ask one. In this room tonight you pronounced me to be a husband. You afterward spoke of additional rites or performances that either should or could be effected. I paid little attention to your words then, but I am hungry to hear them repeated now. As matters stand, am I married past all help?"

"You are as legally and as firmly bound," said the priest, "as though it had been done in a cathedral, in the presence of thousands. The additional observances I referred to are not necessary to the strictest legality of the act, but were advised as a precaution for the future – for convenience of proof in such contingencies as wills, inheritances and the like."

Lorison laughed harshly.

"Many thanks," he said. "Then there is no mistake, and I am the happy benedict. I suppose I should go stand upon the bridal corner, and when my wife gets through walking the streets she will look me up."

Father Rogan regarded him calmly.

"My son," he said, "when a man and woman come to me to be married I always marry them. I do this for the sake of other people whom they might go away and marry if they did not marry each other. As you see, I do not seek your confidence; but your case seems to me to be one not altogether devoid of interest. Very few marriages that have come to my notice have brought such well-expressed regret within so short a time. I will hazard one question: were you not under the impression that you loved the lady you married, at the time you did so?"

"Loved her!" cried Lorison, wildly. "Never so well as now, though she told me she deceived and sinned and stole. Never more than now, when, perhaps, she is laughing at the fool she cajoled and left, with scarcely a word, to return to God only knows what particular line of her former folly."

Father Rogan answered nothing. During the silence that succeeded, he sat with a quiet expectation beaming in his full, lambent eye.

"If you would listen –" began Lorison. The priest held up his hand.

"As I hoped," he said. "I thought you would trust me. Wait but a moment." He brought a long clay pipe, filled and lighted it.

"Now, my son," he said.

Lorison poured a twelve month's accumulated confidence into Father Rogan's ear. He told all; not sparing himself or omitting the facts of his past, the events of the night, or his disturbing conjectures and fears.

"The main point," said the priest, when he had concluded, "seems to me to be this – are you reasonably sure that you love this woman whom you have married?"

"Why," exclaimed Lorison, rising impulsively to his feet – "why should I deny it? But look at me – am fish, flesh or fowl? That is the main point to me, assure you."

"I understand you," said the priest, also rising, and laying down his pipe. "The situation is one that has taxed the endurance of much older men than you – in fact, especially much older men than you. I will try to relieve you from it, and this night. You shall see for yourself into exactly what predicament you have fallen, and how you shall, possibly, be extricated. There is no evidence so credible as that of the eyesight."

Father Rogan moved about the room, and donned a soft black hat. Buttoning his coat to his throat, he laid his hand on the doorknob. "Let us walk," he said.

The two went out upon the street. The priest turned his face down it, and Lorison walked with him through a squalid district, where the houses loomed, awry and desolate-looking, high above them. Presently they turned into a less dismal side street, where the houses were smaller, and, though hinting of the most meagre comfort, lacked the concentrated wretchedness of the more populous byways.

At a segregated, two-story house Father Rogan halted, and mounted the steps with the confidence of a familiar visitor. He ushered Lorison into a narrow hallway, faintly lighted by a cobwebbed hanging lamp. Almost immediately a door to the right opened and a dingy Irish-woman protruded her head.

"Good evening to ye, Mistress Geehan," said the priest, unconsciously, it seemed, falling into a delicately flavored brogue. "And is it yourself can tell me if Norah has gone out again, the night, maybe?"

"Oh, it's yer blissid reverence! Sure and I can tell ye the same. The purty darlin' wint out, as usual, but a bit later. And she says: 'Mother Geehan,' says she, 'it's me last noight out, praise the saints, this noight is!' And, oh, yer reverence, the swate, beautiful drame of a dress she had this time! White satin and silk and ribbons, and lace about the neck and arrums – 'twas a sin, yer reverence, the gold was spint upon it."

The priest heard Lorison catch his breath painfully, and a faint smile flickered across his own clean-cut mouth.

"Well, then, Mistress Geehan," said he, "I'll just step upstairs and see the bit boy for a minute, and I'll take this Gentleman up with me."

"He's awake, thin," said the woman. 'I've just come down from sitting wid him the last hour, tilling him fine shtories of ould County Tyrone. 'Tis a greedy gossoon, it is, yer riverence, for me shtories."

"Small the doubt," said Father Rogan. "There's no rocking would put him to slape the quicker, I'm thinking."

Amid the woman's shrill protest against the retort, the two men ascended the steep stairway. The priest pushed open the door of a room near its top.

"Is that you already, sister?" drawled a sweet, childish voice from the darkness.

"It's only ould Father Denny come to see ye, darlin'; and a foine gentleman I've brought to make ye a gr-r-and call. And ye resaves us fast aslape in bed! Shame on yez manners!"

"Oh, Father Denny, is that you? I'm glad. And will you light the lamp, please? It's on the table by the door. And quit talking like Mother Geehan, Father Denny."

The priest lit the lamp, and Lorison saw a tiny, towsled-haired boy, with a thin, delicate face, sitting up in a small bed in a corner. Quickly, also, his rapid glance considered the room and its contents. It was furnished with more than comfort, and its adornments plainly indicated a woman's discerning taste. An open door beyond revealed the blackness of an adjoining room's interior.

The boy clutched both of Father Rogan's hands. "I'm so glad you came," he said; "but why did you come in the night? Did sister send you?"

"Off wid ye! Am I to be sint about, at me age, as was Terence McShane, of Ballymahone? I come on me own r-r-responsibility."

Lorison had also advanced to the boy's bedside. He was fond of children; and the wee fellow, laving himself down to sleep alone ill that dark room, stirred his heart.

"Aren't you afraid, little man?" he asked, stooping down beside him.

"Sometimes," answered the boy, with a shy smile, "when the rats make too much noise. But nearly every night, when sister goes out, Mother Geehan stays a while with me, and tells me funny stories. I'm not often afraid, sir."

"This brave little gentleman," said Father Rogan, "is a scholar of mine. Every day from half-past six to half-past eight – when sister comes for him – he stops in my study, and we find out what's in the inside of books. He knows multiplication, division and fractions; and he's troubling me to begin wid the chronicles of Ciaran of Clonmaciioise, Corurac McCullenan and Cuan O'Lochain, the gr-r-reat Irish histhorians." The boy was evidently accustomed to the priest's Celtic pleasantries. A little, appreciative grin was all the attention the insinuation of pedantry received.

Lorison, to have saved his life, could not have put to the child one of those vital questions that were wildly beating about, unanswered, in his own brain. The little fellow was very like Norah; he had the same shining hair and candid eyes.

"Oh, Father Denny," cried the boy, suddenly, "I forgot to tell you! Sister is not going away at night any more! She told me so when she kissed me good night as she was leaving. And she said she was so happy, and then she cried. Wasn't that queer? But I'm glad; aren't you?"

"Yes, lad. And now, ye omadhaun, go to sleep, and say good night; we must be going."

"Which shall I do first, Father Denny?"

"Faith, he's caught me again! Wait till I get the sassenach into the annals of Tageruach, the hagiographer; I'll give him enough of the Irish idiom to make him more respectful."

The light was out, and the small, brave voice bidding them good night from the dark room. They groped downstairs, and tore away from the garrulity of Mother Geehan.

Again the priest steered them through the dim ways, but this time in another direction. His conductor was serenely silent, and Lorison followed his example to the extent of seldom speaking. Serene he could not be. His heart beat suffocatingly in his breast. The following of this blind, menacing trail was pregnant with he knew not what humiliating revelation to be delivered at its end.

They came into a more pretentious street, where trade, it could be surmised, flourished by day. And again the priest paused; this time before a lofty building, whose great doors and windows in the lowest floor were carefully shuttered and barred. Its higher apertures were dark, save in the third story, the windows of which were brilliantly lighted. Lorison's ear caught a distant, regular, pleasing thrumming, as of music above. They stood at an angle of the building. Up, along the side nearest them, mounted an iron stairway. At its top was an upright, illuminated parallelogram. Father Rogan had stopped, and stood, musing.

"I will say this much," he remarked, thoughtfully: "I believe you to be a better man than you think yourself to be, and a better man than I thought some hours ago. But do not take this," he added, with a smile, "as much praise. I promised you a possible deliverance from an unhappy perplexity. I will have to modify that promise. I can only remove the mystery that enhanced that perplexity. Your deliverance depends upon yourself. Come."

He led his companion up the stairway. Halfway up, Lorison caught him by the sleeve. "Remember," he gasped, "I love that woman."

"You desired to know.

"I – Go on."

The priest reached the landing at the top of the stairway. Lorison, behind him, saw that the illuminated space was the glass upper half of a door opening into the lighted room. The rhythmic music increased as they neared it; the stairs shook with the mellow vibrations.

Lorison stopped breathing when he set foot upon the highest step, for the priest stood aside, and motioned him to look through the glass of the door.

His eye, accustomed to the darkness, met first a blinding glare, and then he made out the faces and forms of many people, amid an extravagant display of splendid robings – billowy laces, brilliant-hued finery, ribbons, silks and misty drapery. And then he caught the meaning of that jarring hum, and he saw the tired, pale, happy face of his wife, bending, as were a score of others, over her sewing machine – toiling, toiling. Here was the folly she pursued, and the end of his quest.

But not his deliverance, though even then remorse struck him. His shamed soul fluttered once more before it retired to make room for the other and better one. For, to temper his thrill of joy, the shine of the satin and the glimmer of ornaments recalled the disturbing figure of the bespangled Amazon, and the base duplicate histories it by the glare of footlights and stolen diamonds. It is past the wisdom of him who only sets the scenes, either to praise or blame the man. But this time his love overcame his scruples. He took a quick step, and reached out his hand for the doorknob. Father Rogan was quicker to arrest it and draw him back.

"You use my trust in you queerly," said the priest sternly. "What are you about to do?"

"I am going to my wife," said Lorison. "Let me pass."

"Listen," said the priest, holding him firmly by the arm. "I am about to put you in possession of a piece of knowledge of which, thus far, you have scarcely proved deserving. I do not think you ever will; but I will not dwell upon that. You see in that room the woman you married, working for a frugal living for herself, and a generous comfort for an idolized brother. This building belongs to the chief costumer of the city. For months the advance orders for the coming Mardi Gras festivals have kept the work going day and night. I myself secured employment here for Norah. She toils here each night from nine o'clock until daylight, and, besides, carries home with her some of the finer costumes, requiring more delicate needlework, and works there part of the day. Somehow, you two have remained strangely ignorant of each other's lives. Are you convinced now that your wife is not walking the streets?"

"Let me go to her," cried Lorison, again struggling, "and beg her forgiveness!"

"Sir," said the priest, "do you owe me nothing? Be quiet. It seems so often that Heaven lets fall its choicest gifts into hands that must be taught to hold them. Listen again. You forgot that repentant sin must not compromise, but look up, for redemption, to the purest and best. You went to her with the fine-spun sophistry that peace could be found in a mutual guilt; and she, fearful of losing what her heart so craved, thought it worth the price to buy it with a desperate, pure, beautiful lie. I have known her since the day she was born; she is as innocent and unsullied in life and deed as a holy saint. In that lowly street where she dwells she first saw the light, and she has lived there ever since, spending her days in generous self-sacrifice for others. Och, ye spalpeen!" continued Father Rogan, raising his finger in kindly anger at Lorison. "What for, I wonder, could she be after making a fool of hersilf, and shamin' her swate soul with lies, for the like of you!"

"Sir," said Lorison, trembling, "say what you please of me. Doubt it as you must, I will yet prove my gratitude to you, and my devotion to her. But let me speak to her once now, let me kneel for just one moment at her feet, and –"

"Tut, tut!" said the priest. "How many acts of a love drama do you think an old bookworm like me capable of witnessing? Besides, what kind of figures do we cut, spying upon the mysteries of midnight millinery! Go to meet your wife tomorrow, as she ordered you, and obey her thereafter, and maybe some time I shall get forgiveness for the part I have played in this night's work. Off wid yez down the shtairs, now! 'Tis late, and an ould man like me should be takin' his rest."

CALLOWAY'S CODE

THE NEW YORK *Enterprise* sent H. B. Calloway as special correspondent to the Russo-Japanese-Portsmouth war.

For two months Calloway hung about Yokohama and Tokio, shaking dice with the other correspondents for drinks of 'rickshaws – oh, no, that's something to ride in; anyhow, he wasn't earning the salary that his paper was paying him. But that was not Calloway's fault. The little brown men who held the strings of Fate between their fingers were not ready for the readers of the *Enterprise* to season their breakfast bacon and eggs with the battles of the descendants of the gods.

But soon the column of correspondents that were to go out with the First Army tightened their field-glass belts and went down to the Yalu with Kuroki. Calloway was one of these.

Now, this is no history of the battle of the Yalu River. That has been told in detail by the correspondents who gazed at the shrapnel smoke rings from a distance of three miles. But, for justice's sake, let it be understood that the Japanese commander prohibited a nearer view.

Calloway's feat was accomplished before the battle. What he did was to furnish the Enterprise with the biggest beat of the war. That paper published exclusively and in detail the news of the attack on the lines of the Russian General on the same day that it was made. No other paper printed a word about it for two days afterward, except a London paper, whose account was absolutely incorrect and untrue.

Calloway did this in face of the fact that General Kuroki was making, his moves and living his plans with the profoundest secrecy, as far as the world outside his camps was concerned. The correspondents were forbidden to send out any news whatever of his plans; and every message that was allowed on the wires was censored – with rigid severity.

The correspondent for the London paper handed in a cablegram describing, Kuroki's plans; but as it was wrong from beginning to end the censor grinned and let it go through.

So, there they were – Kuroki on one side of the Yalu with forty-two thousand infantry, five thousand cavalry, and one hundred and twenty-four guns. On the other side, Zassulitch waited for him with only twenty-three thousand men, and with a long stretch of river to guard. And Calloway had got hold of some important inside information that he knew would bring the *Enterprise* staff around a cablegram as thick as flies around a Park Row lemonade stand. If he could only get that message past the censor – the new censor who had arrived and taken his post that day!

Calloway did the obviously proper thing. He lit his pipe and sat down on a gun carriage to think it over. And there we must leave him; for the rest of the story belongs to Vesey, a sixteen-dollar-a-week reporter on the *Enterprise.*

II

Calloway's cablegram was handed to the managing editor at four o'clock in the afternoon. He read it three times; and then drew a pocket mirror from a pigeon-hole in his desk, and looked at his reflection carefully. Then he went over to the desk of Boyd, his assistant (he usually called Boyd when he wanted him), and laid the cablegram before him.

"It's from Calloway," he said. "See what you make of it."

The message was dated at Wi-ju, and these were the words of it:

Foregone preconcerted rash witching goes muffled rumor mine dark silent unfortunate richmond existing great hotly brute select mooted parlous beggars ye angel incontrovertible.

Boyd read it twice.

"It's either a cipher or a sunstroke," said he.

"Ever hear of anything like a code in the office – a secret code?" asked the m. e., who had held his desk for only two years. Managing editors come and go.

"None except the vernacular that the lady specials write in," said Boyd. "Couldn't be an acrostic, could it?"

"I thought of that," said the m. e., "but the beginning letters contain only four vowels. It must be a code of some sort."

"Try 'em in groups," suggested Boyd. "Let's see – 'Rash witching goes' – not with me it doesn't. 'Muffled rumor mine' – must have an underground wire. 'Dark silent unfortunate richmond' – no reason why

66

he should knock that town so hard. 'Existing great hotly' – no it doesn't pan out. I'll call Scott."

The city editor came in a hurry, and tried his luck. A city editor must know something about everything; so Scott knew a little about cipher-writing.

"It may be what is called an inverted alphabet cipher," said he. "I'll try that. 'R' seems to be the oftenest used initial letter, with the exception of 'm.' Assuming 'r' to mean 'e,' the most frequently used vowel, we transpose the letters – so."

Scott worked rapidly with his pencil for two minutes; and then showed the first word according to his reading – the word "Scejtzez."

"Great!" cried Boyd. "It's a charade. My first is a Russian general. Go on, Scott."

"No, that won't work," said the city editor. "It's undoubtedly a code. It's impossible to read it without the key. Has the office ever used a cipher code?"

"Just what I was asking," said the m.e. "Hustle everybody up that ought to know. We must get at it some way. Calloway has evidently got hold of something big, and the censor has put the screws on, or he wouldn't have cabled in a lot of chop suey like this."

Throughout the office of the *Enterprise* a dragnet was sent, hauling in such members of the staff as would be likely to know of a code, past or present, by reason of their wisdom, information, natural intelligence, or length of servitude. They got together in a group in the city room, with the m. e. in the centre. No one had heard of a code. All began to explain to the head investigator that newspapers never use a code, anyhow – that is, a cipher code. Of course the Associated Press stuff is a sort of code – an abbreviation, rather – but –.

The m. e. knew all that, and said so. He asked each man how long he had worked on the paper. Not one of them had drawn pay from an *Enterprise* envelope for longer than six years. Calloway had been on the paper twelve years.

"Try old Heffelbauer," said the m. e. "He was here when Park Row was a potato patch."

Heffelbauer was an institution. He was half janitor, half handyman about the office, and half watchman – thus becoming the peer of thirteen and one-half tailors.

Sent for, he came, radiating his nationality. "Heffelbauer," said the m. e., "did you ever hear of a code belonging to the office a long time ago – a private code? You know what a code is, don't you?"

"Yah," said Heffelbauer. "Sure I know vat a code is. Yah, apout dwelf or fifteen year ago der office had a code. Der reborters in der city-room haf it here."

"Ah!" said the m. e. "We're getting on the trail now. Where was it kept, Heffelbauer? What do you know about it?"

"Somedimes," said the retainer, "dey keep it in der little room behind der library room."

"Can you find it," asked the m. e. eagerly. "Do you know where it is?"

"Mein Gott!" said Heffelbauer. "How long you dink a code live? Der reborters call him a maskeet. But von day he butt mit his head der editor, und –"

"Oh, he's talking about a goat," said Boyd. "Get out, Heffelbauer."

Again discomfited, the concerted wit and resource of the *Enterprise* huddled around Calloway's puzzle, considering its mysterious words in vain.

Then Vesey came in.

Vesey was the youngest reporter. He had a thirty-two-inch chest and wore a number fourteen collar; but his bright Scotch plaid suit gave him presence and conferred no obscurity upon his whereabouts. He wore his hat in such a position that people followed him about to see him take it off, convinced that it must be hung upon a peg driven into the back of his head. He was never without an immense, knotted, hard-wood cane with a German-silver tip on its crooked handle. Vesey was the best photograph hustler in the office. Scott said it was because no living human being could resist the personal triumph it was to hand his picture over to Vesey. Vesey always wrote his own news stories, except the big ones, which were sent to the rewrite men. Add to this fact that among all the inhabitants, temples, and groves of the earth nothing existed that could abash Vesey, and his dim sketch is concluded.

Vesey butted into the circle of cipher readers very much as Heffelbauer's "code" would have done, and asked what was up. Some one explained, with the touch of half-familiar condescension that they always used toward him. Vesey reached out and took the cablegram from the m.e.'s hand. Under the protection of some special Providence, he was always doing appalling things like that, and coming off unscathed.

"It's a code," said Vesey. "Anybody got the key?"

"The office has no code," said Boyd, reaching for the message. Vesey held to it.

"Then old Calloway expects us to read it, anyhow," said he. "He's up a tree, or something, and he's made this up so as to get it by the censor. It's up to us. Gee! I wish they had sent, me, too. Say – we can't afford to fall down on our end of it. 'Foregone, preconcerted rash, witching' – h'm."

Vesey sat down on a table corner and began to whistle softly, frowning at the cablegram.

"Let's have it, please," said the m. e. "We've got to get to work on it."

"I believe I've got a line on it," said Vesey. "Give me ten minutes."

He walked to his desk, threw his hat into a waste-basket, spread out flat on his chest like a gorgeous lizard, and started his pencil going. The wit and wisdom of the *Enterprise* remained in a loose group, and smiled at one another, nodding their heads toward Vesey. Then they began to exchange their theories about the cipher.

It took Vesey exactly fifteen minutes. He brought to the m. e. a pad with the code-key written on it.

"I felt the swing of it as soon as I saw it," said Vesey. "Hurrah for old Calloway! He's done the Japs and every paper in town that prints literature instead of news. Take a look at that."

Thus had Vesey set forth the reading of the code:

> Foregone – conclusion
> Preconcerted – arrangement
> Rash – act
> Witching – hour of midnight
> Goes – without saying
> Muffled – report
> Rumour – hath it
> Mine – host
> Dark – horse
> Silent – majority
> Unfortunate – pedestrians*
> Richmond – in the field
> Existing – conditions
> Great – White Way
> Hotly – contested
> Brute – force
> Select – few
> Mooted – question
> Parlous – times

---

* Mr. Vesey afterward explained that the logical journalistic complement of the word "unfortunate" was once the word "victim." But since the automobile became so popular, the correct following word is now "pedestrians." Of course, in Calloway's code it meant infantry.

Beggars – description
Ye – correspondent
Angel – unawares
Incontrovertible – fact

"It's simply newspaper English," explained Vesey. "I've been reporting on the *Enterprise* long enough to know it by heart. Old Calloway gives us the cue word, and we use the word that naturally follows it just as we use 'em in the paper. Read it over, and you'll see how pat they drop into their places. Now, here's the message he intended us to get."

Vesey handed out another sheet of paper.

Concluded arrangement to act at hour of midnight without saying. Report hath it that a large body of cavalry and an overwhelming force of infantry will be thrown into the field. Conditions white. Way contested by only a small force. Question the *Times* description. Its correspondent is unaware of the facts.

"Great stuff!" cried Boyd excitedly. "Kuroki crosses the Yalu tonight and attacks. Oh, we won't do a thing to the sheets that make up with Addison's essays, real estate transfers, and bowling scores!"

"Mr. Vesey," said the m. e., with his jollying-which-you-should-regard-as-a-favor manner, "you have cast a serious reflection upon the literary standards of the paper that employs you. You have also assisted materially in giving us the biggest 'beat' of the year. I will let you know in a day or two whether you are to be discharged or retained at a larger salary. Somebody send Ames to me."

Ames was the king-pin, the snowy-petalled Marguerite, the star-bright looloo of the rewrite men. He saw attempted murder in the pains of green-apple colic, cyclones in the summer zephyr, lost children in every top-spinning urchin, an uprising of the down-trodden masses in every hurling of a derelict potato at a passing automobile. When not rewriting, Ames sat on the porch of his Brooklyn villa playing checkers with his ten-year-old son.

Ames and the "war editor" shut themselves in a room. There was a map in there stuck full of little pins that represented armies and divisions. Their fingers had been itching for days to move those pins along the crooked line of the Yalu. They did so now; and in words of fire Ames translated Calloway's brief message into a front page masterpiece that set the world talking. He told of the secret councils of the Japanese officers; gave Kuroki's flaming speeches in full; counted the cavalry and infantry to a man and a horse; described the quick and silent building of the bridge at Stuikauchen, across which the

Mikado's legions were hurled upon the surprised Zassulitch, whose troops were widely scattered along the river. And the battle! – well, you know what Ames can do with a battle if you give him just one smell of smoke for a foundation. And in the same story, with seemingly supernatural knowledge, he gleefully scored the most profound and ponderous paper in England for the false and misleading account of the intended movements of the Japanese First Army printed in its issue of *the same date.*

Only one error was made; and that was the fault of the cable operator at Wi-ju. Calloway pointed it out after he came back. The word "great" in his code should have been "gage," and its complemental words "of battle." But it went to Ames "conditions white," and of course he took that to mean snow. His description of the Japanese army struggling through the snowstorm, blinded by the whirling flakes, was thrillingly vivid. The artists turned out some effective illustrations that made a hit as pictures of the artillery dragging their guns through the drifts. But, as the attack was made on the first day of May, "conditions white" excited some amusement. But it made no difference to the *Enterprise,* anyway.

It was wonderful. And Calloway was wonderful in having made the new censor believe that his jargon of words meant no more than a complaint of the dearth of news and a petition for more expense money. And Vesey was wonderful. And most wonderful of all are words, and how they make friends one with another, being oft associated, until not even obituary notices them do part.

III

On the second day following, the city editor halted at Vesey's desk where the reporter was writing the story of a man who had broken his leg by falling into a coal-hole – Ames having failed to find a murder motive in it.

"The old man says your salary is to be raised to twenty a week," said Scott.

"All right," said Vesey. "Every little helps. Say – Mr. Scott, which would you say – 'We can state without fear of successful contradiction,' or, 'On the whole it can be safely asserted?'"

CUPID À LA CARTE

"THE DISPOSITIONS OF woman," said Jeff Peters, after various opinions on the subject had been advanced, "run, regular, to diversions. What a woman wants is what you're out of. She wants more of a thing when it's scarce. She likes to have souvenirs of things that never happened. She likes to be reminded of things she never heard of. A one-sided view of objects is disjointing to the female composition."

"Tis a misfortune of mine, begotten by nature and travel," continued Jeff, looking thoughtfully between his elevated feet at the grocery stove, "to look deeper into some subjects than most people do. I've breathed gasoline smoke talking to street crowds in nearly every town in the United States. I've held 'em spellbound with music, oratory, sleight of hand, and prevarications, while I've sold 'em jewelry, medicine, soap, hair-tonic, and junk of other nominations. And during my travels, as a matter of recreation and expiation, I've taken cognizance of some women. It takes a man a lifetime to find out about one particular woman; but if he puts in, say, ten years, industrious and curious, he can acquire the general rudiments of the sex. One lesson I picked up was when I was working the West with a line of Brazilian diamonds and a patent fire kindler just after my trip from Savannah down through the cotton belt with Dalby's Anti-explosive Lamp Oil Powder. 'Twas when the Oklahoma country was in first bloom. Guthrie was rising in the middle of it like a lump of self-raising dough. It was a boom town of the regular kind – you stood in line to get a chance to wash your face; if you ate over ten minutes you had a lodging bill added on; if you slept on a plank at night they charged it to you as board the next morning.

"By nature and doctrines I am addicted to the habit of discovering choice places wherein to feed. So I looked around and found a proposition that exactly cut the mustard. I found a restaurant tent just opened up by an outfit that had drifted in on the tail of the boom.

They had knocked together a box house, where they lived and did the cooking, and served the meals in a tent pitched against the side. That tent was joyful with placards on it calculated to redeem the world-worn pilgrim from the sinfulness of boarding houses and pick-me-up hotels. 'Try Mother's Home-Made Biscuits,' 'What's the Matter with Our Apple Dumplings and Hard Sauce?' 'Hot Cakes and Maple Syrup Like You Ate When a Boy,' 'Our Fried Chicken Never Was Heard to Crow' – there was literature doomed to please the digestions of man! I said to myself that mother's wandering boy should munch there that night. And so it came to pass. And there is where I contracted my case of Mame Dugan.

"Old Man Dugan was six feet by one of Indiana loafer, and he spent his time sitting on his shoulder blades in a rocking-chair in the shanty memorializing the great corn-crop failure of '96. Ma Dugan did the cooking, and Mame waited on the table.

"As soon as I saw Mame I knew there was a mistake in the census reports. There wasn't but one girl in the United States. When you come to specifications it isn't easy. She was about the size of an angel, and she had eyes, and ways about her. When you come to the kind of a girl she was, you'll find a belt of 'em reaching from the Brooklyn Bridge west as far as the courthouse in Council Bluffs, Ia. They earn their own living in stores, restaurants, factories, and offices. They're chummy and honest and free and tender and sassy, and they look life straight in the eye. They've met man face to face, and discovered that he's a poor creature. They've dropped to it that the reports in the Seaside Library about his being a fairy prince lack confirmation.

"Mame was that sort. She was full of life and fun, and breezy; she passed the repartee with the boarders quick as a wink; you'd have smothered laughing. I am disinclined to make excavations into the insides of a personal affection. I am glued to the theory that the diversions and discrepancies of the indisposition known as love should be as private a sentiment as a toothbrush. 'Tis my opinion that the biographies of the heart should be confined with the historical romances of the liver to the advertising pages of the magazines. So, you'll excuse the lack of an itemized bill of my feelings toward Mame.

"Pretty soon I got a regular habit of dropping into the tent to eat at irregular times when there wasn't so many around. Mame would sail in with a smile, in a black dress and white apron, and say: 'Hello, Jeff – why don't you come at mealtime? Want to see how much trouble you can be, of course.

"'Friedchickenbeefsteakporkchopshamandeggspotpie' – and so on. She called me Jeff, but there was no significations attached. Designations was all she meant. The front names of any of us she used as they came to hand. I'd eat about two meals before I left, and string 'em out like a society spread where they changed plates and wives, and josh one another festively between bites. Mame stood for it, pleasant, for it wasn't up to her to take any canvas off the tent by declining dollars just because they were whipped in after meal times.

"It wasn't long until there was another fellow named Ed Collier got the between-meals affliction, and him and me put in bridges between breakfast and dinner, and dinner and supper, that made a three-ringed circus of that tent, and Mame's turn as waiter a continuous performance. That Collier man was saturated with designs and contrivings. He was in well-boring or insurance or claim-jumping, or something – I've forgotten which. He was a man well-lubricated with gentility, and his words were such as recommended you to his point of view. So, Collier and me infested the grub tent with care and activity. Mame was level full of impartiality. 'Twas like a casino hand the way she dealt out her favors – one to Collier and one to me and one to the board, and not a card up her sleeve.

"Me and Collier naturally got acquainted, and gravitated together some on the outside. Divested of his stratagems, he seemed to be a pleasant chap, full of an amiable sort of hostility.

"'I notice you have an affinity for grubbing in the banquet hall after the guests have fled,' says I to him one day, to draw his conclusions.

"'Well, yes,' says Collier, reflecting; 'the tumult of a crowded board seems to harass my sensitive nerves.'

"'It exasperates mine some, too,' says I. 'Nice little girl, don't you think?'

"'I see,' says Collier, laughing. 'Well, now that you mention it, I have noticed that she doesn't seem to displease the optic nerve.'

"'She's a joy to mine,' says I, 'and I'm going after her. Notice is hereby served.'

"'I'll be as candid as you,' admits Collier, 'and if the drug stores don't run out of pepsin I'll give you a run for your money that'll leave you a dyspeptic at the wind-up.'

"So Collier and me begins the race; the grub department lays in new supplies; Mame waits on us, jolly and kind and agreeable, and it looks like an even break, with Cupid and the cook working overtime in Dugan's restaurant.

"'Twas one night in September when I got Mame to take a walk after supper when the things were all cleared away. We strolled out a distance and sat on a pile of lumber at the edge of town. Such opportunities was seldom, so I spoke my piece, explaining how the Brazilian diamonds and the fire kindler were laying up sufficient treasure to guarantee the happiness of two, and that both of 'em together couldn't equal the light from somebody's eyes, and that the name of Dugan should be changed to Peters, or reasons why not would be in order.

"Mame didn't say anything right away. Directly she gave a kind of shudder, and I began to learn something.

"'Jeff,' she says, 'I'm sorry you spoke. I like you as well as any of them, but there isn't a man in the world I'd ever marry, and there never will be. Do you know what a man is in my eye? He's a tomb. He's a sarcophagus for the interment of Beafsteakporkchopsliver'nbaconham-andeggs. He's that and nothing more. For two years I've watched men eat, eat, eat, until they represent nothing on earth to me but ruminant bipeds. They're absolutely nothing but something that goes in front of a knife and fork and plate at the table. They're fixed that way in my mind and memory. I've tried to overcome it, but I can't. I've heard girls rave about their sweethearts, but I never could understand it. A man and a sausage grinder and a pantry awake in me exactly the same sentiments. I went to a matinee once to see an actor the girls were crazy about. I got interested enough to wonder whether he liked his steak rare, medium, or well done, and his eggs over or straight up. That was all. No, Jeff; I'll marry no man and see him sit at the breakfast table and eat, and come back to dinner and eat, and happen in again at supper to eat, eat, eat.'

"'But, Mame,' says I, 'it'll wear off. You've had too much of it. You'll marry some time, of course. Men don't eat always.'

"'As far as my observation goes, they do. No, I'll tell you what I'm going to do.' Mame turns, sudden, to animation and bright eyes. 'There's a girl named Susie Foster in Terre Haute, a chum of mine. She waits in the railroad eating house there. I worked two years in a restaurant in that town. Susie has it worse than I do, because the men who eat at railroad stations gobble. They try to flirt and gobble at the same time. Whew! Susie and I have it all planned out. We're saving our money, and when we get enough we're going to buy a little cottage and five acres we know of, and live together, and grow violets for the Eastern market. A man better not bring his appetite within a mile of that ranch.'

"'Don't girls ever –' I commenced, but Mame heads me off, sharp.

"'No, they don't. They nibble a little bit sometimes; that's all.'

"'I thought the confect –'

"'For goodness' sake, change the subject,' says Mame.

"As I said before, that experience puts me wise that the feminine arrangement ever struggles after deceptions and illusions. Take England – beef made her; wieners elevated Germany; Uncle Sam owes his greatness to fried chicken and pie, but the young ladies of the Shetalkyou schools, they'll never believe it. Shakespeare, they allow, and Rubinstein, and the Rough Riders is what did the trick.

"'Twas a situation calculated to disturb. I couldn't bear to give up Mame; and yet it pained me to think of abandoning the practice of eating. I had acquired the habit too early. For twenty-seven years I had been blindly rushing upon my fate, yielding to the insidious lures of that deadly monster, food. It was too late. I was a ruminant biped for keeps. It was lobster salad to a doughnut that my life was going to be blighted by it.

"I continued to board at the Dugan tent, hoping that Mame would relent. I had sufficient faith in true love to believe that since it has often outlived the absence of a square meal it might, in time, overcome the presence of one. I went on ministering to my fatal vice, although I felt that each time I shoved a potato into my mouth in Mame's presence I might be burying my fondest hopes.

"I think Collier must have spoken to Mame and got the same answer, for one day he orders a cup of coffee and a cracker, and sits nibbling the corner of it like a girl in the parlor, that's filled up in the kitchen, previous, on cold roast and fried cabbage. I caught on and did the same, and maybe we thought we'd made a hit! The next day we tried it again, and out comes old man Dugan fetching in his hands the fairy viands.

"'Kinder off yer feed, ain't ye, gents?' he asks, fatherly and some sardonic. 'Thought I'd spell Mame a bit, seein' the work was light, and my rheumatiz can stand the strain.'

"So back me and Collier had to drop to the heavy grub again. I noticed about that time that I was seized by a most uncommon and devastating appetite. I ate until Mame must have hated to see me darken the door. Afterward I found out that I had been made the victim of the first dark and irreligious trick played on me by Ed Collier. Him and me had been taking drinks together uptown regular, trying to drown our thirst for food. That man had bribed about ten bartenders to always put a big slug of Appletree's Anaconda Appetite

Bitters in every one of my drinks. But the last trick he played me was hardest to forget.

"One day Collier failed to show up at the tent. A man told me he left town that morning. My only rival now was the bill of fare. A few days before he left Collier had presented me with a two-gallon jug of fine whisky which he said a cousin had sent him from Kentucky. I now have reason to believe that it contained Appletree's Anaconda Appetite Bitters almost exclusively. I continued to devour tons of provisions. In Mame's eyes I remained a mere biped, more ruminant than ever.

"About a week after Collier pulled his freight there came a kind of side-show to town, and hoisted a tent near the railroad. I judged it was a sort of fake museum and curiosity business. I called to see Mame one night, and Ma Dugan said that she and Thomas, her younger brother, had gone to the show. That same thing happened for three nights that week. Saturday night I caught her on the way coming back, and got to sit on the steps a while and talk to her. I noticed she looked different. Her eyes were softer, and shiny like. Instead of a Mame Dugan to fly from the voracity of man and raise violets, she seemed to be a Mame more in line as God intended her, approachable, and suited to bask in the light of the Brazilians and the Kindler.

"'You seem to be right smart inveigled,' says I, 'with the Unparalleled Exhibition of the World's Living Curiosities and Wonders.'

"'It's a change,' says Mame.

"'You'll need another,' says I, 'if you keep on going every night.'

"'Don't be cross, Jeff,' says she; 'it takes my mind off business.'

"'Don't the curiosities eat?' I ask.

"'Not all of them. Some of them are wax.'

"'Look out, then, that you don't get stuck,' says I, kind of flip and foolish.

"Mame blushed. I didn't know what to think about her. My hopes raised some that perhaps my attentions had palliated man's awful crime of visibly introducing nourishment into his system. She talked some about the stars, referring to them with respect and politeness, and I drivelled a quantity about united hearts, homes made bright by true affection, and the Kindler. Mame listened without scorn, and I says to myself, 'Jeff, old man, you're removing the hoodoo that has clung to the consumer of victuals; you're setting your heel upon the serpent that lurks in the gravy bowl.'

"Monday night I drop around. Mame is at the Unparalleled Exhibition with Thomas.

"'Now, may the curse of the forty-one seven-sided sea cooks,' says I, 'and the bad luck of the nine impenitent grasshoppers rest upon this self-same sideshow at once and forever more. Amen. I'll go to see it myself to-morrow night and investigate its baleful charm. Shall man that was made to inherit the earth be bereft of his sweetheart first by a knife and fork and then by a ten-cent circus?'

"The next night before starting out for the exhibition tent I inquire and find out that Mame is not at home. She is not at the circus with Thomas this time, for Thomas waylays me in the grass outside of the grub tent with a scheme of his own before I had time to eat supper.

"'What'll you give me, Jeff,' says he, 'if I tell you something?'

"'The value of it, son,' I says.

"'Sis is stuck on a freak,' says Thomas, 'one of the side-show freaks. I don't like him. She does. I overheard 'em talking. Thought maybe you'd like to know. Say, Jeff, does it put you wise two dollars' worth? There's a target rifle up town that—'

"I frisked my pockets and commenced to dribble a stream of halves and quarters into Thomas's hat. The information was of the pile-driver system of news, and it telescoped my intellects for a while. While I was leaking small change and smiling foolish on the outside, and suffering disturbances internally, I was saying, idiotically and pleasantly:

"'Thank you, Thomas – thank you – er – a freak, you said, Thomas. Now, could you make out the monstrosity's entitlements a little clearer, if you please, Thomas?'

"'This is the fellow,' says Thomas, pulling out a yellow handbill from his pocket and shoving it under my nose. 'He's the Champion Faster of the Universe. I guess that's why Sis got soft on him. He don't eat nothing. He's going to fast forty-nine days. This is the sixth. That's him.'

"I looked at the name Thomas pointed out – Professor Eduardo Collieri. 'Ah!' says I, in admiration, 'that's not so bad, Ed Collier. I give you credit for the trick. But I don't give you the girl until she's Mrs. Freak.'

"I hit the sod in the direction of the show. I came up to the rear of the tent, and, as I did so, a man wiggled out like a snake from under the bottom of the canvas, scrambled to his feet, and ran into me like a locoed bronco. I gathered him by the neck and investigated him by the light of the stars. It is Professor Eduardo Collieri, in human habiliments, with a desperate look in one eye and impatience in the other.

"'Hello, Curiosity,' says I. 'Get still a minute and let's have a look at your freakship. How do you like being the willopus-wallopus or the bim-bam from Borneo, or whatever name you are denounced by in the side-show business?'

"'Jeff Peters,' says Collier, in a weak voice. 'Turn me loose, or I'll slug you one. I'm in the extremest kind of a large hurry. Hands off!'

"'Tut, tut, Eddie,' I answers, holding him hard; 'let an old friend gaze on the exhibition of your curiousness. It's an eminent graft you fell onto, my son. But don't speak of assaults and battery, because you're not fit. The best you've got is a lot of nerve and a mighty empty stomach.' And so it was. The man was as weak as a vegetarian cat.

"'I'd argue this case with you, Jeff,' says he, regretful in his style, 'for an unlimited number of rounds if I had half an hour to train in and a slab of beefsteak two feet square to train with. Curse the man, I say, that invented the art of going foodless. May his soul in eternity be chained up within two feet of a bottomless pit of red-hot hash. I'm abandoning the conflict, Jeff; I'm deserting to the enemy. You'll find Miss Dugan inside contemplating the only living mummy and the informed hog. She's a fine girl, Jeff. I'd have beat you out if I could have kept up the grubless habit a little while longer. You'll have to admit that the fasting dodge was aces-up for a while. I figured it out that way. But say, Jeff, it's said that love makes the world go around. Let me tell you, the announcement lacks verification. It's the wind from the dinner horn that does it. I love that Mame Dugan. I've gone six days without food in order to coincide with her sentiments. Only one bite did I have. That was when I knocked the tattooed man down with a war club and got a sandwich he was gobbling. The manager fined me all my salary; but salary wasn't what I was after. 'Twas that girl. I'd give my life for her, but I'd endanger my immortal soul for a beef stew. Hunger is a horrible thing, Jeff. Love and business and family and religion and art and patriotism are nothing but shadows of words when a man's starving!'

"In such language Ed Collier discoursed to me, pathetic. I gathered the diagnosis that his affections and his digestions had been implicated in a scramble and the commissary had won out. I never disliked Ed Collier. I searched my internal admonitions of suitable etiquette to see if I could find a remark of a consoling nature, but there was none convenient.

79

"'I'd be glad, now,' says Ed, 'if you'll let me go. I've been hard hit, but I'll hit the ration supply harder. I'm going to clean out every restaurant in town. I'm going to wade waist deep in sirloins and swim in ham and eggs. It's an awful thing, Jeff Peters, for a man to come to this pass – to give up his girl for something to eat – it's worse than that man Esau, that swapped his copyright for a partridge – but then, hunger's a fierce thing. You'll excuse me, now, Jeff, for I smell a pervasion of ham frying in the distance, and my legs are crying out to stampede in that direction.'

"'A hearty meal to you, Ed Collier,' I says to him, 'and no hard feelings. For myself, I am projected to be an unseldom eater, and I have condolence for your predicaments.'

"There was a sudden big whiff of frying ham smell on the breeze; and the Champion Faster gives a snort and gallops off in the dark toward fodder.

"I wish some of the cultured outfit that are always advertising the extenuating circumstances of love and romance had been there to see. There was Ed Collier, a fine man full of contrivances and flirtations, abandoning the girl of his heart and ripping out into the contiguous territory in the pursuit of sordid grub. 'Twas a rebuke to the poets and a slap at the best-paying element of fiction. An empty stomach is a sure antidote to an overfull heart.

"I was naturally anxious to know how far Mame was infatuated with Collier and his stratagems. I went inside the Unparalleled Exhibition, and there she was. She looked surprised to see me, but unguilty.

"'It's an elegant evening outside,' says I. 'The coolness is quite nice and gratifying, and the stars are lined out, first class, up where they belong. Wouldn't you shake these by-products of the animal kingdom long enough to take a walk with a common human who never was on a program in his life?'

"Mame gave a sort of sly glance around, and I knew what that meant.

"'Oh,' says I, 'I hate to tell you; but the curiosity that lives on wind has flew the coop. He just crawled out under the tent. By this time he has amalgamated himself with half the delicatessen truck in town.'

"'You mean Ed Collier?' says Mame.

"'I do,' I answers; 'and a pity it is that he has gone back to crime again. I met him outside the tent, and he exposed his intentions of devastating the food crop of the world. 'Tis enormously sad when one's ideal descends from his pedestal to make a seventeen-year locust of himself.'

"Mame looked me straight in the eye until she had corkscrewed my reflections.

"'Jeff,' says she, 'it isn't quite like you to talk that way. I don't care to hear Ed Collier ridiculed. A man may do ridiculous things, but they don't look ridiculous to the girl he does 'em for. That was one man in a hundred. He stopped eating just to please me. I'd be hard-hearted and ungrateful if I didn't feel kindly toward him. Could you do what he did?'

"'I know,' says I, seeing the point, 'I'm condemned. I can't help it. The brand of the consumer is upon my brow. Mrs. Eve settled that business for me when she made the dicker with the snake. I fell from the fire into the frying-pan. I guess I'm the Champion Feaster of the Universe.' I spoke humble, and Mame mollified herself a little.

"'Ed Collier and I are good friends,' she said, 'the same as me and you. I gave him the same answer I did you – no marrying for me. I liked to be with Ed and talk with him. There was something mighty pleasant to me in the thought that here was a man who never used a knife and fork, and all for my sake.'

"'Wasn't you in love with him?' I asks, all injudicious. 'Wasn't there a deal on for you to become Mrs. Curiosity?'

"All of us do it sometimes. All of us get jostled out of the line of profitable talk now and then. Mame put on that little lemon *glace* smile that runs between ice and sugar, and says, much too pleasant: 'You're short on credentials for asking that question, Mr. Peters. Suppose you do a forty-nine day fast, just to give you ground to stand on, and then maybe I'll answer it.'

"So, even after Collier was kidnapped out of the way by the revolt of his appetite, my own prospects with Mame didn't seem to be improved. And then business played out in Guthrie.

"I had stayed too long there. The Brazilians I had sold commenced to show signs of wear, and the Kindler refused to light up right frequent on wet mornings. There is always a time, in my business, when the star of success says, 'Move on to the next town.' I was travelling by wagon at that time so as not to miss any of the small towns; so I hitched up a few days later and went down to tell Mame good-bye. I wasn't abandoning the game; I intended running over to Oklahoma City and work it for a week or two. Then I was coming back to institute fresh proceedings against Mame.

"What do I find at the Dugans' but Mame all conspicuous in a blue traveling dress, with her little trunk at the door. It seems that sister Lottie Bell, who is a typewriter in Terre Haute, is going to be married next Thursday, and Mame is off for a week's visit to be an accomplice at the ceremony. Mame is waiting for a freight wagon that is going to take her to Oklahoma, but I condemns the freight wagon with promptness and scorn, and offers to deliver the goods myself. Ma Dugan sees no reason why not, as Mr. Freighter wants pay for the job; so, thirty minutes later Mame and I pull out in my light spring wagon with white canvas cover, and head due south.

"That morning was of a praiseworthy sort. The breeze was lively, and smelled excellent of flowers and grass, and the little cottontail rabbits entertained themselves with skylarking across the road. My two Kentucky bays went for the horizon until it come sailing in so fast you wanted to dodge it like a clothesline. Mame was full of talk and rattled on like a kid about her old home and her school pranks and the things she liked and the hateful ways of those Johnson girls just across the street, way up in Indiana. Not a word was said about Ed Collier or victuals or such solemn subjects. About noon Mame looks and finds that the lunch she had put up in a basket had been left behind. I could have managed quite a collation, but Mame didn't seem to be grieving over nothing to eat, so I made no lamentations. It was a sore subject with me, and I ruled provender in all its branches out of my conversation.

"I am minded to touch light on explanations how I came to lose the way. The road was dim and well grown with grass; and there was Mame by my side confiscating my intellects and attention. The excuses are good or they are not, as they may appear to you. But I lost it, and at dusk that afternoon, when we should have been in Oklahoma City, we were seesawing along the edge of nowhere in some undiscovered river bottom, and the rain was falling in large, wet bunches. Down there in the swamps we saw a little log house on a small knoll of high ground. The bottom grass and the chaparral and the lonesome timber crowded all around it. It seemed to be a melancholy little house, and you felt sorry for it. 'Twas that house for the night, the way I reasoned it. I explained to Mame, and she leaves it to me to decide. She doesn't become galvanic and prosecuting, as most women would, but she says it's all right; she knows I didn't mean to do it.

"We found the house was deserted. It had two empty rooms. There was a little shed in the yard where beasts had once been kept. In a loft of it was a lot of old hay. I put my horses in there and gave them some of it, for which they looked at me sorrowful, expecting apologies. The rest of the hay I carried into the house by armfuls, with a view to accommodations. I also brought in the patent kindler and the Brazilians, neither of which are guaranteed against the action of water.

"Mame and I sat on the wagon seats on the floor, and I lit a lot of the kindler on the hearth, for the night was chilly. If I was any judge, that girl enjoyed it. It was a change for her. It gave her a different point of view. She laughed and talked, and the kindler made a dim light compared to her eyes. I had a pocketful of cigars, and as far as I was concerned there had never been any fall of man. We were at the same old stand in the Garden of Eden. Out there somewhere in the rain and the dark was the river of Zion, and the angel with the flaming sword had not yet put up the keep-off-the-grass sign. I opened up a gross or two of the Brazilians and made Mame put them on – rings, brooches, necklaces, eardrops, bracelets, girdles, and lockets. She flashed and sparkled like a million-dollar princess until she had pink spots in her cheeks and almost cried for a looking-glass.

"When it got late I made a fine bunk on the floor for Mame with the hay and my lap robes and blankets out of the wagon, and persuaded her to lie down. I sat in the other room burning tobacco and listening to the pouring rain and meditating on the many vicissitudes that came to a man during the seventy years or so immediately preceding his funeral.

"I must have dozed a little while before morning, for my eyes were shut, and when I opened them it was daylight, and there stood Mame with her hair all done up neat and correct, and her eyes bright with admiration of existence.

"'Gee whiz, Jeff!' she exclaims, 'but I'm hungry. I could eat a –'

"I looked up and caught her eye. Her smile went back in and she gave me a cold look of suspicion. Then I laughed, and laid down on the floor to laugh easier. It seemed funny to me. By nature and geniality I am a hearty laugher, and I went the limit. When I came to, Mame was sitting with her back to me, all contaminated with dignity.

"'Don't be angry, Mame,' I says, 'for I couldn't help it. It's the funny way you've done up your hair. If you could only see it!'

"'You needn't tell stories, sir,' said Mame, cool and advised. 'My hair is all right. I know what you were laughing about. Why, Jeff, look outside,' she winds up, peeping through a chink between the logs. I opened the little wooden window and looked out. The entire river bottom was flooded, and the knob of land on which the house stood was an island in the middle of a rushing stream of yellow water a hundred yards wide. And it was still raining hard. All we could do was to stay there till the doves brought in the olive branch.

"I am bound to admit that conversations and amusements languished during that day. I was aware that Mame was getting a too prolonged one-sided view of things again, but I had no way to change it. Personally, I was wrapped up in the desire to eat. I had hallucinations of hash and visions of ham, and I kept saying to myself all the time, 'What'll you have to eat, Jeff? – what'll you order now, old man, when the waiter comes?' I picks out to myself all sorts of favourites from the bill of fare, and imagines them coming. I guess it's that way with all hungry men. They can't get their cogitations trained on anything but something to eat. It shows that the little table with the broken-legged caster and the imitation Worcester sauce and the napkin covering up the coffee stains is the paramount issue, after all, instead of the question of immortality or peace between nations.

"I sat there, musing along, arguing with myself quite heated as to how I'd have my steak – with mushrooms, or *a la creole*. Mame was on the other seat, pensive, her head leaning on her hand. 'Let the potatoes come home-fried,' I states in my mind, 'and brown the hash in the pan, with nine poached eggs on the side.' I felt, careful, in my own pockets to see if I could find a peanut or a grain or two of popcorn.

"Night came on again with the river still rising and the rain still falling. I looked at Mame and I noticed that desperate look on her face that a girl always wears when she passes an ice-cream lair. I knew that poor girl was hungry – maybe for the first time in her life. There was that anxious look in her eye that a woman has only when she has missed a meal or feels her skirt coming unfastened in the back.

"It was about eleven o'clock or so on the second night when we sat, gloomy, in our shipwrecked cabin. I kept jerking my mind away from the subject of food, but it kept flopping back again before I could fasten it. I thought of everything good to eat I had ever heard of. I went away back to my kidhood and remembered the hot biscuit sopped in sorghum and bacon gravy with partiality and respect. Then I trailed along up the years, pausing at green apples and salt, flapjacks and maple, lye hominy, fried chicken Old Virginia style, corn on the cob, spareribs and sweet potato pie, and wound up with Georgia Brunswick stew, which is the top notch of good things to eat, because it comprises 'em all.

"They say a drowning man sees a panorama of his whole life pass before him. Well, when a man's starving he sees the ghost of every meal he ever ate set out before him, and he invents new dishes that would make the fortune of a chef. If somebody would collect the last words of men who starved to death, they'd have to sift 'em mighty fine to discover the sentiment, but they'd compile into a cook book that would sell into the millions.

"I guess I must have had my conscience pretty well inflicted with culinary meditations, for, without intending to do so, I says, out loud, to the imaginary waiter, 'Cut it thick and have it rare, with the French fried, and six, soft-scrambled, on toast.'

"Mame turned her head quick as a wing. Her eyes were sparkling and she smiled sudden.

"'Medium for me,' she rattles out, 'with the Juliennes, and three, straight up. Draw one, and brown the wheats, double order to come. Oh, Jeff, wouldn't it be glorious! And then I'd like to have a half fry, and a little chicken curried with rice, and a cup custard with ice cream, and –'

"'Go easy,' I interrupts; 'where's the chicken liver pie, and the kidney *saute* on toast, and the roast lamb, and –'

"'Oh,' cuts in Mame, all excited, 'with mint sauce, and the turkey salad, and stuffed olives, and raspberry tarts, and –'

"'Keep it going,' says I. 'Hurry up with the fried squash, and the hot corn pone with sweet milk, and don't forget the apple dumpling with hard sauce, and the cross-barred dew-berry pie –'

"Yes, for ten minutes we kept up that kind of restaurant repartee. We ranges up and down and backward and forward over the main trunk lines and the branches of the victual subject, and Mame leads the game, for she is apprised in the ramifications of grub, and the dishes she nominates aggravates my yearnings. It seems that there is a feeling that Mame will line up friendly again with food. It seems that she looks upon the obnoxious science of eating with less contempt than before.

"The next morning we find that the flood has subsided. I geared up the bays, and we splashed out through the mud, some precarious, until we found the road again. We were only a few miles wrong, and in two hours we were in Oklahoma City. The first thing we saw was a big restaurant sign, and we piled into there in a hurry. Here I finds myself sitting with Mame at table, with knives and forks and plates between us, and she not scornful, but smiling with starvation and sweetness.

"'Twas a new restaurant and well-stocked. I designated a list of quotations from the bill of fare that made the waiter look out toward the wagon to see how many more might be coming.

"There we were, and there was the order being served. 'Twas a banquet for a dozen, but we felt like a dozen. I looked across the table at Mame and smiled, for I had recollections. Mame was looking at the table like a boy looks at his first stem-winder. Then she looked at me, straight in the face, and two big tears came in her eyes. The waiter was gone after more grub.

"'Jeff,' she says, soft like, 'I've been a foolish girl. I've looked at things from the wrong side. I never felt this way before. Men get hungry every day like this, don't they? They're big and strong, and they do the hard work of the world, and they don't eat just to spite silly waiter girls in restaurants, do they, Jeff? You said once – that is, you asked me – you wanted me to – well, Jeff, if you still care – I'd be glad and willing to have you always sitting across the table from me. Now give me something to eat, quick, please.'

"So, as I've said, a woman needs to change her point of view now and then. They get tired of the same old sights – the same old dinner table, washtub, and sewing machine. Give 'em a touch of the various – a little travel and a little rest, a little tomfoolery along with the tragedies of keeping house, a little petting after the blowing-up, a little upsetting and a little jostling around – and everybody in the game will have chips added to their stack by the play."

"Girl"

IN GILT LETTERS on the ground glass of the door of room No. 962 were the words: "Robbins & Hartley, Brokers." The clerks had gone. It was past five, and with the solid tramp of a drove of prize Percherons, scrub-women were invading the cloud-capped twenty-story office building. A puff of red-hot air flavoured with lemon peelings, soft-coal smoke and train oil came in through the half-open windows.

Robbins, fifty, something of an overweight beau, and addicted to first nights and hotel palm-rooms, pretended to be envious of his partner's commuter's joys.

"Going to be something doing in the humidity line to-night," he said. "You out-of-town chaps will be the people, with your katydids and moonlight and long drinks and things out on the front porch."

Hartley, twenty-nine, serious, thin, good-looking, nervous, sighed and frowned a little.

"Yes," said he, "we always have cool nights in Floralhurst, especially in the winter."

A man with an air of mystery came in the door and went up to Hartley.

"I've found where she lives," he announced in the portentous half-whisper that makes the detective at work a marked being to his fellow men.

Hartley scowled him into a state of dramatic silence and quietude. But by that time Robbins had got his cane and set his tie pin to his liking, and with a debonair nod went out to his metropolitan amusements.

"Here is the address," said the detective in a natural tone, being deprived of an audience to foil.

Hartley took the leaf torn out of the sleuth's dingy memorandum book. On it were pencilled the words "Vivienne Arlington, No. 341 East –th Street, care of Mrs. McComus."

"Moved there a week ago," said the detective. "Now, if you want any shadowing done, Mr. Hartley, I can do you as fine a job in that line as anybody in the city. It will be only $7 a day and expenses. Can send in a daily typewritten report, covering –"

"You needn't go on," interrupted the broker. "It isn't a case of that kind. I merely wanted the address. How much shall I pay you?"

"One day's work," said the sleuth. "A tenner will cover it."

Hartley paid the man and dismissed him. Then he left the office and boarded a Broadway car. At the first large crosstown artery of travel he took an eastbound car that deposited him in a decaying avenue, whose ancient structures once sheltered the pride and glory of the town.

Walking a few squares, he came to the building that he sought. It was a new flathouse, bearing carved upon its cheap stone portal its sonorous name, "The Vallombrosa." Fire-escapes zigzagged down its front – these laden with household goods, drying clothes, and squalling children evicted by the midsummer heat. Here and there a pale rubber plant peeped from the miscellaneous mass, as if wondering to what kingdom it belonged – vegetable, animal or artificial.

Hartley pressed the "McComus" button. The door latch clicked spasmodically – now hospitably, now doubtfully, as though in anxiety whether it might be admitting friends or duns. Hartley entered and began to climb the stairs after the manner of those who seek their friends in city flat-houses – which is the manner of a boy who climbs an apple-tree, stopping when he comes upon what he wants.

On the fourth floor he saw Vivienne standing in an open door. She invited him inside, with a nod and a bright, genuine smile. She placed a chair for him near a window, and poised herself gracefully upon the edge of one of those Jekyll-and-Hyde pieces of furniture that are masked and mysteriously hooded, unguessable bulks by day and inquisitorial racks of torture by night.

Hartley cast a quick, critical, appreciative glance at her before speaking, and told himself that his taste in choosing had been flawless.

Vivienne was about twenty-one. She was of the purest Saxon type. Her hair was a ruddy golden, each filament of the neatly gathered mass shining with its own lustre and delicate graduation of color. In perfect harmony were her ivory-clear complexion and deep sea-blue eyes that looked upon the world with the ingenuous calmness of a mermaid or the pixie of an undiscovered mountain stream. Her frame was strong and yet possessed the grace of absolute naturalness. And yet with all her Northern clearness and frankness of line and coloring, there seemed to be something of the tropics in her – something of langor in the droop of her pose, of love of ease in her ingenious complacency of satisfaction and comfort in the mere act of breathing – something that seemed to claim for her a right as a perfect work of nature to exist and be admired equally with a rare flower or some beautiful, milk-white dove among its sober-hued companions.

She was dressed in a white waist and dark skirt – that discreet masquerade of goose-girl and duchess.

"Vivienne," said Hartley, looking at her pleadingly, "you did not answer my last letter. It was only by nearly a week's search that I found where you had moved to. Why have you kept me in suspense when you knew how anxiously I was waiting to see you and hear from you?"

The girl looked out the window dreamily.

"Mr. Hartley," she said hesitatingly, "I hardly know what to say to you. I realize all the advantages of your offer, and sometimes I feel sure that I could be contented with you. But, again, I am doubtful. I was born a city girl, and I am afraid to bind myself to a quiet suburban life."

"My dear girl," said Hartley, ardently, "have I not told you that you shall have everything that your heart can desire that is in my power to give you? You shall come to the city for the theatres, for shopping and to visit your friends as often as you care to. You can trust me, can you not?"

"To the fullest," she said, turning her frank eyes upon him with a smile. "I know you are the kindest of men, and that the girl you get will be a lucky one. I learned all about you when I was at the Montgomerys'."

"Ah!" exclaimed Hartley, with a tender, reminiscent light in his eye; "I remember well the evening I first saw you at the Montgomerys'. Mrs. Montgomery was sounding your praises to me all the evening. And she hardly did you justice. I shall never forget that supper. Come, Vivienne, promise me. I want you. You'll never regret coming with me. No one else will ever give you as pleasant a home."

The girl sighed and looked down at her folded hands.

A sudden jealous suspicion seized Hartley.

"Tell me, Vivienne," he asked, regarding her keenly, "is there another – is there some one else?"

A rosy flush crept slowly over her fair cheeks and neck.

"You shouldn't ask that, Mr. Hartley," she said, in some confusion.

"But I will tell you. There is one other – but he has no right – I have promised him nothing."

"His name?" demanded Hartley, sternly.

"Townsend."

"Rafford Townsend!" exclaimed Hartley, with a grim tightening of his jaw. "How did that man come to know you? After all I've done for him –"

"His auto has just stopped below," said Vivienne, bending over the window-sill. "He's coming for his answer. Oh I don't know what to do!"

The bell in the flat kitchen whirred. Vivienne hurried to press the latch button.

"Stay here," said Hartley. "I will meet him in the hall."

Townsend, looking like a Spanish grandee in his light tweeds, Panama hat and curling black mustache, came up the stairs three at a time. He stopped at sight of Hartley and looked foolish.

"Go back," said Hartley, firmly, pointing downstairs with his forefinger.

"Hullo!" said Townsend, feigning surprise. "What's up? What are you doing here, old man?"

"Go back," repeated Hartley, inflexibly. "The Law of the Jungle. Do you want the Pack to tear you in pieces? The kill is mine."

"I came here to see a plumber about the bathroom connections," said Townsend, bravely.

"All right," said Hartley. "You shall have that lying plaster to stick upon your traitorous soul. But, go back." Townsend went downstairs, leaving a bitter word to be wafted up the draught of the staircase. Hartley went back to his wooing.

"Vivienne," said he, masterfully. "I have got to have you. I will take no more refusals or dilly-dallying."

"When do you want me?" she asked.

"Now. As soon as you can get ready."

She stood calmly before him and looked him in the eye.

"Do you think for one moment," she said, "that I would enter your home while Héloise is there?"

Hartley cringed as if from an unexpected blow. He folded his arms and paced the carpet once or twice.

"She shall go," he declared grimly. Drops stood upon his brow. "Why should I let that woman make my life miserable? Never have I seen one day of freedom from trouble since I have known her. You are right, Vivienne. Héloise must be sent away before I can take you

90

home. But she shall go. I have decided. I will turn her from my doors."

"When will you do this?" asked the girl.

Hartley clinched his teeth and bent his brows together.

"To-night," he said, resolutely. "I will send her away to-night."

"Then," said Vivienne, "my answer is 'yes.' Come for me when you will."

She looked into his eyes with a sweet, sincere light in her own. Hartley could scarcely believe that her surrender was true, it was so swift and complete.

"Promise me," he said feelingly, "on your word and honor."

"On my word and honor," repeated Vivienne, softly.

At the door he turned and gazed at her happily, but yet as one who scarcely trusts the foundations of his joy.

"Tomorrow," he said, with a forefinger of reminder uplifted.

"Tomorrow," she repeated with a smile of truth and candour.

In an hour and forty minutes Hartley stepped off the train at Floralhurst. A brisk walk of ten minutes brought him to the gate of a handsome two-story cottage set upon a wide and well-tended lawn. Halfway to the house he was met by a woman with jet-black braided hair and flowing white summer gown, who half strangled him without apparent cause.

When they stepped into the hall she said:

"Mamma's here. The auto is coming for her in half an hour. She came to dinner, but there's no dinner."

"I've something to tell you," said Hartley. "I thought to break it to you gently, but since your mother is here we may as well out with it."

He stooped and whispered something at her ear.

His wife screamed. Her mother came running into the hall. The dark-haired woman screamed again – the joyful scream of a well-beloved and petted woman.

"Oh, mamma!" she cried ecstatically, "what do you think? Vivienne is coming to cook for us! She is the one that stayed with the Montgomeries a whole year. And now, Billy, dear," she concluded, "you must go right down into the kitchen and discharge Héloise. She has been drunk again the whole day long."

MEMOIRS OF A YELLOW DOG

I DON'T SUPPOSE it will knock any of you people off your perch to read a contribution from an animal. Mr. Kipling and a good many others have demonstrated the fact that animals can express themselves in remunerative English, and no magazine goes to press nowadays without an animal story in it, except the old-style monthlies that are still running pictures of Bryan and the Mont Pelee horror.

But you needn't look for any stuck-up literature in my piece, such as Bearoo, the bear, and Snakoo, the snake, and Tammanoo, the tiger, talk in the jungle books. A yellow dog that's spent most of his life in a cheap New York flat, sleeping in a corner on an old sateen underskirt (the one she spilled port wine on at the Lady Longshoremen's banquet), mustn't be expected to perform any tricks with the art of speech.

I was born a yellow pup; date, locality, pedigree and weight unknown. The first thing I can recollect, an old woman had me in a basket at Broadway and Twenty-third trying to sell me to a fat lady. Old Mother Hubbard was boosting me to beat the band as a genuine Pomeranian-Hambletonian-Red Irish-Cochin-China-Stoke-Pogis fox terrier. The fat lady chased a V around among the samples of gros grain flannelette in her shopping bag till she cornered it, and gave up. From that moment I was a pet – a mamma's own wootsey quidlums. Say, gentle reader, did you ever have a 200-pound woman breathing a flavor of Camembert cheese and Peau d'Espagne pick you up and wallop her nose all over you, remarking all the time in an Emma Eames tone of voice "Oh, oo's um oodlum, doodlum, woodlum, toodlum, bitsy-witsy skoodlums!"

From pedigreed yellow pup I grew up to be an anonymous yellow cur looking like a cross between an Angora cat and a box of lemons. But my mistress never tumbled. She thought that the two primeval pups that Noah chased into the ark were but a collateral branch of my ancestors. It took two policemen to keep her from entering me at the Madison Square Garden for the Siberian bloodhound prize.

I'll tell you about that flat. The house was the ordinary thing in New York, paved with Parian marble in the entrance hall and cobblestones above the first floor. Our flat was three – well, not flights – climbs up. My mistress rented it unfurnished, and put in the regular things – 1903 antique upholstered parlor set, oil chromo of geishas in a Harlem tea house, rubber plant and husband.

By Sirius! there was a biped I felt sorry for. He was a little man with sandy hair and whiskers a good deal like mine. Henpecked? – well, toucans and flamingoes and pelicans all had their bills in him. He wiped the dishes and listened to my mistress tell about the cheap, ragged things the lady with the squirrel-skin coat on the second floor hung out on her line to dry. And every evening while she was getting supper she made him take me out on the end of a string for a walk.

If men knew how women pass the time when they are alone they'd never marry. Laura Lean Jibbey, peanut brittle, a little almond cream on the neck muscles, dishes unwashed, half an hour's talk with the iceman, reading a package of old letters, a couple of pickles and two bottles of malt extract, one hour peeking through a hole in the window shade into the flat across the air-shaft – that's about all there is to it. Twenty minutes before time for him to come home from work she straightens up the house, fixes her rat so it won't show, and gets out a lot of sewing for a ten-minute bluff.

I led a dog's life in that flat. Most all day I lay there in my corner watching that fat woman kill time. I slept sometimes and had pipe dreams about being out chasing cats into basements and growling at old ladies with black mittens, as a dog was intended to do. Then she would pounce upon me with a lot of that drivelling poodle palaver and kiss me on the nose – but what could I do? A dog can't chew cloves.

I began to feel sorry for Hubby, dog my cats if I didn't. We looked so much alike that people noticed it when we went out; so we shook the streets that Morgan's cab drives down, and took to climbing the piles of last December's snow on the streets where cheap people live.

One evening when we were thus promenading, and I was trying to look like a prize St. Bernard, and the old man was trying to look like he wouldn't have murdered the first organ-grinder he heard play Mendelssohn's wedding-march, I looked up at him and said, in my way:

"What are you looking so sour about, you oakum trimmed lobster? She don't kiss you. You don't have to sit on her lap and listen to talk that would make the book of a musical comedy sound like the maxims of Epictetus. You ought to be thankful you're not a dog. Brace up, Benedick, and bid the blues begone."

The matrimonial mishap looked down at me with almost canine intelligence in his face.

"Why, doggie," says he, "good doggie. You almost look like you could speak. What is it, doggie – cats."

Cats! Could speak!

But, of course, he couldn't understand. Humans were denied the speech of animals. The only common ground of communication upon which dogs and men can get together is in fiction.

In the flat across the hall from us lived a lady with a black-and-tan terrier. Her husband strung it and took it out every evening, but he always came home cheerful and whistling. One day I touched noses with the black-and tan in the hall, and I struck him for an elucidation.

"See here, Wiggle-and-Skip," I says, "you know that it ain't the nature of a real man to play dry nurse to a dog in public. I never saw one leashed to a bow-wow yet that didn't look like he'd like to lick every other man that looked at him. But your boss comes in every day as perky and set up as an amateur prestidigitator doing the egg trick. How does he do it? Don't tell me he likes it."

"Him?" says the black-and-tan. "Why, he uses Nature's Own Remedy. He gets spifflicated. At first when we go out he's as shy as the man on the steamer who would rather play pedro when they make 'em all jackpots. By the time we've been in eight saloons he don't care whether the thing on the end of his line is a dog or a catfish. I've lost two inches of my tail trying to sidestep those swinging doors."

The pointer I got from that terrier – Vaudeville please copy – set me to thinking.

One evening about 6 o'clock my mistress ordered him to get busy and do the ozone act for Lovey. I have concealed it until now, but that is what she called me. The black-and-tan was called "Tweetness." I consider that I have the bulge on him as far as you could chase a rabbit. Still "Lovey" is something of a nomenclatural tin can on the tail of one's self-respect.

At a quiet place on a safe street I tightened the line of my custodian in front of an attractive, refined saloon. I made a dead-ahead scramble for the doors, whining like a dog in the press dispatches that lets the family know that little Alice is bogged while gathering lilies in the brook.

"Why, darn my eyes," says the old man, with a grin; "darn my eyes if the saffron-colored son of a seltzer lemonade ain't asking me in to take a drink. Lemme see – how long's it been since I saved shoe leather by keeping one foot on the foot-rest? I believe I'll –"

I knew I had him. Hot Scotches he took, sitting at a table. For an hour he kept the Campbells coming. I sat by his side rapping for the waiter with my tail, and eating free lunch such as mamma in her flat never equalled with her homemade truck bought at a delicatessen store eight minutes before papa comes home.

When the products of Scotland were all exhausted except the rye bread the old man unwound me from the table leg and played me outside like a fisherman plays a salmon. Out there he took off my collar and threw it into the street.

"Poor doggie," says he; "good doggie. She shan't kiss you any more. 'S a darned shame. Good doggie, go away and get run over by a street car and be happy."

I refused to leave. I leaped and frisked around the old man's legs happy as a pug on a rug.

"You old flea-headed woodchuck-chaser," I said to him – "you moon-baying, rabbit-pointing, egg-stealing old beagle, can't you see that I don't want to leave you? Can't you see that we're both Pups in the Wood and the missis is the cruel uncle after you with the dish towel and me with the flea liniment and a pink bow to tie on my tail. Why not cut that all out and be pards forever more?"

Maybe you'll say he didn't understand – maybe he didn't. But he kind of got a grip on the Hot Scotches, and stood still for a minute, thinking.

"Doggie," says he, finally, "we don't live more than a dozen lives on this earth, and very few of us live to be more than 300. If I ever see that flat any more I'm a flat, and if you do you're flatter; and that's no flattery. I'm offering 60 to 1 that Westward Ho wins out by the length of a dachshund."

There was no string, but I frolicked along with my master to the twenty-third Street ferry. And the cats on the route saw reason to give thanks that prehensile claws had been given to them.

On the Jersey side my master said to a stranger who stood eating a currant bun

"Me and my doggie, we are bound for the Rocky Mountains."

But what pleased me most was when my old man pulled both of

my ears until I howled, and said, "You common, monkey-headed, rat-tailed, sulphur-colored son of a door mat, do you know what I'm going to call you?"

I thought of "Lovey," and I whined dolefully.

"I'm going to call you 'Pete'," says my master; and if I'd had five tails I couldn't have done enough wagging to do justice to the occasion.

NEMESIS AND
THE CANDY MAN

"WE SAIL AT eight in the morning on the celtic," said Honoria, plucking a loose thread from her lace sleeve.

"I heard so," said young Ives, dropping his hat, and muffing it as he tried to catch it, "and I came around to wish you a pleasant voyage."

"Of course you heard it," said Honoria, coldly sweet, "since we have had no opportunity of informing you ourselves."

Ives looked at her pleadingly, but with little hope.

Outside in the street a high-pitched voice chanted, not unmusically, a commercial gamut of "Cand-de-ee-ee-s! Nice, fresh cand-ee-ee-ee-ees!"

"It's our old candy man," said Honoria, leaning out the window and beckoning. "I want some of his motto kisses. There's nothing in the Broadway shops half so good."

The candy man stopped his pushcart in front of the old Madison Avenue home. He had a holiday and festival air unusual to street peddlers. His tie was new and bright red, and a horseshoe pin, almost life-size, glittered speciously from its folds. His brown, thin face was crinkled into a semi-foolish smile. Striped cuffs with dog-head buttons covered the tan on his wrists.

"I do believe he's going to get married," said Honoria, pityingly. "I never saw him taken that way before. And today is the first time in months that he has cried his wares, I am sure."

Ives threw a coin to the sidewalk. The candy man knows his customers. He filled a paper bag, climbed the old-fashioned stoop and banded it in. "I remember –" said Ives.

"Wait," said Honoria.

She took a small portfolio from the drawer of a writing desk and from the portfolio a slip of flimsy paper one-quarter of an inch by two inches in size.

"This," said Honoria, inflexibly, "was wrapped about the first one we opened."

"It was a year ago," apologized Ives, as he held out his hand for it, "As long as skies above are blue To you, my love, I will be true."

This he read from the slip of flimsy paper.

"We were to have sailed a fortnight ago," said Honoria, gossipingly. "It has been such a warm summer. The town is quite deserted. There is nowhere to go. Yet I am told that one or two of the roof gardens are amusing. The singing – and the dancing – on one or two seem to have met with approval." Ives did not wince. When you are in the ring you are not surprised when your adversary taps you on the ribs.

"I followed the candy man that time," said Ives, irrelevantly, "and gave him five dollars at the corner of Broadway."

He reached for the paper bag in Honoria's lap, took out one of the square, wrapped confections and slowly unrolled it.

"Sara Chillingworth's father," said Honoria, "has given her an automobile."

"Read that," said Ives, handing over the slip that had been wrapped around the square of candy.

"Life teaches us – how to live,

Love teaches us – to forgive."

Honoria's checks turned pink. "Honoria!" cried Ives, starting up from his chair.

"Miss Clinton," corrected Honoria, rising like Venus from the head on the surf. "I warned you not to speak that name again."

"Honoria," repeated Ives, "you must bear me. I know I do not deserve your forgiveness, but I must have it. There is a madness that possesses one sometimes for which his better nature is not responsible. I throw everything else but you to the winds. I strike off the chains that have bound me. I renounce the siren that lured me from you. Let the bought verse of that street peddler plead for me. It is you only whom I can love. Let your love forgive, and I swear to you that mine will be true 'as long as skies above are blue.'"

On the west side, between Sixth and Seventh Avenues, an alley cuts the block in the middle. It perishes in a little court in the centre of the block. The district is theatrical; the inhabitants, the bubbling froth of half a dozen nations. The atmosphere is Bohemian, the language polyglot, the locality precarious. In the court at the rear of the alley lived the candy man. At seven o'clock be pushed his cart into the narrow entrance, rested it upon the irregular stone slats and sat upon one of the handles to cool himself. There was a great draught of cool wind through the alley.

There was a window above the spot where be always stopped his pushcart. In the cool of the afternoon, Mlle. Adele, drawing card of the Aerial Roof Garden, sat at the window and took the air. Generally her ponderous mass of dark auburn hair was down, that the breeze might have the felicity of aiding Sidonié, the maid, in drying and airing it. About her shoulders – the point of her that the photographers always made the most of – was loosely draped a heliotrope scarf. Her arms to the elbow were bare – there were no sculptors there to rave over them – but even the stolid bricks in the walls of the alley should not have been so insensate as to disapprove. While she sat thus Felice, another maid, anointed and bathed the small feet that twinkled and so charmed the nightly Aerial audiences.

Gradually Mademoiselle began to notice the candy man stopping to mop his brow and cool himself beneath her window. In the hands of her maids she was deprived for the time of her vocation – the charming and binding to her chariot of man. To lose time was displeasing to Mademoiselle. Here was the candy man – no fit game for her darts, truly – but of the sex upon which she had been born to make war.

After casting upon him looks of unseeing coldness for a dozen times, one afternoon she suddenly thawed and poured down upon him a smile that put to shame the sweets upon his cart.

"Candy man," she said, cooingly, while Sidonie followed her impulsive dive, brushing the heavy auburn hair, "don't you think I am beautiful?"

The candy man laughed harshly, and looked up, with his thin jaw set, while he wiped his forehead with a red-and-blue handkerchief.

"Yer'd make a dandy magazine cover," he said, grudgingly. "Beautiful or not is for them that cares. It's not my line. If yer lookin' for bouquets apply elsewhere between nine and twelve. I think we'll have rain."

Truly, fascinating a candy man is like killing rabbits in a deep snow; but the hunter's blood is widely diffused. Mademoiselle tugged a great coil of hair from Sidonie's bands and let it fall out the window.

"Candy man, have you a sweetheart anywhere with hair as long and soft as that? And with an arm so round?" She flexed an arm like Galatea's after the miracle across the window-sill.

The candy man cackled shrilly as he arranged a stock of butterscotch that had tumbled down.

"Smoke up!" said he, vulgarly. "Nothin' doin' in the complimentary line. I'm too wise to be bam-boozled by a switch of hair and a newly massaged arm. Oh, I guess you'll make good in the calcium, all right, with plenty of powder and paint on and the orchestra playing 'Under the Old Apple Tree.' But don't put on your hat and chase downstairs to fly to the Little Church Around the Corner with me. I've been up

against peroxide and make-up boxes before. Say, all joking aside –
don't you think we'll have rain?"

"Candy man," said Mademoiselle softly, with her lips curving and
her chin dimpling, "don't you think I'm pretty?"

The candy man grinned. "Savin' money, ain't yer?" said he, "by
bein' yer own press agent. I smoke, but I haven't seen yer mug on any
of the five-cent cigar boxes. It'd take a new brand of woman to get me
goin', anyway. I know 'em from sidecombs to shoelaces. Gimme a
good day's sales and steak-and-onions at seven and a pipe and an
evenin' paper back there in the court, and I'll not trouble Lillian
Russell herself to wink at me, if you please."

Mademoiselle pouted.

"Candy man," she said, softly and deeply, "yet you shall say that I
am beautiful. All men say so and so shall you."

The candy man laughed and pulled out his pipe.

"Well," said be, "I must be goin' in. There is a story in the evenin'
paper that I am readin'. Men are divin' in the seas for a treasure, and
pirates are watchin' them from behind a reef. And there ain't a woman
on land or water or in the air. Good-evenin'." And he trundled his
pushcart down the alley and back to the musty court where he lived.

Incredibly to him who has not learned woman, Mademoiselle sat
at the window each day and spread her nets for the ignominious game.
Once she kept a grand cavalier waiting in her reception chamber for
half an hour while she battered in vain the candy man's tough
philosophy. His rough laugh chafed her vanity to its core. Daily he sat
on his cart in the breeze of the alley while her hair was being
ministered to, and daily the shafts of her beauty rebounded from his
dull bosom pointless and ineffectual. Unworthy pique brightened her
eyes. Pride-hurt she glowed upon him in a way that would have sent
her higher adorers into an egoistic paradise. The candy man's hard
eyes looked upon her with a half-concealed derision that urged her to
the use of the sharpest arrow in her beauty's quiver.

One afternoon she leaned far over the sill, and she did not
challenge and torment him as usual.

"Candy man," said she, "stand up and look into my eyes."

He stood up and looked into her eyes, with his harsh laugh like the
sawing of wood. He took out his pipe, fumbled with it, and put it back
into big pocket with a trembling band.

"That will do," said Mademoiselle, with a slow smile. "I must go
now to my masseuse. Good-evening." The next evening at seven the
candy man came and rested his cart under the window. But was it the

candy man? His clothes were a bright new check. His necktie was a flaming red, adorned by a glittering horseshoe pin, almost life-size. His shoes were polished; the tan of his cheeks had paled – his hands had been washed. The window was empty, and he waited under it with his nose upward, like a hound hoping for a bone.

Mademoiselle came, with Sidonie carrying her load of hair. She looked at the candy man and smiled a slow smile that faded away into ennui. Instantly she knew that the game was bagged; and so quickly she wearied of the chase. She began to talk to Sidonie.

"Been a fine day," said the candy man, hollowly. "First time in a month I've felt first-class. Hit it up down old Madison, hollering out like I useter. Think it'll rain to-morrow?"

Mademoiselle laid two round arms on the cushion on the window-sill, and a dimpled chin upon them.

"Candy man," said she, softly, "do you not love me?"

The candy man stood up and leaned against the brick wall.

"Lady," said he, chokingly, "I've got $800 saved up. Did I say you wasn't beautiful? Take it every bit of it and buy a collar for your dog with it."

A sound as of a hundred silvery bells tinkled in the room of Mademoiselle. The laughter filled the alley and trickled back into the court, as strange a thing to enter there as sunlight itself. Mademoiselle was amused. Sidonie, a wise echo, added a sepulchral but faithful contralto. The laughter of the two seemed at last to penetrate the candy man. He fumbled with his horseshoe pin. At length Mademoiselle, exhausted, turned her flushed, beautiful face to the window. "Candy man," said she, "go away. When I laugh Sidonie pulls my hair. I can but laugh while you remain there."

"Here is a note for Mademoiselle," said Felice, coming to the window in the room.

"There is no justice," said the candy man, lifting the handle of his cart and moving away.

Three yards he moved, and stopped. Loud shriek after shriek came from the window of Mademoiselle. Quickly he ran back. He heard a body thumping upon the floor and a sound as though heels beat alternately upon it.

"What is it?" be called.

Sidonie's severe head came into the window.

"Mademoiselle is overcome by bad news," she said. "One whom she loved with all her soul has gone – you may have beard of him – he is Monsieur Ives. He sails across the ocean to-morrow. Oh, you men!"

No Story

TO AVOID HAVING this book hurled into corner of the room by the suspicious reader, I will assert in time that this is not a newspaper story. You will encounter no shirt-sleeved, omniscient city editor, no prodigy "cub" reporter just off the farm, no scoop, no story – no anything.

But if you will concede me the setting of the first scene in the reporters' room of the Morning Beacon, I will repay the favor by keeping strictly my promises set forth above.

I was doing space-work on the Beacon, hoping to be put on a salary. Someone had cleared with a rake or a shovel a small space for me at the end of a long table piled high with exchanges, Congressional Records, and old files. There I did my work. I wrote whatever the city whispered or roared or chuckled to me on my diligent wanderings about its streets. My income was not regular.

One day Tripp came in and leaned on my table. Tripp was something in the mechanical department – I think he had something to do with the pictures, for he smelled of photographers' supplies, and his hands were always stained and cut up with acids. He was about twenty-five and looked forty. Half of his face was covered with short, curly red whiskers that looked like a door-mat with the "welcome" left off. He was pale and unhealthy and miserable and fawning, and an assiduous borrower of sums ranging from twenty-five cents to a dollar. One dollar was his limit. He knew the extent of his credit as well as the Chemical National Bank knows the amount of H20 that collateral will show on analysis. When he sat on my table he held one hand with the other to keep both from shaking. Whiskey. He had a spurious air of lightness and bravado about him that deceived no one, but was useful in his borrowing because it was so pitifully and perceptibly assumed.

This day I had coaxed from the cashier five shining silver dollars as a grumbling advance on a story that the Sunday editor had reluctantly accepted. So if I was not feeling at peace with the world, at least an armistice had been declared; and I was beginning with ardor to write a description of the Brooklyn Bridge by moonlight.

"Well, Tripp," said I, looking up at him rather impatiently, "how goes it?" He was looking to-day more miserable, more cringing and haggard and downtrodden than I had ever seen him. He was at that stage of misery where he drew your pity so fully that you longed to kick him.

"Have you got a dollar?" asked Tripp, with his most fawning look and his dog-like eyes that blinked in the narrow space between his high-growing matted beard and his low-growing matted hair.

"I have," said I; and again I said, "I have," more loudly and inhospitably, "and four besides. And I had hard work corkscrewing them out of old Atkinson, I can tell you. And I drew them," I continued, "to meet a want – a hiatus – a demand – a need – an exigency – a requirement of exactly five dollars."

I was driven to emphasis by the premonition that I was to lose one of the dollars on the spot.

"I don't want to borrow any," said Tripp, and I breathed again. "I thought you'd like to get put onto a good story," he went on. "I've got a rattling fine one for you. You ought to make it run a column at least. It'll make a dandy if you work it up right. It'll probably cost you a dollar or two to get the stuff. I don't want anything out of it myself."

I became placated. The proposition showed that Tripp appreciated past favors, although he did not return them. If he had been wise enough to strike me for a quarter then he would have got it.

"What is the story ?" I asked, poising my pencil with a finely calculated editorial air.

"I'll tell you," said Tripp. "It's a girl. A beauty. One of the howlingest Amsden's Junes you ever saw. Rosebuds covered with dew-violets in their mossy bed – and truck like that. She's lived on Long Island twenty years and never saw New York City before. I ran against her on Thirty-fourth Street. She'd just got in on the East River ferry. I tell you, she's a beauty that would take the hydrogen out of all the peroxides in the world. She stopped me on the street and asked me where she could find George Brown. Asked me where she could find George Brown in New York City! What do you think of that?

"I talked to her, and found that she was going to marry a young farmer named Dodd – Hiram Dodd – next week. But it seems that George Brown still holds the championship in her youthful fancy. George had greased his cowhide boots some years ago, and came to the city to make his fortune. But he forgot to remember to show up again at Greenburg, and Hiram got in as second-best choice. But when it comes to the scratch Ada – her name's Ada Lowery – saddles a nag and rides eight miles to the railroad station and catches the 6.45 A.M. train for the city. Looking for George, you know – you understand about women – George wasn't there, so she wanted him.

"Well, you know, I couldn't leave her loose in Wolftown-on-the-Hudson. I suppose she thought the first person she inquired of would say: 'George Brown ? – why, yes – lemme see – he's a short man with light-blue eyes, ain't he? Oh yes – you'll find George on One Hundred and Twenty- fifth Street, right next to the grocery. He's bill-clerk in a saddle-and-harness store.' That's about how innocent and beautiful she is. You know those little Long Island water-front villages like Greenburg a couple of duck-farms for sport, and clams and about nine summer visitors for industries. That's the kind of a place she comes from. But, say – you ought to see her!

"What could I do? I don't know what money looks like in the morning. And she'd paid her last cent of pocket-money for her railroad ticket except a quarter, which she had squandered on gum-drops. She was eating them out of a paper bag. I took her to a boarding-house on Thirty-second Street where I used to live, and hocked her. She's in soak for a dollar. That's old Mother McGinnis' price per day. I'll show you the house."

"What words are these, Tripp?" said I. "I thought you said you had a story. Every ferryboat that crosses the East River brings or takes away girls from Long Island."

The premature lines on Tripp's face grew deeper. He frowned seriously from his tangle of hair. He separated his hands and emphasized his answer with one shaking forefinger.

"Can't you see," he said, "what a rattling fine story it would make? You could do it fine. All about the romance, you know, and describe the girl, and put a lot of stuff in it about true love, and sling in a few stickfuls of funny business – joshing the Long Islanders about being green, and, well – you know how to do it. You ought to get fifteen dollars out of it, anyhow. And it'll cost you only about four dollars. You'll make a clear profit of eleven."

"How will it cost me four dollars?" I asked, suspiciously.

"One dollar to Mrs. McGinnis," Tripp answered, promptly, "and two dollars to pay the girl's fare back home."

"And the fourth dimension?" I inquired, making a rapid mental calculation.

"One dollar to me," said Tripp. "For whiskey. Are you on?"

I smiled enigmatically and spread my elbows as if to begin writing again. But this grim, abject, specious, subservient, burr-like wreck of a man would not be shaken off. His forehead suddenly became shiningly moist.

"Don't you see," he said, with a sort of desperate calmness, "that this girl has got to be sent home to-day – not to-night nor to-morrow, but to-day? I can't do anything for her. You know, I'm the janitor and corresponding secretary of the Down-and-Out Club. I thought you could make a newspaper story out of it and win out a piece of money on general results. But, anyhow, don't you see that she's got to get back home before night?"

And then I began to feel that dull, leaden, soul-depressing sensation known as the sense of duty. Why should that sense fall upon one as a weight and a burden? I knew that I was doomed that day to give up the bulk of my store of hard-wrung coin to the relief of this Ada Lowery. But I swore to myself that Tripp's whiskey dollar would not be forthcoming. He might play knight-errant at my expense, but he would indulge in no assail afterward, commemorating my weakness and gullibility. In a kind of chilly anger I put on my coat and hat.

Tripp, submissive, cringing, vainly endeavoring to please, conducted me via the street-cars to the human pawn-shop of Mother McGinnis. I paid the fares. It seemed that the collodion-scented Don Quixote and the smallest minted coin were strangers.

Tripp pulled the bell at the door of the mouldly red-brick boarding- house. At its faint tinkle he paled, and crouched as a rabbit makes ready to spring away at the sound of a hunting-dog. I guessed what a life he had led, terror-haunted by the coming footsteps of landladies.

"Give me one of the dollars – quick!" he said.

The door opened six inches. Mother McGinnis stood there with white eyes – they were white, I say – and a yellow face, holding together at her throat with one hand a dingy pink flannel dressing-sack. Tripp thrust the dollar through the space without a word, and it bought us entry.

"She's in the parlor," said the McGinnis, turning the back of her sack upon us.

In the dim parlor a girl sat at the cracked marble centre-table weeping comfortably and eating gum-drops. She was a flawless beauty. Crying had only made her brilliant eyes brighter. When she crunched a gum-drop you thought only of the poetry of motion and envied the senseless confection. Eve at the age of five minutes must have been a ringer for Miss Ada Lowery at nineteen or twenty. I was introduced, and a gum-drop suffered neglect while she conveyed to me a naive interest, such as a puppy dog (a prize winner) might bestow upon a crawling beetle or a frog.

Tripp took his stand by the table, with the fingers of one hand spread upon it, as an attorney or a master of ceremonies might have stood. But he looked the master of nothing. His faded coat was buttoned high, as if it sought to be charitable to deficiencies of tie and linen.

I thought of a Scotch terrier at the sight of his shifty eyes in the glade between his tangled hair and beard. For one ignoble moment I felt ashamed of having been introduced as his friend in the presence of so much beauty in distress. But evidently Tripp meant to conduct the ceremonies, whatever they might be. I thought I detected in his actions and pose an intention of foisting the situation upon me as material for a newspaper story, in a lingering hope of extracting from me his whiskey dollar.

"My friend" (I shuddered), "Mr. Chalmers," said Tripp, "will tell you, Miss Lowery, the same that I did. He's a reporter, and he can hand out the talk better than I can. That's why I brought him with me." (Tripp, wasn't it the silver-tongued orator you wanted?) "He's wise to a lot of things, and he'll tell you now what's best to do."

I stood on one foot, as it were, as I sat in my rickety chair.

"Why – er – Miss Lowery," I began, secretly enraged at Tripp's awkward opening, "I am at your service, of course, but – er – as I haven't been apprized of the circumstances of the case, I – er –"

"Oh," said Miss Lowery, beaming for a moment, "it ain't as bad as that – there ain't any circumstances. It's the first time I've ever been in New York except once when I was five years old, and I had no idea it was such a big town. And I met Mr. – Mr. Snip on the street and asked him about a friend of mine, and he brought me here and asked me to wait."

"I advise you, Miss Lowery," said Tripp, "to tell Mr. Chalmers all. He's a friend of mine" (I was getting used to it by this time), "and he'll give you the right tip."

"Why, certainly," said Miss Ada, chewing a gum-drop toward me. "There ain't anything to tell except that – well, everything's fixed for me to marry Hiram Dodd next Thursday evening. He has got two hundred acres of land with a lot of shore-front, and one of the best truck-farms on the Island. But this morning I had my horse saddled up –

he's a white horse named Dancer – and I rode over to the station. I told 'em at home I was going to spend the day with Susie Adams. It was a story, I guess, but I don't care. And I came to New York on the train, and I met Mr. – Mr. Flip on the street and asked him if he knew where I could find G – G –"

"Now, Miss Lowery," broke in Tripp, loudly, and with much bad taste, I thought, as she hesitated with her word, "you like this young man, Hiram Dodd, don't you? He's all right, and good to you, ain't he?"

"Of course I like him," said Miss Lowery emphatically. "He's all right. And of course he's good to me. So is everybody."

I could have sworn it myself. Throughout Miss Ada Lowery's life all men would be to good to her. They would strive, contrive, struggle, and compete to hold umbrellas over her hat, check her trunk, pick up her handkerchief, buy for her soda at the fountain.

"But," went on Miss Lowery, "last night got to thinking about G – George, and I –"

Down went the bright gold head upon dimpled, clasped hands on the table. Such a beautiful April storm! Unrestrainedly sobbed. I wished I could have comforted her. But I was not George. And I was glad I was not Hiram – and yet I was sorry, too.

By-and-by the shower passed. She straightened up, brave and half-way smiling. She would have made a splendid wife, for crying only made her eyes more bright and tender. She took a gum-drop and began her story.

"I guess I'm a terrible hayseed," she said between her little gulps and sighs, "but I can't help it. G – George Brown and I were sweethearts since he was eight and I was five. When he was nineteen – that was four years ago – he left Greenburg and went to the city. He said he was going to be a policeman or a railroad president or something. And then he was coming back for me. But I never heard from him any more. And I – I – liked him."

Another flow of tears seemed imminent, but Tripp hurled himself into the crevasse and dammed it. Confound him, I could see his game. He was trying to make a story of it for his sordid ends and profit.

"Go on, Mr. Chalmers," said he, "and tell the lady what's the proper caper. That's what I told her – you'd hand it to her straight. Spiel up."

I coughed, and tried to feel less wrathful toward Tripp. I saw my duty. Cunningly I had been inveigled, but I was securely trapped. Tripp's first dictum to me had been just and correct. The young lady must be sent back to Greenburg that day. She must be argued with, convinced, assured, instructed, ticketed, and returned without delay. I hated Hiram and despised George; but duty must be done.

Noblesse oblige and only five silver dollars are not strictly romantic compatibles, but sometimes they can be made to jibe. It was mine to be Sir Oracle, and then pay the freight. So I assumed an air that mingled Solomon's with that of the general passenger agent of the Long Island Railroad.

"Miss Lowery," said I, as impressively as I could, "life is rather a queer proposition, after all." There was a familiar sound to these words after I had spoken them, and I hoped Miss Lowery had never heard Mr. Cohan's song. "Those whom we first love we seldom wed. Our earlier romances, tinged with the magic radiance of youth, often fail to materialize." The last three words sounded somewhat trite when they struck the air. "But those fondly cherished dreams," I went on, "may cast a pleasant afterglow on our future lives, however impracticable and vague they may have been. But life is full of realities as well as visions and dreams. One cannot live on memories. May I ask, Miss Lowery, if you think you could pass a happy – that is, a contented and harmonious life with Mr. –er – Dodd – if in other ways than romantic recollections he seems to – er – fill the bill, as I might say?"

"Oh, He's all right," answered Miss Lowery. "Yes, I could get along with him fine. He's promised me an automobile and a motor-boat. But somehow, when it got so close to the time I was to marry him, I couldn't help wishing – well, just thinking about George. Something must have happened to him or he'd have written. On the day he left, he and me got a hammer and a chisel and cut a dime into two pieces. I took one piece and he took the other, and we promised to be true to each other and always keep the pieces till we saw each other again. I've got mine at home now in a ring-box in the top drawer of my dresser. I guess I was silly to come up here looking for him. I never realized what a big place it is."

And then Tripp joined in with a little grating laugh that he had, still trying to drag in a little story or drama to earn the miserable dollar that he craved.

"Oh, the boys from the country forget a lot when they come to the city and learn something. I guess George, maybe, is on the bum, or got roped in by some other girl, or maybe gone to the dogs on account of whiskey or the races. You listen to Mr. Chalmers and go back home, and you'll be all right."

But now the time was come for action, for the hands of the clock were moving close to noon. Frowning upon Tripp, I argued gently and philosophically with Miss Lowery, delicately convincing her of the importance of returning home at once. And I impressed upon her the truth that it would not be absolutely necessary to her future happiness that she mention to He the wonders or the fact of her visit to the city that had swallowed up the unlucky George.

She said she had left her horse (unfortunate Rosinante) tied to a tree near the railroad station. Tripp and I gave her instructions to mount the patient steed as soon as she arrived and ride home as fast as possible. There she was to recount the exciting adventure of a day spent with Susie Adams. She could "fix" Susie – I was sure of that – and all would be well.

And then, being susceptible to the barbed arrows of beauty, I warmed to the adventure. The three of us hurried to the ferry, and there I found the price of a ticket to Greenburg to be but a dollar and eighty cents. I bought one, and a red, red rose with the twenty cents for Miss Lowery. We saw her aboard her ferryboat, and stood watching her wave her handkerchief at us until it was the tiniest white patch imaginable. And then Tripp and I faced each other, brought back to earth, left dry and desolate in the shade of the sombre verities of life.

The spell wrought by beauty and romance was dwindling. I looked at Tripp and almost sneered. He looked more careworn, contemptible, and disreputable than ever. I fingered the two silver dollars remaining in my pocket and looked at him with the half-closed eyelids of contempt. He mustered up an imitation of resistance.

"Can't you get a story out of it?" he asked, huskily. "Some sort of a story, even if you have to fake part of it?"

"Not a line," said I. "I can fancy the look on Grimes' face if I should try to put over any slush like this. But we've helped the little lady out, and that'll have to be our only reward."

"I'm sorry," said Tripp, almost inaudibly. "I'm sorry you're out your money. Now, it seemed to me like a find of a big story, you know – that is, a sort of thing that would write up pretty well."

"Let's try to forget it," said I, with a praiseworthy attempt at gayety, "and take the next car 'cross town."

I steeled myself against his unexpressed but palpable desire. He should not coax, cajole, or wring from me the dollar he craved. I had had enough of that wild-goose chase.

Tripp feebly unbuttoned his coat of the faded pattern and glossy seams to reach for something that had once been a handkerchief deep down in some obscure and cavernous pocket. As he did so I caught the shine of a cheap silver-plated watch-chain across his vest, and something dangling from it caused me to stretch forth my hand and seize it curiously. It was the half of a silver dime that had been cut in halves with a chisel.

"What!" I said, looking at him keenly.

"Oh yes," he responded, dully. "George Brown, alias Tripp. What's the use?"

Barring the W. C. T. U., I'd like to know if anybody disapproves of my having produced promptly from my pocket Tripp's whiskey dollar and unhesitatingly laying it in his hand.

PSYCHE AND
THE PSKYSCRAPER

IF YOU ARE a philosopher you can do this thing: you can go to the top
of a high building, look down upon your fellow-men 300 feet below,
and despise them as insects. Like the irresponsible black waterbugs on
summer ponds, they crawl and circle and hustle about idiotically
without aim or purpose. They do not even move with the admirable
intelligence of ants, for ants always know when they are going home.
The ant is of a lowly station, but he will often reach home and get his
slippers on while you are left at your elevated station.

Man, then, to the housetopped philosopher, appears to be but a
creeping, contemptible beetle. Brokers, poets, millionaires,
bootblacks, beauties, hod-carriers and politicians become little black
specks dodging bigger black specks in streets no wider than your
thumb.

From this high view the city itself becomes degraded to an
unintelligible mass of distorted buildings and impossible perspectives;
the revered ocean is a duck pond; the earth itself a lost golf ball. All
the minutiae of life are gone. The philosopher gazes into the infinite
heavens above him, and allows his soul to expand to the influence of
his new view. He feels that he is the heir to Eternity and the child of
Time. Space, too, should be his by the right of his immortal heritage,
and he thrills at the thought that some day his kind shall traverse
those mysterious aerial roads between planet and planet. The tiny
world beneath his feet upon which this towering structure of steel rests
as a speck of dust upon a Himalayan mountain – it is but one of a
countless number of such whirling atoms. What are the ambitions, the
achievements, the paltry conquests and loves of those restless black
insects below compared with the serene and awful immensity of the
universe that lies above and around their insignificant city?

It is guaranteed that the philosopher will have these thoughts.
They have been expressly compiled from the philosophies of the
world and set down with the proper interrogation point at the end of

them to represent the invariable musings of deep thinkers on high places. And when the philosopher takes the elevator down his mind is broader, his heart is at peace, and his conception of the cosmogony of creation is as wide as the buckle of Orion's summer belt.

But if your name happened to be Daisy, and you worked in an Eighth Avenue candy store and lived in a little cold hall bedroom, five feet by eight, and earned $6 per week, and ate ten-cent lunches and were nineteen years old, and got up at 6:30 and worked till 9, and never had studied philosophy, maybe things wouldn't look that way to you from the top of a skyscraper.

Two sighed for the hand of Daisy, the unphilosophical. One was Joe, who kept the smallest store in New York. It was about the size of a tool-box of the D. P. W., and was stuck like a swallow's nest against a corner of a down-town skyscraper. Its stock consisted of fruit, candies, newspapers, song books, cigarettes, and lemonade in season. When stern winter shook his congealed locks and Joe had to move himself and the fruit inside, there was exactly room in the store for the proprietor, his wares, a stove the size of a vinegar cruet, and one customer.

Joe was not of the nation that keeps us forever in a furore with fugues and fruit. He was a capable American youth who was laying by money, and wanted Daisy to help him spend it. Three times he had asked her.

"I got money saved up, Daisy," was his love song; "and you know how bad I want you. That store of mine ain't very big, but –"

"Oh, ain't it?" would be the antiphony of the unphilosophical one. "Why, I heard Wanamaker's was trying to get you to sublet part of your floor space to them for next year." Daisy passed Joe's corner every morning and evening.

"Hello, Two-by-Four!" was her usual greeting. "Seems to me your store looks emptier. You must have sold a pack of chewing gum."

"Ain't much room in here, sure," Joe would answer, with his slow grin, "except for you, Daise. Me and the store are waitin' for you whenever you'll take us. Don't you think you might before long?"

"Store!" – a fine scorn was expressed by Daisy's uptilted nose – "sardine box! Waitin' for me, you say? Gee! you'd have to throw out about a hundred pounds of candy before I could get inside of it, Joe."

"I wouldn't mind an even swap like that," said Joe, complimentary.

Daisy's existence was limited in every way. She had to walk sideways between the counter and the shelves in the candy store. In her own hall bedroom coziness had been carried close to cohesiveness. The walls were so near to one another that the paper on them made a perfect Babel of noise. She could light the gas with one hand and close the door with the other without taking her eyes off the reflection of her brown pompadour in the mirror. She had Joe's picture in a gilt frame on the dresser, and sometimes – but her next thought would always be of Joe's funny little store tacked like a soap box to the corner of that great building, and away would go her sentiment in a breeze of laughter.

Daisy's other suitor followed Joe by several months. He came to board in the house where she lived. His name was Dabster, and he was a philosopher. Though young, attainments stood out upon him like continental labels on a Passaic (N. J.) suitcase. Knowledge he had kidnapped from cyclopedias and handbooks of useful information; but as for wisdom, when she passed he was left sniffling in the road without so much as the number of her motor car. He could and would tell you the proportion of water and muscle-making properties of peas and veal, the shortest verse in the Bible, the number of pounds of shingle nails required to fasten 256 shingles laid four inches to the weather, the population of Kankakee, Ill., the theories of Spinoza, the name of Mr. H. McKay Twombly's second hall footman, the length of the Hoosac Tunnel, the best time to set a hen, the salary of the railway post-office messenger between Driftwood and Red Bank Furnace, Pa., and the number of bones in the foreleg of a cat.

The weight of learning was no handicap to Dabster. His statistics were the sprigs of parsley with which he garnished the feast of small talk that he would set before you if he conceived that to be your taste. And again he used them as breastworks in foraging at the boardinghouse. Firing at you a volley of figures concerning the weight of a lineal foot of bar-iron 5 x 2¾ inches, and the average annual rainfall at Fort Snelling, Minn., he would transfix with his fork the best piece of chicken on the dish while you were trying to rally sufficiently to ask him weakly why does a hen cross the road.

Thus, brightly armed, and further equipped with a measure of good looks, of a hair-oily, shopping-district-at-three-in-the-afternoon kind, it seems that Joe, of the Lilliputian emporium, had a rival worthy of his steel. But Joe carried no steel. There wouldn't have been room in his store to draw it if he had.

One Saturday afternoon, about four o'clock, Daisy and Mr. Dabster stopped before Joe's booth. Dabster wore a silk hat, and – well, Daisy was a woman, and that hat had no chance to get back in its box until

Joe had seen it. A stick of pineapple chewing gum was the ostensible object of the call. Joe supplied it through the open side of his store. He did not pale or falter at sight of the hat.

"Mr. Dabster's going to take me on top of the building to observe the view," said Daisy, after she had introduced her admirers. "I never was on a skyscraper. I guess it must be awfully nice and funny up there."

"H'm!" said Joe.

"The panorama," said Mr. Dabster, "exposed to the gaze from the top of a lofty building is not only sublime, but instructive. Miss Daisy has a decided pleasure in store for her."

"It's windy up there, too, as well as here," said Joe. "Are you dressed warm enough, Daise?"

"Sure thing! I'm all lined," said Daisy, smiling slyly at his clouded brow. "You look just like a mummy in a case, Joe. Ain't you just put in an invoice of a pint of peanuts or another apple? Your stock looks awful over-stocked."

Daisy giggled at her favorite joke; and Joe had to smile with her.

"Your quarters are somewhat limited, Mr. – er – er," remarked Dabster, "in comparison with the size of this building. I understand the area of its side to be about 340 by 100 feet. That would make you occupy a proportionate space as if half of Beloochistan were placed upon a territory as large as the United States east of the Rocky Mountains, with the Province of Ontario and Belgium added."

"Is that so, sport?" said Joe, genially. "You are Weisenheimer on figures, all right. How many square pounds of baled hay do you think a jackass could eat if he stopped brayin' long enough to keep still a minute and five eighths?"

A few minutes later Daisy and Mr. Dabster stepped from an elevator to the top floor of the skyscraper. Then up a short, steep stairway and out upon the roof. Dabster led her to the parapet so she could look down at the black dots moving in the street below.

"What are they?" she asked, trembling. She had never before been on a height like this before.

And then Dabster must needs play the philosopher on the tower, and conduct her soul forth to meet the immensity of space.

"Bipeds," he said, solemnly. "See what they become even at the small elevation of 340 feet – mere crawling insects going to and fro at random."

"Oh, they ain't anything of the kind," exclaimed Daisy, suddenly – "they're folks! I saw an automobile. Oh, gee! are we that high up?"

"Walk over this way," said Dabster.

He showed her the great city lying like an orderly array of toys far below, starred here and there, early as it was, by the first beacon lights of the winter afternoon. And then the bay and sea to the south and east vanishing mysteriously into the sky.

"I don't like it," declared Daisy, with troubled blue eyes. "Say we go down."

But the philosopher was not to be denied his opportunity. He would let her behold the grandeur of his mind, the half-nelson he had on the infinite, and the memory he had for statistics. And then she would never more be content to buy chewing gum at the smallest store in New York. And so he began to prate of the smallness of human affairs, and how that even so slight a removal from earth made man and his works look like one-tenth part of a dollar thrice computed. And that one should consider the sidereal system and the maxims of Epictetus and be comforted.

"You don't carry me with you," said Daisy. "Say, I think it's awful to be up so high that folks look like fleas. One of them we saw might have been Joe. Why, Jiminy! we might as well be in New Jersey! Say, I'm afraid up here!"

The philosopher smiled fatuously.

"The earth," said he, "is itself only as a grain of wheat in space. Look up there."

Daisy gazed upward apprehensively. The short day was spent and the stars were coming out above.

"Yonder star," said Dabster, "is Venus, the evening star. She is 66,000,000 miles from the sun."

"Fudge!" said Daisy, with a brief flash of spirit, "where do you think I come from – Brooklyn? Susie Price, in our store – her brother sent her a ticket to go to San Francisco – that's only three thousand miles."

The philosopher smiled indulgently.

"Our world," he said, "is 91,000,000 miles from the sun. There are eighteen stars of the first magnitude that are 211,000 times further from us than the sun is. If one of them should be extinguished it would be three years before we would see its light go out. There are six thousand stars of the sixth magnitude. It takes thirty-six years for the light of one of them to reach the earth. With an eighteen-foot telescope we can see 43,000,000 stars, including those of the thirteenth magnitude, whose light takes 2,700 years to reach us. Each of these stars –"

"You're lyin'," cried Daisy, angrily. "You're tryin' to scare me. And you have; I want to go down!"

She stamped her foot.

"Arcturus –" began the philosopher, soothingly, but he was interrupted by a demonstration out of the vastness of the nature that he was endeavoring to portray with his memory instead of his heart. For to the heart-expounder of nature the stars were set in the firmament expressly to give soft light to lovers wandering happily beneath them; and if you stand tiptoe some September night with your sweetheart on your arm you can almost touch them with your hand. Three years for their light to reach us, indeed!

Out of the west leaped a meteor, lighting the roof of the skyscraper almost to midday. Its fiery parabola was limned against the sky toward the east. It hissed as it went, and Daisy screamed.

"Take me down," she cried, vehemently, "you – you mental arithmetic!"

Dabster got her to the elevator, and inside of it. She was wild-eyed, and she shuddered when the express made its debilitating drop.

Outside the revolving door of the skyscraper the philosopher lost her. She vanished; and he stood, bewildered, without figures or statistics to aid him.

Joe had a lull in trade, and by squirming among his stock succeeded in lighting a cigarette and getting one cold foot against the attenuated stove.

The door was burst open, and Daisy, laughing, crying, scattering fruit and candies, tumbled into his arms.

"Oh, Joe, I've been up on the skyscraper. Ain't it cozy and warm and homelike in here! I'm ready for you, Joe, whenever you want me."

School And School

I

OLD JEROME WARREN lived in a hundred-thousand-dollar house at 35 East Fifty-Soforth Street. He was a down-town broker, so rich that he could afford to walk – for his health – a few blocks in the direction of his office every morning, and then call a cab.

He had an adopted son, the son of an old friend named Gilbert – Cyril Scott could play him nicely – who was becoming a successful painter as fast as he could squeeze the paint out of his tubes. Another member of the household was Barbara Ross, a stepniece. Man is born to trouble; so, as old Jerome had no family of his own, he took up the burdens of others.

Gilbert and Barbara got along swimmingly. There was a tacit and tactical understanding all round that the two would stand up under a floral bell some high noon, and promise the minister to keep old Jerome's money in a state of high commotion. But at this point complications must be introduced.

Thirty years before, when old Jerome was young Jerome, there was a brother of his named Dick. Dick went West to seek his or somebody else's fortune. Nothing was heard of him until one day old Jerome had a letter from his brother. It was badly written on ruled paper that smelled of salt bacon and coffee-grounds. The writing was asthmatic and the spelling St. Vitusy.

It appeared that instead of Dick having forced Fortune to stand and deliver, he had been held up himself, and made to give hostages to the enemy. That is, as his letter disclosed, he was on the point of pegging out with a complication of disorders that even whiskey had failed to check. All that his thirty years of prospecting had netted him was one daughter, nineteen years old, as per invoice, whom he was shipping East, charges prepaid, for Jerome to clothe, feed, educate, comfort, and cherish for the rest of her natural life or until matrimony should them part.

Old Jerome was a board-walk. Everybody knows that the world is supported by the shoulders of Atlas; and that Atlas stands on a rail-fence; and that the rail-fence is built on a turtle's back. Now, the turtle has to stand on something; and that is a board-walk made of men like old Jerome.

I do not know whether immortality shall accrue to man; but if not so, I would like to know when men like old Jerome get what is due them?

They met Nevada Warren at the station. She was a little girl, deeply sunburned and wholesomely good-looking, with a manner that was frankly unsophisticated, yet one that not even a cigar-drummer would intrude upon without thinking twice. Looking at her, somehow you would expect to see her in a short skirt and leather leggings, shooting glass balls or taming mustangs. But in her plain white waist and black skirt she sent you guessing again. With an easy exhibition of strength she swung along a heavy valise, which the uniformed porters tried in vain to wrest from her.

"I am sure we shall be the best of friends," said Barbara, pecking at the firm, sunburned cheek.

"I hope so," said Nevada.

"Dear little niece," said old Jerome, "you are as welcome to my home as if it were your father's own."

"Thanks," said Nevada.

"And I am going to call you 'cousin,'" said Gilbert, with his charming smile.

"Take the valise, please," said Nevada. "It weighs a million pounds. It's got samples from six of dad's old mines in it," she explained to Barbara. "I calculate they'd assay about nine cents to the thousand tons, but I promised him to bring them along."

II

It is a common custom to refer to the usual complication between one man and two ladies, or one lady and two men, or a lady and a man and a nobleman, or – well, any of those problems – as the triangle. But they are never unqualified triangles. They are always isosceles – never equilateral. So, upon the coming of Nevada Warren, she and Gilbert and Barbara Ross lined up into such a figurative triangle; and of that triangle Barbara formed the hypotenuse.

One morning old Jerome was lingering long after breakfast over the dullest morning paper in the city before setting forth to his down-town fly-trap. He had become quite fond of Nevada, finding in her much of his dead brother's quiet independence ànd unsuspicious frankness.

A maid brought in a note for Miss Nevada Warren.

"A messenger-boy delivered it at the door, please," she said. "He's waiting for an answer."

Nevada, who was whistling a Spanish waltz between her teeth, and watching the carriages and autos roll by in the street, took the envelope. She knew it was from Gilbert, before she opened it, by the little gold palette in the upper left-hand corner.

After tearing it open she pored over the contents for a while, absorbedly. Then, with a serious face, she went and stood at her uncle's elbow.

"Uncle Jerome, Gilbert is a nice boy, isn't he?"

"Why, bless the child!" said old Jerome, crackling his paper loudly; "of course he is. I raised him myself."

"He wouldn't write anything to anybody that wasn't exactly – I mean that everybody couldn't know and read, would he?"

"I'd just like to see him try it," said uncle, tearing a handful from his newspaper. "Why, what –"

"Read this note he just sent me, uncle, and see if you think it's all right and proper. You see, I don't know much about city people and their ways."

Old Jerome threw his paper down and set both his feet upon it. He took Gilbert's note and fiercely perused it twice, and then a third time.

"Why, child," said he, "you had me almost excited, although I was sure of that boy. He's a duplicate of his father, and he was a gilt-edged diamond. He only asks if you and Barbara will be ready at four o'clock this afternoon for an automobile drive over to Long Island. I don't see anything to criticise in it except the stationery. I always did hate that shade of blue."

"Would it be all right to go?" asked Nevada, eagerly.

"Yes, yes, yes, child; of course. Why not? Still, it pleases me to see you so careful and candid. Go, by all means."

"I didn't know," said Nevada, demurely. "I thought I'd ask you. Couldn't you go with us, uncle?"

"I? No, no, no, no! I've ridden once in a car that boy was driving. Never again! But it's entirely proper for you and Barbara to go. Yes, yes. But I will not. No, no, no, no!"

Nevada flew to the door, and said to the maid:

"You bet we'll go. I'll answer for Miss Barbara. Tell the boy to say to Mr. Warren, 'You bet we'll go.'"

"Nevada," called old Jerome, "pardon me, my dear, but wouldn't it be as well to send him a note in reply? Just a line would do."

"No, I won't bother about that," said Nevada, gayly. "Gilbert will understand – he always does. I never rode in an automobile in my life; but I've paddled a canoe down Little Devil River through the Lost Horse Canon, and if it's any livelier than that I'd like to know!"

III

Two months are supposed to have elapsed.

Barbara sat in the study of the hundred-thousand-dollar house. It was a good place for her. Many places are provided in the world where men and women may repair for the purpose of extricating themselves from divers difficulties. There are cloisters, wailing-places, watering-places, confessionals, hermitages, lawyer's offices, beauty parlors, air-ships, and studies; and the greatest of these are studies.

It usually takes a hypotenuse a long time to discover that it is the longest side of a triangle. But it's a long line that has no turning.

Barbara was alone. Uncle Jerome and Nevada had gone to the theatre. Barbara had not cared to go. She wanted to stay at home and study in the study. If you, miss, were a stunning New York girl, and saw every day that a brown, ingenuous Western witch was getting hobbles and a lasso on the young man you wanted for yourself, you, too, would lose taste for the oxidized-silver setting of a musical comedy.

Barbara sat by the quartered-oak library table. Her right arm rested upon the table, and her dextral fingers nervously manipulated a sealed letter. The letter was addressed to Nevada Warren; and in the upper left-hand corner of the envelope was Gilbert's little gold palette. It had been delivered at nine o'clock, after Nevada had left.

Barbara would have given her pearl necklace to know what the letter contained; but she could not open and read it by the aid of steam, or a pen-handle, or a hair-pin, or any of the generally approved methods, because her position in society forbade such an act. She had tried to read some of the lines of the letter by holding the envelope up to a strong light and pressing it hard against the paper, but Gilbert had too good a taste in stationery to make that possible.

At eleven-thirty the theatre-goers returned. It was a delicious winter night. Even so far as from the cab to the door they were powdered thickly with the big flakes downpouring diagonally from the cast. Old Jerome growled good-naturedly about villanous cab service and blockaded streets. Nevada, colored like a rose, with sapphire eyes, babbled of the stormy nights in the mountains around dad's cabin. During all these wintry apostrophes, Barbara, cold at heart, sawed wood – the only appropriate thing she could think of to do.

Old Jerome went immediately up-stairs to hot-water-bottles and quinine. Nevada fluttered into the study, the only cheerfully lighted room, subsided into an arm-chair, and, while at the interminable task of unbuttoning her elbow gloves, gave oral testimony as to the demerits of the "show."

"Yes, I think Mr. Fields is really amusing – sometimes," said Barbara. "Here is a letter for you, dear, that came by special delivery just after you had gone."

"Who is it from?" asked Nevada, tugging at a button.

"Well, really," said Barbara, with a smile, "I can only guess. The envelope has that queer little thing in one corner that Gilbert calls a palette, but which looks to me rather like a gilt heart on a school-girl's valentine."

"I wonder what he's writing to me about," remarked Nevada, listlessly.

"We're all alike," said Barbara; "all women. We try to find out what is in a letter by studying the postmark. As a last resort we use scissors, and read it from the bottom upward. Here it is."

She made a motion as if to toss the letter across the table to Nevada.

"Great catamounts!" exclaimed Nevada. "These center-fire buttons are a nuisance. I'd rather wear buckskins. Oh, Barbara, please shuck the hide off that letter and read it. It'll be midnight before I get these gloves off!"

"Why, dear, you don't want me to open Gilbert's letter to you? It's for you, and you wouldn't wish any one else to read it, of course!"

Nevada raised her steady, calm, sapphire eyes from her gloves.

"Nobody writes me anything that everybody mightn't read," she said. "Go on, Barbara. Maybe Gilbert wants us to go out in his car again to-morrow."

Curiosity can do more things than kill a cat; and if emotions, well recognized as feminine, are inimical to feline life, then jealousy would soon leave the whole world catless. Barbara opened the letter, with an indulgent, slightly bored air.

"Well, dear," said she, "I'll read it if you want me to."

She slit the envelope, and read the missive with swift-travelling eyes; read it again, and cast a quick, shrewd glance at Nevada, who, for the time, seemed to consider gloves as the world of her interest, and letters from rising artists as no more than messages from Mars.

For a quarter of a minute Barbara looked at Nevada with a strange steadfastness; and then a smile so small that it widened her mouth only the sixteenth part of an inch, and narrowed her eyes no more than a twentieth, flashed like an inspired thought across her face.

Since the beginning no woman has been a mystery to another woman. Swift as light travels, each penetrates the heart and mind of another, sifts her sister's words of their cunningest disguises, reads her most hidden desires, and plucks the sophistry from her wiliest talk like hairs from a comb, twiddling them sardonically between her thumb and fingers before letting them float away on the breezes of fundamental doubt. Long ago Eve's son rang the door-bell of the family residence in Paradise Park, bearing a strange lady on his arm, whom he introduced. Eve took her daughter-in-law aside and lifted a classic eyebrow.

"The Land of Nod," said the bride, languidly flirting the leaf of a palm. "I suppose you've been there, of course?"

"Not lately," said Eve, absolutely unstaggered. "Don't you think the apple-sauce they serve over there is execrable? I rather like that mulberry-leaf tunic effect, dear; but, of course, the real fig goods are not to be had over there. Come over behind this lilac-bush while the gentlemen split a celery tonic. I think the caterpillar-holes have made your dress open a little in the back."

So, then and there – according to the records – was the alliance formed by the only two who's-who ladies in the world. Then it was agreed that woman should forever remain as clear as a pane of glass – though glass was yet to be discovered – to other women, and that she should palm herself off on man as a mystery.

Barbara seemed to hesitate.

"Really, Nevada," she said, with a little show of embarrassment, "you shouldn't have insisted on my opening this. I – I'm sure it wasn't meant for any one else to know."

Nevada forgot her gloves for a moment.

"Then read it aloud," she said. "Since you've already read it, what's the difference? If Mr. Warren has written to me something that any one else oughtn't to know, that is all the more reason why everybody should know it."

"Well," said Barbara, "this is what it says:

'Dearest Nevada – Come to my studio at twelve o'clock to-night.

Do not fail.'" Barbara rose and dropped the note in Nevada's lap. "I'm awfully sorry," she said, "that I knew. It isn't like Gilbert. There must be some mistake. Just consider that I am ignorant of it, will you, dear? I must go up-stairs now, I have such a headache. I'm sure I don't understand the note. Perhaps Gilbert has been dining too well, and will explain. Good night!"

IV

Nevada tiptoed to the hall, and heard Barbara's door close upstairs. The bronze clock in the study told the hour of twelve was fifteen minutes away. She ran swiftly to the front door, and let herself out into the snow-storm. Gilbert Warren's studio was six squares away.

By aerial ferry the white, silent forces of the storm attacked the city from beyond the sullen East River. Already the snow lay a foot deep on the pavements, the drifts heaping themselves like scaling-ladders against the walls of the besieged town. The Avenue was as quiet as a street in Pompeii. Cabs now and then skimmed past like white-winged gulls over a moonlit ocean; and less frequent motor-cars-sustaining the comparison – hissed through the foaming waves like submarine boats on their jocund, perilous journeys.

Nevada plunged like a wind-driven storm-petrel on her way. She looked up at the ragged sierras of cloud-capped buildings that rose above the streets, shaded by the night lights and the congealed vapors to gray, drab, ashen, lavender, dun, and cerulean tints. They were so like the wintry mountains of her Western home that she felt a satisfaction such as the hundred-thousand-dollar house had seldom brought her.

A policeman caused her to waver on a corner, just by his eye and weight.

"Hello, Mabel!" said he. "Kind of late for you to be out, ain't it?"

"I – I am just going to the drug store," said Nevada, hurrying past him.

The excuse serves as a passport for the most sophisticated. Does it prove that woman never progresses, or that she sprang from Adam's rib, full-fledged in intellect and wiles?

Turning eastward, the direct blast cut down Nevada's speed one-half. She made zigzag tracks in the snow; but she was as tough as a pinon sapling, and bowed to it as gracefully. Suddenly the studio-building loomed before her, a familiar landmark, like a cliff above some well-remembered canon. The haunt of business and its hostile neighbor, art, was darkened and silent. The elevator stopped at ten.

Up eight flights of Stygian stairs Nevada climbed, and rapped firmly at the door numbered "89." She had been there many times before, with Barbara and Uncle Jerome.

Gilbert opened the door. He had a crayon pencil in one hand, a green shade over his eyes, and a pipe in his mouth. The pipe dropped to the floor.

"Am I late?" asked Nevada. "I came as quick as I could. Uncle and me were at the theatre this evening. Here I am, Gilbert!"

Gilbert did a Pygmalion-and-Galatea act. He changed from a statue of stupefaction to a young man with a problem to tackle. He admitted Nevada, got a whiskbroom, and began to brush the snow from her clothes. A great lamp, with a green shade, hung over an easel, where the artist had been sketching in crayon.

"You wanted me," said Nevada simply, "and I came. You said so in your letter. What did you send for me for?"

"You read my letter?" inquired Gilbert, sparring for wind.

"Barbara read it to me. I saw it afterward. It said: 'Come to my studio at twelve to-night, and do not fail.' I thought you were sick, of course, but you don't seem to be."

"Aha!" said Gilbert irrelevantly. "I'll tell you why I asked you to come, Nevada. I want you to marry me immediately – to-night. What's a little snow-storm? Will you do it?"

"You might have noticed that I would, long ago," said Nevada. "And I'm rather stuck on the snow-storm idea, myself. I surely would hate one of these flowery church noon-weddings. Gilbert, I didn't know you had grit enough to propose it this way. Let's shock 'em – it's our funeral, ain't it?"

"You bet!" said Gilbert. "Where did I hear that expression?" he added to himself. "Wait a minute, Nevada; I want to do a little 'phoning."

He shut himself in a little dressing-room, and called upon the lightnings of tile heavens – condensed into unromantic numbers and districts.

"That you, Jack? You confounded sleepyhead! Yes, wake up; this is me – or I – oh, bother the difference in grammar! I'm going to be married right away. Yes! Wake up your sister – don't answer me back; bring her along, too – you must! Remind Agnes of the time I saved her from drowning in Lake Ronkonkoma – I know it's caddish to refer to it, but she must come with you. Yes. Nevada is here, waiting. We've been engaged quite a while. Some opposition among the relatives, you know, and we have to pull it off this way. We're waiting here for you. Don't let Agnes out-talk you – bring her! You will? Good old boy! I'll order a carriage to call for you, double-quick time. Confound you, Jack, you're all right!"

Gilbert returned to the room where Nevada waited.

"My old friend, Jack Peyton, and his sister were to have been here at a quarter to twelve," he explained; "but Jack is so confoundedly slow. I've just 'phoned them to hurry. They'll be here in a few minutes. I'm the happiest man in the world, Nevada! What did you do with the letter I sent you to-day?"

"I've got it cinched here," said Nevada, pulling it out from beneath her opera-cloak.

Gilbert drew the letter from the envelope and looked it over carefully. Then he looked at Nevada thoughtfully.

"Didn't you think it rather queer that I should ask you to come to my studio at midnight?" he asked.

"Why, no," said Nevada, rounding her eyes. "Not if you needed me. Out West, when a pal sends you a hurry call – ain't that what you say here? – we get there first and talk about it after the row is over. And it's usually snowing there, too, when things happen. So I didn't mind."

Gilbert rushed into another room, and came back burdened with overcoats warranted to turn wind, rain, or snow.

"Put this raincoat on," he said, holding it for her. "We have a quarter of a mile to go. Old Jack and his sister will be here in a few minutes." He began to struggle into a heavy coat. "Oh, Nevada," he said, "just look at the head-lines on the front page of that evening paper on the table, will you? It's about your section of the West, and I know it will interest you."

He waited a full minute, pretending to find trouble in the getting on of his overcoat, and then turned. Nevada had not moved. She was looking at him with strange and pensive directness. Her cheeks had a flush on them beyond the color that had been contributed by the wind and snow; but her eyes were steady.

"I was going to tell you," she said, "anyhow, before you – before we – before – well, before anything. Dad never gave me a day of schooling. I never learned to read or write a darned word. Now if –"

Pounding their uncertain way up-stairs, the feet of Jack, the somnolent, and Agnes, the grateful, were heard.

V

When Mr. and Mrs. Gilbert Warren were spinning softly homeward in a closed carriage, after the ceremony, Gilbert said:

"Nevada, would you really like to know what I wrote you in the letter that you received tonight?"

"Fire away!" said his bride.

"Word for word," said Gilbert, "it was this: 'My dear Miss Warren. You were right about the flower. It was a hydrangea, and not a lilac.'"

"All right," said Nevada. "But let's forget it. The joke's on Barbara, anyway!"

THE ADVENTURES
OF SHAMROCK JOLNES

I AM SO fortunate as to count Shamrock Jolnes, the great New York detective, among my muster of friends. Jolnes is what is called the "inside man" of the city detective force. He is an expert in the use of the typewriter, and it is his duty, whenever there is a "murder mystery" to be solved, to sit at a desk telephone at headquarters and take down the message of "cranks" who phone in their confessions to having committed the crime.

But on certain "off" days when confessions are coming in slowly and three or four newspapers have run to earth as many different guilty persons, Jolnes will knock about the town with me, exhibiting, to my great delight and instruction, his marvelous powers of observation and deduction.

The other day I dropped in at Headquarters and found the great detective gazing thoughtfully at a string that was tied tightly around his little finger.

"Good morning, Whatsup," he said, without turning his head. "I'm glad to notice that you've had your house fitted up with electric lights at last."

"Will you please tell me," I said, in surprise, "how you knew that? I am sure that I never mentioned the fact to any one, and the wiring was a rush order not completed until this morning."

"Nothing easier," said Jolnes, genially. "As you came in I caught the odor of the cigar you are smoking. I know an expensive cigar; and I know that not more than three men in New York can afford to smoke cigars and pay gas bills too at the present time. That was an easy one. But I am working just now on a little problem of my own."

"Why have you that string on your finger?" I asked.

"That's the problem," said Jolnes. "My wife tied that on this morning to remind me of something I was to send up to the house. Sit down, Whatsup, and excuse me for a few moments."

The distinguished detective went to a wall telephone, and stood with the receiver to his ear for probably ten minutes.

"Were you listening to a confession?" I asked, when he had returned to his chair.

"Perhaps," said Jolnes, with a smile, "it might be called something of the sort. To be frank with you, Whatsup, I've cut out the dope. I've been increasing the quantity for so long that morphine doesn't have much effect on me any more. I've got to have something more powerful. That telephone I just went to is connected with a room in the Waldorf where there's an author's reading in progress. Now, to get at the solution of this string."

After five minutes of silent pondering, Jolnes looked at me, with a smile, and nodded his head.

"Wonderful man!" I exclaimed; "already?"

"It is quite simple," he said, holding up his finger. You see that knot? That is to prevent my forgetting. It is, therefore, a forget-me-knot. A forget-me-not is a flower. It was a sack of flour that I was to send home!"

"Beautiful!" I could not help crying out in admiration.

"Suppose we go out for a ramble," suggested Jolnes.

"There is only one case of importance on hand now. Old man McCarty, one hundred and four years old, died from eating too many bananas. The evidence points so strongly to the Mafia that the police have surrounded the Second Avenue Katzenjammer Cambrinus Club No. 2, and the capture of the assassin is only the matter of a few hours. The detective force has not yet been called on for assistance."

Jolnes and I went out and up the street toward the corner, where we were to catch a surface car.

Halfway up the block we met Rheingelder, an acquaintance of ours, who held a City Hall position.

"Good morning, Rheingelder," said Jolnes, halting.

"Nice breakfast that was you had this morning."

Always on the lookout for the detective's remarkable feats of deduction, I saw Jolnes's eyes flash for an instant upon a long yellow splash on the shirt bosom and a smaller one upon the chin of Rheingelder – both undoubtedly made by the yolk of an egg.

"Oh, dot is some of your detectiveness," said Rheingelder, shaking all over with a smile. "Vell, I bet you trinks and cigars all around dot you cannot tell vot I haf eaten for breakfast."

"Done," said Jolnes. "Sausage, pumpernickel, and coffee."

Rheingelder admitted the correctness of the surmise and paid the bet. When we had proceeded on our way I said to Jolnes:

"I thought you looked at the egg spilled on his chin and shirt front."

"I did," said Jolnes. "That is where I began my deduction. Rheingelder is a very economical, saving man. Yesterday eggs dropped in the market to twenty-eight cents per dozen. Today they are quoted at forty-two. Rheingelder ate eggs yesterday, and today he went back to his usual fare. A little thing like this isn't anything, Whatsup; it belongs to the primary arithmetic class."

When we boarded the street car we found the seats all occupied – principally by ladies. Jolnes and I stood on the rear platform. About the middle of the it there sat an elderly man with a short, gray beard, who looked to be the typical, well-dressed New Yorker. At successive corners other ladies climbed aboard, and soon three or four of them were standing over the man, clinging to straps and glaring meaningly at the man who occupied the coveted seat. But he resolutely retained his place.

"We New Yorkers," I remarked to Jolnes, "have about lost our manners, as far as the exercise of them in public goes."

"Perhaps so," said Jolnes, lightly; "but the man you evidently refer to happens to be a very chivalrous and courteous gentleman from Old Virginia. He is spending a few days in New York with his wife and two daughters, and he leaves for the South tonight."

"You know him, then?" I said, in amazement.

"I never saw him before we stepped on the car," declared the detective, smilingly.

"By the gold tooth of the Witch of Endor!" I cried, "if you can construe all that from his appearance you are dealing in nothing else than black art."

"The habit of observation – nothing more," said Jolnes. "If the old gentleman gets off the car before we do, I think I can demonstrate to you the accuracy of my deduction."

Three blocks farther along the gentleman rose to leave the car. Jolnes addressed him at the door: "Pardon me, sir, but are you not Colonel Hunter, of Norfolk, Virginia?"

"No, suh," was the extremely courteous answer. "My name, suh, is Ellison – Major Winfield R. Ellison, from Fairfax County, in the same state. I know a good many people, suh, in Norfolk – the Goodriches, the Tollivers, and the Crabtrees, suh, but I never had the pleasure of meeting yo' friend, Colonel Hunter. I am happy to say, suh, that I am going back to Virginia tonight, after having spent a week in yo' city with my wife and three daughters. I shall be in Norfolk in about ten days, and if you will give me yo' name, suh, I will take pleasure in looking up Colonel Hunter and telling him that you inquired after him, suh."

"Thank you," said Jolnes; "tell him that Reynolds sent his regards, if you will be so kind."

I glanced at the great New York detective and saw that a look of intense chagrin had come upon his clear-cut features. Failure in the slightest point always galled Shamrock Jolnes.

"Did you say your *three* daughters?" he asked of the Virginia gentleman.

"Yes, suh, my three daughters, all as fine girls as there are in Fairfax County," was the answer. With that Major Ellison stopped the car and began to descend the step.

Shamrock Jolnes clutched his arm. "One moment, Sir," he begged, in an urbane voice in which I alone detected the anxiety – "am I not right in believing that one of the young ladies is an adopted daughter?"

"You are, suh," admitted the major, from the ground, "but how the devil you knew it, suh, is mo' than I can tell."

"And mo' than I can tell, too," I said, as the car went on.

Jolnes was restored to his calm, observant serenity by having wrested victory from his apparent failure; so after we got off the car he invited me into a cafe promising to reveal the process of his latest wonderful feat.

"In the first place," he began after we were comfortably seated, "I knew the gentleman was no New Yorker because be was flushed and uneasy and restless on account of the ladies that were standing, although he did not rise and give them his seat. I decided from his appearance that he was a Southerner rather than a Westerner."

"Next I began to figure out his reason for not relinquishing his seat to a lady when he evidently felt strongly, but not overpoweringly, impelled to do so. I very quickly decided upon that. I noticed that one of his eyes had received a severe jab in one corner, which was red and inflamed, and that all over his face were tiny round marks about the size of the end of an uncut lead pencil. Also upon both of his patentleather shoes were a number of deep imprints shaped like ovals cut off square at one end."

"Now, there is only one district in New York City where a man is bound to receive scars and wounds and indentations of that sort – and that is along the sidewalks of Twenty-third Street and a portion of Sixth Avenue south of there. I knew from the imprints of trampling French heels on his feet and the marks of countless jabs in the face from umbrella and parasols carried by women in the shopping district that he bad been in conflict with the amazonian troops. And as he was a man of intelligent appearance, I knew he would not have braved such dangers unless he bad been dragged thither by his own women folk. Therefore, when he got on the car his anger at the treatment he had received was sufficient to make him keep his seat in spite of his traditions of Southern chivalry."

"That is all very well," I said, "but why did you insist upon daughters and especially two daughters? Why couldn't a wife alone have taken him shopping?"

"There had to be daughters," said Jolnes, calmly. "If he had only a wife, and she near his own age, he could have bluffed her into going alone. If he had a young wife she would prefer to go alone. So there you are."

"I'll admit that," I said; "but, now, why two daughters? And how, in the name of all the prophets, did you guess that one was adopted when he told you he had three?"

"Don't say guess," said Jolnes, with a touch of pride in his air; "there is no such word in the lexicon of ratiocination. In Major Ellison's buttonhole there was a carnation and a rosebud backed by a geranium leaf. No woman ever combined a carnation and a rosebud into a boutonnière. Close your eyes, Whatsup, and give the logic of your imagination a chance. Cannot you see the lovely Adele fastening the carnation to the lapel so that papa may be gay upon the street? And then the romping Edith May dancing up with sisterly jealousy to add her rosebud to the adornment?"

"And then," I cried, beginning to feel enthusiasm, "when he declared that he had three daughters –"

"I could see," said Jolnes, "one in the background who added no flower; and I knew that she must be –"

"Adopted!" I broke in. "I give you every credit; but how did you know he was leaving for the South tonight?"

"In his breast pocket," said the great detective, "something large and oval made a protuberance. Good liquor is scarce on trains, and it is a long journey from New York to Fairfax County."

"Again, I must bow to you," I said. "And tell me this, so that my last shred of doubt will be cleared away; why did you decide that he was from Virgirna?"

"It was very faint, I admit," answered Shamrock Jolnes, "but no trained observer could have failed to detect the odor of mint in the car."

THE COP AND THE ANTHEM

ON HIS BENCH in Madison Square, Soapy moved uneasily. When wild geese honk high of nights, and when women without sealskin coats grow kind to their husbands, and when Soapy moves uneasily on his bench in the park, you may know that winter is near at hand.

A dead leaf fell in Soapy's lap. That was Jack Frost's card. Jack is kind to the regular denizens of Madison Square and gives fair warning of his annual call. At the corners of four streets he hands his pasteboard to the North Wind, footman of the mansion of All Outdoors, so that the inhabitants thereof may make ready.

Soapy's mind became cognizant of the fact that the time had come for him to resolve himself into a singular Committee of Ways and Means to provide against the coming rigor. And therefore he moved uneasily on his bench.

The hibernatorial ambitions of Soapy were not of the highest. In them were no considerations of Mediterranean cruises, of soporific Southern skies or drifting in the Vesuvian Bay. Three months on the Island was what his soul craved. Three months of assured board and bed and congenial company, safe from Boreas and blue Coats, seemed to Soapy the essence of things desirable.

For years the hospitable Blackwell's had been his winter quarters. Just as his more fortunate fellow New Yorkers had bought their tickets to Palm Beach and the Riviera each winter, so Soapy had made his humble arrangements for his annual hegira to the Island. And now the time was come. On the previous night three Sabbath newspapers, distributed beneath his coat, about his ankles and over his lap, had failed to repulse the cold as he slept on his bench near the spurring fountain in the ancient square. So the Island loomed big and timely in Soapy's mind. He scorned the provisions made in the name of charity for the city's dependents. In Soapy's opinion the Law was more benign than Philanthropy.There was an endless round of institutions, municipal and eleemosynary, on which he might set out and receive lodging and food accordant with the simple life. But to one of Soapy's proud spirit the gifts of charity are encumbered. If not in coin you must pay in humiliation of spirit for every benefit received at the hands of philanthropy. As Caesar had his Brutus, every bed of charity must have its toll of a bath, every loaf of bread its compensation of a private and personal inquisition. Wherefore it is better to be a guest of the law, which, though conducted by rules, does not meddle unduly with a gentleman's private affairs.

Soapy, having decided to go to the Island, at once set about accomplishing his desire. There were many easy ways of doing this. The pleasantest was to dine luxuriously at some expensive restaurant; and then, after declaring Insolvency, be handed over quietly and without uproar to a policeman. An accommodating magistrate would do the rest.

Soapy left his bench and strolled out of the square and across the level sea of asphalt, where Broadway and Fifth Avenue flow together. Up Broadway he turned, and halted at a glittering cafe where are gathered together nightly the choicest products of the grape, the silkworm, and the protoplasm.

Soapy had confidence in himself from the lowest button of his vest upward. He was shaven, and his coat was decent and his neat black, ready-tied four-in-hand had been presented to him by a lady missionary on Thanksgiving Day. If he could reach a table in the restaurant unsuspected success would be his. The portion of him that would show above the table would raise no doubt in the waiter's mind. A roasted mallard duck, thought Soapy, would be about the thing – with a bottle of Chablis, and then Camembert, a demi-tasse and a cigar. One dollar for the cigar would be enough. The total would not be so high as to call forth any supreme manifestation of revenge from the cafe management; and yet the meat would leave him filled and happy for the journey to his winter refuge.

But as Soapy set foot inside the restaurant door the head waiter's eye fell upon his frayed trousers and decadent shoes. Strong and ready hands turned him about and conveyed him in silence and haste to the sidewalk and averted the ignoble fate of the menaced Mallard.

Soapy turned off Broadway. It seemed that his route to the coveted Island was not to be an epicurean one. Some other way of entering limbo must be thought of.

At a corner of Sixth Avenue electric lights and cunningly displayed wares behind plateglass made a shop window conspicuous.

Soapy took a cobblestone and dashed it through the glass. People came running around the corner, a policeman in the lead. Soapy stood still, with his hands in his pockets, arid smiled at the sight of brass buttons.

"Where's the man that done that?" inquired the officer, excitedly.

"Don't you figure out that I might have had something to do with it?" said Soapy, not without sarcasm, but friendly, as one greets good fortune.

The policeman's mind refused to accept Soapy even as a clue. Men who smash windows do not remain to parley with the law's minions. They take to their heels. The policeman saw a man halfway down the block running to catch a cat. With drawn club he joined in the pursuit. Soapy, with disgust in his heart, loafed along, twice unsuccessful.

On the opposite side of the street was a restaurant of no great pretensions. It catered to large appetites and modest purses. Its crockery and atmosphere were thick; its soup and napery thin. Into this place Soapy took his accusive shoes and telltale trousers without challenge. At a table he sat and consumed beefsteak, flapjacks, doughnuts and pie. And then to the waiter he betrayed the fact that the minutest coin and himself were strangers.

"Now, get busy and call a cop," said Soapy. "And don't keep a gentleman waiting."

"No cop for youse," said the waiter, with a voice like butter cakes and an eye like the cherry in a Manhattan cocktail. "Hey, Con!"

Neatly upon his left ear on the callous pavement two waiters pitched Soapy. He arose joint by joint, as a carpenter's rule opens, and beat the dust from his clothes. Arrest seemed but a rosy dream. The Island seemed very far away. A policeman who stood before a drug store two doors away laughed and walked down the street.

Five blocks Soapy traveled before his courage permitted him to woo capture again. This time the opportunity presented what he fatuously termed to himself a "cinch." A young woman of a modest and pleasing guise was standing before a show window gazing with sprightly interest at its display of shaving mugs and inkstands, and two yards from the window a large policeman of severe demeanor leaned against a water plug.

It was Soapy's design to assume the role of the despicable and execrated "masher." The refined and elegant appearance of his victim and the contiguity of the conscientious cop encouraged him to believe that he would soon feel the pleasant official clutch upon his arm that would insure his winter quarters on the right little, tight little isle.

Soapy straightened the lady missionary's ready-made tie, dragged his shrinking cuffs into the open, set his hat at a killing cant and sidled toward the young woman. He made eyes at her, was taken with sudden coughs and "hems," smiled, smirked and went brazenly through the impudent and contemptible litany of the "masher." With half an eye Soapy saw that the policeman was watching him fixedly. The young woman moved away a few steps, and again bestowed her absorbed attention upon the shaving mugs. Soapy followed, boldly stepping to her side, raised his hat and said:

"Ah there, Bedelia! Don't you want to come and play in my yard?"

The policeman was still looking. The persecuted young woman had but to beckon a finger and Soapy would be practically en route for his insular haven. Already be imagined he could feel the cozy warmth of the station-house. The young woman faced him and, stretching out a hand, caught Soapy's coat sleeve.

"Sure, Mike," she said, joyfully, "if you'll blow me to a pail of suds. I'd have spoke to you sooner' but the cop was watching."

With the young woman playing the clinging ivy to his oak Soapy walked past the policeman overcome with gloom. He seemed doomed to liberty.

At the next corner he shook off his companion and ran. He halted in the district where by night are found the lightest streets, hearts, vows and librettos. Women in furs and men in greatcoats moved gaily in the wintry air. A sudden fear seized Soapy that some dreadful enchantment had rendered him immune to arrest. The thought brought a little of panic upon it, and when he came upon another policeman lounging grandly in front of a transplendent theatre he caught at the immediate straw of "disorderly conduct."

On the sidewalk Soapy began to yell drunken gibberish at the top of his harsh voice. He danced, howled, raved, and otherwise disturbed the welkin.

The policeman twirled his club, turned his back to Soapy and remarked to a citizen.

"'Tis one of them Yale lads celebratin' the goose egg they give to the Hartford College. Noisy; but no harm. We've instructions to lave them be."

Disconsolate, Soapy ceased his unavailing racket. Would never a policeman lay hands on him? In his fancy the Island seemed an unattainable Arcadia. He buttoned his thin coat against the chilling wind.

In a cigar store he saw a well-dressed man lighting a cigar at a swinging light. His silk umbrella he had set by the door on entering. Soapy stepped inside, secured the umbrella and sauntered off with it slowly. The man at the cigar light followed hastily.

"My umbrella," he said, sternly.

"Oh, is it?" sneered Soapy, adding insult to petit larceny. "Well, why don't you call a policeman? I took it. Your umbrella? Why don't you call a cop? There stands one on the corner."

The umbrella owner slowed his steps. Soapy did likewise, with a presentiment that luck would again run against him. The policeman looked at the two curiously.

"Of course," said the umbrella man – "that is – well, you know how these mistakes occur – I – if it's your umbrella I hope you'll excuse me – I picked it up this morning in a restaurant – If you recognize it as yours, why – I hope you'll –"

"Of course it's mine," said Soapy, viciously.

The ex-umbrella man retreated. The policeman hurried to assist a tall blonde in an opera cloak across the street in front of a street car that was approaching two blocks away.

Soapy walked eastward through a street damaged by improvements. He hurled the umbrella wrathfully into an excavation. He muttered against the men who wear helmets and carry clubs. Because he wanted to fall into their clutches, they seemed to regard him as a king who could do no wrong.

At length Soapy reached one of the avenues to the east where the glitter and turmoil was but faint. He set his face down this toward Madison Square, for the homing instinct survives even when the home is a park bench.

But on an unusually quiet corner Soapy came to a standstill. Here was an old church, quaint and rambling and gabled. Through one violet-stained window a soft light glowed, where, no doubt, the organist loitered over the keys, making sure of his mastery of the coming Sabbath anthem. For there drifted out to Soapy's ears sweet music that caught and held him transfixed against the convolutions of the iron fence.

The moon was above, lustrous and serene; vehicles and pedestrians were few; sparrows twittered sleepily in the eaves – for a little while the scene might have been a country churchyard. And the anthem that the organist played cemented Soapy to the iron fence, for he had known it well in the days when his life contained such things as mothers and roses and ambitions and friends and immaculate thoughts and collars.

The conjunction of Soapy's receptive state of mind and the influences about the old church wrought a sudden and wonderful change in his soul. He viewed with swift horror the pit into which he had tumbled, the degraded days, unworthy desires, dead hopes, wrecked faculties and base motives that made up his existence.

And also in a moment his heart responded thrillingly to this novel mood. An instantaneous and strong impulse moved him to battle with his desperate fate. He would pull himself out of the mire; he would make a man of himself again; he would conquer the evil that had taken possession of him. There was time; he was comparatively young yet: he would resurrect his old eager ambitions and pursue them without faltering. Those solemn but sweet organ notes had set up a revolution in him. Tomorrow he would go into the roaring downtown district and find work. A fur importer had once offered him a place as driver. He would find him to-morrow and ask for the position. He would be somebody in the world. He would –

Soapy felt a hand laid on his arm. He looked quickly around into the broad face of a policeman.

"What are you doin' here?" asked the officer.

"Nothin'," said Soapy.

"Then come along," said the policeman.

"Three months on the Island," said the Magistrate in the Police Court the next morning.

THE DETECTIVE DETECTOR

I WAS WALKING in Central Park with Avery Knight, the great New York burglar, highwayman, and murderer.

"But, my dear Knight," said I, "it sounds incredible. You have undoubtedly performed some of the most wonderful feats in your profession known to modern crime. You have committed some marvelous deeds under the very noses of the police – you have boldly entered the homes of millionaires and held them up with an empty gun while you made free with their silver and jewels; you have sandbagged citizens in the glare of Broadway's electric lights; you have killed and robbed with superb openness and absolute impunity – but when you boast that within forty-eight hours after committing a murder you can run down and actually bring me face to face with the detective assigned to apprehend you, I must beg leave to express my doubts – remember, you are in New York."

Avery Knight smiled indulgently.

"You pique my professional pride, doctor," he said in a nettled tone. "I will convince you."

About twelve yards in advance of us a prosperous-looking citizen was rounding a clump of bushes where the walk curved. Knight suddenly drew a revolver and shot the man in the back. His victim fell and lay without moving.

The great murderer went up to him leisurely and took from his clothes his money, watch, and a valuable ring and cravat pin. He then rejoined me smiling calmly, and we continued our walk.

Ten steps and we met a policeman running toward the spot where the shot had been fired. Avery Knight stopped him.

"I have just killed a man," he announced, seriously, "and robbed him of his possessions."

"G'wan," said the policeman, angrily, "or I'll run yez in! Want yer name in the papers, don't yez? I never knew the cranks to come around so quick after a shootin' before. Out of th' park, now, for yours, or I'll fan yez."

"What you have done," I said, argumentatively, as Knight and I walked on, "was easy. But when you come to the task of hunting down the detective that they send upon your trail you will find that you have undertaken a difficult feat."

"Perhaps so," said Knight, lightly. "I will admit that my success depends in a degree upon the sort of man they start after me. If it should be an ordinary plain-clothes man I might fail to gain a sight of him. If they honor me by giving the case to some one of their celebrated sleuths I do not fear to match my cunning and powers of induction against his."

On the next afternoon Knight entered my office with a satisfied look on his keen countenance.

"How goes the mysterious murder?" I asked.

"As usual," said Knight, smilingly. "I have put in the morning at the police station and at the inquest. It seems that a card case of mine containing cards with my name and address was found near the body. They have three witnesses who saw the shooting and gave a description of me. The case has been placed in the hands of Shamrock Jolnes, the famous detective. He left Headquarters at 11:30 on the assignment. I waited at my address until two, thinking he might call there."

I laughed, tauntingly.

"You will never see Jolnes," I continued, "until this murder has been forgotten, two or three weeks from now. I had a better opinion of your shrewdness, Knight. During the three hours and a half that you waited he has got out of your ken. He is after you on true induction theories now, and no wrongdoer has yet been known to come upon him while thus engaged. I advise you to give it up."

"Doctor," said Knight, with a sudden glint in his keen gray eye and a squaring of his chin, "in spite of the record your city holds of something like a dozen homicides without a subsequent meeting of the perpetrator, and the sleuth in charge of the case, I will undertake to break that record. To-morrow I will take you to Shamrock Jolnes — I will unmask him before you and prove to you that it is not an impossibility for an officer of the law and a manslayer to stand face to face in your city."

"Do it," said I, "and you'll have the sincere thanks of the Police Department."

On the next day Knight called for me in a cab.

"I've been on one or two false scents, doctor," he admitted. "I know something of detectives' methods, and I followed out a few of them, expecting to find Jolnes at the other end. The pistol being a .45-caliber, I thought surely I would find him at work on the clue in Forty-fifth Street. Then, again, I looked for the detective at the Columbia University, as the man's being shot in the back naturally suggested hazing. But I could not find a trace of him."

"Nor will you," I said, emphatically.

"Not by ordinary methods," said Knight. "I might walk up and down Broadway for a month without success. But you have aroused my pride, doctor; and if I fail to show you Shamrock Jolnes this day, I promise you I will never kill or rob in your city again."

"Nonsense, man," I replied. "When our burglars walk into our houses and politely demand, thousands of dollars' worth of jewels, and then dine and bang the piano an hour or two before leaving, how do you, a mere murderer, expect to come in contact with the detective that is looking for you?"

Avery Knight, sat lost in thought for a while. At length he looked up brightly.

"Doc," said he, "I have it. Put on your hat, and come with me. In half an hour I guarantee that you shall stand in the presence of Shamrock Jolnes."

I entered a cab with Avery Knight. I did not hear his instructions to the driver, but the vehicle set out at a smart pace up Broadway, turning presently into Fifth Avenue, and proceeding northward again. It was with a rapidly beating heart that I accompanied this wonderful and gifted assassin, whose analytical genius and superb self-confidence had prompted him to make me the tremendous promise of bringing me into the presence of a murderer and the New York detective in pursuit of him simultaneously. Even yet I could not believe it possible.

"Are you sure that you are not being led into some trap?" I asked. "Suppose that your clue, whatever it is, should bring us only into the presence of the Commissioner of Police and a couple of dozen cops!"

"My dear doctor," said Knight, a little stiffly. "I would remind you that I am no gambler."

"I beg your pardon," said I. "But I do not think you will find Jolnes."

The cab stopped before one of the handsomest residences on the avenue. Walking up and down in front of the house was a man with long red whiskers, with a detective's badge showing on the lapel of his coat. Now and then the man would remove his whiskers to wipe his face, and then I would recognize at once the well-known features of the great New York detective. Jolnes was keeping a sharp watch upon the doors and windows of the house.

"Well, doctor," said Knight, unable to repress a note of triumph in his voice, "have you seen?"

"It is wonderful – wonderful!" I could not help exclaiming as our cab started on its return trip. "But how did you do it? By what process of induction –"

"My dear doctor," interrupted the great murderer, "the inductive theory is what the detectives use. My process is more modern. I call it the saltatorial theory. Without bothering with the tedious mental phenomena necessary to the solution of a mystery from slight clues, I jump at once to a conclusion. I will explain to you the method I employed in this case.

"In the first place, I argued that as the crime was committed in New York City in broad daylight, in a public place and under peculiarly atrocious circumstances, and that as the most skilful sleuth available was let loose upon the case, the perpetrator would never be discovered. Do you not think my postulation justified by precedent?"

"Perhaps so," I replied, doggedly. "But if Big Bill Dev –"

"Stop that," interrupted Knight, with a smile, "I've heard that several times. It's too late now. I will proceed.

"If homicides in New York went undiscovered, I reasoned, although the best detective talent was employed to ferret them out, it must be true that the detectives went about their work in the wrong way. And not only in the wrong way, but exactly opposite from the right way. That was my clue.

"I slew the man in Central Park. Now, let me describe myself to you.

"I am tall, with a black beard, and I hate publicity. I have no money to speak of; I do not like oatmeal, and it is the one ambition of my life to die rich. I am of a cold and heartless disposition. I do not care for my fellowmen and I never give a cent to beggars or charity.

"Now, my dear doctor, that is the true description of myself, the man whom that shrewd detective was to hunt down. You who are familiar with the history of crime in New York of late should be able to foretell the result. When I promised you to exhibit to your incredulous gaze the sleuth who was set upon me, you laughed at me because you said that detectives and murderers never met in New York. I have demonstrated to you that the theory is possible."

"But how did you do it?" I asked again.

"It was very simple," replied the distinguished murderer. "I assumed that the detective would go exactly opposite to the clues he had. I have given you a description of myself. Therefore, he must necessarily set to work and trail a short man with a white beard who likes to be in the papers, who is very wealthy, is fond of oatmeal, wants to die poor, and is of an extremely generous and philanthropic disposition. When thus far is reached the mind hesitates no longer. I conveyed you at once to the spot where Shamrock Jolnes was piping off Andrew Carnegie's residence."

"Knight," said I, "you're a wonder. If there was no danger of your reforming, what a rounds man you'd make for the Nineteenth Precinct!"

THE DIAMOND OF KALI

THE ORIGINAL NEWS item concerning the diamond of the goddess Kali was handed in to the city editor. He smiled and held it for a moment above the wastebasket. Then he laid it back on his desk and said: "Try the Sunday people; they might work something out of it."

The Sunday editor glanced the item over and said: "H'm!" Afterward he sent for a reporter and expanded his comment.

"You might see General Ludlow," he said, "and make a story out of this if you can. Diamond stories are a drug; but this one is big enough to be found by a scrubwoman wrapped up in a piece of newspaper and tucked under the corner of the hall linoleum. Find out first if the General has a daughter who intends to go on the stage. If not, you can go ahead with the story. Run cuts of the Kohinoor and J. P. Morgan's collection, and work in pictures of the Kimberley mines and Barney Barnato. Fill in with a tabulated comparison of the values of diamonds, radium, and veal cutlets since the meat strike; and let it run to a half page."

On the following day the reporter turned in his story. The Sunday editor let his eye sprint along its lines. "H'm!" he said again. This time the copy went into the waste-basket with scarcely a flutter.

The reporter stiffened a little around the lips; but he was whistling softly and contentedly between his teeth when I went over to talk with him about it an hour later.

"I don't blame the 'old man'," said he, magnanimously, "for cutting it out. It did sound like funny business; but it happened exactly as I wrote it. Say, why don't you fish that story out of the w. b. and use it? Seems to me it's as good as the tommyrot you write."

I accepted the tip, and if you read further you will learn the facts about the diamond of the goddess Kali as vouched for by one of the most reliable reporters on the staff.

Gen. Marcellus B. Ludlow lives in one of those decaying but venerated old red-brick mansions in the West Twenties. The General is a member of an old New York family that does not advertise. He is a globe-trotter by birth, a gentleman by predilection, a millionaire by the mercy of Heaven, and a connoisseur of precious stones by occupation.

The reporter was admitted promptly when he made himself known at the General's residence at about eight thirty on the evening that he received the assignment. In the magnificent library he was greeted by the distinguished traveler and connoisseur, a tall, erect gentleman in the early fifties, with a nearly white moustache, and a bearing so soldierly that one perceived in him scarcely a trace of the National Guardsman. His weather-beaten countenance lit up with a charming smile of interest when the reporter made known his errand.

"Ah, you have heard of my latest find. I shall be glad to show you what I conceive to be one of the six most valuable blue diamonds in existence."

The General opened a small safe in a corner of the library and brought forth a plush-covered box. Opening this, he exposed to the reporter's bewildered gaze a huge and brilliant diamond – nearly as large as a hailstone.

"This stone," said the General, "is something more than a mere jewel. It once formed the central eye of the three-eyed goddess Kali, who is worshipped by one of the fiercest and most fanatical tribes of India. If you will arrange yourself comfortably I will give you a brief history of it for your paper."

General Ludlow brought a decanter of whiskey and glasses from a cabinet, and set a comfortable armchair for the lucky scribe.

"The Phansigars, or Thugs, of India," began the General, "are the most dangerous and dreaded of the tribes of North India. They are extremists in religion, and worship the horrid goddess Kali in the form of images. Their rites are interesting and bloody. The robbing and murdering of travellers are taught as a worthy and obligatory deed by their strange religious code. Their worship of the three-eyed goddess Kali is conducted so secretly that no traveler has ever heretofore had the honor of witnessing the ceremonies. That distinction was reserved for myself.

"While at Sakaranpur, between Delhi and Khelat, I used to explore the jungle in every direction in the hope of learning something new about these mysterious Phansigars.

"One evening at twilight I was making my way through a teakwood forest, when I came upon a deep circular depression in an open space, in the center of which was a rude stone temple. I was sure that this was one of the temples of the Thugs, so I concealed myself in the undergrowth to watch.

"When the moon rose the depression in the clearing was suddenly filled with hundreds of shadowy, swiftly gliding forms. Then a door opened in the temple, exposing a brightly illuminated image of the goddess Kali, before which a white-robed priest began a barbarous incantation, while the tribe of worshippers prostrated themselves upon the earth.

"But what interested me most was the central eye of the huge wooden idol. I could see by its flashing brilliancy that it was an immense diamond of the purest water.

"After the rites were concluded the Thugs slipped away into the forest as silently as they had come. The priest stood for a few minutes in the door of the temple enjoying the cool of the night before closing his rather warm quarters. Suddenly a dark, lithe shadow slipped down into the hollow, leaped upon the priest, and struck him down with a glittering knife. Then the murderer sprang at the image of the goddess like a cat and pried out the glowing central eye of Kali with his weapon. Straight toward me he ran with his royal prize. When he was within two paces I rose to my feet and struck him with all my force between the eyes. He rolled over senseless and the magnificent jewel fell from his hand. That is the splendid blue diamond you have just seen – a stone worthy of a monarch's crown."

"That's a corking story," said the reporter. "That decanter is exactly like the one that John W. Gates always sets out during an interview."

"Pardon me," said General Ludlow, "for forgetting hospitality in the excitement of my narrative. Help yourself."

"Here's looking at you," said the reporter. "What I am afraid of now," said the General, lowering his voice, "is that I may be robbed of the diamond. The jewel that formed an eye of their goddess is their most sacred symbol. Somehow the tribe suspected me of having it; and members of the band have followed me half around the earth. They are the most cunning and cruel fanatics in the world, and their religious vows would compel them to assassinate the unbeliever who has desecrated their sacred treasure."

"Once in Lucknow three of their agents, disguised as servants in a hotel, endeavoured to strangle me with a twisted cloth. Again, in London, two Thugs, made up as street musicians, climbed into my window at night and attacked me. They have even tracked me to this country. My life is never safe. A month ago, while I was at a hotel in the Berkshires, three of them sprang upon me from the roadside weeds. I saved myself then by my knowledge of their customs."

"How was that, General?" asked the reporter.

"There was a cow grazing near by," said General Ludlow, "a gentle Jersey cow. I ran to her side and stood. The three Thugs ceased their attack, knelt and struck the ground thrice with their foreheads. Then, after many respectful salaams, they departed." "Afraid the cow would hook?" asked the reporter.

"No; the cow is a sacred animal to the Phansigars. Next to their goddess they worship the cow. They have never been known to commit any deed of violence in the presence of the animal they reverence."

"It's a mighty interesting story," said the reporter. "If you don't mind I'll take another drink, and then a few notes."

"I will join you," said General Ludlow, with a courteous wave of his hand.

"If I were you," advised the reporter, "I'd take that sparkler to Texas. Get on a cow ranch there, and the Pharisees –"

"Phansigars," corrected the General.

"Oh, yes; the fancy guys would run up against a long horn every time they made a break."

General Ludlow closed the diamond case and thrust it into his bosom.

"The spies of the tribe have found me out in New York," he said, straightening his tall figure. "I'm familiar with the East Indian cast of countenance, and I know that my every movement is watched. They will undoubtedly attempt to rob and murder me here."

"Here?" exclaimed the reporter, seizing the decanter and pouring out a liberal amount of its contents.

"At any moment," said the General. "But as a soldier and a connoisseur I shall sell my life and my diamond as dearly as I can."

At this point of the reporter's story there is a certain vagueness, but it can be gathered that there was a loud crashing noise at the rear of the house they were in. General Ludlow buttoned his coat closely and sprang for the door. But the reporter clutched him firmly with one hand, while he held the decanter with the other.

"Tell me before we fly," he urged, in a voice thick with some inward turmoil, "do any of your daughters contemplate going on the stage?"

"I have no daughters – fly for your life – the Phansigars are upon us!" cried the General.

The two men dashed out of the front door of the house. The hour was late. As their feet struck the side-walk strange men of dark and forbidding appearance seemed to rise up out of the earth and encompass them. One with Asiatic features pressed close to the General and droned in a terrible voice:

"Buy cast clo'!"

Another, dark-whiskered and sinister, sped lithely to his side and began in a whining voice:

"Say, mister, have yer got a dime fer a poor feller what –"

They hurried on, but only into the arms of a black-eyed, dusky-browed being, who held out his hat under their noses, while a confederate of Oriental hue turned the handle of a street organ near by.

Twenty steps farther on General Ludlow and the reporter found themselves in the midst of half a dozen villainous-looking men with high-turned coat collars and faces bristling with unshaven beards.

"Run for it!" hissed the General. "They have discovered the possessor of the diamond of the goddess Kali."

The two men took to their heels. The avengers of the goddess pursued.

"Oh, Lordy!" groaned the reporter, "there isn't a cow this side of Brooklyn. We're lost!"

When near the corner they both fell over an iron object that rose from the sidewalk close to the gutter. Clinging to it desperately, they awaited their fate.

"If I only had a cow!" moaned the reporter – "or another nip from that decanter, General!"

As soon as the pursuers observed where their victims had found refuge they suddenly fell back and retreated to a considerable distance.

"They are waiting for reinforcements in order to attack us," said General Ludlow.

But the reporter emitted a ringing laugh, and hurled his hat triumphantly into the air.

"Guess again," he shouted, and leaned heavily upon the iron object. "Your old fancy guys or thugs, whatever you call 'em, are up to date. Dear General, this is a pump we've stranded upon – same as a cow in New York (hic!) see? Thas'h why the 'nfuriated smoked guys don't attack us – see? Sacred an'mal, the pump in N' York, my dear General!"

But further down in the shadows of Twenty-eighth Street the marauders were holding a parley.

"Come on, Reddy," said one. "Let's go frisk the old 'un. He's been showin' a sparkler as big as a hen egg all around Eighth Avenue for two weeks past."

"Not on your silhouette," decided Reddy. "You see 'em rallyin' round The Pump? They're friends of Bill's. Bill won't stand for nothin' of this kind in his district since he got that bid to Esopus."

This exhausts the facts concerning the Kali diamond. But it is deemed not inconsequent to close with the following brief (paid) item that appeared two days later in a morning paper.

"It is rumored that a niece of Gen. Marcellus B. Ludlow, of New York City, will appear on the stage next season."

"Her diamonds are said to be extremely valuable and of much historic interest."

The Duel

THE GODS, LYING beside their nectar on 'Lympus and peeping over the edge of the cliff, perceive a difference in cities. Although it would seem that to their vision towns must appear as large or small ant-hills without special characteristics, yet it is not so. Studying the habits of ants from so great a height should be but a mild diversion when coupled with the soft drink that mythology tells us is their only solace. But doubtless they have amused themselves by the comparison of villages and towns; and it will be no news to them (nor, perhaps, to many mortals), that in one particularity New York stands unique among the cities of the world. This shall be the theme of a little story addressed to the man who sits smoking with his Sabbath-slippered feet on another chair, and to the woman who snatches the paper for a moment while boiling greens or a narcotized baby leaves her free. With these I love to sit upon the ground and tell sad stories of the death of Kings.

New York City is inhabited by 4,000,000 mysterious strangers; thus beating Bird Centre by three millions and half a dozen nine's. They came here in various ways and for many reasons – Hendrik Hudson, the art schools, green goods, the stork, the annual dressmakers' convention, the Pennsylvania Railroad, love of money, the stage, cheap excursion rates, brains, personal column ads., heavy walking shoes, ambition, freight trains – all these have had a hand in making up the population.

But every man Jack when he first sets foot on the stones of Manhattan has got to fight. He has got to fight at once until either he or his adversary wins. There is no resting between rounds, for there are no rounds. It is slugging from the first. It is a fight to a finish.

Your opponent is the City. You must do battle with it from the time the ferry-boat lands you on the island until either it is yours or it has conquered you. It is the same whether you have a million in your pocket or only the price of a week's lodging.

The battle is to decide whether you shall become a New Yorker or turn the rankest outlander and Philistine. You must be one or the other. You cannot remain neutral. You must be for or against – lover or enemy – bosom friend or outcast. And, oh, the city is a general in the ring. Not only by blows does it seek to subdue you. It woos you to its heart with the subtlety of a siren. It is a combination of Delilah, green Chartreuse, Beethoven, chloral and John L. in his best days.

In other cities you may wander and abide as a stranger man as long as you please. You may live in Chicago until your hair whitens, and be a citizen and still prate of beans if Boston mothered you, and without rebuke. You may become a civic pillar in any other town but Knickerbocker's, and all the time publicly sneering at its buildings, comparing them with the architecture of Colonel Telfair's residence in Jackson, Miss., whence you hail, and you will not be set upon. But in New York you must be either a New Yorker or an invader of a modern Troy, concealed in the wooden horse of your conceited provincialism. And this dreary preamble is only to introduce to you the unimportant figures of William and Jack.

They came out of the West together, where they had been friends. They came to dig their fortunes out of the big city. Father Knickerbocker met them at the ferry, giving one a right-hander on the nose and the other an upper-cut with his left, just to let them know that the fight was on.

William was for business; Jack was for Art. Both were young and ambitious; so they countered and clinched. I think they were from Nebraska or possibly Missouri or Minnesota. Anyhow, they were out for success and scraps and scads, and they tackled the city like two Lochinvars with brass knucks and a pull at the City Hall. Four years afterward William and Jack met at luncheon. The business man blew in like a March wind, hurled his silk hat at a waiter, dropped into the chair that was pushed under him, seized the bill of fare, and had ordered as far as cheese before the artist had time to do more than nod. After the nod a humorous smile came into his eyes.

"Billy," he said, "you're done for. The city has gobbled you up. It has taken you and cut you to its pattern and stamped you with its brand. You are so nearly like ten thousand men I have seen to-day that you couldn't be picked out from them if it weren't for your laundry marks."

"Camembert," finished William. "What's that? Oh, you've still got your hammer out for New York, have you? Well, little old Noisyville-on-the-Subway is good enough for me. It's giving me mine. And, say,

I used to think the West was the whole round world – only slightly flattened at the poles whenever Bryan ran. I used to yell myself hoarse about the free expense, and hang my hat on the horizon, and say cutting things in the grocery to little soap drummers from the East. But I'd never seen New York, then, Jack. Me for it from the rathskellers up. Sixth Avenue is the West to me now. Have you heard this fellow Crusoe sing? The desert isle for him, I say, but my wife made me go. Give me May Irwin or E. S. Willard any time."

"Poor Billy," said the artist, delicately fingering a cigarette. "You remember, when we were on our way to the East how we talked about this great, wonderful city, and how we meant to conquer it and never let it get the best of us? We were going to be just the same fellows we had always been, and never let it master us. It has downed you, old man. You have changed from a maverick into a butterick."

"Don't see exactly what you are driving at," said William. "I don't wear an alpaca coat with blue trousers and a seersucker vest on dress occasions, like I used to do at home. You talk about being cut to a pattern – well, ain't the pattern all right? When you're in Rome you've got to do as the Dagoes do. This town seems to me to have other alleged metropolises skinned to flag stations. According to the railroad schedule I've got in mind, Chicago and Saint Jo and Paris, France, are asterisk stops – which means you wave a red flag and get on every other Tuesday. I like this little suburb of Tarrytown-on-the-Hudson. There's something or somebody doing all the time. I'm clearing $8,000 a year selling automatic pumps, and I'm living like kings-up. Why, yesterday, I was introduced to John W. Gates. I took an auto ride with a wine agent's sister. I saw two men run over by a street car, and I seen Edna May play in the evening. Talk about the West, why, the other night I woke everybody up in the hotel hollering. I dreamed I was walking on a board sidewalk in Oshkosh. What have you got against this town, Jack? There's only one thing in it that I don't care for, and that's a ferryboat."

The artist gazed dreamily at the cartridge paper on the wall. "This town," said he, "is a leech. It drains the blood of the country. Whoever comes to it accepts a challenge to a duel. Abandoning the figure of the leech, it is a juggernaut, a Moloch, a monster to which the innocence, the genius, and the beauty of the land must pay tribute. Hand to hand every newcomer must struggle with the leviathan. You've lost, Billy. It shall never conquer me. I hate it as one hates sin or pestilence or – the color work in a ten-cent magazine. I despise its very vastness and power. It has the poorest millionaires, the littlest great men, the lowest skyscrapers, the dolefulest pleasures of any town I ever saw. It has caught you, old man, but I will never run beside its chariot wheels. It glosses itself as the Chinaman glosses his collars. Give me the domestic finish. I could stand a town ruled by wealth or one ruled by an aristocracy; but this is one controlled by its lowest ingredients. Claiming culture, it is the crudest; asseverating its pre-eminence, it is the basest; denying all outside values and virtue, it is the narrowest. Give me the pure and the open heart of the West country. I would go back there to-morrow if I could."

"Don't you like this *filet mignon*?" said William. "Shucks, now, what's the use to knock the town! It's the greatest ever. I couldn't sell one automatic pump between Harrisburg and Tommy O'Keefe's saloon, in Sacramento, where I sell twenty here. And have you seen Sara Bernardt in 'Andrew Mack' yet?"

"The town's got you, Billy," said Jack.

"All right," said William. "I'm going to buy a cottage on Lake Ronkonkoma next summer."

At midnight Jack raised his window and sat close to it. He caught his breath at what he saw, though he had seen and felt it a hundred times.

Far below and around lay the city like a ragged purple dream. The irregular houses were like the broken exteriors of cliffs lining deep gulches and winding streams. Some were mountainous; some lay in long, desert canons. Such was the background of the wonderful, cruel, enchanting, bewildering, fatal, great city. But into this background were cut myriads of brilliant parallelograms and circles and squares through which glowed many colored lights. And out of the violet and purple depths ascended like the city's soul sounds and odors and thrills that make up the civic body. There arose the breath of gaiety unrestrained, of love, of hate, of all the passions that man can know. There below him lay all things, good or bad, that can be brought from the four corners of the earth to instruct, please, thrill, enrich, despoil, elevate, cast down, nurture or kill. Thus the flavor of it came up to him and went into his blood.

There was a knock on his door. A telegram had come for him. It came from the West, and these were its words:

Come back and the answer will be yes.
                    DOLLY.

He kept the boy waiting ten minutes, and then wrote the reply:

"Impossible to leave here at present." Then he sat at the window again and let the city put its cup of mandragora to his lips again.

After all it isn't a story; but I wanted to know which one of the heroes won the battle against the city. So I went to a very learned friend and laid the case before him. What he said was: "Please don't bother me; I have Christmas presents to buy."

So there it rests; and you will have to decide for yourself.

THE FURNISHED ROOM

RESTLESS, SHIFTING, FUGACIOUS as time itself is a certain vast bulk of the population of the red brick district of the lower West Side. Homeless, they have a hundred homes. They flit from furnished room to furnished room, transients forever – transients in abode, transients in heart and mind. They sing "Home, Sweet Home" in ragtime; they carry their lares et penates in a bandbox; their vine is entwined about a picture hat; a rubber plant is their fig tree.

Hence the houses of this district, having had a thousand dwellers, should have a thousand tales to tell, mostly dull ones, no doubt; but it would be strange if there could not be found a ghost or two in the wake of all these vagrant guests.

One evening after dark a young man prowled among these crumbling red mansions, ringing their bells. At the twelfth he rested his lean band-baggage upon the step and wiped the dust from his hatband and forehead. The bell sounded faint and far away in some remote, hollow depths.

To the door of this, the twelfth house whose bell he had rung, came a housekeeper who made him think of an unwholesome, surfeited worm that had eaten its nut to a hollow shell and now sought to fill the vacancy with edible lodgers.

He asked if there was a room to let.

"Come in," said the housekeeper. Her voice came from her throat; her throat seemed lined with fur. "I have the third-floor back, vacant since a week back. Should you wish to look at it?"

The young man followed her up the stairs. A faint light from no particular source mitigated the shadows of the halls. They trod noiselessly upon a stair carpet that its own loom would have forsworn. It seemed to have become vegetable; to have degenerated in that rank, sunless air to lush lichen or spreading moss that grew in patches to the stair-case and was viscid under the foot like organic matter. At each turn of the stairs were vacant niches in the wall. Perhaps plants had once been set within them. If so they had died in that foul and tainted air. It may be that statues of the saints had stood there, but it was not difficult to conceive that imps and devils had dragged them forth in the darkness and down to the unholy depths of some furnished pit below.

"This is the room," said the housekeeper, from her furry throat. "It's a nice room. It ain't often vacant. I had some most elegant people in it last summer – no trouble at all, and paid in advance to the minute. The water's at the end of the hall. Sprawls and Mooney kept it three months. They done a vaudeville sketch. Miss B'retta Sprowls – you may have heard of her – Oh, that was just the stage names – right there over the dresser is where the marriage certificate hung, framed. The gas is here, and you see there is plenty of closet room. It's a room everybody likes. It never stays idle long."

"Do you have many theatrical people rooming here?" asked the young man.

"They comes and goes. A good proportion of my lodgers is connected with the theatres. Yes, sir, this is the theatrical district. Actor people never stays long anywhere. I get my share. Yes, they comes and they goes."

He engaged the room, paying for a week in advance. He was tired, he said, and would take possession at once. He counted out the money. The loom had been made ready, she said, even to towels and water. As the housekeeper moved away he put, for the thousandth time, the question that he carried at the end of his tongue.

"A young girl – Miss Vashner – Miss Eloise Vashner – do you remember such a one among your lodgers? She would be singing on the stage, most likely. A fair girl, of medium height and slender, with reddish, gold hair and dark mole near her left eyebrow."

"No, I don't remember the name. Them stage people have names they change as often as their rooms. They comes and they goes. No, I don't call that one to mind."

No. Always no. Five months of ceaseless interrogation and the inevitable negative. So much time spent by day in questioning managers, agents, schools and choruses; by night among the audiences of theatres from all-star casts down to music halls so low that he dreaded to find what he most hoped for. He who had loved her best had tried to find her. He was sure that since her disappearance from home this great, watergirt city held her somewhere, but it was like a monstrous quicksand, shifting its particles constantly, with no foundation, its upper granules of today buried tomorrow in ooze and slime.

The furnished room received its latest guest with a first glow of pseudo-hospitality, a hectic, haggard, perfunctory welcome like the specious smile of a demirep. The sophistical comfort came in reflected gleams from the decayed furniture, the ragged brocade upholstery of a couch and two chairs, a foot-wide cheap pier glass between the two windows, from one or two gilt picture frames and a brass bedstead in a corner.

The guest reclined, inert, upon a chair, while the room, confused in speech as though it were an apartment in Babel, tried to discourse to him of its diverse tenantry.

A polychromatic rug like some brilliant-flowered, rectangular, tropical islet lay surrounded by a billowy sea of soiled matting. Upon the gay-papered wall were those pictures that pursue the homeless one from house to house – The Huguenot Lovers, The First Quarrel, The Wedding Breakfast, Psyche at the Fountain. The mantel's chastely severe outline was ingloriously veiled behind some pert drapery drawn rakishly askew like the sashes of the Amazonian ballet. Upon it was some desolate flotsam cast aside by the room's marooned when a lucky Sail had borne them to a fresh port – a trifling vase or two, pictures of actresses, a medicine bottle, some stray cards out of a deck.

One by one, as the characters of a cryptograph became explicit, the little signs left by the furnished rooms' procession of guests developed a significance. The threadbare space in the rug in front of the dresser told that lovely woman had marched in the throng. The tiny fingerprints on the wall spoke of little prisoners trying to feel their way to sun and air. A splattered stain, raying like the shadow of a bursting bomb, witnessed where a hurled glass or bottle had splintered with its contents against the wall. Across the pier glass had been scrawled with a diamond in staggering letters the name "Marie." It seemed that the succession of dwellers in the furnished room had turned in fury – perhaps tempted beyond forbearance by its garish coldness – and wreaked upon it their passions. The furniture was chipped and bruised; the couch, distorted by bursting springs, seemed a horrible monster that had been slain during the stress of some grotesque convulsion. Some more potent upheaval had cloven a great slice from the marble mantel. Each plank in the floor owned its particular cant and shriek as from a separate arid individual agony. It seemed incredible that all this malice and injury had been wrought upon the room by those who had called it for a time their home; and yet it may have been the cheated home instinct surviving blindly, the resentful rage at false household gods that had kindled their wrath. A hut that is our own we can sweep and adorn and cherish.

The young tenant in the chair allowed these thoughts to file, soft-shod, through his mind, while there drifted into the room furnished sounds and furnished scents. He heard in one room a tittering and incontinent, slack laughter; in others the monologue of a scold, the rattling of dice, a lullaby, and one crying dully; above him a banjo tinkled with spirit. Doors banged somewhere; the elevated trains roared intermittently; a cat yowled miserably upon a back fence. And he breathed the breath of the house – a dank savor rather than a smell – a cold, musty effluvium as from underground vaults mingled with the reeking exhalations of linoleum and mildewed and rotten woodwork.

Then suddenly, as he rested there, the room was filled with the strong, sweet odor of mignonette. It came as upon a single buffet of wind with such sureness and fragrance and emphasis that it almost seemed a living visitant. And the man cried aloud: "What, dear?" as if he had been called, and sprang up and faced about. The rich odor clung to him and wrapped him around. He reached out his arms for it, all his senses for the time confused and commingled. How could one be peremptorily called by an odor? Surely it must have been a sound. But, was it not the sound that had touched, that had caressed him?

"She has been in this room," he cried, and he sprang to wrest from it a token, for he knew he would recognize the smallest thing that had belonged to her or that she had touched. This enveloping scent of mignonette, the odor that she had loved and made her own – whence came it?

The room had been but carelessly set in order. Scattered upon the flimsy dresser scarf were half a dozen hairpin – those discreet, indistinguishable friends of womankind, feminine of gender, infinite of mood and uncommunicative of tense. These he ignored, conscious of their triumphant lack of identity. Ransacking the drawers of the dresser he came upon a discarded, tiny, ragged handkerchief. He pressed it to his face. It was racy and insolent with heliotrope; he hurled it to the floor. In another drawer he found odd buttons, a theatre programme, a pawnbroker's card, two lost marshmallows, a book on the divination of dreams. In the last was a woman's black satin hair bow, which halted him, poised between ice and fire. But the black satin bow also is femininity's demure, impersonal common ornament and tells no tales.

And then he traversed the room like a hound on the scent, skimming the walls, considering the comers of the bulging matting on his hands and knees, rummaging mantel and tables, the curtains and hangings, the drunken cabinet in the corner, for a visible sign, unable to perceive that She was there beside, around, against, within, above him, clinging to him, wooing him, calling him so poignantly through the finer senses that even his grosser ones became cognizant of the call. Once again he answered loudly: "Yes, dear –" and turned, wild-eyed, to gaze on vacancy, for he could not yet discern form and color and love and outstretched arms in the odor of mignonette. Oh, God! whence that odor, and since when have odors had a voice to call? Thus he groped.

He burrowed in crevices and corners, and found corks and cigarettes. These he passed in passive contempt. But once he found in a fold of the matting a halfsmoked cigar, and this he ground beneath his heel with a green and trenchant oath. He sifted the room from end to end. He found dreary and ignoble small records of many a peripatetic tenant; but of her whom he sought, and who may have lodged there, and whose spirit seemed to hover there, he found no trace.

And then he thought of the housekeeper. He ran from the haunted room downstairs and to a door that showed a crack of light. She came out to his knock, He smothered his excitement as best he could.

"Will you tell me, madam," he besought her, "who occupied the room I have before I came?"

"Yes, sir. I can tell you again. 'Twas Sprowls and Mooney, as I said. Miss B'retta Sprowls it was in the theatres, but Missis Mooney she was. My house is well-known for respectability. The marriage certificate hung, framed, on a nail over –"

"What kind of a lady was Miss Sprowls – in looks, I mean?"

"Why, black-haired, sir, short, and stout, with a comical face. They left a week ago Tuesday."

"And before they occupied it?"

"Why, there was a single gentleman connected with the draying business. He left owing me a week. Before him was Missis Crowder and her two children, that stayed four months; and back of them was old Mr. Doyle, whose sons paid for him. He kept the room six months. That goes back a year, sir, and further I do not remember."

He thanked her and crept back to his loom. The room was dead. The essence that had vivified it was gone. The perfume of mignotnette had departed. In its place was the old, stale odor of moldy house furniture, of atmosphere in storage.

The ebbing of his hope drained his faith. He sat staring at the yellow, singing gaslight. Soon he walked to the bed and began to tear the sheets into strips. With the blade of his knife he drove them tightly into every crevice around windows and door. When all was snug and taut he turned out the light, turned the gas full on again and laid himself gratefully upon the bed.

* * *

It was Mrs. McCool's night to go with the can for beer. So she fetched it and sat with Mrs. Purdy in one of those subterranean retreats where housekeepers foregather and the worm dieth seldom.

"I rented out my third-floor-back this evening," said Mrs. Purdy, across a fine circle of foam. "A young man took it. He went up to bed two hours ago."

"Now, did ye, Mrs. Purdy, ma'am?" said Mrs. McCool, with intense admiration. "You do be a wonder for rentin' rooms of that kind. And did ye tell him, then?" she concluded in a husky whisper laden with mystery.

"Rooms," said Mrs. Purdy, in her furriest tones, "are furnished for to rent. I did not tell him, Mrs. McCool."

"'Tis right ye are, ma'am; 'tis by renting rooms we kape alive. Ye have the rale sense for business, ma'am. There be many people will rayjict the rentin' of a room if they be told a suicide has been after dyin' in the bed of it."

"As you say, we has our living to be making," remarked Mrs. Purdy.

"Yis, ma'am; 'tis true. 'Tis just one wake ago this day I helped ye lay out the third-floor-back. A pretty slip of a colleen she was to be killin' herself wid the gas, a swate little face she had, Mrs. Purdy, ma'am."

"She'd a-been called handsome, as you say," said Mrs. Purdy, assenting but critical, "but for that mole she had a-growin' by her left eyebrow. Do fill up your glass again, Mrs. McCool."

THE GIFT OF THE MAGI

ONE DOLLAR AND eighty seven cents. That was all. And sixty cents of it was in pennies. Pennies saved one and two at a time by bull-dozing the grocer and the vegetable man and the butcher until one's cheeks burned with the silent imputation of parsimony that such close dealing implied. Three times Della counted it. One dollar and eighty seven cents. And the next day would be Christmas.

There was clearly nothing to do but flop down on the shabby little couch and howl. So Della did it. Which instigates the moral reflection that life is made up of sobs, sniffles, and smiles, with sniffles predominating.

While the mistress of the home is gradually subsiding from the first stage to the second, take a look at the home. A furnished flat at $8 per week. It did not exactly beggar description, but it certainly had that word on the lookout for the mendicancy squad.

In the vestibule below was a letterbox into which no letter would go, and an electric button from which no mortal finger could coax a ring. Also appertaining thereunto was a card bearing the name "Mr. James Dillingham Young."

The "Dillingham" had been flung to the breeze during a former period of prosperity when its possessor was being paid $30 per week.

Now, when the income was shrunk to $20, the letters of "Dillingham" looked blurred, as though they were thinking seriously of contracting to a modest and unassuming D.

But whenever Mr. James Dillingham Young came home and reached his flat above, he was called "Jim" and greatly hugged by Mrs. James Dillingham Young, already introduced to you as Della. Which is all very good.

Della finished her cry and attended to her cheeks with the powder rag. She stood by the window and looked out dully at a gray cat walking a gray fence in a gray backyard. Tomorrow would be Christmas Day, and she had only $1.87 with which to buy Jim a present. She had been saving every penny she could for months, with this result.

Twenty dollars a week doesn't go far. Expenses had been greater than she had calculated. They always are. Only $1.87 to buy a present for Jim. Her Jim. Many a happy hour she had spent planning for something nice for him. Something fine and rare and sterling – something just a little bit near to being worthy of the honor of being owned by Jim.

There was a pier-glass between the windows of the room. Perhaps you have seen a pier-glass in an $8 flat. A very thin and very agile person may, by observing his reflection in a rapid sequence of longitudinal strips, obtain a fairly accurate conception of his looks. Della, being slender, had mastered the art.

Suddenly she whirled from the window and stood before the glass. Her eyes were shining brilliantly, but her face had lost its color within twenty seconds. Rapidly she pulled down her hair and let it fall to its full length.

Now, there were two possessions of the James Dillingham Youngs in which they both took a mighty pride. One was Jim's gold watch that had been his father's and his grandfather's. The other was Della's hair. Had the Queen of Sheba lived in the flat across the airshaft, Della would have let her hair hang out the window some day to dry just to depreciate Her Majesty's jewels and gifts. Had King Solomon been the janitor, with all his treasures piled up in the basement, Jim would have pulled out his watch every time he passed, just to see him pluck at his beard from envy.

So now Della's beautiful hair fell about her rippling and shining like a cascade of brown waters. It reached below her knee and made itself almost a garment for her. And then she did it up again nervously and quickly. Once she faltered for a minute and stood still while a tear or two splashed on the worn red carpet.

On went her old brown jacket; on went her old brown hat. With a whirl of skirts and with the brilliant sparkle still in her eyes, she fluttered out the door and down the stairs to the street. Where she stopped, the sign read: "Mme. Sofronie. Hair Goods of All Kinds."

One flight up Della ran, and collected herself, panting. Madame, large, too white, chilly, hardly looked the "Sofronie."

"Will you buy my hair?" asked Della.

"I buy hair," said Madame. "Take ye hat off and let's have a sight at the looks of it." Down rippled the brown cascade.

"Twenty dollars," said Madame, lifting the mass with a practiced hand.

"Give it to me quick," said Della.

Oh, and the next two hours tripped by on rosy wings. Forget the hashed metaphor. She was ransacking the stores for Jim's present.

She found it at last. It surely had been made for Jim and no one else. There was no other like it in any of the stores, and she had turned all of them inside out. It was a platinum fob chain simple and chaste in design, properly proclaiming its value by substance alone and not by meretricious ornamentation – as all good things should do.

It was even worthy of The Watch. As soon as she saw it she knew that it must be Jim's. It was like him. Quietness and value – the description applied to both. Twenty one dollars they took from her for it, and she hurried home with the 87 cents. With that chain on his watch Jim might be properly anxious about the time in any company. Grand as the watch was, he sometimes looked at it on the sly on account of the old leather strap that he used in place of a chain.

When Della reached home her intoxication gave way a little to prudence and reason. She got out her curling irons and lighted the gas and went to work repairing the ravages made by generosity added to love. Which is always a tremendous task, dear friends – a mammoth task.

Within forty minutes her head was covered with tiny, close-lying curls that made her look wonderfully like a truant schoolboy. She looked at her reflection in the mirror long, carefully, and critically.

"If Jim doesn't kill me," she said to herself, "before he takes a second look at me, he'll say I look like a Coney Island chorus girl. But what could I do – oh! what could I do with a dollar and eighty seven cents?"

At 7 o'clock the coffee was made and the frying pan was on the back of the stove and ready to cook the chops.

Jim was never late. Della doubled the fob chain in her hand and sat on the corner of the table near the door that he always entered. Then she heard his step on the stairway down on the first flight, and she turned white for just a moment.

Della had a habit of saying little silent prayers about the simplest everyday things, and now she whispered: "Please God, make him think I am still pretty."

The door opened and Jim stepped in and closed it. He looked thin and very serious. Poor fellow, he was only twenty two – and to be burdened with a family! He needed a new overcoat and he was without gloves.

Jim stopped inside the door, as immovable as a setter at the scent of quail. His eyes were fixed upon Della, and there was an expression in them that she could not read, and it terrified her. It was not anger, nor surprise, nor disapproval, nor horror, nor any of the sentiments that she had been prepared for. He simply stared at her fixedly with that peculiar expression on his face.

Della wriggled off the table and went for him.

"Jim, darling," she cried, "don't look at me that way. I had my hair cut off and sold it because I couldn't have lived through Christmas without giving you a present. It'll grow out again – you won't mind, will you? I just had to do it. My hair grows awfully fast. Say *Merry Christmas!*, Jim, and let's be happy. You don't know what a nice – what a beautiful, nice gift I've got for you."

"You've cut off your hair?" asked Jim, laboriously, as if he had not arrived at that patent fact yet even after the hardest mental labor.

"Cut it off and sold it," said Della. "Don't you like me just as well, anyhow? I'm me without my hair, ain't I?"

Jim looked around the room curiously.

"You say your hair is gone?" he said, with an air almost of idiocy.

"You needn't look for it," said Della. "It's sold, I tell you – sold and gone, too. It's Christmas Eve, boy. Be good to me, for it went for you. Maybe the hairs of my head were numbered," she went on with a sudden serious sweetness, "but nobody could ever count my love for you. Shall I put the chops on, Jim?"

Out of his trance Jim seemed quickly to wake. He enfolded his Della. For ten seconds let us regard with discreet scrutiny some inconsequential object in the other direction. Eight dollars a week or a million a year – what is the difference? A mathematician or a wit would give you the wrong answer. The magi brought valuable gifts, but that was not among them. This dark assertion will be illuminated later on.

Jim drew a package from his overcoat pocket and threw it on the table.

"Don't make any mistake, Dell," he said, "about me. I don't think there's anything in the way of a haircut or a shave or a shampoo that could make me like my girl any less. But if you'll unwrap that package you may see why you had me going a while at first."

White fingers and nimble tore at the string and paper. And then an ecstatic scream of joy; and then, alas! a quick feminine change to hysterical tears and wails, necessitating the immediate employment of all the comforting powers of the lord of the flat.

For there lay The Combs – the set of combs, side and back, that Della had worshipped for so long in a Broadway window. Beautiful combs, pure tortoise shell, with jeweled rims – just the shade to wear in the beautiful vanished hair.

They were expensive combs, she knew, and her heart had simply craved and yearned over them without the least hope of possession. And now they were hers, but the tresses that should have adorned the coveted adornments were gone.

But she hugged them to her bosom, and at length she was able to look up with dim eyes and say: "My hair grows so fast, Jim!"

And then Della leaped up like a little singed cat and cried, "Oh, oh!"

Jim had not yet seen his beautiful present. She held it out to him eagerly upon her open palm. The dull precious metal seemed to flash with a reflection of her bright and ardent spirit.

"Isn't it a dandy, Jim? I hunted all over town to find it. You'll have to look at the time a hundred times a day now. Give me your watch. I want to see how it looks on it."

Instead of obeying, Jim tumbled down on the couch and put his hands under the back of his head and smiled.

"Dell," said he, "let's put our Christmas presents away and keep 'em a while. They're too nice to use just at present – I sold the watch, to get the money to buy your combs. And now suppose you put the chops on."

The magi, as you know, were wise men – wonderfully wise men – who brought gifts to the Babe in the manger. They invented the art of giving Christmas presents. Being wise, their gifts were no doubt wise ones, possibly bearing the privilege of exchange in case of duplication. And here I have lamely related to you the uneventful chronicle of two foolish children in a flat who most unwisely sacrificed for each other the greatest treasures of their house. But in a last word to the wise of these days, let it be said that of all who give gifts, these two were the wisest.

Of all who give and receive gifts, such as they are the wisest.

Everywhere they are the wisest.

They are the magi.

THE HANDBOOK OF HYMEN

TIS THE OPINION of myself, Sanderson Pratt, who sets this down, that the educational system of the United States should be in the hands of the weather bureau. I can give you good reasons for it; and you can't tell me why our college professors shouldn't be transferred to the meteorological department. They have been learned to read; and they could very easily glance at the morning papers and then wire in to the main office what kind of weather to expect. But there's the other side of the proposition. I am going on to tell you how the weather furnished me and Idaho Green with an elegant education.

We was up in the Bitter Root Mountains over the Montana line prospecting for gold. A chin-whiskered man in Walla-Walla, carrying a line of hope as excess baggage, had grubstaked us; and there we was in the foothills pecking away, with enough grub on hand to last an army through a peace conference.

Along one day comes a mail-rider over the mountains from Carlos, and stops to eat three cans of greengages, and leave us a newspaper of modern date. This paper prints a system of premonitions of the weather, and the card it dealt Bitter Root Mountains from the bottom of the deck was "warmer and fair, with light westerly breezes."

That evening it began to snow, with the wind strong in the east. Me and Idaho moved camp into an old empty cabin higher up the mountain, thinking it was only a November flurry. But after falling three foot on a level it went to work in earnest; and we knew we was snowed in. We got in plenty of firewood before it got deep, and we had grub enough for two months, so we let the elements rage and cut up all they thought proper.

If you want to instigate the art of manslaughter just shut two men up in a eighteen by twenty-foot cabin for a month. Human nature won't stand it.

When the first snowflakes fell me and Idaho Green laughed at each other's jokes and praised the stuff we turned out of a skillet and called bread. At the end of three weeks Idaho makes this kind of a edict to me. Says he:

"I never exactly heard sour milk dropping out of a balloon on the bottom of a tin pan, but I have an idea it would be music of the spears compared to this attenuated stream of asphyxiated thought that emanates out of your organs of conversation. The kind of half-masticated noises that you emit every day puts me in mind of a cow's cud, only she's lady enough to keep hers to herself, and you ain't."

"Mr. Green," says I, "you having been a friend of mine once, I have some hesitations in confessing to you that if I had my choice for society between you and a common yellow, three-legged cur pup, one of the inmates of this cabin here would be wagging a tail just at present."

This way we goes on for two or three days, and then we quits speaking to one another. We divides up the cooking implements, and Idaho cooks his grub on one side of the fireplace, and me on the other. The snow is up to the windows, and we have to keep a fire all day.

You see me and Idaho never had any education beyond reading and doing "if John had three apples and James five" on a slate. We never felt any special need for a university degree, though we had acquired a species of intrinsic intelligence in knocking around the world that we could use in emergencies. But, snowbound in that cabin in the Bitter Roots, we felt for the first time that if we had studied Homer or Greek and fractions and the higher branches of information, we'd have had some resources in the line of meditation and private thought. I've seen them Eastern college fellows working in camps all through the West, and I never noticed but what education was less of a drawback to 'em than you would think. Why, once over on Snake River, when Andrew McWilliams' saddle horse got the botts, he sent a buckboard ten miles for one of these strangers that claimed to be a botanist. But that horse died.

One morning Idaho was poking around with a stick on top of a little shelf that was too high to reach. Two books fell down to the floor. I started toward 'em, but caught Idaho's eye. He speaks for the first time in a week.

"Don't burn your fingers," says he. "In spite of the fact that you're only fit to be the companion of a sleeping mud-turtle, I'll give you a square deal. And that's more than your parents did when they turned you loose in the world with the sociability of a rattle-snake and the bedside manner of a frozen turnip. I'll play you a game of seven-up, the winner to pick up his choice of the book, the loser to take the other."

We played; and Idaho won. He picked up his book; and I took mine. Then each of us got on his side of the house and went to reading.

I never was as glad to see a ten-ounce nugget as I was that book. And Idaho took at his like a kid looks at a stick of candy.

Mine was a little book about five by six inches called "Herkimer's Handbook of Indispensable Information." I may be wrong, but I think that was the greatest book that ever was written. I've got it to-day; and I can stump you or any man fifty times in five minutes with the information in it. Talk about Solomon or the New York *Tribune*! Herkimer had cases on both of 'em. That man must have put in fifty years and travelled a million miles to find out all that stuff. There was the population of all cities in it, and the way to tell a girl's age, and the number of teeth a camel has. It told you the longest tunnel in the world, the number of the stars, how long it takes for chicken pox to break out, what a lady's neck ought to measure, the veto powers of Governors, the dates of the Roman aqueducts, how many pounds of rice going without three beers a day would buy, the average annual temperature of Augusta, Maine, the quantity of seed required to plant an acre of carrots in drills, antidotes for poisons, the number of hairs on a blond lady's head, how to preserve eggs, the height of all the mountains in the world, and the dates of all wars and battles, and how to restore drowned persons, and sunstroke, and the number of tacks in a pound, and how to make dynamite and flowers and beds, and what to do before the doctor comes – and a hundred times as many things besides. If there was anything Herkimer didn't know I didn't miss it out of the book.

I sat and read that book for four hours. All the wonders of education was compressed in it. I forgot the snow, and I forgot that me and old Idaho was on the outs. He was sitting still on a stool reading away with a kind of partly soft and partly mysterious look shining through his tan-bark whiskers.

"Idaho," says I, "what kind of a book is yours?"

Idaho must have forgot, too, for he answered moderate, without any slander or malignity.

"Why," says he, "this here seems to be a volume by Homer K. M."

"Homer K. M. what?" I asks.

"Why, just Homer K. M.," says he.

"You're a liar," says I, a little riled that Idaho should try to put me up a tree. "No man is going 'round signing books with his initials. If it's Homer K. M. Spoopendyke, or Homer K. M. McSweeney, or Homer K. M. Jones, why don't you say so like a man instead of biting off the end of it like a calf chewing off the tail of a shirt on a clothesline?"

"I put it to you straight, Sandy," says Idaho, quiet. "It's a poem book," says he, "by Homer K. M. I couldn't get color out of it at first, but there's a vein if you follow it up. I wouldn't have missed this book for a pair of red blankets."

"You're welcome to it," says I. "What I want is a disinterested statement of facts for the mind to work on, and that's what I seem to find in the book I've drawn."

"What you've got," says Idaho, "is statistics, the lowest grade of information that exists. They'll poison your mind. Give me old K. M.'s system of surmises. He seems to be a kind of a wine agent. His regular toast is 'nothing doing,' and he seems to have a grouch, but he keeps it so well-lubricated with booze that his worst kicks sound like an invitation to split a quart. But it's poetry," says Idaho, "and I have sensations of scorn for that truck of yours that tries to convey sense in feet and inches. When it comes to explaining the instinct of philosophy through the art of nature, old K. M. has got your man beat by drills, rows, paragraphs, chest measurement, and average annual rainfall."

So that's the way me and Idaho had it. Day and night all the excitement we got was studying our books. That snowstorm sure fixed us with a fine lot of attainments apiece. By the time the snow melted, if you had stepped up to me suddenly and said: "Sanderson Pratt, what would it cost per square foot to lay a roof with twenty by twenty-eight tin at nine dollars and fifty cents per box?" I'd have told you as quick as light could travel the length of a spade handle at the rate of one hundred and ninety-two thousand miles per second. How many can do it? You wake up most any man you know in the middle of the night, and ask him quick to tell you the number of bones in the human skeleton exclusive of the teeth, or what percentage of the vote of the Nebraska Legislature overrules a veto. Will he tell you? Try him and see.

About what benefit Idaho got out of his poetry book I didn't exactly know. Idaho boosted the wine-agent every time he opened his mouth; but I wasn't so sure.

This Homer K. M., from what leaked out of his libretto through Idaho, seemed to me to be a kind of a dog who looked at life like it was a tin can tied to his tail. After running himself half to death, he sits down, hangs his tongue out, and looks at the can and says:

"Oh, well, since we can't shake the growler, let's get it filled at the corner, and all have a drink on me."

Besides that, it seems he was a Persian; and I never hear of Persia producing anything worth mentioning unless it was Turkish rugs and Maltese cats.

That spring me and Idaho struck pay ore. It was a habit of ours to sell out quick and keep moving. We unloaded our grubstaker for eight thousand dollars apiece; and then we drifted down to this little town of Rosa, on the Salmon river, to rest up, and get some human grub, and have our whiskers harvested.

Rosa was no mining-camp. It laid in the valley, and was as free of uproar and pestilence as one of them rural towns in the country. There was a three-mile trolley line champing its bit in the environs; and me and Idaho spent a week riding on one of the cars, dropping off at nights at the Sunset View Hotel. Being now well read as well as travelled, we was soon *pro re nata* with the best society in Rosa, and was invited out to the most dressed-up and high-toned entertainments. It was at a piano recital and quail-eating contest in the city hall, for the benefit of the fire company, that me and Idaho first met Mrs. De Ormond Sampson, the queen of Rosa society.

Mrs. Sampson was a widow, and owned the only two-story house in town. It was painted yellow, and whichever way you looked from you could see it as plain as egg on the chin of an O'Grady on a Friday. Twenty-two men in Rosa besides me and Idaho was trying to stake a claim on that yellow house.

There was a dance after the song books and quail bones had been raked out of the Hall. Twenty-three of the bunch galloped over to Mrs. Sampson and asked for a dance. I side-stepped the two-step, and asked permission to escort her home. That's where I made a hit.

On the way home says she:

"Ain't the stars lovely and bright to-night, Mr. Pratt?"

"For the chance they've got," says I, "they're humping themselves in a mighty creditable way. That big one you see is sixty-six million miles distant. It took thirty-six years for its light to reach us. With an eighteen-foot telescope you can see forty-three millions of 'em, including them of the thirteenth magnitude, which, if one was to go out now, you would keep on seeing it for twenty-seven hundred years."

"My!" says Mrs. Sampson. "I never knew that before. How warm it is! I'm as damp as I can be from dancing so much."

"That's easy to account for," says I, "when you happen to know that you've got two million sweat-glands working all at once. If every one of your perspiratory ducts, which are a quarter of an inch long, was placed end to end, they would reach a distance of seven miles."

"Lawsy!" says Mrs. Sampson. "It sounds like an irrigation ditch you was describing, Mr. Pratt. How do you get all this knowledge of information?"

"From observation, Mrs. Sampson," I tells her. "I keep my eyes open when I go about the world."

"Mr. Pratt," says she, "I always did admire a man of education. There are so few scholars among the sap-headed plug-uglies of this town that it is a real pleasure to converse with a gentleman of culture. I'd be gratified to have you call at my house whenever you feel so inclined."

And that was the way I got the goodwill of the lady in the yellow house. Every Tuesday and Friday evening I used to go there and tell her about the wonders of the universe as discovered, tabulated, and compiled from nature by Herkimer. Idaho and the other gay Lutherans of the town got every minute of the rest of the week that they could.

I never imagined that Idaho was trying to work on Mrs. Sampson with old K. M.'s rules of courtship till one afternoon when I was on my way over to take her a basket of wild hog-plums. I met the lady coming down the lane that led to her house. Her eyes was snapping, and her hat made a dangerous dip over one eye.

"Mr. Pratt," she opens up, "this Mr. Green is a friend of yours, I believe."

"For nine years," says I.

"Cut him out," says she. "He's no gentleman!"

"Why ma'am," says I, "he's a plain incumbent of the mountains, with asperities and the usual failings of a spendthrift and a liar, but I never on the most momentous occasion had the heart to deny that he was a gentleman. It may be that in haberdashery and the sense of arrogance and display Idaho offends the eye, but inside, ma'am, I've found him impervious to the lower grades of crime and obesity. After nine years of Idaho's society, Mrs. Sampson," I winds up, "I should hate to impute him, and I should hate to see him imputed."

"It's right plausible of you, Mr. Pratt," says Mrs. Sampson, "to take up the curmudgeons in your friend's behalf; but it don't alter the fact that he has made proposals to me sufficiently obnoxious to ruffle the ignominy of any lady."

"Why, now, now, now!" says I. "Old Idaho do that! I could believe it of myself, sooner. I never knew but one thing to deride in him; and a blizzard was responsible for that. Once while we was snow-bound in the mountains he became a prey to a kind of spurious and uneven poetry, which may have corrupted his demeanour."

"It has," says Mrs. Sampson. "Ever since I knew him he has been reciting to me a lot of irreligious rhymes by some person he calls Ruby Ott, and who is no better than she should be, if you judge by her poetry."

"Then Idaho has struck a new book," says I, "for the one he had was by a man who writes under the *nom de plume* of K. M."

"He'd better have stuck to it," says Mrs. Sampson, "whatever it was. And to-day he caps the vortex. I get a bunch of flowers from him, and on 'em is pinned a note. Now, Mr. Pratt, you know a lady when you see her; and you know how I stand in Rosa society. Do you think for a moment that I'd skip out to the woods with a man along with a jug of wine and a loaf of bread, and go singing and cavorting up and down under the trees with him? I take a little claret with my meals, but I'm not in the habit of packing a jug of it into the brush and raising Cain in any such style as that. And of course he'd bring his book of verses along, too. He said so. Let him go on his scandalous picnics alone! Or let him take his Ruby Ott with him. I reckon she wouldn't kick unless it was on account of there being too much bread along. And what do you think of your gentleman friend now, Mr. Pratt?"

"Well, 'm," says I, "it may be that Idaho's invitation was a kind of poetry, and meant no harm. May be it belonged to the class of rhymes they call figurative. They offend law and order, but they get sent through the mails on the grounds that they mean something that they don't say. I'd be glad on Idaho's account if you'd overlook it," says I, and let us extricate our minds from the low regions of poetry to the higher planes of fact and fancy. On a beautiful afternoon like this, Mrs. Sampson," I goes on, "we should let our thoughts dwell accordingly. Though it is warm here, we should remember that at the equator the line of perpetual frost is at an altitude of fifteen thousand feet. Between the latitudes of forty degrees and forty-nine degrees it is from four thousand to nine thousand feet."

"Oh, Mr. Pratt," says Mrs. Sampson, "it's such a comfort to hear you say them beautiful facts after getting such a jar from that minx of a Ruby's poetry!"

"Let us sit on this log at the roadside," says I, "and forget the inhumanity and ribaldry of the poets. It is in the glorious columns of ascertained facts and legalised measures that beauty is to be found. In this very log we sit upon, Mrs. Sampson," says I, "is statistics more wonderful than any poem. The rings show it was sixty years old. At the depth of two thousand feet it would become coal in three thousand years. The deepest coal mine in the world is at Killingworth, near Newcastle. A box four feet long, three feet wide, and two feet eight inches deep will hold one ton of coal. If an artery is cut, compress it above the wound. A man's leg contains thirty bones. The Tower of London was burned in 1841."

"Go on, Mr. Pratt," says Mrs. Sampson. "Them ideas is so original and soothing. I think statistics are just as lovely as they can be."

But it wasn't till two weeks later that I got all that was coming to me out of Herkimer.

One night I was waked up by folks hollering "Fire!" all around. I jumped up and dressed and went out of the hotel to enjoy the scene. When I see it was Mrs. Sampson's house, I gave forth a kind of yell, and I was there in two minutes.

The whole lower story of the yellow house was in flames, and every masculine, feminine, and canine in Rosa was there, screeching and barking and getting in the way of the firemen. I saw Idaho trying to get away from six firemen who were holding him. They was telling him the whole place was on fire downstairs, and no man could go in it and come out alive.

"Where's Mrs. Sampson?" I asks.

"She hasn't been seen," says one of the firemen. "She sleeps upstairs. We've tried to get in, but we can't, and our company hasn't got any ladders yet."

I runs around to the light of the big blaze, and pulls the Handbook out of my inside pocket. I kind of laughed when I felt it in my hands – I reckon I was some daffy with the sensation of excitement.

"Herky, old boy," I says to it, as I flipped over the pages, "you ain't ever lied to me yet, and you ain't ever throwed me down at a scratch yet. Tell me what, old boy, tell me what!" says I.

I turned to "What to do in Case of Accidents," on page 117. I run my finger down the page, and struck it. Good old Herkimer, he never overlooked anything! It said:

Suffocation from Inhaling Smoke or Gas. – There is nothing better than flaxseed. Place a few seed in the outer corner of the eye.

I shoved the Handbook back in my pocket, and grabbed a boy that was running by.

"Here," says I, giving him some money, "run to the drug store and bring a dollar's worth of flaxseed. Hurry, and you'll get another one for yourself. Now," I sings out to the crowd, "we'll have Mrs. Sampson!" And I throws away my coat and hat.

Four of the firemen and citizens grabs hold of me. It's sure death, they say, to go in the house, for the floors was beginning to fall through.

"How in blazes," I sings out, kind of laughing yet, but not feeling like it, "do you expect me to put flaxseed in a eye without the eye?"

I jabbed each elbow in a fireman's face, kicked the bark off of one citizen's shin, and tripped the other one with a side hold. And then I busted into the house. If I die first I'll write you a letter and tell you if it's any worse down there than the inside of that yellow house was; but don't believe it yet. I was a heap more cooked than the hurry-up orders of broiled chicken that you get in restaurants. The fire and smoke had me down on the floor twice, and was about to shame Herkimer, but the firemen helped me with their little stream of water, and I got to Mrs. Sampson's room. She'd lost consciousness from the smoke, so I wrapped her in the bed clothes and got her on my shoulder. Well, the floors wasn't as bad as they said, or I never could have done it – not by no means.

I carried her out fifty yards from the house and laid her on the grass. Then, of course, every one of them other twenty-two plaintiff's to the lady's hand crowded around with tin dippers of water ready to save her. And up runs the boy with the flaxseed.

I unwrapped the covers from Mrs. Sampson's head. She opened her eyes and says:

"Is that you, Mr. Pratt?"

"S-s-sh," says I. "Don't talk till you've had the remedy."

I runs my arm around her neck and raises her head, gentle, and breaks the bag of flaxseed with the other hand; and as easy as I could I bends over and slips three or four of the seeds in the outer corner of her eye.

Up gallops the village doc by this time, and snorts around, and grabs at Mrs. Sampson's pulse, and wants to know what I mean by any such sandblasted nonsense.

"Well, old Jalap and Jerusalem oakseed," says I, "I'm no regular practitioner, but I'll show you my authority, anyway."

They fetched my coat, and I gets out the Handbook.

"Look on page 117," says I, "at the remedy for suffocation by smoke or gas. Flaxseed in the outer corner of the eye, it says. I don't know whether it works as a smoke consumer or whether it hikes the compound gastro-hippopotamus nerve into action, but Herkimer says it, and he was called to the case first. If you want to make it a consultation, there's no objection."

Old doc takes the book and looks at it by means of his specs and a fireman's lantern.

"Well, Mr. Pratt," says he, "you evidently got on the wrong line in reading your diagnosis. The recipe for suffocation says: 'Get the patient into fresh air as quickly as possible, and place in a reclining position.' The flaxseed remedy is for 'Dust and Cinders in the Eye,' on the line above. But, after all —"

"See here," interrupts Mrs. Sampson, "I reckon I've got something to say in this consultation. That flaxseed done me more good than anything I ever tried." And then she raises up her head and lays it back on my arm again, and says: "Put some in the other eye, Sandy dear."

And so if you was to stop off at Rosa to-morrow, or any other day, you'd see a fine new yellow house with Mrs. Pratt, that was Mrs. Sampson, embellishing and adorning it. And if you was to step inside you'd see on the marble-top centre table in the parlour "Herkimer's Handbook of Indispensable Information," all rebound in red morocco, and ready to be consulted on any subject pertaining to human happiness and wisdom.

THE HYPOTHESES OF FAILURE

LAWYER GOOCH BESTOWED his undivided attention upon the engrossing arts of his profession. But one flight of fancy did he allow his mind to entertain. He was fond of likening his suite of office rooms to the bottom of a ship. The rooms were three in number, with a door opening from one to another. These doors could also be closed.

"Ships," Lawyer Gooch would say, "are constructed for safety, with separate, water-tight compartments in their bottoms. If one compartment springs a leak it fills with water; but the good ship goes on unhurt. Were it not for the separating bulkheads one leak would sink the vessel. Now it often happens that while I am occupied with clients, other clients with conflicting interests call. With the assistance of Archibald – an office boy with a future – I cause the dangerous influx to be diverted into separate compartments, while I sound with my legal plummet the depth of each. If necessary, they may be haled into the hallway and permitted to escape by way of the stairs, which we may term the lee scuppers. Thus the good ship of business is kept afloat; whereas if the element that supports her were allowed to mingle freely in her hold we might be swamped – ha, ha, ha!"

The law is dry. Good jokes are few. Surely it might be permitted Lawyer Gooch to mitigate the bore of briefs, the tedium of torts and the prosiness of processes with even so light a levy upon the good property of humor.

Lawyer Gooch's practice leaned largely to the settlement of marital infelicities. Did matrimony languish through complications, he mediated, soothed and arbitrated. Did it suffer from implications, he readjusted, defended and championed. Did it arrive at the extremity of duplications, he always got light sentences for his clients.

But not always was Lawyer Gooch the keen, armed, wily belligerent, ready with his two-edged sword to lop off the shackles of

Hymen. He had been known to build up instead of demolishing, to reunite instead of severing, to lead erring and foolish ones back into the fold instead of scattering the flock. Often had he by his eloquent and moving appeals sent husband and wife, weeping, back into each other's arms. Frequently he had coached childhood so successfully that, at the psychological moment (and at a given signal) the plaintive pipe of "Papa, won't you turn home adain to me and muvver?" had won the day and upheld the pillars of a tottering home.

Unprejudiced persons admitted that Lawyer Gooch received as big fees from these revoked clients as would have been paid him had the cases been contested in court. Prejudiced ones intimated that his fees were doubled. because the penitent couples always came back later for the divorce, anyhow.

There came a season in June when the legal ship of Lawyer Gooch (to borrow his own figure) was nearly becalmed. The divorce mill grinds slowly in June. It is the month of Cupid and Hymen.

Lawyer Gooch, then, sat idle in the middle room of his clientless suite. A small anteroom connected – or rather separated – this apartment from the hallway. Here was stationed Archibald, who wrested from visitors their cards or oral nomenclature which he bore to his master while they waited.

Suddenly, on this day, there came a great knocking at the outermost door.

Archibald, opening it, was thrust aside as superfluous by the visitor, who without due reverence at once penetrated to the office of Lawyer Gooch and threw himself with good-natured insolence into a comfortable chair facing that gentlemen.

"You are Phineas C. Gooch, attorney-at-law?" said the visitor, his tone of voice and inflection making his words at once a question, an assertion and an accusation.

Before committing himself by a reply, the lawyer estimated his possible client in one of his brief but shrewd and calculating glances.

The man was of the emphatic type – large-sized, active, bold and debonair in demeanour, vain beyond a doubt, slightly swaggering, ready and at ease. He was well-clothed, but with a shade too much ornateness. He was seeking a lawyer; but if that fact would seem to saddle him with troubles they were not patent in his beaming eye and courageous air.

"My name is Gooch," at length the lawyer admitted. Upon pressure he would also have confessed to the Phineas C. But he did not consider it good practice to volunteer information. "I did not receive your card," he continued, by way of rebuke, "so I –"

"I know you didn't," remarked the visitor, coolly; "And you won't just yet. Light up?" He threw a leg over an arm of his chair, and tossed a handful of rich-hued cigars upon the table. Lawyer Gooch knew the brand. He thawed just enough to accept the invitation to smoke.

"You are a divorce lawyer," said the cardless visitor. This time there was no interrogation in his voice. Nor did his words constitute a simple assertion. They formed a charge – a denunciation – as one would say to a dog: "You are a dog." Lawyer Gooch was silent under the imputation.

"You handle," continued the visitor, "all the various ramifications of busted-up connubiality. You are a surgeon, we might saw, who extracts Cupid's darts when he shoots 'em into the wrong parties. You furnish patent, incandescent lights for premises where the torch of Hymen has burned so low you can't light a cigar at it. Am I right, Mr. Gooch?"

"I have undertaken cases," said the lawyer, guardedly, "in the line to which your figurative speech seems to refer. Do you wish to consult me professionally, Mr. –" The lawyer paused, with significance.

"Not yet," said the other, with an arch wave of his cigar, "not just yet. Let us approach the subject with the caution that should have been used in the original act that makes this pow-wow necessary. There exists a matrimonial jumble to be straightened out. But before I give you names I want your honest – well, anyhow, your professional opinion on the merits of the mix-up. I want you to size up the catastrophe – abstractly – you understand? I'm Mr. Nobody; and I've got a story to tell you. Then you say what's what. Do you get my wireless?"

"You want to state a hypothetical case?" suggested Lawyer Gooch.

"That's the word I was after. 'Apothecary' was the best shot I could make at it in my mind. The hypothetical goes. I'll state the case. Suppose there's a woman – a deuced fine-looking woman – who has run away from her husband and home? She's badly mashed on another man who went to her town to work up some real estate business. Now, we may as well call this woman's husband Thomas R. Billings, for that's his name. I'm giving you straight tips on the cognomens. The Lothario chap is Henry K. Jessup. The Billingses lived in a little town called Susanville – a good many miles from here. Now, Jessup leaves Susanville two weeks ago. The next day Mrs. Billings follows him.

She's dead gone on this man Jessup; you can bet your law library on that."

Lawyer Gooch's client said this with such unctuous satisfaction that even the callous lawyer experienced a slight ripple of repulsion. He now saw clearly in his fatuous visitor the conceit of the lady-killer, the egoistic complacency of the successful trifler.

"Now," continued the visitor, "suppose this Mrs. Billings wasn't happy at home? We'll say she and her husband didn't gee worth a cent. They've got incompatibility to burn. The things she likes, Billings wouldn't have as a gift with trading-stamps. It's Tabby and Rover with them all the time. She's an educated woman in science and culture, and she reads things out loud at meetings. Billings is not on. He don't appreciate progress and obelisks and ethics, and things of that sort. Old Billings is simply a blink when it comes to such things. The lady is out and out above his class. Now, lawyer, don't it look like a fair equalization of rights and wrongs that a woman like that should be allowed to throw down Billings and take the man that can appreciate her?"

"Incompatibility," said Lawyer Gooch, "is undoubtedly the source of much marital discord and unhappiness. Where it is positively proved, divorce would seem to be the equitable remedy. Are you – excuse me – is this man Jessup one to whom the lady may safely trust her future?"

"Oh, you can bet on Jessup," said the client, with a confident wag of his head. "Jessup's all right. He'll do the square thing. Why, he left Susanville just to keep people from talking about Mrs. Billings. But she followed him up, and now, of course, he'll stick to her. When she gets a divorce, all legal and proper, Jessup the proper thing."

"And now," said Lawyer Gooch, "continuing the hypo – if you prefer, and supposing that my services should be required in the case, what –"

The client rose impulsively to his feet.

"Oh, dang the hypothetical business," he exclaimed, impatiently. "Let's let her drop, and get down to straight talk. You ought to know who I am by this time. I want that woman to have her divorce. I'll pay for it. The day you set Mrs. Billings free I'll pay you five hundred dollars."

Lawyer Gooch's client banged his fist upon the table to punctuate his generosity.

"If that is the case –" began the lawyer.

"Lady to see you, sir," bawled Archibald, bouncing in from his anteroom. He had orders to always announce immediately any client that might come. There was no sense in turning business away.

Lawyer Gooch took client number one by the arm and led him suavely into one of the adjoining rooms. "Favor me by remaining here a few minutes, sir," said he. "I will return and resume our consultation with the least possible delay. I am rather expecting a visit from a very wealthy old lady in connection with a will. I will not keep you waiting long."

The breezy gentleman seated himself with obliging acquiescence, aud took up a magazine. The lawyer returned to the middle office, carefully closing behind him the connecting door.

"Show the lady in, Archibald," he said to the office boy, who was awaiting the order.

A tall lady, of commanding presence and sternly handsome, entered the room. She wore robes – robes, not clothes – ample and fluent. In her eye could be perceived the lambent flame of genius and soul. In her hand was a green bag of the capacity of a bushel, and an umbrella that also seemed to wear a robe, ample and fluent. She accepted a chair.

"Are you Mr. Phineas C. Gooch, the lawyer?" she asked, in formal and unconciliatory tones.

"I am," answered Lawyer Gooch, without circumlocution. He never circumlocuted when dealing with a woman. Women circumlocute. Time is wasted when both sides in debate employ the same tactics.

"As a lawyer, sir," began the lady, "you may have acquired some knowledge of the human heart. Do you believe that the pusillanimous and petty conventions of our artificial social life should stand as an obstacle in the way of a noble and affectionate heart when it finds its true mate among the miserable and worthless wretches in the world that are called men?"

"Madam," said Lawyer Gooch, in the tone that he used in curbing his female clients, "this is an office for conducting the practice of law. I am a lawyer, not a philosopher, nor the editor of an 'Answers to the Lovelorn' column of a newspaper. I have other clients waiting. I will ask you kindly to come to the point."

"Well, you needn't get so stiff around the gills about it," said the lady, with a snap of her luminous eyes and a startling gyration of her umbrella. "Business is what I've come for. I want your opinion in the matter of a suit for divorce, as the vulgar would call it, but which is really only the readjustment of the false and ignoble conditions that the short-sighted laws of man have interposed between a loving –"

"I beg your pardon, madam," interrupted Lawyer Gooch, with some impatience, "for reminding you again that this is a law office. Perhaps Mrs. Wilcox –"

"Mrs. Wilcox is all right," cut in the lady, with a hint of asperity. "And so are Tolstoi, and Mrs. Gertrude Atherton, and Omar Khayyam, and Mr. Edward Bok. I've read 'em all. I would like to discuss with you the divine right of the soul as opposed to the freedom-destroying restrictions of a bigoted and narrow-minded society. But I will proceed to business. I would prefer to lay the matter before you in an impersonal way until you pass upon its merits. That is to describe it as a supposable instance, without –"

"You wish to state a hypothetical case?" said Lawyer Gooch.

"I was going to say that," said the lady, sharply. "Now, suppose there is a woman who is all soul and heart and aspirations for a complete existence. This woman has a husband who is far below her in intellect, in taste – in everything. Bah! he is a brute. He despises literature. He sneers at the lofty thoughts of the world's great thinkers. He thinks only of real estate and such sordid things. He is no mate for a woman with soul. We will say that this unfortunate wife one day meets with her ideal – a man with brain and heart and force. She loves him. Although this man feels the thrill of a new-found affinity he is too noble, too honourable to declare himself. He flies from the presence of his beloved. She flies after him, trampling, with superb indifference, upon the fetters with which an unenlightened social system would bind her. Now, what will a divorce cost? Eliza Ann Timmins, the poetess of Sycamore Gap, got one for three hundred and forty dollars. Can I – I mean can this lady I speak of get one that cheap?"

"Madam," said Lawyer Gooch, "your last two or three sentences delight me with their intelligence and clearness. Can we not now abandon the hypothetical and come down to names and business?"

"I should say so," exclaimed the lady, adopting the practical with admirable readiness. "Thomas R. Billings is the name of the low brute who stands between the happiness of his legal – his legal, but not his spiritual – wife and Henry K. Jessup, the noble man whom nature intended for her mate. I," concluded the client, with an air of dramatic revelation, "am Mrs. Billings!"

"Gentlemen to see you, sir," shouted Archibald, invading the room almost at a handspring. Lawyer Gooch arose from his chair.

"Mrs. Billings," he said courteously, "allow me to conduct you into the adjoining office apartment for a few minutes. I am expecting a very wealthy old gentleman on business connected with a will. In a very short while I will join you, and continue our consultation."

With his accustomed chivalrous manner, Lawyer Gooch ushered his soulful client into the remaining unoccupied room, and came out, closing the door with circumspection.

The next visitor introduced by Archibald was a thin, nervous, irritable-looking man of middle age, with a worried and apprehensive expression of countenance. He carried in one hand a small satchel, which he set down upon the floor beside the chair which the lawyer placed for him. His clothing was of good quality, but it was worn without regard to neatness or style, and appeared to be covered with the dust of travel.

"You make a specialty of divorce cases," he said, in, an agitated but business-like tone.

"I may say," began Lawyer Gooch, "that my practice has not altogether avoided –"

"I know you do," interrupted client number three. "You needn't tell me. I've heard all about you. I have a case to lay before you without necessarily disclosing any connection that I might have with it – that is –"

"You wish," said Lawyer Gooch, "to state a hypothetical case.

"You may call it that. I am a plain man of business. I will be as brief as possible. We will first take up a hypothetical woman. We will say she is married uncongenially. In many ways she is a superior woman. Physically she is considered to be handsome. She is devoted to what she calls literature – poetry and prose, and such stuff. Her husband is a plain man in the business walks of life. Their home has not been happy, although the husband has tried to make it so. Some time ago a man – a stranger – came to the peaceful town in which they lived and engaged in some real estate operations. This woman met him, and became unaccountably infatuated with him. Her attentions became so open that the man felt the community to be no safe place for him, so he left it. She abandoned husband and home, and followed him. She forsook – her home, where she was provided with every comfort, to follow this man who had inspired her with such a strange affection. Is there anything more to be deplored," concluded the client, in a trembling voice, "than the wrecking of a home by a woman's uncalculating folly?"

Lawyer Gooch delivered the cautious opinion that there was not.

"This man she has gone to join," resumed the visitor, "is not the man to make her happy. It is a wild and foolish self-deception that makes her think he will. Her husband, in spite of their many disagreements, is the only one capable of dealing with her sensitive and peculiar nature. But this she does not realize now."

"Would you consider a divorce the logical cure in the case you present?" asked Lawyer Gooch, who felt that the conversation was wandering too far from the field of business.

"A divorce!" exclaimed the client, feelingly – almost tearfully. "No, no – not that. I have read, Mr. Gooch, of many instances where your sympathy and kindly interest led you to act as a mediator between estranged husband and wife, and brought them together again. Let us drop the hypothetical case – I need conceal no longer that it is I who am the sufferer in this sad affair – the names you shall have – Thomas R. Billings and wife – and Henry K. Jessup, the man with whom she is infatuated."

Client number three laid his hand upon Mr. Gooch's arm. Deep emotion was written upon his careworn face. "For Heaven's sake", he said fervently, "help me in this hour of trouble. Seek, out Mrs. Billings, and persuade her to abandon this distressing pursuit of her lamentable folly. Tell her, Mr. Gooch, that her husband is willing to receive her back to his heart and home – promise her anything that will induce her to return. I have heard of your success in these matters. Mrs. Billings cannot be very far away. I am worn out with travel and weariness. Twice during the pursuit I saw her, but various circumstances prevented our having an interview. Will you undertake this mission for me, Mr. Gooch, and earn my everlasting gratitude?"

"It is true," said Lawyer Gooch, frowning slightly at the other's last words, but immediately calling up an expression of virtuous benevolence, "that on a number of occasions I have been successful in persuading couples who sought the severing of their matrimonial bonds to think better of their rash intentions an⁴ return to their homes reconciled. But I assure you that the work is often exceedingly difficult. The amount of argument, perseverance, and, if I may be allowed to say it, eloquence that it requires would astonish you. But this is a case in which my sympathies would be wholly enlisted. I feel deeply for you sir, and I would be most happy to see husband and wife reunited. But my time," concluded the lawyer, looking at his watch as if suddenly reminded of the fact, "is valuable."

"I am aware of that," said the client, "and if you will take the case and persuade Mrs. Billings to return home and leave the man alone that she is following – on that day I will pay you the sum of one thousand dollars. I have made a little money in real estate during the recent boom in Susanville, and I will not begrudge that amount."

"Retain your seat for a few moments, please," said Lawyer Gooch, arising, and again consulting his watch. "I have another client waiting in an adjoining room whom I had very nearly forgotten. I will return in the briefest possible space."

The situation was now one that fully satisfied Lawyer Gooch's love of intricacy and complication. He revelled in cases that presented such subtle problems and possibilities. It pleased him to think that he was master of the happiness and fate of the three individuals who sat, unconcious of one another's presence, within his reach. His old figure of the ship glided into his mind. But now the figure failed, for to have filled every compartment of an actual vessel would have been to endanger her safety; with his compartments full, his ship of affairs could but sail on to the advantageous port of a fine, fat fee. The thing for him to do, of course, was to wring the best bargain he could from some one of his anxious cargo.

First he called to the office boy: "Lock the outer door, Archibald, and admit no one." Then he moved, with long, silent strides into the room in which client number one waited. That gentleman sat, patiently scanning the pictures in the magazine, with a cigar in his mouth and his feet upon a table.

"Well," he remarked, cheerfully, as the lawyer entered, "have you made up your mind? Does five hundred dollars go for getting the fair lady a divorce?"

"You mean that as a retainer?" asked Lawyer Gooch, softly interrogative.

"Hey? No; for the whole job. It's enough, ain't it?"

"My fee," said Lawyer Gooch, "would be one thousand five hundred dollars. Five hundred dollars down, and the remainder upon issuance of the divorce."

A loud whistle came from client number one. His feet descended to the floor.

"Guess we can't close the deal," he said, arising, "I cleaned up five hunderd dollars in a little real estate dicker down in Susanville. I'd do anything I could to free the lady, but it out-sizes my pile."

"Could you stand one thousand two hundred dollars?" asked the lawyer, insinuatingly.

"Five hundred is my limit, I tell you. Guess I'll have to hunt up a cheaper lawyer." The client put on his hat.

"Out this way, please," said Lawyer Gooch, opening the door that led into the hallway.

As the gentleman flowed out of the compartment and down the stairs, Lawyer Gooch smiled to himself. "Exit Mr. Jessup," he murmured, as he fingered the Henry Clay tuft of hair at his ear. "And now for the forsaken husband." He returned to the middle office, and assumed a businesslike manner.

"I understand," he said to client number three, "that you agree to pay one thousand dollars if I bring about, or am instrumental in bringing about, the return of Mrs. Billings to her home, and her abandonment of her infatuated pursuit of the man for whom she has conceived such a violent fancy. Also that the case is now unreservedly in my hands on that basis. Is that correct?"

"Entirely," said the other, eagerly. "And I can produce the cash any time at two hours' notice."

Lawyer Gooch stood up at his full height. His thin figure seemed to expand. His thumbs sought the armholes of his vest. Upon his face was a look of sympathetic benignity that he always wore during such undertakings.

."Then, sir," he said, in kindly tones, "I think I can promise you an early relief from your troubles. I have that much confidence in my powers of argument and persuasion, in the natural impulses of the human heart toward good, and in the strong influence of a husband's unfaltering love. Mrs. Billings, sir, is here – in that room – "the lawyer's long arm pointed to the door. "I will call her in at once; and our united pleadings –"

Lawyer Gooch paused, for client number three had leaped from his chair as if propelled by steel springs, and clutched his satchel.

"What the devil," he exclaimed, harshly, "do you mean? That woman in there! I thought I shook her off forty miles back."

He ran to the open window, looked out below, and threw one leg over the sill.

"Stop!" cried Lawyer Gooch, in amazement. "What would you do? Come, Mr. Billings, and face your erring but innocent wife. Our combined entreaties cannot fail to –"

"Billings!" shouted the now thoroughly moved client. "I'll Billings you, you old idiot!"

Turning, he hurled his satchel with fury at the lawyer's head. It struck that astounded peacemaker between the eyes, causing him to stagger backward a pace or two. When Lawyer Gooch recovered his wits he saw that his client had disappeared. Rushing to the window, he leaned out, and saw the recreant gathering himself up from the top of a shed upon which he had dropped from the second-story window. Without stopping to collect his hat he then plunged downward the remaining ten feet to the alley, up which he flew with prodigious celerity until the surrounding building swallowed him up from view.

Lawyer Gooch passed his hand tremblingly across his brow. It was a habitual act with him, serving to clear his thoughts. Perhaps also it now seemed to soothe the spot where a very hard alligator-hide satchel had struck.

The satchel lay upon the floor, wide open, with its contents spilled about. Mechanically, Lawyer Gooch stooped to gather up the articles. The first was a collar; and the omniscient eye of the man of law perceived, wonderingly, the initials H.K.J. marked upon it. Then came a comb, a brush, a folded map, and a piece of soap. lastly, a handful of old business letters, addressed – every one of them – to "Henry K. Jessup, Esq."

Lawyer Gooch closed the satchel, and set it upon the table. He hesitated for a moment, and then put on his hat and walked into the office boy's anteroom.

"Archibald," he said mildly, as he opened the hall door, "I am going around to the Supreme Court rooms. In five minutes you may step into the inner office, and inform the lady who is waiting there that" – here Lawyer Gooch made use of the vernacular – "that there's nothing doing."

THE LAST LEAF

The Pathetic Story of Two Girl Artists in Old New York and a Gray-Haired
Failure Who Made Successful Sacrifice at the End.

IN A LITTLE district west of Washington Square the streets have run crazy and broken themselves into small strips called "places." These "places" make strange angles and curves. One street crosses itself a time or two. An artist once discovered a valuable possibility in this street. Suppose a collector with a bill for paints, paper and canvas should, in traversing this route, suddenly meet himself coming back, without a cent having been paid on account!

So, to quaint old Greenwich Village the art people soon came prowling, hunting for north windows and eighteenth-century gables and Dutch attics and low rents. Then they imported some pewter mugs and a chafing dish or two from Sixth Avenue, and became a "colony."

At the top of a squatty, three-story brick Sue and Johnsy had their studio. "Johnsy" was familiar for Joanna. One was from Maine; the other from California. They had met at the table d'hote of an Eighth Street "Delmonico's," and found their tastes in art, chicory salad and bishop sleeves so congenial that the joint studio resulted.

That was in May. In November a cold, unseen stranger, whom the doctors called Pneumonia, stalked about the colony, touching one here and there with his icy fingers. Over on the east side this ravager strode boldly, smiting his victims by scores, but his feet trod slowly through the maze of the narrow and moss-grown "places."

Mr. Pneumonia was not what you would call a chivalric old gentleman. A mite of a little woman with blood thinned by California zephyrs was hardly fair game for the red-fisted, short-breathed old duffer. But Johnsy he smote; and she lay, scarcely moving, on her painted iron bedstead, looking through the small Dutch window-panes at the blank side of the next brick house.

One morning the busy doctor invited Sue into the halfway with shaggy, gray eyebrow.

"She has one chance in – let us say, ten," he said, as he shook down the mercury in his clinical thermometer. "And that chance is for her to want to live. This way people have of lining-up on the side of the undertaker makes the entire pharmacopoeia look silly. Your little lady has made up her mind that she's not going to get well. Has she anything on her mind?"

"She – she wanted to paint the Bay of Naples some day," said Sue.

"Paint? – bosh! Has she anything on her mind worth thinking about twice – a man, for instance?"

"A man?" said Sue, with a jew-sharp twang in her voice. "Is a man worth – but, no, doctor; there is nothing of the kind."

"Well, it is the weakness, then," said the doctor. "I will do all that science, so far as it may filter through my efforts, can accomplish. But whenever my patient begins to count the carriages in her funeral procession I subtract 50 per cent from the curative power of medicines. If you will get her to ask one question about the new winter styles in cloak sleeves I will promise you a one-in-five chance for her, instead of one-in-ten."

After the doctor had gone Sue went into the workroom and cried a Japanese napkin to a pulp. Then she swaggered into Johnsy's room with her drawing board, whistling ragtime.

Johnsy lay scarcely making a ripple under the bedclothes, with her face toward the window. Sue stopped whistling, thinking she was asleep.

She arranged her board and began a pen-and-ink drawing to illustrate a magazine story. Young artists must pave their way to Art by drawing pictures for magazine stories that young authors write to pave their way to Literature.

As Sue was sketching a pair of elegant horseshow riding trousers and a monocle on the figure of the hero, an Idaho cowboy, she heard a low sound, several times repeated. She went quickly to the bedside.

Johnsy's eyes were open wide. She was looking out the window and counting – counting backward.

"Twelve," she said, and a little later "eleven"; and then "ten," and "nine'; – and then "eight" and "seven," almost together.

Sue looked solicitously out of the window. What was there to count? There was only a bare, dreary yard to be seen, and the blank side of the brick house twenty feet away. An old, old ivy vine, gnarled and decayed at the roots, climbed half way up the brick wall. The cold breath of autumn had stricken its leaves from the vine until its skeleton branches clung, almost bare, to the crumbling bricks.

"What is it, dear?" asked Sue.

"Six," said Johnsy, in almost a whisper. "They're falling faster now. Three days ago there were almost a hundred. It made my head ache to count them. But now it's easy. There goes another one. There are only five left now."

"Five what, dear? Tell your Sudie."

"Leaves. On the ivy vine. When the last one falls I must go, too. I've known that for three days. Didn't the doctor tell you?"

"Oh, I never heard of such nonsense," complained Sue, with magnificent scorn. "What have old ivy leaves to do with your getting well? And you used to love that vine, so, you naughty girl. Don't be a goosey. Why, the doctor told me this morning that your chances for getting well real soon were – let's see exactly what he said – he said the chances were ten to one! Why, that's almost as good a chance as we have in New York when we ride on the street cars or walk past a new building. Try to take some broth now, and let Sudie go back to her drawing, so she can sell the editor man with it, and buy port wine for her sick child, and pork chops for her greedy self."

"You needn't get any more wine?" said Johnsy, keeping her eyes fixed out the window. "There goes another. No, I don't want any broth. That leaves just four. I want to see the last one fall before it gets dark. Then I'll go, too."

"Johnsy, dear" said Sue, bending over her, "will you promise me to keep your eyes dosed, and not look out the window until I am done working? I must hand those drawings in by tomorrow I need the light, or I would draw the shade down."

"Couldn't you draw in the other room?" asked Johnsy, coldly.

"I'd rather be here by you," said Sue. "Besides, I don't want you to keep looking at those silly ivy leaves."

"Tell me as soon as you have finished," said Johnsy, closing her eyes, and lying white and still as a fallen statue, "because I want to see the last one fall. I'm tired of waiting. I'm tired of thinking. I want to turn loose my hold on everything, and go sailing down, down, just like one of those poor, tired leaves."

"Try to sleep," said Sue. "I must call Behrman up to be my model for the old hermit miner. I'll not be gone a minute. Don't try to move 'til I come back."

Old Behrman was a painter who lived on the ground floor beneath them. He was past sixty and had a Michael Angelo's Moses beard curling down from the head of a satyr along the body of an imp. Behrman was a failure in art. Forty years he had wielded the brush without getting near enough to touch the hem of his Mistress's robe. He had been always about to paint a masterpiece, but had never yet begun it. For several years he had painted nothing except now and then a daub in the line of commerce or advertising. He earned a little by serving as a model to those young artists in the colony who could not pay the price of a professional. He drank gin to excess, and still talked of his coming masterpiece. For the rest he was a fierce little old man, who scoffed terribly at softness in any one, and who regarded himself as especial mastiff-in-waiting to protect the two young artists in the studio above.

Sue found Behrman smelling strongly of juniper berries in his dimly lighted den below. In one comer was a blank canvas on an easel that had been waiting there for twenty-five years to receive the first line of the masterpiece. She told him of Johnsy's fancy, and how she feared she would, indeed, light and fragile as a leaf herself, float away, when her slight hold upon the world grew weaker.

Old Behrman, with his red eyes plainly streaming, shouted his contempt and derision for such idiotic imaginings.

"Vass!" he cried. "Is dere people in de world mit der foolishness to die because leafs dey drop off from a confounded vine? I haf not heard of such a thing. No, I will not bose as a model for your fool hermit-dunder-head. Vy do you allow dot silly business to come in der brain of her? Ach, dot poor leetle Miss Yohnsy."

"She is very ill and weak," said Sue, "and the fever has left her mind morbid and full of strange fancies. Very well, Mr. Behrman, if you do not care to pose for me, you needn't. But I think you are a horrid old-old flibbertigibbet."

"You are just like a woman!" yelled Behrman. "Who said I will not bose? Go on. I come mit you. For half an hour I haf peen trying to say dot I am ready to bose. Got! ids is not any blase in which one so goof as Miss Yohnsy shall lie sick. Some day I vill baint a masterpiece, and ve shall all go away. Gott! yes."

Johnsy was sleeping when they went upstairs. Sue pulled the shade down to the window-sill, and motioned Behrman into the other room. In there they peered out the window fearfully at the ivy vine. Then they looked at each other for a moment without speaking. A persistent, cold rain was falling, mingled with snow. Behrman, in his old blue shirt, took his seat as the hermit miner on an upturned kettle for a rock.

When Sue awoke from an hour's sleep the next morning she found Johnsy with dull, wide-open eyes staring at the drawn green shade.

"Pull it up; I want to see," she ordered, in a whisper.

Wearily Sue obeyed.

But lo! after the beating rain and fierce gusts of wind that had endured through the livelong night, there yet stood out against the brick wall one ivy leaf. It was the last on the vine. Still dark green near its stem, but with its serrated edges tinted with the yellow of dissolution and decay, it hung bravely from a branch some twenty feet above the ground.

"It is the last one," said Johnsy. "I thought it would surely fall during the night. I heard the wind. It will fall today, and I shall die at the same time."

"Dear, dear!" said Sue, leaning her worn face down to the pillow, "think of me, if you won't think of yourself. What would I do?"

But Johnsy did not answer. The lonesomest thing in all the world is a soul when it is making ready to go on its mysterious, far journey. The fancy seemed to possess her more strongly as one by one the ties that bound her to friendship and to earth were loosed.

The day wore away, and even through the twilight they could see the lone ivy leaf clinging to its stem against the wall. And then, with the coming of the night the north wind was again loosed, while the rain still beat against the windows and pattered down from the low Dutch eaves.

When it was light enough Johnsy, the merciless, commanded that the shade be raised.

The ivy leaf was still there.

Johnsy lay for a long time looking at it. And then she called to Sue, who was stirring her chicken broth over the gas stove.

"I've been a bad girl, Sudie," said Johnsy. "Something has made that last leaf stay there to show me how wicked I was. It is a sin to want to die. You may bring me a little broth now, and some milk with a little port in it, and – no, bring me a hand-mirror first, and then pack some pillows about me, and I will sit up and watch you cook?"

An hour later she said:

"Sudie, some day I hope to paint the Bay of Naples."

The doctor came in the afternoon, and Sue had an excuse to go into the hallway as he left.

"Even chances," said the doctor, taking Sue's thin, shaking hand in his. "With good nursing you'll win. And now I must see another case I have downstairs. Behrman, his name is – some kind of an artist I believe. Pneumonia, too. He is an old, weak man, and the attack is acute. There is no hope for him; but he goes to the hospital to-day to be made more comfortable."

The next day the doctor said to Sue: "She's out of danger. You've won. Nutrition and care now – that's all."

And that afternoon Sue came to the bed where Johnsy lay, contentedly knitting a very blue and very useless woollen shoulder scarf, and put one arm around her, pillows and all.

"I have something to tell you, white mouse," she said. "Mr. Behrman died of pneumonia today in the hospital. He was ill only two days. The janitor found him on the morning of the first day in his room. downstairs helpless with pain. His shoes and clothing were wet through and icy cold. They couldn't imagine where he had been on such a dreadful night. And then they found a lantern, still lighted, and a ladder that had been dragged from its place, and some scattered brushes, and a palette with green and yellow colors mixed on it, and – look out the window, dear, at the last ivy leaf on the wall. Didn't you wonder why it never fluttered or moved when the wind blew? Ah, darling, it's Behrman's masterpiece – he painted it there the night that the last leaf fell."

THE MARRY MONTH OF MAY

PRITHEE, SMITE THE poet in the eye when he would sing to you praises of the month of May. It is a month presided over by the spirits of mischief and madness. Pixies and flibbertigibbets haunt the budding woods: Puck and his train of midgets are busy in town and country.

In May nature holds up at us a chiding finger, bidding us remember that we are not gods, but overconceited members of her own great family. She reminds us that we are brothers to the chowder-doomed clam and the donkey; lineal scions of the pansy and the chimpanzee, and but cousins-german to the cooing doves, the quacking ducks and the housemaids and policemen in the parks.

In May Cupid shoots blindfolded – millionaires marry stenographers; wise professors woo white-aproned gum-chewers behind quick-lunch counters; schoolma'ams make big bad boys remain after school; lads with ladders steal lightly over lawns where Juliet waits in her trellissed window with her telescope packed; young couples out for a walk come home married; old chaps put on white spats and promenade near the Normal School; even married men, grown unwontedly tender and sentimental, whack their spouses on the back and growl: "How goes it, old girl?"

This May, who is no goddess, but Circe, masquerading at the dance given in honor of the fair débutante, Summer, puts the kibosh on us all.

Old Mr. Coulson groaned a little, and then sat up straight in his invalid's chair. He had the gout very bad in one foot, a house near Gramercy Park, half a million dollars and a daughter. And he had a housekeeper, Mrs. Widdup. The fact and the name deserve a sentence each. They have it.

When May poked Mr. Coulson he became elder brother to the turtle-dove. In the window near which he sat were boxes of jonquils, of hyacinths, geraniums and pansies. The breeze brought their odor into the room. Immediately there was a well-contested round between the breath of the flowers and the able and active effluvium from gout liniment. The liniment won easily; but not before the flowers got an uppercut to old Mr. Coulson's nose. The deadly work of the implacable, false enchantress May was done.

Across the park to the olfactories of Mr. Coulson came other unmistakable, characteristic, copyrighted smells of spring that belong to the-big-city-above-the-Subway, alone. The smells of hot asphalt, underground caverns, gasoline, patchouli, orange peel, sewer gas, Albany grabs, Egyptian cigarettes, mortar and the undried ink on newspapers. The inblowing air was sweet and mild. Sparrows wrangled happily everywhere outdoors. Never trust May.

Mr. Coulson twisted the ends of his white mustache, cursed his foot, and pounded a bell on the table by his side.

In came Mrs. Widdup. She was comely to the eye, fair, flustered, forty and foxy.

"Higgins is out, sir," she said, with a smile suggestive of vibratory massage. "He went to post a letter. Can I do anything for you, sir?"

"It's time for my aconite," said old Mr. Coulson. "Drop it for me. The bottle's there. Three drops. In water. D – that is, confound Higgins! There's nobody in this house cares if I die here in this chair for want of attention."

Mrs. Widdup sighed deeply.

"Don't be saying that, sir," she said. "There's them that would care more than any one knows. Thirteen drops, you said, sir?"

"Three," said old man Coulson.

He took his dose and then Mrs. Widdup's hand. She blushed. Oh, yes, it can be done. Just hold your breath and compress the diaphragm.

"Mrs. Widdup," said Mr. Coulson, "the springtime's full upon us."

"Ain't that right?" said Mrs. Widdup. "The air's real warm. And there's bock-beer signs on every corner. And the park's all yaller and pink and blue with flowers; and I have such shooting pains up my legs and body."

"'In the spring,'" quoted Mr. Coulson, curling his mustache, "'ay – that is, a man's – fancy lightly turns to thoughts of love.'"

"Lawsy, now!" exclaimed Mrs. Widdup; "ain't that right? Seems like it's in the air."

"'In the spring,'" continued old Mr. Coulson, "'a livelier iris shines upon the burnished dove.'"

"They do be lively, the Irish," sighed Mrs. Widdup pensively.

"Mrs. Widdup," said Mr. Coulson, making a face at a twinge of his gouty foot, "this would be a lonesome house without you. I'm an – that is, I'm an elderly man – but I'm worth a comfortable lot of money. If half a million dollars' worth of Government bonds and the true affection of a heart that, though no longer beating with the first ardour of youth, can still throb with genuine –"

The loud noise of an overturned chair near the portières of the adjoining room interrupted the venerable and scarcely suspecting victim of May.

In stalked Miss Van Meeker Constantia Coulson, bony, durable, tall, high-nosed, frigid, well-bred, thirty-five, in-the-neighborhood-of-Gramercy-Parkish. She put up a lorgnette. Mrs. Widdup hastily stooped and arranged the bandages on Mr. Coulson's gouty foot.

"I thought Higgins was with you," said Miss Van Meeker Constantia.

"Higgins went out," explained her father, "and Mrs. Widdup answered the bell. That is better now, Mrs. Widdup, thank you. No; there is nothing else I require."

The housekeeper retired, pink under the cool, inquiring stare of Miss Coulson.

"This spring weather is lovely, isn't it, daughter?" said the old man, consciously conscious.

"That's just it," replied Miss Van Meeker Constantia Coulson, somewhat obscurely. "When does Mrs. Widdup start on her vacation, papa?"

"I believe she said a week from to-day," said Mr. Coulson.

Miss Van Meeker Constantia stood for a minute at the window gazing, toward the little park, flooded with the mellow afternoon sunlight. With the eye of a botanist she viewed the flowers – most potent weapons of insidious May. With the cool pulses of a virgin of Cologne she withstood the attack of the ethereal mildness. The arrows of the pleasant sunshine fell back, frostbitten, from the cold panoply of her unthrilled bosom. The odor of the flowers waked no soft sentiments in the unexplored recesses of her dormant heart. The chirp of the sparrows gave her a pain. She mocked at May.

But although Miss Coulson was proof against the season, she was keen enough to estimate its power. She knew that elderly men and thick-waisted women jumped as educated fleas in the ridiculous train of May, the merry mocker of the months. She had heard of foolish old gentlemen marrying their housekeepers before. What a humiliating thing, after all, was this feeling called love!

The next morning at 8 o'clock, when the iceman called, the cook told him that Miss Coulson wanted to see him in the basement.

"Well, ain't I the Olcott and Depew; not mentioning the first name at all?" said the iceman, admiringly, of himself.

As a concession he rolled his sleeves down, dropped his icehooks on a syringe and went back. When Miss Van Meeker Constantia Coulson addressed him he took off his hat.

"There is a rear entrance to this basement," said Miss Coulson, "which can be reached by driving into the vacant lot next door, where they are excavating for a building. I want you to bring in that way within two hours 1,000 pounds of ice. You may have to bring another man or two to help you. I will show you where I want it placed. I also want 1,000 pounds a day delivered the same way for the next four days. Your company may charge the ice on our regular bill. This is for your extra trouble."

Miss Coulson tendered a ten-dollar bill. The iceman bowed, and held his hat in his two hands behind him.

"Now if you'll excuse me, lady. It'll be a pleasure to fix things up for you any way you please."

Alas for May!

About noon Mr. Coulson knocked two glasses off his table, broke the spring of his bell and yelled for Higgins at the same time.

"Bring an axe," commanded Mr. Coulson, sardonically, "or send out for a quart of prussic acid, or have a policeman come in and shoot me. I'd rather that than be frozen to death."

"It does seem to be getting cool, Sir," said Higgins. "I hadn't noticed it before. I'll close the window, Sir."

"Do," said Mr. Coulson. "They call this spring, do they? If it keeps up long I'll go back to Palm Beach. House feels like a morgue."

Later Miss Coulson dutifully came in to inquire how the gout was progressing.

"Stantia," said the old man, "how is the weather outdoors?"

"Bright," answered Miss Coulson, "but chilly."

"Feels like the dead of winter to me," said Mr. Coulson.

"An instance," said Constantia, gazing abstractedly out the window, "of 'winter lingering in the lap of spring,' though the metaphor is not in the most refined taste."

A little later she walked down by the side of the little park and on westward to Broadway to accomplish a little shopping.

A little later than that Mrs. Widdup entered the invalid's room.

"Did you ring, Sir?" she asked, dimpling in many places. "I asked Higgins to go to the drug store, and I thought I heard your bell."

"I did not," said Mr. Coulson.

"I'm afraid," said Mrs. Widdup, "I interrupted you sir, yesterday when you were about to say something."

"How comes it, Mrs. Widdup," said old man Coulson sternly, "that I find it so cold in this house?"

"Cold, Sir?" said the housekeeper, "why, now, since you speak of it it do seem cold in this room. But, outdoors it's as warm and fine as June, sir. And how this weather do seem to make one's heart jump out of one's shirt waist, sir. And the ivy all leaved out on the side of the house, and the hand-organs playing, and the children dancing on the sidewalk – 'tis a great time for speaking out what's in the heart. You were saying yesterday, sir –"

"Woman!" roared Mr. Coulson; "you are a fool. I pay you to take care of this house. I am freezing to death in my own room, and you come in and drivel to me about ivy and hand-organs. Get me an overcoat at once. See that all doors and windows are closed below. An old, fat, irresponsible, one-sided object like you prating about springtime and flowers in the middle of winter! When Higgins comes back, tell him to bring me a hot rum punch. And now get out!"

But who shall shame the bright face of May? Rogue though she be and disturber of sane men's peace, no wise virgins cunning nor cold storage shall make her bow her head in the bright galaxy of months.

Oh, yes, the story was not quite finished.

A night passed, and Higgins helped old man Coulson in the morning to his chair by the window. The cold of the room was gone. Heavenly odors and fragrant mildness entered.

In hurried Mrs. Widdup, and stood by his chair. Mr. Coulson reached his bony hand and grasped her plump one.

"Mrs. Widdup," he said, "this house would be no home without you. I have half a million dollars. If that and the true affection of a heart no longer in its youthful prime, but still not cold, could –"

"I found out what made it cold," said Mrs. Widdup, leanin' against his chair. "'Twas ice – tons of it – in the basement and in the furnace room, everywhere. I shut off the registers that it was coming through into your room, Mr. Coulson, poor soul! And now it's Maytime again."

"A true heart," went on old man Coulson, a little wanderingly, "that the springtime has brought to life again, and – but what will my daughter say, Mrs. Widdup?"

"Never fear, sir," said Mrs. Widdup, cheerfully. "Miss Coulson, she ran away with the iceman last night, sir!"

THE POET AND THE PEASANT

THE OTHER DAY a poet friend of mine, who has lived in close communion with nature all his life, wrote a poem and took it to an editor.

It was a living pastoral, full of the genuine breath of the fields, the song of birds, and the pleasant chatter of trickling streams.

When the poet called again to see about it, with hopes of a beefsteak dinner in his heart, it was handed back to him with the comment:

"Too artificial."

Several of us met over spaghetti and Duchess county chianti, and swallowed indignation with slippery forkfuls.

And there we dug a pit for the editor. With us was Conant, a well-arrived writer of fiction – a man who had trod on asphalt all his life, and who had never looked upon bucolic scenes except with sensations of disgust from the windows of express trains. Conant wrote a poem and called it "The Doe and the Brook." It was a fine specimen of the kind of work you would expect from a poet who had strayed with Amaryllis only as far as the florist's windows, and whose sole ornithological discussion had been carried on with a waiter. Conant signed this poem, and we sent it to the same editor. But this has very little to do with the story.

Just as the editor was reading the first line of the poem, on the next morning, a being stumbled off the West Shore ferryboat, and loped slowly up Forty-second Street.

The invader was a young man with light blue eyes, a hanging lip and hair the exact color of the little orphan's (afterward discovered to be the earl's daughter) in one of Mr. Blaney's plays. His trousers were corduroy, his coat short-sleeved, with buttons in the middle of his back. One bootleg was outside the corduroys. You looked expectantly, though in vain, at his straw hat for ear holes, its shape inaugurating the suspicion that it had been ravaged from a former equine possessor. In his hand was a valise – description of it is an impossible task; a Boston man would not have carried his lunch and law books to his office in it. And above one ear, in his hair, was a wisp of hay – the rustic's letter of credit, his badge of innocence, the last clinging touch of the Garden of Eden lingering to shame the gold-brick men.

Knowingly, smilingly, the city crowds passed him by. They saw the raw stranger stand in the gutter and stretch his neck at the tall buildings. At this they ceased to smile, and even to look at him. It had been done so often. A few glanced at the antique valise to see what Coney "attraction" or brand of chewing gum he might be thus dinning into his memory. But for the most part he was ignored. Even the newsboys looked bored when he scampered like a circus clown out of the way of cabs and street cars.

At Eighth Avenue stood "Bunco Harry," with his dyed mustache and shiny, good-natured eyes. Harry was too good an artist not to be pained at the sight of an actor overdoing his part. He edged up to the countryman, who had stopped to open his mouth at a jewelry store window, and shook his head.

"Too thick, pal," he said, critically – "too thick by a couple of inches. I don't know what your lay is; but you've got the properties too thick. That hay, now – why, they don't even allow that on Proctor's circuit any more."

"I don't understand you, mister," said the green one. "I'm not lookin' for any circus. I've just run down from Ulster County to look at the town, bein' that the hayin's over with. Gosh! but it's a whopper. I thought Poughkeepsie was some punkins; but this here town is five times as big."

"Oh, well," said "Bunco Harry," raising his eyebrows, "I didn't mean to butt in. You don't have to tell. I thought you ought to tone down a little, so I tried to put you wise. Wish you success at your graft, whatever it is. Come and have a drink, anyhow."

"I wouldn't mind having a glass of lager beer," acknowledged the other. They went to a cafe frequented by men with smooth faces and shifty eyes, and sat at their drinks.

"I'm glad I come across you, mister," said Haylocks. "How'd you like to play a game or two of seven-up? I've got the keerds." He fished them out of Noah's valise – a rare, inimitable deck, greasy with bacon suppers and grimy with the soil of cornfields. "Bunco Harry" laughed loud and briefly.

"Not for me, sport," he said, firmly. "I don't go against that make-up of yours for a cent. But I still say you've overdone it. The Reubs haven't dressed like that since '79. I doubt if you could work Brooklyn for a key-winding watch with that layout."

"Oh, you needn't think I ain't got the money," boasted Haylocks. He drew forth a tightly rolled mass of bills as large as a teacup, and laid it on the table.

"Got that for my share of grandmother's farm," he announced.

"There's $950 in that roll. Thought I'd come to the city and look around for a likely business to go into."

"Bunco Harry" took up the roll of money and looked at it with almost respect in his smiling eyes.

"I've seen worse," he said, critically. "But you'll never do it in them clothes. You want to get light tan shoes and a black suit and a straw hat with a colored band, and talk a good deal about Pittsburg and freight differentials, and drink sherry for breakfast in order to work off phony stuff like that."

"What's his line?" asked two or three shifty-eyed men of "Bunco Harry" after Haylocks had gathered up his impugned money and departed.

"The queer, I guess," said Harry. "Or else he's one of Jerome's men. Or some guy with a new graft. He's too much hayseed. Maybe that his – I wonder now – oh, no, it couldn't have been real money."

Haylocks wandered on. Thirst probably assailed him again, for he dived into a dark groggery on a side street and bought beer. At first sight of him their eyes brightened; but when his insistent and exaggerated rusticity became apparent their expressions changed to wary suspicion.

Haylocks swung his valise across the bar.

"Keep that a while for me, mister," he said, chewing at the end of a virulent claybank cigar. "I'll be back after I knock around a spell. And keep your eye on it, for there's $950 inside of it, though maybe you wouldn't think so to look at me."

Somewhere outside a phonograph struck up a band piece, and Haylocks was off for it, his coat-tail buttons flopping in the middle of his back.

"Divvy, Mike," said the men hanging upon the bar, winking openly at one another.

"Honest, now," said the bartender, kicking the valise to one side. "You don't think I'd fall to that, do you? Anybody can see he ain't no jay. One of McAdoo's come-on squad, I guess. He's a shine if he made himself up. There ain't no parts of the country now where they dress like that since they run rural free delivery to Providence, Rhode Island. If he's got nine-fifty in that valise it's a ninety-eight cent Waterbury that's stopped at ten minutes to ten."

When Haylocks had exhausted the resources of Mr. Edison to amuse he returned for his valise. And then down Broadway he gallivanted, culling the sights with his eager blue eyes. But still and evermore Broadway rejected him with curt glances and sardonic smiles. He was the oldest of the "gags" that the city must endure. He was so flagrantly impossible, so ultra rustic, so exaggerated beyond the most freakish products of the barnyard, the hayfield and the vaudeville stage, that he excited only weariness and suspicion. And the wisp of hay in his hair was so genuine, so fresh and redolent of the meadows, so clamorously rural that even a shellgame man would have put up his peas and folded his table at the sight of it. Haylocks seated himself upon a flight of stone steps and once more exhumed his roll of yellow-backs from the valise. The outer one, a twenty, he shucked off and beckoned to a newsboy.

"Son," said he, "run somewhere and get this changed for me. I'm mighty nigh out of chicken feed. I guess you'll get a nickel if you'll hurry up."

A hurt look appeared through the dirt on the newsy's face.

"Aw, watchert'ink! G'wan and get yer funny bill changed yerself. Dey ain't no farm clothes yer got on. G'wan wit yer stage money."

On a corner lounged a keen-eyed steerer for a gambling-house. He was Haylocks, and his expression suddenly grew cold and virtuous.

"Mister," said the rural one. "I've heard of places in this here town where a fellow could have a good game of old sledge or peg a card at keno. I got $950 in this valise, and I come down from old Ulster to see the sights. Know where a fellow could get action on about $9 or $10? I'm goin' to have some sport, and then maybe I'll buy out a business of some kind."

The steerer looked pained, and investigated a white speck on his left forefinger nail.

"Cheese it, old man," he murmured, reproachfully. "The Central Office must be bughouse to send you out looking like such a gillie. You couldn't get within two blocks of a sidewalk crap game in them Tony Pastor props. The recent Mr. Scotty from Death Valley has got you beat a crosstown block in the way of Elizabethan scenery and mechanical accessories. Let it be skiddoo for yours. Nay, I know of no gilded halls where one may bet a patrol wagon on the ace."

Rebuffed once again by the great city that is so swift to detect artificialities, Haylocks sat upon the curb and presented his thoughts to hold a conference.

"It's my clothes," said he; "durned if it ain't. They think I'm a hayseed and won't have nothin' to do with me. Nobody never made fun of this hat in Ulster County. I guess if you want folks to notice you in New York you must dress up like they do."

So Haylocks went shopping in the bazaars where men spake through their noses and rubbed their hands and ran the tape line ecstatically over the buldge in his inside pocket where reposed a red nubbin of corn with an even number of rows. And messengers bearing parcels and boxes streamed to his hotel on Broadway within the lights of Long Acre.

At 9 o'clock in the evening one descended to the sidewalk whom Ulster County would have foresworn. Bright tan were his shoes; his hat the latest block. His light gray trousers were deeply creased; a gay blue silk handkerchief flapped from the breast pocket of his elegant English walking coat. His collar might have graced a laundry window; his blond hair was trimmed close; the wisp of hay was gone.

For an instant he stood, resplendent, with the leisurely air of a boulevardier concocting in his mind the route for his evening pleasures. And then he turned down the gay, bright street with the easy and graceful tread of a millionaire.

But in the instant that he had paused the wisest and keenest eyes in the city had enveloped him in their field of vision. A stout man with gray eyes picked two of his friends with a lift of his eyebrows from the row of loungers in front of the hotel.

"The juiciest jay I've seen in six months," said the man with gray eyes. "Come along."

It was half-past eleven when a man galloped into the West Forty-seventh Street Police Station with the story of his wrongs.

"Nine hundred and fifty dollars," he gasped, "all my share of grandmother's farm."

The desk seargeant wrung from him the name Jabez Bulltongue, of Locust Valley farm, Ulster County, and then bagan to take descriptions of the strong-arm gentlemen.

When Conant went to see the editor about the fate of his poem, he was received over the head of the office boy into the inner office that is decorated with the statuettes by Rodin and J. G. Brown.

"When I read the first line of 'The Doe and the Brook,'" said the editor, "I knew it to be the work of one whose life has been heart to heart with Nature. The finished art of the line did not blind me to that fact. To use a somewhat homely comparison, it was as if a wild, free child of the woods and fields were to don the garb of fashion and walk down Broadway. Beneath the apparel the man would show."

"Thanks," said Conant. "I suppose the check will be round on Thursday, as usual."

The morals of this story have somehow gotten mixed. You can take your choice of "Stay on the Farm" or "Don't Write Poetry."

THE MOMENT OF VICTORY

BEN GRANGER IS a war veteran aged twenty-nine – which should enable you to guess the war. He is also principal merchant and postmaster of Cadiz, a little town over which the breezes from the Gulf of Mexico perpetually blow.

Ben helped to hurl the Don from his stronghold in the Greater Antilles; and then, hiking across half the world, he marched as a corporal-usher up and down the blazing tropic aisles of the open-air college in which the Filipino was schooled. Now, with his bayonet beaten into a cheese-slicer, he rallies his corporal's guard of cronies in the shade of his well-whittled porch, instead of in the matted jungles of Mindanao. Always have his interest and choice been for deeds rather than for words; but the consideration and digestion of motives is not beyond him, as this story, which is his, will attest.

"What is it," he asked me one moonlit eve, as we sat among his boxes and barrels, "that generally makes men go through dangers, and fire, and trouble, and starvation, and battle, and such rucouses? What does a man do it for? Why does he try to outdo his fellow-humans, and be braver and stronger and more daring and showy than even his best friends are? What's his game? What does he expect to get out of it? He din't do it just for the fresh air and exercise. What would you say, now, Bill, that an ordinary man expects, generally speaking, for his efforts along the line of ambition and extraordinary hustling in the marketplaces, forums, shooting-galleries, lyceums, battle-fields, links, cinder-paths, and arenas of the civilized and vice versa places of the world?"

"Well, Ben," said I, with judicial seriousness, "I think we might safely limit the number of motives of a man who seeks fame to three – to ambition, which is a desire for popular applause; to avarice, which looks to the material side of success; and to love of some woman whom he either possesses or desires to possess."

Ben pondered over my words while a mocking-bird on the top of a mesquite by the porch trilled a dozen bars.

"I reckon," said he, "that your diagnosis about covers the case according to the rules laid down in the copy-books and historical readers. But what I had in my mind was the case of Willie Robbins, a person I used to know. I'll tell you about him before I close up the store, if you don't mind listening.

"Willie was one of our social set up in San Augustine. I was clerking there then for Brady & Murchison, wholesale dry-goods and ranch supplies. Willie and I belonged to the same german club and athletic association and military company. He played the triangle in our serenading and quartet crowd that used to ring the welkin three nights a week somewhere in town.

"Willie jibed with his name considerable. He weighed about as much as a hundred pounds of veal in his summer suitings, and he had a 'where-is-Mary?' expression on his features so plain that you could almost see the wool growing on him.

"And yet you couldn't fence him away from the girls with barbed wire. You know that kind of young fellows – a kind of a mixture of fools and angels – they rush in and fear to tread at the same time; but they never fail to tread when they get the chance. He was always on hand when 'a joyful occasion was had,' as the morning paper would say, looking as happy as a king full, and at the same time as uncomfortable as a raw oyster served with sweet pickles. He danced like he had hind hobbles on; and he had a vocabulary of about three hundred and fifty words that he made stretch over four germans a week, and plagiarized from to get him through two ice-cream suppers and a Sunday-night call. He seemed to me to be a sort of a mixture of Maltese kitten, sensitive plant, and a member of a stranded Two Orphans company.

"I'll give you an estimate of his physiological and pictorial make-up, and then I'll stick spurs into the sides of my narrative.

"Willie inclined to the Caucasian in his coloring and manner of style. His hair was opalescent and his conversation fragmentary. His eyes were the same blue shade as the china dog's on the right-hand corner of your Aunt Ellen's mantelpiece. He took things as they come, and I never felt any hostility against him. I let him live, and so did others.

"But what does this Willie do but coax his heart out of his boots and lose it to Myra Allison, the liveliest, brightest, keenest, smartest, and prettiest girl in San Augustine. I tell you, she had the blackest eyes, the shiniest curls, and the most tantalizing – Oh, no, you're off – I wasn't a victim. I might have been, but I knew better. I kept out. Joe Granberry was It from the start. He had everybody else beat a couple of leagues and thence east to a stake and mound. But, anyhow, Myra was a nine-pound, full-merino, fall-clip fleece, sacked and loaded on a four-horse team for San Antone.

"One night there was an ice-cream sociable at Mrs. Colonel Spraggins', in San Augustine. We fellows had a big room up-stairs opened up for us to put our hats and things in, and to comb our hair and put on the clean collars we brought along inside the sweat-bands of our hats – in short, a room to fix up in just like they have everywhere at high-toned doings. A little farther down the hall was the girls' room, which they used to powder up in, and so forth. Downstairs we – that is, the San Augustine Social Cotillion and Merrymakers' Club – had a stretcher put down in the parlor where our dance was going on.

"Willie Robbins and me happened to be up in our – cloak-room, I believe we called it when Myra Allison skipped through the hall on her way down-stairs from the girls' room. Willie was standing before the mirror, deeply interested in smoothing down the blond grass-plot on his head, which seemed to give him lots of trouble. Myra was always full of life and devilment. She stopped and stuck her head in our door. She certainly was good-looking. But I knew how Joe Granberry stood with her. So did Willie; but he kept on ba-a-a-ing after her and following her around. He had a system of persistence that didn't coincide with pale hair and light eyes.

"'Hello, Willie!' says Myra. 'What are you doing to yourself in the glass?'

"'I'm trying to look fly,' says Willie.

"'Well, you never could be fly,' says Myra, with her special laugh, which was the provokingest sound I ever heard except the rattle of an empty canteen against my saddle-horn.

"I looked around at Willie after Myra had gone. He had a kind of a lily-white look on him which seemed to show that her remark had, as you might say, disrupted his soul. I never noticed anything in what she said that sounded particularly destructive to a man's ideas of self-consciousness; but he was set back to an extent you could scarcely imagine.

"After we went down-stairs with our clean collars on, Willie never went near Myra again that night. After all, he seemed to be a diluted kind of a skim-milk sort of a chap, and I never wondered that Joe Granberry beat him out.

"The next day the battleship Maine was blown up, and then pretty soon somebody – I reckon it was Joe Bailey, or Ben Tillman, or maybe the Government-declared war against Spain.

"Well, everybody south of Mason & Hamlin's line knew that the North by itself couldn't whip a whole country the size of Spain. So the Yankees commenced to holler for help, and the Johnny Rebs answered the call. 'We're coming, Father William, a hundred thousand strong – and then some,' was the way they sang it. And the old party lines drawn by Sherman's march and the Kuklux and nine-cent cotton and the Jim Crow street-car ordinances faded away. We became one undivided. country, with no North, very little East, a good-sized chunk of West, and a South that loomed up as big as the first foreign label on a new eight-dollar suit-case.

"Of course the dogs of war weren't a complete pack without a yelp from the San Augustine Rifles, Company D, of the Fourteenth Texas Regiment. Our company was among the first to land in Cuba and strike terror into the hearts of the foe. I'm not going to give you a history of the war, I'm just dragging it in to fill out my story about Willie Robbins, just as the Republican party dragged it in to help out the election in 1898.

"If anybody ever had heroitis, it was that Willie Robbins. From the minute he set foot on the soil of the tyrants of Castile he seemed to engulf danger as a cat laps up cream. He certainly astonished every man in our company, from the captain up. You'd have expected him to gravitate naturally to the job of an orderly to the colonel, or typewriter in the commissary – but not any. He created the part of the flaxen-haired boy hero who lives and gets back home with the goods, instead of dying with an important despatch in his hands at his colonel's feet.

"Our company got into a section of Cuban scenery where one of the messiest and most unsung portions of the campaign occurred. We were out every day capering around in the bushes, and having little skirmishes with the Spanish troops that looked more like kind of tired-out feuds than anything else. The war was a joke to us, and of no interest to them. We never could see it any other way than as a howling farce-comedy that the San Augustine Rifles were actually fighting to uphold the Stars and Stripes. And the blamed little senors didn't get enough pay to make them care whether they were patriots or traitors. Now and then somebody would get killed. It seemed like a waste of life to me. I was at Coney Island when I went to New York once, and one of them down-hill skidding apparatuses they call 'roller-coasters' flew the track and killed a man in a brown sack-suit. Whenever the Spaniards shot one of our men, it struck me as just about as unnecessary and regrettable as that was.

"But I'm dropping Willie Robbins out of the conversation.

"He was out for bloodshed, laurels, ambition, medals, recommendations, and all other forms of military glory. And he didn't seem to be afraid of any of the recognized forms of military danger, such as Spaniards, cannon-balls, canned beef, gunpowder, or nepotism. He went forth with his pallid hair and china-blue eyes and ate up Spaniards like you would sardines a la canopy. Wars and rumbles of wars never flustered him. He would stand guard-duty, mosquitoes, hardtack, treat, and fire with equally perfect unanimity. No blondes in history ever come in comparison distance of him except the Jack of Diamonds and Queen Catherine of Russia.

"I remember, one time, a little caballard of Spanish men sauntered out from behind a patch of sugar-cane and shot Bob Turner, the first sergeant of our company, while we were eating dinner. As required by the army regulations, we fellows went through the usual tactics of falling into line, saluting the enemy, and loading and firing, kneeling.

"That wasn't the Texas way of scrapping; but, being a very important addendum and annex to the regular army, the San Augustine Rifles had to conform to the red-tape system of getting even.

"By the time we had got out our 'Upton's Tactics,' turned to page fifty-seven, said 'one – two – three – one – two – three' a couple of times, and got blank cartridges into our Springfields, the Spanish outfit had smiled repeatedly, rolled and lit cigarettes by squads, and walked away contemptuously.

"I went straight to Captain Floyd, and says to him: 'Sam, I don't think this war is a straight game. You know as well as I do that Bob Turner was one of the whitest fellows that ever threw a leg over a saddle, and now these wirepullers in Washington have fixed his clock. He's politically and ostensibly dead. It ain't fair. Why should they keep this thing up? If they want Spain licked, why don't they turn the San Augustine Rifles and Joe Seely's ranger company and a car-load of West Texas deputy-sheriffs onto these Spaniards, and let us exonerate them from the face of the earth? I never did,' says I, 'care much about fighting by the Lord Chesterfield ring rules. I'm going to hand in my resignation and go home if anybody else I am personally acquainted with gets hurt in this war. If you can get somebody in my place, Sam,' says I, 'I'll quit the first of next week. I don't want to work in an army that don't give its help a chance. Never mind my wages,' says I, 'let the Secretary of the Treasury keep 'em.'

"'Well, Ben,' says the captain to me, 'your allegations and estimations of the tactics of war, government, patriotism, guard-mounting, and democracy are all right. But I've looked into the system of international arbitration and the ethics of justifiable slaughter a little closer, maybe, than you have. Now, you can hand in your resignation the first of next week if you are so minded. But if you do,' says Sam, 'I'll order a corporal's guard to take you over by that limestone bluff on the creek and shoot enough lead into you to ballast a submarine air-ship. I'm captain of this company, and I've swore allegiance to the Amalgamated States regardless of sectional, secessional, and Congressional differences. Have you got any smoking-tobacco?' winds up Sam. 'Mine got wet when I swum the creek this morning.'

"The reason I drag all this non ex parte evidence in is because Willie Robbins was standing there listening to us. I was a second sergeant and he was a private then, but among us Texans and Westerners there never was as much tactics and subordination as there was in the regular army. We never called our captain anything but 'Sam' except when there was a lot of major-generals and admirals around, so as to preserve the discipline.

"And says Willie Robbins to me, in a sharp construction of voice much unbecoming to his light hair and previous record:

"'You ought to be shot, Ben, for emitting any such sentiments. A man that won't fight for his country is worse than a, horse-thief. If I was the cap, I'd put you in the guard-house for thirty days on round steak and tamales. War,' says Willie, 'is great and glorious. I didn't know you were a coward.'

"'I'm not,' says I. 'If I was, I'd knock some of the pallidness off of your marble brow. I'm lenient with you,' I says, 'just as I am with the Spaniards, because you have always reminded me of something with mushrooms on the side. Why, you little Lady of Shalott,' says I, 'you underdone leader of cotillions, you glassy fashion and moulded form, you white-pine soldier made in the Cisalpine Alps in Germany for the late New Year trade, do you know of whom you are talking to? We've been in the same social circle,' says I, 'and I've put up with you because you seemed so meek and self-unsatisfying. I don't understand why you have so sudden taken a personal interest in chivalrousness and murder. Your nature's undergone a complete revelation. Now, how is it?'

"'Well, you wouldn't understand, Ben,' says Willie, giving one of his refined smiles and turning away.

"'Come back here!' says I, catching him by the tail of his khaki coat. 'You've made me kind of mad, in spite of the aloofness in which I have heretofore held you. You are out for making a success in this hero business, and I believe I know what for. You are doing it either because you are crazy or because you expect to catch some girl by it. Now, if it's a girl, I've got something here to show you.'

"I wouldn't have done it, but I was plumb mad. I pulled a San Augustine paper out of my hip-pocket, and showed him an item. It was a half a column about the marriage of Myra Allison and Joe Granberry.

"Willie laughed, and I saw I hadn't touched him.

"'Oh,' says he, 'everybody knew that was going to happen. I heard about that a week ago.' And then he gave me the laugh again.

"'All right,' says I. 'Then why do you so recklessly chase the bright rainbow of fame? Do you expect to be elected President, or do you belong to a suicide club?'

"And then Captain Sam interferes.

"'You gentlemen quit jawing and go back to your quarters,' says he, 'or I'll have you escorted to the guard-house. Now, scat, both of you! Before you go, which one of you has got any chewing-tobacco?'

"'We're off, Sam,' says I. 'It's supper-time, anyhow. But what do you think of what we was talking about? I've noticed you throwing out a good many grappling-hooks for this here balloon called fame – What's ambition, anyhow? What does a man risk his life day after day for? Do you know of anything he gets in the end that can pay him for the trouble? I want to go back home,' says I. 'I don't care whether Cuba sinks or swims, and I don't give a pipeful of rabbit tobacco whether Queen Sophia Christina or Charlie Culberson rules these fairy isles; and I don't want my name on any list except the list of survivors. But I've noticed you, Sam,' says I, 'seeking the bubble notoriety in the cannon's larynx a number of times. Now, what do you do it for? Is it ambition, business, or some freckle-faced Pheebe at home that you are heroing for?'

"'Well, Ben,' says Sam, kind of hefting his sword out from between his knees, 'as your superior officer I could court-martial you for attempted cowardice and desertion. But I won't. And I'll tell you why I'm trying for promotion and the usual honors of war and conquest. A major gets more pay than a captain, and I need the money.'

"'Correct for you!' says I. 'I can understand that. Your system of fame-seeking is rooted in the deepest soil of patriotism. But I can't comprehend,' says I, 'why Willie Robbins, whose folks at home are well-off, and who used to be as meek and undesirous of notice as a cat with cream on his whiskers, should all at once develop into a warrior bold with the most fire-eating kind of proclivities. And the girl in his case seems to have been eliminated by marriage to another fellow. I reckon,' says I, 'it's a plain case of just common ambition. He wants his name, maybe, to go thundering down the coroners of time. It must be that.'

"Well, without itemizing his deeds, Willie sure made good as a hero. He simply spent most of his time on his knees begging our captain to send him on forlorn hopes and dangerous scouting expeditions. In every fight he was the first man to mix it at close quarters with the Don Alfonsos. He got three or four bullets planted in various parts of his autonomy. Once he went off with a detail of eight men and captured a whole company of Spanish. He kept Captain Floyd busy writing out recommendations of his bravery to send in to headquarters; and he began to accumulate medals for all kinds of things – heroism and target-shooting and valor and tactics and uninsubordination, and all the little accomplishments that look good to the third assistant secretaries of the War Department.

"Finally, Captain Floyd got promoted to be a major-general, or a knight commander of the main herd, or something like that. He pounded around on a white horse, all desecrated up with gold-leaf and hen-feathers and a Good Templar's hat, and wasn't allowed by the regulations to speak to us. And Willie Robbins was made captain of our company.

"And maybe he didn't go after the wreath of fame then! As far as I could see it was him that ended the war. He got eighteen of us boys – friends of his, too – killed in battles that he stirred up himself, and that didn't seem to me necessary at all. One night he took twelve of us and waded through a little nil about a hundred and ninety yards wide, and climbed a couple of mountains, and sneaked through a mile of neglected shrubbery and a couple of rock-quarries and into a rye-straw village, and captured a Spanish general named, as they said, Benny Veedus. Benny seemed to me hardly worth the trouble, being a blackish man without shoes or cuffs, and anxious to surrender and throw himself on the commissary of his foe.

"But that job gave Willie the big boost he wanted. The San Augustine News and the Galveston, St. Louis, New York, and Kansas

City papers printed his picture and columns of stuff about him. Old San Augustine simply went crazy over its 'gallant son.' The News had an editorial tearfully begging the Government to call off the regular army and the national guard, and let Willie carry on the rest of the war single-handed. It said that a refusal to do so would be regarded as a proof that the Northern jealousy of the South was still as rampant as ever.

"If the war hadn't ended pretty soon, I don't know to what heights of gold braid and encomiums Willie would have climbed; but it did. There was a secession of hostilities just three days after he was appointed a colonel, and got in three more medals by registered mail, and shot two Spaniards while they were drinking lemonade in an ambuscade.

"Our company went back to San Augustine when the war was over. There wasn't anywhere else for it to go. And what do you think? The old town notified us in print, by wire cable, special delivery, and a nigger named Saul sent on a gray mule to San Antone, that they was going to give us the biggest blow-out, complimentary, alimentary, and elementary, that ever disturbed the kildees on the sand-flats outside of the immediate contiguity of the city.

"I say 'we,' but it was all meant for ex-Private, Captain de facto, and Colonel-elect Willie Robbins. The town was crazy about him. They notified us that the reception they were going to put up would make the Mardi Gras in New Orleans look like an afternoon tea in Bury St. Edmunds with a curate's aunt.

"Well, the San Augustine Rifles got back home on schedule time. Everybody was at the depot giving forth Roosevelt-Democrat — they used to be called Rebel — yells. There was two brass-bands, and the mayor, and schoolgirls in white frightening the street-car horses by throwing Cherokee roses in the streets, and — well, maybe you've seen a celebration by a town that was inland and out of water.

"They wanted Brevet-Colonel Willie to get into a carriage and be drawn by prominent citizens and some of the city aldermen to the armory, but he stuck to his company and marched at the head of it up Sam Houston Avenue. The buildings on both sides was covered with flags and audiences, and everybody hollered 'Robbins!' or 'Hello, Willie!' as we marched up in files of fours. I never saw a illustriouser-looking human in my life than Willie was. He had at least seven or eight medals and diplomas and decorations on the breast of his khaki coat; he was sunburnt the color of a saddle, and he certainly done himself proud.

"They told us at the depot that the courthouse was to be illuminated at half-past seven, and there would be speeches and chili-con-came at the Palace Hotel. Miss Delphine Thompson was to read an original poem by James Whitcomb Ryan, and Constable Hooker had promised us a salute of nine guns from Chicago that he had arrested that day.

"After we had disbanded in the armory, Willie says to me:

"'Want to walk out a piece with me?'

"'Why, yes,' says I, 'if it ain't so far that we can't hear the tumult and the shouting die away. I'm hungry myself,' says I, 'and I'm pining for some home grub, but I'll go with you.'

"Willie steered me down some side streets till we came to a little white cottage in a new lot with a twenty-by-thirty-foot lawn decorated with brickbats and old barrel-staves.

"'Halt and give the countersign,' says I to Willie. 'Don't you know this dugout? It's the bird's-nest that Joe Granberry built before he married Myra Allison. What you going there for?'

"But Willie already had the gate open. He walked up the brick walk to the steps, and I went with him. Myra was sitting in a rocking-chair on the porch, sewing. Her hair was smoothed back kind of hasty and tied in a knot. I never noticed till then that she had freckles. Joe was at one side of the porch, in his shirtsleeves, with no collar on, and no signs of a shave, trying to scrape out a hole among the brickbats and tin cans to plant a little fruit-tree in. He looked up but never said a word, and neither did Myra.

"Willie was sure dandy-looking in his uniform, with medals strung on his breast and his new gold-handled sword. You'd never have taken him for the little white-headed snipe that the girls used to order about and make fun of. He just stood there for a minute, looking at Myra with a peculiar little smile on his face; and then he says to her, slow, and kind of holding on to his words with his teeth:

"'Oh, I don't know! Maybe I could if I tried!'

"That was all that was said. Willie raised his hat, and we walked away.

"And, somehow, when he said that, I remembered, all of a sudden, the night of that dance and Willie brushing his hair before the looking-glass, and Myra sticking her head in the door to guy him.

"When we got back to Sam Houston Avenue, Willie says:

"'Well, so long, Ben. I'm going down home and get off my shoes and take a rest.'

"'You?' says I. 'What's the matter with you? Ain't the court-house jammed with everybody in town waiting to honor the hero? And two brass-bands, and recitations and flags and jags and grub to follow waiting for you?'

"Willie sighs.

"'All right, Ben,' says he. 'Darned if I didn't forget all about that.'

"And that's why I say," concluded Ben Granger, "that you can't tell where ambition begins any more than you can where it is going to wind up."

THE PRINCESS AND THE PUMA

THERE HAD TO be a king and queen, of course. The king was a terrible old man who wore six-shooters and spurs, and shouted in such a tremendous voice that the rattlers on the prairie would run into their holes under the prickly pear. Before there was a royal family they called the man "Whispering Ben." When he came to own 50,000 acres of land and more cattle than he could count, they called him O'Donnell "the Cattle King."

The queen had been a Mexican girl from Laredo. She made a good, mild, Coloradoclaro wife, and even succeeded in teaching Ben to modify his voice sufficiently while in the house to keep the dishes from being broken. When Ben got to be king she would sit on the gallery of Espinosa Ranch and weave rush mats. When wealth became so irresistible and oppressive that upholstered chairs and a centre table were brought down from San Antone in the wagons, she bowed her smooth, dark head, and shared the fate of the Danaë.

To avoid *lèse-majesté* you have been presented first to the king and queen. They do not enter the story, which might be called "The Chronicle of the Princess, the Happy Thought, and the Lion that Bungled his Job."

Josefa O'Donnell was the surviving daughter, the princess. From her mother she inherited warmth of nature and a dusky, semi-tropic beauty. From Ben O'Donnell the royal she acquired a store in intrepidity, common sense, and the faculty of ruling. The combination was worth going miles to see. Josefa while riding her pony at a gallop could put five out of six bullets through a tomato-can swinging at the end of a string. She could play for hours with a white kitten she owned, dressing it in all manner of absurd clothes. Scorning a pencil, she could tell you out of her head what 1,545 two-year-olds would bring on the hoof, at $8.50 per head. Roughly speaking, the Espinosal Ranch is forty miles long and thirty broad – but mostly leased land. Josefa, on her pony, had prospected over every mile of it. Every cowpuncher on the range knew her by sight and was a loyal vassal. Ripley Givens, foreman of one of the Espinosal outfits, saw her one day, and made up his mind to form a royal matrimonial alliance. Presumptuous? No. In those days in the Nueces country a man was a man. And, after all, the title of cattle king does not presuppose blood royal. Often it only signifies that its owner wears the crown in token of his magnificent qualities in the art of cattle stealing.

One day Ripley Givens rode over to the Double Elm Ranch to inquire about a bunch of strayed yearlings. He was late in setting out on his return trip, and it was sundown when he struck the White Horse Crossing of the Nueces. From there to his own camp it was sixteen miles. To the Espinosal ranchhouse it was twelve. Givens was tired. He decided to pass the night at the Crossing.

There was a fine water hole in the river-bed. The banks were thickly covered with great trees, undergrown with brush. Back from the water hole fifty yards was a stretch of curly mesquite grass – supper for his horse and bed for himself. Givens staked his horse, and spread out his saddle blankets to dry. He sat down with his back against a tree and rolled a cigarette. From somewhere in the dense timber along the river came a sudden, rageful, shivering wail. The pony danced at the end of his rope and blew a whistling snort of comprehending fear. Givens puffed at his cigarette, but he reached leisurely for his pistol-belt, which lay on the grass, and twirled the cylinder of his weapon tentatively. A great gar plunged with a loud splash into the water hole. A little brown rabbit skipped around a bunch of catclaw and sat twitching his whiskers and looking humorously at Givens. The pony went on eating grass.

It is well to be reasonably watchful when a Mexican lion sings soprano along the arroyos at sundown. The burden of his song may be that young calves and fat lambs are scarce, and that he has a carnivorous desire for your acquaintance.

In the grass lay an empty fruit can, cast there by some former sojourner. Givens caught sight of it with a grunt of satisfaction. In his coat pocket tied behind his saddle was a handful or two of ground coffee. Black coffee and cigarettes! What ranchero could desire more?

In two minutes he had a little fire going clearly. He started, with his can, for the water hole. When within fifteen yards of its edge he saw, between the bushes, a side-saddled pony with down-dropped reins cropping grass a little distance to his left. Just rising from her hands and knees on the brink of the water hole was Josefa O'Donnell. She had been drinking water, and she brushed the sand from the palms of her hands. Ten yards away, to her right, half concealed by a clump of sacuista, Givens saw the crouching form of the Mexican lion. His amber eyelids glared hungrily; six feet from them was the tip of the tail stretched straight, like a pointer's. His hind-quarters rocked with the motion of the cat tribe preliminary to leaping.

Givens did what he could. His six-shooter was thirty-five yards away lying on the grass. He gave a loud yell, and dashed between the lion and the princess.

The "rucus," as Givens called it afterward, was brief and somewhat confused. When he arrived on the line of attack he saw a dim streak in the air, and heard a couple of faint cracks. Then a hundred pounds of Mexican lion plumped down upon his head and flattened him, with a heavy jar, to the ground. He remembered calling out: "Let up, now – no fair gouging!" and then he crawled from under the lion like a worm, with his mouth full of grass and dirt, and a big lump on the back of his head where it had struck the root of a water-elm. The lion lay motionless. Givens, feeling aggrieved, and suspicious of fouls, shook his fist at the lion, and shouted: "I'll rastle you again for twenty –" and then he got back to himself.

Josefa was standing in her tracks, quietly reloading her silver-mounted .38. It had not been a difficult shot. The lion's head made an easier mark than a tomato-can swinging at the end of a string. There was a provoking, teasing, maddening smile upon her mouth and in her dark eyes. The would-be-rescuing knight felt the fire of his fiasco burn down to his soul. Here had been his chance, the chance that he had dreamed of; and Momus, and not Cupid, had presided over it. The satyrs in the wood were, no doubt, holding their sides in hilarious, silent laughter. There had been something like vaudeville – say Signor Givens and his funny knockabout act with the stuffed lion.

"Is that you, Mr. Givens?" said Josefa, in her deliberate, saccharine contralto. "You nearly spoiled my shot when you yelled. Did you hurt your head when you fell?"

"Oh, no," said Givens, quietly; "that didn't hurt." He stooped ignominiously and dragged his best Stetson hat from under the beast. It was crushed and wrinkled to a fine comedy effect. Then he knelt down and softly stroked the fierce, open-jawed head of the dead lion.

"Poor old Bill!" he exclaimed, mournfully.

"What's that?" asked Josefa, sharply.

"Of course you didn't know, Miss Josefa," said Givens, with an air of one allowing magnanimity to triumph over grief. "Nobody can blame you. I tried to save him, but I couldn't let you know in time."

"Save who?"

"Why, Bill. I've been looking for him all day. You see, he's been our camp pet for two years. Poor old fellow, he wouldn't have hurt a cottontail rabbit. It'll break the boys all up when they hear about it. But you couldn't tell, of course, that Bill was just trying to play with you."

Josefa's black eyes burned steadily upon him. Ripley Givens met the test successfully. He stood rumpling the yellow-brown curls on his head pensively. In his eyes was regret, not unmingled with a gentle reproach. His smooth features were set to a pattern of indisputable sorrow. Josefa wavered.

"What was your pet doing here?" she asked, making a last stand. "There's no camp near the White Horse Crossing."

"The old rascal ran away from camp yesterday," answered Givens, readily. "It's a wonder the coyotes didn't scare him to death. You see, Jim Webster, our horse wrangler, brought a little terrier pup into camp last week. The pup made life miserable for Bill – he used to chase him around and chew his hind legs for hours at a time. Every night when bedtime came Bill would sneak under one of the boys' blankets and sleep to keep the pup from finding him. I reckon he must have been worried pretty desperate or he wouldn't have run away. He was always afraid to get out of sight of camp."

Josefa looked at the body of the fierce animal. Givens gently patted one of the formidable paws that could have killed a yearling calf with one blow. Slowly a red flush widened upon the dark olive face of the girl. Was it the signal of shame of the true sportsman who has brought down ignoble quarry? Her eyes grew softer, and the lowered lids drove away all their bright mockery.

"I'm very sorry," she said, humbly; "but he looked so big, and jumped so high that –." "Poor old Bill was hungry," interrupted Givens, in quick defence of the deceased. "We always made him jump for his supper in camp. He would lie down and roll over for a piece of meat. When he saw you he thought he was going to get something to eat from you."

Suddenly Josefa's eyes opened wide.

"I might have shot you!" she exclaimed. "You ran right in between. You risked your life to save your pet! That was fine, Mr. Givens. I like a man who is kind to animals."

Yes; there was even admiration in her gaze now. After all, there was a hero rising out of the ruins of the anti-climax. The look on Givens's face would have secured him a high position in the S.P.C.A.

"I always loved 'em," said he; "horses, dogs, Mexican lions, cows, alligators –"

"I hate alligators," instantly demurred Josefa; "crawly, muddy things!"

"Did I say alligators?" said Givens. "I meant antelopes, of course."

Josefa's conscience drove her to make further amends. She held out her hand penitently. There was a bright, unshed drop in each of her eyes.

"Please forgive me, Mr. Givens, won't you? I'm only a girl, you know, and I was frightened at first. I'm very, very sorry I shot Bill. You don't know how ashamed I feel. I wouldn't have done it for anything."

Givens took the proffered hand. He held it for a time while he allowed the generosity of his nature to overcome his grief at the loss of Bill. At last it was clear that he had forgiven her.

"Please don't speak of it any more, Miss Josefa. 'Twas enough to frighten any young lady the way Bill looked. I'll explain it all right to the boys."

"Are you really sure you don't hate me?" Josefa came closer to him impulsively. Her eyes were sweet – oh, sweet and pleading with gracious penitence. "I would hate any one who would kill my kitten. And how daring and kind of you to risk being shot when you tried to save him! How very few men would have done that!" Victory wrested from defeat! Vaudeville turned into drama! Bravo, Ripley Givens!

It was now twilight. Of course Miss Josefa could not be allowed to ride on to the ranch-house alone. Givens resaddled his pony in spite of that animal's reproachful glances, and rode with her. Side by side they galloped across the smooth grass, the princess and the man who was kind to animals. The prairie odors of fruitful earth and delicate bloom were thick and sweet around them. Coyotes yelping over there on the hill! No fear. And yet –

Josefa rode closer. A little hand seemed to grope. Givens found it with his own. The ponies kept an even gait. The hands lingered together, and the owner of one explained.

"I never was frightened before, but just think! How terrible it would be to meet a really wild lion! Poor Bill! I'm so glad you came with me!"

O'Donnell was sitting on the ranch gallery

"Hello, Rip!" he shouted – "that you?"

"He rode in with me," said Josefa. "I lost my way and was late."

"Much obliged," called the cattle king. "Stop over, Rip, and ride to camp in the morning."

But Givens would not. He would push on to camp. There was a bunch of steers to start off on the trail at daybreak. He said good-night, and trotted away.

An hour later, when the lights were out, Josefa, in her night-robe, came to her door and called to the king in his own room across the brick-paved hallway:

"Say, Pop, you know that old Mexican lion they call the 'Gotch-eared Devil' – the one that killed Gonzales, Mr. Martin's sheep herder, and about fifty calves on the Salada range? Well, I settled his hash this afternoon over at the White Horse Crossing. Put two balls in his head with my .38 while he was on the jump. I knew him by the slice gone from his left ear that old Gonzales cut off with his machete. You couldn't have made a better shot yourself, Daddy."

"Bully for you!" thundered Whispering Ben from the darkness of the royal chamber.

THE SKYLIGHT ROOM

FIRST MRS. PARKER would show you the double parlors. You would not dare to interrupt her description of their advantages and of the merits of the gentleman who had occupied them for eight years. Then you would manage to stammer forth the confession that you were neither a doctor nor a dentist.

Mrs. Parker's manner of receiving the admission was such that you could never afterward entertain the same feeling toward your parents, who had neglected to train you up in one of the professions that fitted Mrs. Parker's parlors.

Next you ascended one flight of stairs and looked at the second-floor-back at $8. Convinced by her second-floor manner that it was worth the $12 that Mr. Toosenberry always paid for it until he left to take charge of his brother's orange plantation in Florida near Palm Beach, where Mrs. McIntyre always spent the winters that had the double front room with private bath, you managed to babble that you wanted something still cheaper.

If you survived Mrs. Parker's scorn, you were taken to look at Mr. Skidder's large hall room on the third floor. Mr. Skidder's room was not vacant. He wrote plays and smoked cigarettes in it all day long. But every room-hunter was made to visit his room to admire the lambrequins. After each visit, Mr. Skidder, from the fright caused by possible eviction, would pay something on his rent.

Then – oh, then – if you still stood on one foot, with your hot hand clutching the three moist dollars in your pocket, and hoarsely proclaimed your hideous arid culpable poverty, never – more would Mrs. Parker be cicerone of yours. She would honk loudly the word "Clara," she would show you her back, and march downstairs. Then Clara, the colored [African-American] maid, would escort you up the carpeted ladder that served for the fourth flight, and show you the Skylight Room.

It occupied 7 x 8 feet of floor space in the middle of the hall. On each side of it was a dark lumber closet or storeroom.

In it was an iron cot, a washstand and a chair. A shelf was the dresser. Its four bare walls seemed to close in upon you like the sides of a coin. Your hand crept to your the glass of the little skylight you saw a square of blue infinity.

"Two dollars, suh," Clara would say in her half-contemptuous, half-Tuskegeenial tones.

One day Miss Leeson came hunting for a room. She carried a typewriter made to be lugged around by a much larger lady. She was a very little girl, with eyes and hair that had kept on growing after she had stopped and that always looked as if they were saying: "Goodness me! Why didn't you keep up with us?"

Mrs. Parker showed her the double parlors. "In this closet," she said, "one could keep a skeleton or an anesthetic or coal –"

"But I am neither a doctor nor a dentist," said Miss Leeson, with a shiver.

Mrs. Parker gave her the incredulous, pitying, sneering, icy stare that she kept for those who failed to qualify as doctors or dentists, and led the way to the second-floor-back.

"Eight dollars?" said Miss Leeson. "Dear me! I'm not Hetty if I do look green. I'm just a poor little working girl. Show me something higher and lower."

Mr. Skidder jumped and strewed the floor with cigarette stubs at the rap on his door.

"Excuse me, Mr. Skidder," said Mrs. Parker, with her demon's smile at his pale looks. "I didn't know you were in. I asked the lady to have a look at your lambrequins."

"They're too lovely for anything," said Miss Leeson, smiling in exactly the way the angels do.

After they had gone Mr. Skidder got very busy erasing the tall, black-haired heroine from his latest (unproduced) play and insetted a small, roguish one with heavy, bright hair and vivacious features.

"Anna Held'll jump at it," said Mr. Skidder to himself, putting his feet up against the lambrequins and disappearing in a cloud of smoke like an aerial cuttlefish.

Presently the tocsin call of "Clara!" sounded to the world the state of Miss Leeson's purse. A dark goblin seized her, mounted a Stygian stairway, thrust her into a vault with a glimmer of light in its top and muttered the menacing and cabalistic words:

"Two dollars!"

"I'll take it!" sighed Miss Leeson, sinking down upon the squeaky iron bed.

Every day Miss Leeson went out to work. At night she brought home papers with handwriting on them and made copies with her typewriter. Sometimes she had no work at night, and then she would sit on the steps of the high stoop with the other roomers. Miss Leeson was not intended for a skylight room when the plans were drawn for her creation. She was gay-hearted and full of tender, whimsical fancies. Once she let Mr. Skidder read to her three acts of his great (unpublished) comedy, "It's No Kid; or,The Heir of the Subway."

There was rejoicing among the gentlemen roomers whenever Miss Leeson had time to sit on the steps for an hour or two. But Miss Longnecker, the tall blonde who taught in a public school and said, "Well, really!" to everything you said, sat on the top step and sniffed. And Miss Dorn, who shot at the moving ducks at Coney [Island] every Sunday and worked in a department store, sat on the bottom step and sniffed. Miss Leeson sat on the middle step and the men would quickly group around her.

Especially Mr. Skidder, who had cast her in his mind for the star part in a private, romantic (unspoken) drama in real life. And especially Mr. Hoover, who was forty-five, fat, flush and foolish. And especially very young Mr. Evans, who set up a hollow cough to induce her to ask him to leave off cigarettes. The men voted her "the funniest and jolliest ever," but the sniffs on the top step and the lower step were implacable.

* * *

I pray you to let the drama halt while Chorus stalks to the footlights and drops an epicedian tear upon the fatness of Mr. Hoover. Tune the pipes to the tragedy of tallow, the bane of bulk, the calamity of corpulence. Tried out, Falstaff might have rendered more romance to the ton than would have Romeo's rickety ribs to the ounce. A lover may sigh, but he must not puff. To the train of Momus are the fat men remanded. In vain beats the faithfullest heart above a 52-inch belt. Avaunt, Hoover!

Hoover, forty-five, flush and foolish, might carry off Helen herself; Hoover, forty-five, flush, foolish and fat is meat for perdition. There was never a chance for you anyhow, Hoover.

As Mrs. Parker's roomers sat thus one summer's evening, Miss

Leeson looked up into the firmament and cried with her little gay laugh:

"Why, there's Billy Jackson! I can see him from down here, too."

All looked up-some at the windows of skyscrapers, some casting about for an airship, Jackson-guided.

"It's that star," explained Miss Leeson, pointing with a tiny finger. "Not the big one that winkles – the steady blue one near it. I can see it every night through my skylight. I named it Billy Jackson."

"Well, really!" said Miss Longnecker. "I didn't know you were an astronomer, Miss Leeson."

"Oh, yes," said the small star gazer, "I know as much as any of them about the style of sleeves they're going to wear next fall in Mars."

"Well, really!" said Miss Longnecker. "The star you refer to is Gamma, of the constellation Cassiopeia, it is nearly of the second magnitude, arid its meridian passage is –"

"Said the very young Mr. Evans, "I think Hilly Jackson is a much better name for it,"

"Same here," said Mr. Hoover, loudly breathing defiance to Miss Longnecker. "I think Miss Leeson has just as much right to name stars as any of those old astrologers had?"

"Well, really!" said Miss Longnecker.

"I wonder whether it's a shooting star," remarked Miss Dorn. "I hit nine ducks and a rabbit out of ten in the gallery at Coney Sunday."

"He doesn't show up very well from down here," said Miss Leeson. "You ought to see him from my room. You know you can see stars even in the daytime from the bottom of a well. At night my room is like the shaft of a coal mine, and it makes Billy Jackson look like the big diamond pin that Night fastens her kimono with."

There came a time after that when Miss Leeson brought no formidable papers home to copy. And when she went out in the morning, instead of working, she went from office to office and let her heart melt away in the drip of cold refusals transmitted through insolent office boys. This went on.

There came an evening when she wearily climbed Mrs. Parker's stoop at the hour when she always returned from her dinner at the restaurant. But she had had no dinner.

As she stepped into the hall Mr. Hoover met her and seized his chance. He asked her to marry him, and his fatness hovered above her like an avalanche. She dodged, and caught the balustrade. He tried for her hand, and she raised it and smote him weakly in the face. Step by step she went up, dragging herself by the railing. She passed Mr. Skidder's door as he was red-inking a stage direction for Myrtle Delorme (Miss Leeson) in his (unaccepted) comedy, to "pirouette across stage from L to the side of the Count." Up the carpeted ladder she crawled at last and opened the door of the skylight room.

She was too weak to light the lamp to undress. She fell upon the iron cot, her fragile body scarcely hollowing the worn springs. And in that Erehus of a room she slowly raised her heavy eyelids, and smiled.

For Billy Jackson was shining down on her, calm and bright and constant through the skylight. There was no world about her. She was sunk in a pit of blackness, with but that small square of pallid light framing the star that she had so whimsically and oh, so ineffectually, named. Miss Longnecker must be right. It was Gamma, of the constellation Cassiopeia, and not Billy Jackson. And yet she could not let it be Gamma.

As she lay on her back, she tried twice to raise her arm. The third time she got two thin fingers to her lips and blew a kiss out of the black pit to Billy Jackson. Her arm fell back limply.

"Good-bye, Billy," she murmured, faintly. "You're millions of miles away and you won't even twinkle once. But you kept where I could see you most of the time up there when there wasn't anything else but darkness to look at, didn't you? ... Millions of miles.... Good bye, Billy Jackson."

* * *

Clara, the colored maid, found the door locked at 10 the next day, and they forced it open. Vinegar, and the slapping of wrists and burnt feathers proving of no avail, some one ran to phone for an ambulance.

In due time it backed up to the door with much gong-clanging, and the capable young medico, in his white linen coat, ready, active, confident, with his smooth face half debonair, half grim, danced up the steps.

"Ambulance call to 49," he said, briefly. "What's the trouble?"

"Oh, yes, doctor," sniffed Mrs. Parker, as though her trouble that there should be trouble in the house was the greater. "I can't think what can be the matter with her. Nothing we could do would bring her to. It's a young woman, a Miss Elsi – yes, a Miss Elsie Leesson. Never before in my house –"

"What room?" cried the doctor in a terrible voice, to which Mrs. Parker was a stranger.

"The skylight room. It –"

Evidently the ambulance doctor was familiar with the location of skylight rooms. He was gone up the stairs, four at a time. Mrs. Parker followed slowly, as her dignity demanded.

On the first landing she met him coming back bearing the astronomer in his arms. He stopped and let loose the practised scalpel of his tongue, not loudly. Gradually Mrs. Parker crumpled as a stiff garment that slips down from a nail. Ever afterwards there remained crumples in her mind and body. Sometimes her curious roomers would ask her what the doctor said to her.

"Let that be," she would answer. "If I can get forgiveness for having heard it I will be satisfied."

The ambulance physician strode with his burden through the pack of hounds that follow the curiosity chase, and even they fell back along the sidewalk abashed, for his face was that of one who bears his own dead.

They noticed that he did not lay down upon the bed prepared for it in the ambulance the form that he carried, and all that he said was: "Drive like h – l, Wilson," to the driver.

That is all. Is it a story? In the next morning's paper I saw a little news item, and the last sentence of it may help you (as it helped me) to weld the incidents togetber. It recounted the reception into Bellevue Hospital of a young woman who had been removed from No. 49 East Street, suffering from debility induced by starvation. It concluded with these words:

"Dr. William Jackson, the ambulance physician who attended the case, says the patient will recover."

THE SLEUTHS

IN THE BIG city a man will disappear with the suddenness and completeness of the flame of a candle that is blown out. All the agencies of inquisition – the hounds of the trail, the sleuths of the city's labyrinths, the closet detectives of theory and induction – will be invoked to the search. Most often the man's face will be seen no more. Sometimes he will reappear in Sheboygan or in the wilds of Terre Haute, calling himself one of the synonyms of "Smith," and without memory of events up to a certain time, including his grocer's bill. Sometimes it will be found, after dragging the rivers, and polling the restaurants to see if he may be waiting for a well-done sirloin, that he has moved next door.

This snuffing out of a human being like the erasure of a chalk man from a blackboard is one of the most impressive themes in dramaturgy.

The case of Mary Snyder, in point, should not be without interest.

A man of middle age, of the name of Meeks, came from the West to New York to find his sister, Mrs. Mary Snyder, a widow, aged fifty-two, who had been living for a year in a tenement house in a crowded neighborhood.

At her address he was told that Mary Snyder had moved away longer than a month before. No one could tell him her new address.

On coming out Mr. Meeks addressed a policeman who was standing on the corner, and explained his dilemma.

"My sister is very poor," he said, "and I am anxious to find her. I have recently made quite a lot of money in a lead mine, and I want her to share my prosperity. There is no use in advertising her, because she cannot read."

The policeman pulled his moustache and looked so thoughtful and mighty that Meeks could almost feel the joyful tears of his sister Mary dropping upon his bright blue tie.

"You go down in the Canal Street neighborhood," said the

policeman, "and get a job drivin' the biggest dray you can find. There's old women always gettin' knocked over by drays down there. You might see 'er among 'em. If you don't want to do that you better go 'round to headquarters and get 'em to put a fly cop onto the dame."

At police headquarters, Meeks received ready assistance. A general alarm was sent out, and copies of a photograph of Mary Snyder that her brother had were distributed among the stations. In Mulberry Street the chief assigned Detective Mullins to the case.

The detective took Meeks aside and said:

"This is not a very difficult case to unravel. Shave off your whiskers, fill your pockets with good cigars, and meet me in the cafe of the Waldorf at three o'clock this afternoon."

Meeks obeyed. He found Mullins there. They had a bottle of wine, while the detective asked questions concerning the missing woman.

"Now," said Mullins, "New York is a big city, but we've got the detective business systematized. There are two ways we can go about finding your sister. We will try one of 'em first. You say she's fifty-two?"

"A little past," said Meeks.

The detective conducted the Westerner to a branch advertising office of one of the largest dailies. There he wrote the following "ad" and submitted it to Meeks:

"Wanted, at once – one hundred attractive chorus girls for a new musical comedy. Apply all day at No. – Broadway."

Meeks was indignant.

"My sister," said he, "is a poor, hard-working, elderly woman. I do not see what aid an advertisement of this kind would be toward finding her."

"All right," said the detective. "I guess you don't know New York. But if you've got a grouch against this scheme we'll try the other one. It's a sure thing. But it'll cost you more."

"Never mind the expense," said Meeks; "we'll try it."

The sleuth led him back to the Waldorf. "Engage a couple of bedrooms and a parlor," he advised, "and let's go up."

This was done, and the two were shown to a superb suite on the fourth floor. Meeks looked puzzled. The detective sank into a velvet armchair, and pulled out his cigar case.

"I forgot to suggest, old man," he said, "that you should have taken the rooms by the month. They wouldn't have stuck you so much for 'em."

"By the month!" exclaimed Meeks. "What do you mean?"

"Oh, it'll take time to work the game this way. I told you it would cost you more. We'll have to wait till spring. There'll be a new city directory out then. Very likely your sister's name and address will be in it."

Meeks rid himself of the city detective at once. On the next day some one advised him to consult Shamrock Jolnes, New York's famous private detective, who demanded fabulous fees, but performed miracles in the way of solving mysteries and crimes.

After waiting for two hours in the anteroom of the great detective's apartment, Meeks was shown into his presence. Jolnes sat in a purple dressing-gown at an inlaid ivory chess table, with a magazine before him, trying to solve the mystery of "They." The famous sleuth's thin, intellectual face, piercing eyes, and rate per word are too well-known to need description.

Meeks set forth his errand. "My fee, if successful, will be $500," said Shamrock Jolnes.

Meeks bowed his agreement to the price.

"I will undertake your case, Mr. Meeks," said Jolnes, finally. "The disappearance of people in this city has always been an interesting problem to me. I remember a case that I brought to a successful outcome a year ago. A family bearing the name of Clark disappeared suddenly from a small flat in which they were living. I watched the flat building for two months for a clue. One day it struck me that a certain milkman and a grocer's boy always walked backward when they carried their wares upstairs. Following out by induction the idea that this observation gave me, I at once located the missing family. They had moved into the flat across the hall and changed their name to Kralc." Shamrock Jolnes and his client went to the tenement house where Mary Snyder had lived, and the detective demanded to be shown the room in which she had lived. It had been occupied by no tenant since her disappearance.

The room was small, dingy, and poorly furnished. Meeks seated himself dejectedly on a broken chair, while the great detective searched the walls and floor and the few sticks of old, rickety furniture for a clue.

At the end of half an hour Jolnes had collected a few seemingly unintelligible articles – a cheap black hat pin, a piece torn off a theatre programme, and the end of a small torn card on which was the word "left" and the characters "C 12."

Shamrock Jolnes leaned against the mantel for ten minutes, with his head resting upon his hand, and an absorbed look upon his intellectual face. At the end of that time he exclaimed, with animation:

"Come, Mr. Meeks; the problem is solved. I can take you directly to the house where your sister is living. And you may have no fears concerning her welfare, for she is amply provided with funds – for the present at least."

Meeks felt joy and wonder in equal proportions.

"How did you manage it?" he asked, with admiration in his tones.

Perhaps Jolnes's only weakness was a professional pride in his wonderful achievements in induction. He was ever ready to astound and charm his listeners by describing his methods.

"By elimination," said Jolnes, spreading his clues upon a little table, "I got rid of certain parts of the city to which Mrs. Snyder might have removed. You see this hatpin? That eliminates Brooklyn. No woman attempts to board a car at the Brooklyn Bridge without being sure that she carries a hatpin with which to fight her way into a seat. And now I will demonstrate to you that she could not have gone to Harlem. Behind this door are two hooks in the wall. Upon one of these Mrs. Snyder has hung her bonnet, and upon the other her shawl. You will observe that the bottom of the hanging shawl has gradually made a soiled streak against the plastered wall. The mark is clean-cut, proving that there is no fringe on the shawl. Now, was there ever a case where a middle-aged woman, wearing a shawl, boarded a Harlem train without there being a fringe on the shawl to catch in the gate and delay the passengers behind her? So we eliminate Harlem.

"Therefore I conclude that Mrs. Snyder has not moved very far away. On this torn piece of card you see the word 'Left,' the letter 'C,' and the number '12.' Now, I happen to know that No. 12 Avenue C is a first-class boarding house, far beyond your sister's means – as we suppose. But then I find this piece of a theatre programme, crumpled into an odd shape. What meaning does it convey. None to you, very likely, Mr. Meeks; but it is eloquent to one whose habits and training take cognizance of the smallest things.

"You have told me that your sister was a scrub woman. She scrubbed the floors of offices and hallways. Let us assume that she procured such work to perform in a theatre. Where is valuable jewelry lost the oftenest, Mr. Meeks? In the theatres, of course. Look at that piece of programme, Mr. Meeks. Observe the round impression in it. It has been wrapped around a ring – perhaps a ring of great value. Mrs. Snyder found the ring while at work in the theatre. She hastily tore off a piece of a programme, wrapped the ring carefully, and thrust it into her bosom. The next day she disposed of it, and, with her increased means, looked about her for a more comfortable place in which to live. When I reach thus far in the chain I see nothing impossible about No. 12 Avenue C. It is there we will find your sister, Mr. Meeks."

Shamrock Jolnes concluded his convincing speech with the smile of a successful artist. Meeks's admiration was too great for words. Together they went to No. 12 Avenue C. It was an old-fashioned brownstone house in a prosperous and respectable neighborhood.

They rang the bell, and on inquiring were told that no Mrs. Snyder was known there, and that not within six months had a new occupant come to the house.

When they reached the sidewalk again, Meeks examined the clues which he had brought away from his sister's old room.

"I am no detective," he remarked to Jolnes as he raised the piece of theatre programme to his nose, "but it seems to me that instead of a ring having been wrapped in this paper it was one of those round peppermint drops. And this piece with the address on it looks to me like the end of a seat coupon – No. 12, row C, left aisle."

Shamrock Jolnes had a far-away look in his eyes.

"I think you would do well to consult Juggins," said he. "Who is Juggins?" asked Meeks.

"He is the leader," said Jolnes, "of a new modern school of detectives. Their methods are different from ours, but it is said that Juggins has solved some extremely puzzling cases. I will take you to him."

They found the greater Juggins in his office. He was a small man with light hair, deeply absorbed in reading one of the bourgeois works of Nathaniel Hawthorne.

The two great detectives of different schools shook hands with ceremony, and Meeks was introduced.

"State the facts," said Juggins, going on with his reading.

When Meeks ceased, the greater one closed his book and said: "Do I understand that your sister is fifty-two years of age, with a large mole on the side of her nose, and that she is a very poor widow, making a scanty living by scrubbing, and with a very homely face and figure?"

"That describes her exactly," admitted Meeks. Juggins rose and put on his hat.

"In fifteen minutes," he said, "I will return, bringing you her present address."

Shamrock Jolnes turned pale, but forced a smile.

Within the specified time Juggins returned and consulted a little slip of paper held in his hand.

"Your sister, Mary Snyder," he announced calmly, "will be found at No. 162 Chilton street. She is living in the back hall bedroom, five flights up. The house is only four blocks from here," he continued, addressing Meeks. "Suppose you go and verify the statement and then return here. Mr. Jolnes will await you, I dare say."

Meeks hurried away. In twenty minutes he was back again, with a beaming face.

"She is there and well!" he cried. "Name your fee!"

"Two dollars," said Juggins.

When Meeks had settled his bill and departed, Shamrock Jolnes stood with his hat in his hand before Juggins.

"If it would not be asking too much," he stammered – "if you would favor me so far – would you object to –"

"Certainly not," said Juggins pleasantly. "I will tell you how I did it. You remember the description of Mrs. Snyder? Did you ever know a woman like that who wasn't paying weekly instalments on an enlarged crayon portrait of herself? The biggest factory of that kind in the country is just around the corner. I went there and got her address off the books. That's all."

THE SNOW MAN

EDITORIAL NOTE. — BEFORE the fatal illness of William Sydney Porter (known through his literary work as "O. Henry") this American master of short-story writing had begun for Hampton's Magazine the story printed below. Illness crept upon him rapidly and he was compelled to give up writing about at the point where the girl enters the story.

When he realized that he could do no more (it was his lifelong habit to write with a pencil, never dictating to a stenographer), O. Henry told in detail the remainder of "The Snow Man" to Harris Merton Lyon, whom he had often spoken of as one of the most effective short-story writers of the present time. Mr. Porter had delineated all of the characters, leaving only the rounding out of the plot in the final pages to Mr. Lyon.

Housed and windowpaned from it, the greatest wonder to little children is the snow. To men, it is something like a crucible in which their world melts into a white star ten million miles away. The man who can stand the test is a Snow Man; and this is his reading by Fahrenheit, Reaumur, or Moses's carven tablets of stone.

Night had fluttered a sable pinion above the canyon of Big Lost River, and I urged my horse toward the Bay Horse Ranch because the snow was deepening. The flakes were as large as an hour's circular tatting by Miss Wilkins's ablest spinster, betokening a heavy snowfall and less entertainment and more adventure than the completion of the tatting could promise. I knew Ross Curtis of the Bay Horse, and that I would be welcome as a snow-bound pilgrim, both for hospitality's sake and because Ross had few chances to confide in living creatures who did not neigh, bellow, bleat, yelp, or howl during his discourse.

The ranch house was just within the jaws of the canyon where its builder may have fatuously fancied that the timbered and rocky walls on both sides would have protected it from the wintry Colorado winds; but I feared the drift. Even now through the endless, bottomless rift in the hills — the speaking tube of the four winds — came roaring the voice of the proprietor to the little room on the top floor.

At my "hello," a ranch hand came from an outer building and

received my thankful horse. In another minute, Ross and I sat by a stove in the dining-room of the four-room ranch house, while the big, simple welcome of the household lay at my disposal. Fanned by the whizzing norther, the fine, dry snow was sifted and bolted through the cracks and knotholes of the logs. The cook room, without a separating door, appended.

In there I could see a short, sturdy, leisurely and weather-beaten man moving with professional sureness about his red-hot stove. His face was stolid and unreadable – something like that of a great thinker, or of one who had no thoughts to conceal. I thought his eye seemed unwarrantably superior to the elements and to the man, but quickly attributed that to the characteristic self-importance of a petty chef. "Camp cook" was the niche that I gave him in the Hall of Types; and he fitted it as an apple fits a dumpling.

Cold it was in spite of the glowing stove; and Ross and I sat and talked, shuddering frequently, half from nerves and half from the freezing draughts. So he brought the bottle and the cook brought boiling water, and we made prodigious hot toddies against the attacks of Boreas. We clinked glasses often. They sounded like icicles dropping from the eaves, or like the tinkle of a thousand prisms on a Louis XIV chandelier that I once heard at a boarder's dance in the parlor of a ten-a-week boarding-house in Gramercy Square transit.

Silence in the terrible beauty of the snow and of the Sphinx and of the stars; but they who believe that all things, from a without-wine table d'hote to the crucifixion, may be interpreted through music, might have found a nocturne or a symphony to express the isolation of that blotted-out world. The clink of glass and bottle, the aeolian chorus of the wind in the house crannies, its deeper trombone through the canyon below, and the Wagnerian crash of the cook's pots and pans, united in a fit, discordant melody, I thought. No less welcome an accompaniment was the sizzling of broiling ham and venison cutlet indorsed by the solvent fumes of true Java, bringing rich promises of comfort to our yearning souls.

The cook brought the smoking supper to the table. He nodded to me democratically as he cast the heavy plates around as though he were pitching quoits or hurling the discus. I looked at him with some appraisement and curiosity and much conciliation. There was no prophet to tell us when that drifting evil outside might cease to fall; and it is well, when snow-bound, to stand somewhere within the radius of the cook's favorable consideration. But I could read neither favor nor disapproval in the face and manner of our pot-wrestler.

He was about five feet nine inches, and two hundred pounds of commonplace, bull-necked, pink-faced, callous calm. He wore brown duck trousers too tight and too short, and a blue flannel shirt with sleeves rolled above his elbows. There was a sort of grim, steady scowl on his features that looked to me as though he had fixed it there purposely as a protection against the weakness of an inherent amiability that, he fancied, were better concealed. And then I let supper usurp his brief occupancy of my thoughts.

"Draw up, George," said Ross. "Let's all eat while the grub's hot."

"You fellows go on and chew," answered the cook. "I ate mine in the kitchen before sun-down."

"Think it'll be a big snow, George?" asked the ranchman.

George had turned to reenter the cook room. He moved slowly around and, looking at his face, it seemed to me that he was turning over the wisdom and knowledge of centuries in his head.

"It might," was his delayed reply.

At the door of the kitchen he stopped and looked back at us. Both Ross and I held our knives and forks poised and gave him our regard. Some men have the power of drawing the attention of others without speaking a word. Their attitude is more effective than a shout.

"And again it mightn't," said George, and went back to his stove.

After we had eaten, he came in and gathered the emptied dishes. He stood for a moment, while his spurious frown deepened.

"It might stop any minute," he said, "or it might keep up for days."

At the farther end of the cook room I saw George pour hot water into his dishpan, light his pipe, and put the tableware through its required lavation. He then carefully unwrapped from a piece of old saddle blanket a paperback book, and settled himself to read by his dim oil lamp.

And then the ranchman threw tobacco on the cleared table and set forth again the bottles and glasses; and I saw that I stood in a deep channel through which the long dammed flood of his discourse would soon be booming. But I was half content, comparing my fate with that of the late Thomas Tucker, who had to sing for his supper, thus doubling the burdens of both himself and his host.

"Snow is a hell of a thing," said Ross, by way of a foreword. "It ain't, somehow, it seems to me, salubrious. I can stand water and mud and two inches below zero and a hundred and ten in the shade and medium-sized cyclones, but this here fuzzy white stuff naturally gets me all locoed. I reckon the reason it rattles you is because it changes the look of things so much. It's like you had a wife and left her in the morning with the same old blue cotton wrapper on, and rides in of a night and runs across her all outfitted in a white silk evening frock, waving an ostrich-feather fan, and monkeying with a posy of lily flowers. Wouldn't it make you look for your pocket compass? You'd be liable to kiss her before you collected your presence of mind."

By and by, the flood of Ross's talk was drawn up into the clouds (so it pleased me to fancy) and there condensed into the finer snowflakes of thought; and we sat silent about the stove, as good friends and bitter enemies will do. I thought of Boss's preamble about the mysterious influence upon man exerted by that ermine-lined monster that now covered our little world, and knew he was right.

Of all the curious knickknacks, mysteries, puzzles, Indian gifts, rat-traps, and well-disguised blessings that the gods chuck down to us from the Olympian peaks, the most disquieting and evil-bringing is the snow. By scientific analysis it is absolute beauty and purity – so, at the beginning we look doubtfully at chemistry.

It falls upon the world, and lo! we live in another. It hides in a night the old scars and familiar places with which we have grown heart-sick or enamored. So, as quietly as we can, we hustle on our embroidered robes and hie us on Prince Camaralzaman's horse or in the reindeer sleigh into the white country where the seven colors converge. This is when our fancy can overcome the bane of it.

But in certain spots of the earth comes the snow-madness, made known by people turned wild and distracted by the bewildering veil that has obscured the only world they know. In the cities, the white fairy who sets the brains of her dupes whirling by a wave of her wand is cast for the comedy role. Her diamond shoe buckles glitter like frost; with a pirouette she invites the spotless carnival.

But in the waste places the snow is sardonic. Sponging out the world of the outliers, it gives no foothold on another sphere in return. It makes of the earth a firmament under foot; it leaves us clawing and stumbling in space in an inimical fifth element whose evil outdoes its strangeness and beauty. There Nature, low comedienne, plays her tricks on man. Though she has put him forth as her highest product, it appears that she has fashioned him with what seems almost incredible carelessness and indexterity. One-sided and without balance, with his two halves unequally fashioned and joined, must he ever jog his eccentric way. The snow falls, the darkness caps it, and the ridiculous man-biped strays in accurate circles until he succumbs in the ruins of his defective architecture.

In the throat of the thirsty the snow is vitriol. In appearance as plausible as the breakfast food of the angels, it is as hot in the mouth as ginger, increasing the pangs of the water-famished. It is a derivative from water, air, and some cold, uncanny fire from which the caloric has been extracted. Good has been said of it; even the poets, crazed by its spell and shivering in their attics under its touch, have indited permanent melodies commemorative of its beauty.

Still, to the saddest overcoated optimist it is a plague – a corroding plague that Pharaoh successfully side-stepped. It beneficently covers the wheat fields, swelling the crop – and the Flour Trust gets us by the throat like a sudden quinsy. It spreads the tail of its white kirtle over the red seams of the rugged north – and the Alaskan short story is born. Etiolated perfidy, it shelters the mountain traveler burrowing from the icy air – and, melting to-morrow, drowns his brother in the valley below.

At its worst it is lock and key and crucible, and the wand of Circe. When it corrals man in lonely ranches, mountain cabins, and forest huts, the snow makes apes and tigers of the hardiest. It turns the bosoms of weaker ones to glass, their tongues to infants' rattles, their hearts to lawlessness and spleen. It is not all from the isolation; the snow is not merely a blockader; it is a Chemical Test. It is a good man who can show a reaction that is not chiefly composed of a drachm or two of potash and magnesia, with traces of Adam, Ananias, Nebuchadnezzar, and the fretful porcupine.

This is no story, you say; well, let it begin.

There was a knock at the door (is the opening not full of context and reminiscence oh, best buyers of best sellers?).

We drew the latch, and in stumbled Etienne Girod (as he afterward named himself). But just then he was no more than a worm struggling for life, enveloped in a killing white chrysalis.

We dug down through snow, overcoats, mufflers, and waterproofs, and dragged forth a living thing with a Van Dyck beard and marvelous diamond rings. We put it through the approved curriculum of snow-rubbing, hot milk, and teaspoonful doses of whiskey, working him up to a graduating class entitled to a diploma of three fingers of rye in half a glassful of hot water. One of the ranch boys had already come from the quarters at Ross's bugle-like yell and kicked the stranger's staggering pony to some sheltered corral where beasts were entertained.

Let a paragraphic biography of Girod intervene.

Etienne was an opera singer originally, we gathered; but adversity and the snow had made him non compos vocis. The adversity consisted of the stranded San Salvador Opera Company, a period of hotel second-story work, and then a career as a professional palmist, jumping from town to town. For, like other professional palmists, every time he worked the Heart Line too strongly he immediately moved along the Line of Least Resistance. Though Etienne did not confide this to us, we surmised that he had moved out into the dusk about twenty minutes ahead of a constable, and had thus encountered the snow. In his most sacred blue language he dilated upon the subject of snow; for Etienne was Paris-born and loved the snow with the same passion that an orchid does.

"Mee-ser-rhable!" commented Etienne, and took another three fingers.

"Complete, cast-iron, pussy-footed, blank ... blank!" said Ross, and followed suit.

"Rotten," said I.

The cook said nothing. He stood in the door weighing our outburst; and insistently from behind that frozen visage I got two messages (via the M. A. M. wireless). One was that George considered our vituperation against the snow childish; the other was that George did not love Dagoes. Inasmuch as Etienne was a Frenchman, I concluded I had the message wrong. So I queried the other: "Bright eyes, you don't really mean Dagoes, do you?" and over the wireless came three deathly, psychic taps: "Yes." Then I reflected that to George all foreigners were probably "Dagoes." I had once known another camp cook who had thought Mons., Sig., and Millie (Trans-Mississippi for Mlle.) were Italian given names; this cook used to marvel therefore at the paucity of Neo-Roman precognomens, and therefore why not –

I have said that snow is a test of men. For one day, two days, Etienne stood at the window, Fletcherizing his finger nails and shrieking and moaning at the monotony. To me, Etienne was just about as unbearable as the snow; and so, seeking relief. I went out on the second day to look at my horse, slipped on a stone, broke my collarbone, and thereafter underwent not the snow test, but the test of flat-on-the-back. A test that comes once too often for any man to stand.

However, I bore up cheerfully. I was now merely a spectator, and from my couch in the big room I could lie and watch the human interplay with that detached, impassive, impersonal feeling which French writers tell us is so valuable to the litterateur, and American writers to the faro-dealer.

"I shall go crazy in this abominable, mee-ser-rhable place!" was Etienne's constant prediction.

"Never knew Mark Twain to bore me before," said Ross, over and over. He sat by the other window, hour after hour, a box of Pittsburg stogies of the length, strength, and odor of a Pittsburg graft scandal deposited on one side of him, and "Roughing It," "The Jumping Frog," and "Life on the Mississippi" on the other. For every chapter he lit a new stogy, puffing furiously. This in time, gave him a recurrent premonition of cramps, gastritis, smoker's colic or whatever it is they have in Pittsburg after a too deep indulgence in graft scandals. To fend off the colic, Ross resorted time and again to Old Doctor Still's Amber-Colored U. S. A. Colic Cure. Result, after forty-eight hours – nerves.

"Positive fact I never knew Mark Twain to make me tired before. Positive fact." Ross slammed "Roughing It" on the floor. "When you're snowbound this way you want tragedy, I guess. Humor just seems to bring out all your cussedness. You read a man's poor, pitiful attempts to be funny and it makes you so nervous you want to tear the book up, get out your bandana, and have a good, long cry."

At the other end of the room, the Frenchman took his finger nails out of his mouth long enough to exclaim: "Humor! Humor at such a time as thees! My God, I shall go crazy in thees abominable –"

"Supper," announced George.

These meals were not the meals of Rabelais who said, "the great God makes the planets and we make the platters neat." By that time, the ranch-house meals were not affairs of gusto; they were mental distraction, not bodily provender. What they were to be later shall never be forgotten by Ross or me or Etienne.

After supper, the stogies and finger nails began again. My shoulder ached wretchedly, and with half-closed eyes I tried to forget it by watching the deft movements of the stolid cook.

Suddenly I saw him cock his ear, like a dog. Then, with a swift step, he moved to the door, threw it open, and stood there.

The rest of us had heard nothing.

"What is it, George?" asked Ross.

The cook reached out his hand into the darkness alongside the jamb. With careful precision he prodded something. Then he made one careful step into the snow. His back muscles bulged a little under the arms as he stooped and lightly lifted a burden. Another step inside the door, which he shut methodically behind him, and he dumped the burden at a safe distance from the fire.

He stood up and fixed us with a solemn eye. None of us moved under that Orphic suspense until, "A woman," remarked George.

Miss Willie Adams was her name. Vocation, school-teacher. Present avocation, getting lost in the snow. Age, yum-yum (the Persian for twenty). Take to the woods if you would describe Miss Adams. A willow for grace; a hickory for fibre; a birch for the clear whiteness of her skin; for eyes, the blue sky seen through treetops; the silk in cocoons for her hair; her voice, the murmur of the evening June wind in the leaves; her mouth, the berries of the wintergreen; fingers as light as ferns; her toe as small as a deer track. General impression upon the dazed beholder – you could not see the forest for the trees.

Psychology, with a capital P and the foot of a lynx, at this juncture stalks into the ranch house. Three men, a cook, a pretty young woman – all snowbound. Count me out of it, as I did not count, anyway. I never did, with women. Count the cook out, if you like. But note the effect upon Ross and Etienne Girod.

Ross dumped Mark Twain in a trunk and locked the trunk. Also, he discarded the Pittsburg scandals. Also, he shaved off a three days' beard.

Etienne, being French, began on the beard first. He pomaded it, from a little tube of grease Hongroise in his vest pocket. He combed it with a little aluminum comb from the same vest pocket. He trimmed it with manicure scissors from the same vest pocket. His light and Gallic spirits underwent a sudden, miraculous change. He hummed a blithe San Salvador Opera Company tune; he grinned, smirked, bowed, pirouetted, twiddled, twaddled, twisted, and tooralooed. Gayly, the notorious troubadour, could not have equalled Etienne.

Ross's method of advance was brusque, domineering. "Little woman," he said, "you're welcome here!" – and with what he thought subtle double meaning – "welcome to stay here as long as you like, snow or no snow."

Miss Adams thanked him a little wildly, some of the wintergreen berries creeping into the birch bark. She looked around hurriedly as if seeking escape. But there was none, save the kitchen and the room allotted her. She made an excuse and disappeared into her own room.

Later I, feigning sleep, heard the following:

"Mees Adams, I was almost to perish – die of monotony w'en your fair and beautiful face appear in thees mee-ser-rhable house." I opened my starboard eye. The beard was being curled furiously around a finger, the Svengali eye was rolling, the chair was being hunched closer to the school-teacher's. "I am French – you see – temperamental – nervous! I cannot endure thees dull hours in thees ranch house; but – a woman comes! Ah!" The shoulders gave nine 'rahs and a tiger. "What a difference! All is light and gay; ever'ting smile w'en you smile. You have 'eart, beauty, grace. My 'eart comes back to me w'en I feel your 'eart. So!" He laid his hand upon his vest pocket. From this vantage point he suddenly snatched at the school-teacher's own hand, "Ah! Mees Adams, if I could only tell you how I ad –"

"Dinner," remarked George. He was standing just behind the Frenchman's ear. His eyes looked straight into the school-teacher's eyes. After thirty seconds of survey, his lips moved, deep in the flinty, frozen maelstrom of his face: "Dinner," he concluded, "will be ready in two minutes."

Miss Adams jumped to her feet, relieved. "I must get ready for dinner," she said brightly, and went into her room.

Ross came in fifteen minutes late. After the dishes had been cleaned away, I waited until a propitious time when the room was temporarily ours alone, and told him what had happened.

He became so excited that he lit a stogy without thinking. "Yeller-hided, unwashed, palm-readin' skunk," he said under his breath. "I'll shoot him full o' holes if he don't watch out – talkin' that way to my wife!"

I gave a jump that set my collarbone back another week. "Your wife!" I gasped.

"Well, I mean to make her that," he announced.

The air in the ranch house the rest of that day was tense with pent-up emotions, oh, best buyers of best sellers.

Ross watched Miss Adams as a hawk does a hen; he watched Etienne as a hawk does a scarecrow, Etienne watched Miss Adams as a weasel does a henhouse. He paid no attention to Ross.

The condition of Miss Adams, in the role of sought-after, was feverish. Lately escaped from the agony and long torture of the white cold, where for hours Nature had kept the little school-teacher's vision locked in and turned upon herself, nobody knows through what profound feminine introspections she had gone. Now, suddenly cast among men, instead of finding relief and security, she beheld herself plunged anew into other discomforts. Even in her own room she could hear the loud voices of her imposed suitors. "I'll blow you full o' holes!" shouted Ross. "Witnesses," shrieked Etienne, waving his hand at the cook and me. She could not have known the previous harassed condition of the men, fretting under indoor conditions. All she knew was, that where she had expected the frank freemasonry of the West, she found the subtle tangle of two men's minds, bent upon exacting whatever romance there might be in her situation.

She tried to dodge Ross and the Frenchman by spells of nursing me. They also came over to help nurse. This combination aroused such a natural state of invalid cussedness on my part that they were all forced to retire. Once she did manage to whisper: "I am so worried here. I don't know what to do."

To which I replied, gently, hitching up my shoulder, that I was a hunch-savant and that the Eighth House under this sign, the Moon being in Virgo, showed that everything would turn out all right.

But twenty minutes later I saw Etienne reading her palm and felt that perhaps I might have to recast her horoscope, and try for a dark man coming with a bundle.

Toward sunset, Etienne left the house for a few moments and Ross, who had been sitting taciturn and morose, having unlocked Mark Twain, made another dash. It was typical Ross talk.

He stood in front of her and looked down majestically at that cool and perfect spot where Miss Adams' forehead met the neat part in her fragrant hair. First, however, he cast a desperate glance at me. I was in a profound slumber.

"Little woman," he began, "it's certainly tough for a man like me to see you bothered this way. You" – gulp – "you have been alone in this world too long. You need a protector. I might say that at a time like this you need a protector the worst kind – a protector who would take a three-ring delight in smashing the saffron-colored kisser off of any yeller-skinned skunk that made himself obnoxious to you. Hem. Hem. I am a lonely man, Miss Adams. I have so far had to carry on my life without the" – gulp – "sweet radiance" – gulp – "of a woman around the house. I feel especially doggoned lonely at a time like this, when I am pretty near locoed from havin' to stall indoors, and hence it was with delight I welcomed your first appearance in this here shack. Since then I have been packed jam full of more different kinds of feelings, ornery, mean, dizzy, and superb, than has fallen my way in years."

Miss Adams made a useless movement toward escape. The Ross chin stuck firm. "I don't want to annoy you, Miss Adams, but, by heck, if it comes to that you'll have to be annoyed. And I'll have to have my say. This palm-ticklin' slob of a Frenchman ought to be kicked off the place and if you'll say the word, off he goes. But I don't want to do the wrong thing. You've got to show a preference. I'm gettin' around to the point, Miss – Miss Willie, in my own brick fashion. I've stood about all I can stand these last two days and somethin's got to happen. The suspense hereabouts is enough to hang a sheepherder. Miss Willie" – he lassooed her hand by main force – "just say the word. You need somebody to take your part all your life long. Will you mar –"

"Supper," remarked George, tersely, from the kitchen door.

Miss Adams hurried away.

Ross turned angrily. "You –"

"I have been revolving it in my head," said George.

He brought the coffee pot forward heavily. Then bravely the big platter of pork and beans. Then somberly the potatoes. Then profoundly the biscuits. "I have been revolving it in my mind. There ain't no use waitin' any longer for Swengalley. Might as well eat now."

From my excellent vantage-point on the couch I watched the progress of that meal. Ross, muddled, glowering, disappointed; Etienne, eternally blandishing, attentive, ogling; Miss Adams, nervous, picking at her food, hesitant about answering questions, almost hysterical; now and then the solid, flitting shadow of the cook, passing behind their backs like a Dreadnaught in a fog.

I used to own a clock which gurgled in its throat three minutes before it struck the hour. I know, therefore, the slow freight of anticipation. For I have awakened at three in the morning, heard the clock gurgle, and waited those three minutes for the three strokes I knew were to come. Alors. In Ross's ranch house that night the slow freight of Climax whistled in the distance.

Etienne began it after supper. Miss Adams had suddenly displayed a lively interest in the kitchen layout and I could see her in there, chatting brightly at George – not with him – the while he ducked his head and rattled his pans.

"My fren'," said Etienne, exhaling a large cloud from his cigarette and patting Ross lightly on the shoulder with a bediamonded hand which, hung limp from a yard or more of bony arm, "I see I mus' be frank with you. Firs', because we are rivals; second, because you take these matters so serious. I – I am Frenchman. I love the women" – he threw back his curls, bared his yellow teeth, and blew an unsavory kiss toward the kitchen. "It is, I suppose, a trait of my nation. All Frenchmen love the women – pretty women. Now, look: Here I am!" He spread out his arms. "Cold outside! I detes' the col-l-l! Snow! I abominate the mees-ser-rhable snow! Two men! This –" pointing to me – "an' this!" Pointing to' Ross. "I am distracted! For two whole days I stan' at the window an' tear my 'air! I am nervous, upset, pr-r-ro-foun'ly distress inside my 'ead! An' suddenly – be'old! A woman, a nice, pretty, charming, innocen' young woman! I, naturally, rejoice. I become myself again – gay, light-'earted, 'appy. I address myself to mademoiselle; it passes the time. That, m'sieu', is wot the women are for – pass the time! Entertainment – like the music, like the wine!"

"They appeal to the mood, the caprice, the temperamen'. To play with thees woman, follow her through her humor, pursue her – ah! that is the mos' delightful way to sen' the hours about their business."

Ross banged the table. "Shut up, you miserable yeller pup!" he roared. "I object to your pursuin' anything or anybody in my house. Now, you listen to me, you –" He picked up the box of stogies and used it on the table as an emphasizer. The noise of it awoke the attention of the girl in the kitchen. Unheeded, she crept into the room. "I don't know anything about your French ways of lovemakin' an' I don't care. In my section of the country, it's the best man wins. And I'm the best man here, and don't you forget it! This girl's goin' to be mine. There ain't g'oing to be any playing, or philandering, or palm reading about it. I've made up my mind I'll have this girl, and that settles it. My word is the law in this neck o' the woods. She's mine, and as soon as she says she's mine, you pull out." The box made one final, tremendous punctuation point.

Etienne's bravado was unruffled. "Ah! that is no way to win a woman," he smiled, easily. "I make prophecy you will never win 'er that way. No. Not thees woman. She mus' be played along an' then keessed, this charming, delicious little creature. One kees! An' then you 'ave her." Again he displayed his unpleasant teeth. "I make you a bet I will kees her –"

As a cheerful chronicler of deeds done well, it joys me to relate that the hand which fell upon Etienne's amorous lips was not his own. There was one sudden sound, as of a mule kicking a lath fence, and then – through the swinging doors of oblivion for Etienne.

I had seen this blow delivered. It was an aloof, unstudied, almost absent-minded affair. I had thought the cook was rehearsing the proper method of turning a flapjack.

Silently, lost in thought, he stood there scratching his head. Then he began rolling down his sleeves.

"You'd better get your things on, Miss, and we'll get out of here," he decided. "Wrap up warm."

I heard her heave a little sigh of relief as she went to get her cloak, sweater, and hat.

Ross jumped to his feet, and said: "George, what are you goin' to do?"

George, who had been headed in my direction, slowly swivelled around and faced his employer. "Bein' a camp cook, I ain't over-burdened with hosses," George enlightened us. "Therefore, I am going to try to borrow this feller's here."

For the first time in four days my soul gave a genuine cheer. "If it's for Lochinvar purposes, go as far as you like," I said, grandly.

The cook studied me a moment, as if trying to find an insult in my words. "No," he replied. "It's for mine and the young lady's purposes, and we'll go only three miles – to Hicksville. Now let me tell you somethin', Ross." Suddenly I was confronted with the cook's chunky back and I heard a low, curt, carrying voice shoot through the room at my host. George had wheeled just as Ross started to speak. "You're nutty. That's what's the matter with you. You can't stand the snow. You're getting nervouser, and nuttier every day. That and this Dago" – he jerked a thumb at the half-dead Frenchman in the corner – "has got you to the point where I thought I better horn in. I got to revolving it around in my mind and I seen if somethin' wasn't done, and done soon, there'd be murder around here and maybe" – his head gave an imperceptible list toward the girl's room – "worse."

He stopped, but he held up a stubby finger to keep any one else from speaking. Then he plowed slowly through the drift of his ideas. "About this here woman. I know you, Ross, and I know what you reely think about women. If she hadn't happened in here durin' this here snow, you'd never have given two thoughts to the whole woman question. Likewise, when the storm clears, and you and the boys go hustlin' out, this here whole business 'll clear out of your head and you won't think of a skirt again until Kingdom Come. Just because o' this snow here, don't forget you're living in the selfsame world you was in four days ago. And you're the same man, too. Now, what's the use o' getting all snarled up over four days of stickin' in the house? That there's what I been revolvin' in my mind and this here's the decision I've come to."

He plodded to the door and shouted to one of the ranch hands to saddle my horse.

Ross lit a stogy and stood thoughtful in the middle of the room. Then he began: "I've a durn good notion, George, to knock your confounded head off and throw you into that snowbank, if –"

"You're wrong, mister. That ain't a durned good notion you've got. It's durned bad. Look here!" He pointed steadily out of doors until we were both forced to follow his finger. "You're in here for more'n a week yet." After allowing this fact to sink in, he barked out at Ross: "Can you cook?" Then at me: "Can you cook?" Then he looked at the wreck of Etienne and sniffed.

There was an embarrassing silence as Ross and I thought solemnly of a foodless week.

"If you just use hoss sense," concluded George, "and don't go for to hurt my feelin's, all I want to do is to take this young gal down to Hicksville; and then I'll head back here and cook fer you."

The horse and Miss Adams arrived simultaneously, both of them very serious and quiet. The horse because he knew what he had before him in that weather; the girl because of what she had left behind.

Then all at once I awoke to a realization of what the cook was doing. "My God, man!" I cried, "aren't you afraid to go out in that snow?"

Behind my back I heard Ross mutter, "Not him."

George lifted the girl daintily up behind the saddle, drew on his gloves, put his foot in the stirrup, and turned to inspect me leisurely.

As I passed slowly in his review, I saw in my mind's eye the algebraic equation of Snow, the equals sign, and the answer in the man before me.

"Snow is my last name," said George. He swung into the saddle and they started cautiously out into the darkening swirl of fresh new currency just issuing from the Snowdrop Mint. The girl, to keep her place, clung happily to the sturdy figure of the camp cook.

I brought three things away from Ross Curtis's ranch house – yes, four. One was the appreciation of snow, which I have so humbly tried here to render; (2) was a collarbone, of which I am extra careful; (3) was a memory of what it is to eat very extremely bad food for a week; and (4) was the cause of (3) a little note delivered at the end of the week and hand-painted in blue pencil on a sheet of meat paper.

"I cannot come back there to that there job. Mrs. Snow say no, George. I been revolvin' it in my mind; considerin' circumstances she's right."

THE SPARROWS
IN MADISON SQUARE

THE YOUNG MAN in straitened circumstances who comes to New York City to enter literature has but one thing to do, provided he has studied carefully his field in advance. He must go straight to Madison Square, write an article about the sparrows there, and sell it to the *Sun* for $15.

I cannot recall either a novel or a story dealing with the popular theme of the young writer from the provinces who comes to the metropolis to win fame and fortune with his pen in which the hero does not get his start that way. It does seem strange that some author, in casting about for startlingly original plots, has not hit upon the idea of having his hero write about the bluebirds in Union Square and sell it to the *Herald*. But a search through the files of metropolitan fiction counts up overwhelmingly for the sparrows and the old Garden Square, and the *Sun* always writes the check.

Of course it is easy to understand why this first city venture of the budding author is always successful. He is primed by necessity to a superlative effort; mid the iron and stone and marble of the roaring city he has found this spot of singing birds and green grass and trees; every tender sentiment in his nature is baffling with the sweet pain of homesickness; his genius is aroused as it never may be again; the birds chirp, the tree branches sway, the noise of wheels is forgotten; he writes with his soul in his pen – and he sells it to the *Sun* for $15.

I had read of this custom during many years before I came to New York. When my friends were using their strongest arguments to dissuade me from coming, I only smiled serenely. They did not know of that sparrow graft I had up my sleeve.

When I arrived in New York, and the car took me straight from the ferry up Twenty-third Street to Madison Square, I could hear that $15 check rustling in my inside pocket.

I obtained lodging at an unhyphenated hostelry, and the next morning I was on a bench in Madison Square almost by the time the sparrows were awake. Their melodious chirping, the benignant spring foliage of the noble trees and the clean, fragrant grass reminded me so potently of the old farm I had left that tears almost came into my eyes.

Then, all in a moment, I felt my inspiration. The brave, piercing notes of those cheerful small birds formed a keynote to a wonderful, light, fanciful song of hope and joy and altruism. Like myself, they were creatures with hearts pitched to the tune of woods and fields; as I was, so were they captives by circumstance in the discordant, dull city – yet with how much grace and glee they bore the restraint!

And then the early morning people began to pass through the square to their work – sullen people, with sidelong glances and glum faces, hurrying, hurrying, hurrying. And I got my theme cut out clear from the bird notes, and wrought it into a lesson, and a poem, and a carnival dance, and a lullaby; and then translated it all into prose and began to write.

For two hours my pencil traveled over my pad with scarcely a rest. Then I went to the little room I had rented for two days, and there I cut it to half, and then mailed it, white-hot, to the *Sun*.

The next morning I was up by daylight and spent two cents of my capital for a paper. If the word "sparrow" was in it I was unable to find it. I took it up to my room and spread it out on the bed and went over it, column by column. Something was wrong.

Three hours afterward the postman brought me a large envelope containing my MS. and a piece of inexpensive paper, about 3 inches by 4 – I suppose some of you have seen them – upon which was written in violet ink, "With the *Sun's* thanks."

I went over to the square and sat upon a bench. No; I did not think it necessary to eat any breakfast that morning. The confounded pests of sparrows were making the square hideous with their idiotic "cheep, cheep." I never saw birds so persistently noisy, impudent, and disagreeable in all my life.

By this time, according to all traditions, I should have been standing in the office of the editor of the *Sun*. That personage – a tall, grave, white-haired man – would strike a silver bell as he grasped my hand and wiped a suspicious moisture from his glasses.

"Mr. McChesney," he would be saying when a subordinate appeared, "this is Mr. Henry, the young man who sent in that exquisite gem about the sparrows in Madison Square. You may give him a desk at once. Your salary, sir, will be $80 a week, to begin with."

This was what I had been led to expect by all writers who have evolved romances of literary New York.

Something was decidedly wrong with tradition. I could not assume the blame, so I fixed it upon the sparrows. I began to hate them with intensity and heat.

At that moment an individual wearing an excess of whiskers, two hats, and a pestilential air slid into the seat beside me.

"Say, Willie," he muttered cajolingly, "could you cough up a dime out of your coffers for a cup of coffee this morning?"

"I'm lung-weary, my friend," said I. "The best I can do is three cents."

"And you look like a gentleman, too," said he. "What brung you down? – boozer?"

"Birds," I said fiercely. "The brown-throated songsters carolling songs of hope and cheer to weary man toiling amid the city's dust and din. The little feathered couriers from the meadows and woods chirping sweetly to us of blue skies and flowering fields. The confounded little squint-eyed nuisances yawping like a flock of steam pianos, and stuffing themselves like aldermen with grass seeds and bugs, while a man sits on a bench and goes without his breakfast. Yes, sir, birds! look at them!"

As I spoke I picked up a dead tree branch that lay by the bench, and hurled it with all my force into a close congregation of the sparrows on the grass. The flock flew to the trees with a babel of shrill cries; but two of them remained prostrate upon the turf.

In a moment my unsavory friend had leaped over the row of benches and secured the fluttering victims, which he thrust hurriedly into his pockets. Then he beckoned me with a dirty forefinger.

"Come on, cully," he said hoarsely. "You're in on the feed."

Thank you very much!

Weakly I followed my dingy acquaintance. He led me away from the park down a side street and through a crack in a fence into a vacant lot where some excavating had been going on. Behind a pile of old stones and lumber he paused, and took out his birds.

"I got matches," said he. "You got any paper to start a fire with?"

I drew forth my manuscript story of the sparrows, and offered it for burnt sacrifice. There were old planks, splinters, and chips for our fire. My frowsy friend produced from some interior of his frayed clothing half a loaf of bread, pepper, and salt.

In ten minutes each of us was holding a sparrow spitted upon a stick over the leaping flames.

"Say," said my fellow bivouacker, "this ain't so bad when a fellow's hungry. It reminds me of when I struck New York first – about fifteen years ago. I come in from the West to see if I could get a job on a newspaper. I hit the Madison Square Park the first mornin' after, and was sitting around on the benches. I noticed the sparrows chirpin', and the grass and trees so nice and green that I thought I was back in the country again. Then I got some papers out of my pocket, and –"

"I know," I interrupted. "You sent it to the *Sun* and got $15."

"Say," said my friend, suspiciously, "you seem to know a good deal. Where was you? I went to sleep on the bench there, in the sun, and somebody touched me for every cent I had – $15."

THE WHIRLIGIG OF LIFE

JUSTICE-OF-THE-PEACE Benaja Widdup sat in the door of his office smoking his elder-stem pipe. Halfway to the zenith the Cumberland range rose blue-gray in the afternoon haze. A speckled hen swaggered down the main street of the "settlement," cackling foolishly.

Up the road came a sound of creaking axles, and then a slow cloud of dust, and then a bull-cart bearing Ransie Bilbro and his wife. The cart stopped at the Justice's door, and the two climbed down. Ransie was a narrow six feet of sallow brown skin and yellow hair. The imperturbability of the mountains hung upon him like a suit of armor. The woman was calicoed, angled, snuff-brushed, and weary with unknown desires. Through it all gleamed a faint protest of cheated youth unconscious of its loss.

The Justice of the Peace slipped his feet into his shoes, for the sake of dignity, and moved to let them enter.

"We-all," said the woman, in a voice like the wind blowing through pine boughs, "wants a divo'ce." She looked at Ransie to see if he noted any flaw or ambiguity or evasion or partiality or self-partisanship in her statement of their business.

"A divo'ce," repeated Ransie, with a solemn Dod. "We-all can't git along together nohow. It's lonesome enough fur to live in the mount'ins when a man and a woman keers fur one another. But when she's a-spittin' like a wildcat or a-sullenin' like a hoot-owl in the cabin, a man ain't got no call to live with her."

"When he's a no-'count varmint," said the woman, "without any especial warmth, a-traipsin' along of scalawags and moonshiners and a-layin' on his back pizen 'ith co'n whiskey, and a-pesterin' folks with a pack o' hungry, triflin' houn's to feed!"

"When she keeps a-throwin' skillet lids," came Ransie's antiphony, "and slings b'ilin' water on the best coon-dog in the Cumberlands, and sets herself agin' cookin' a man's victuals, and keeps him awake o' nights accusin' him of a sight of doin's!"

"When he's al'ays a-fightin' the revenues, and gits a hard name in the mount'ins fur a mean man, who's gwine to be able fur to sleep o' nights?"

The Justice of the Peace stirred deliberately to his duties. He placed his one chair and a wooden stool for his petitioners. He opened his book of statutes on the table and scanned the index. Presently he wiped his spectacles and shifted his inkstand.

"The law and the statutes," said he, "air silent on the subjeck of divo'ce as fur as the jurisdiction of this co't air concerned. But, accordin' to equity and the Constitution and the golden rule, it's a bad barg'in that can't run both ways. If a justice of the peace can marry a couple, it's plain that he is bound to be able to divo'ce 'em. This here office will issue a decree of divo'ce and abide by the decision of the Supreme Co't to hold it good."

Ransie Bilbro drew a small tobacco-bag from his trousers pocket. Out of this he shook upon the table a five-dollar note. "Sold a b'arskin and two foxes fur that," he remarked. "It's all the money we got."

"The regular price of a divo'ce in this co't," said the Justice, "air five dollars." He stuffed the bill into the pocket of his homespun vest with a deceptive air of indifference. With much bodily toil and mental travail he wrote the decree upon half a sheet of foolscap, and then copied it upon the other. Ransie Bilbro and his wife listened to his reading of the document that was to give them freedom:

"Know all men by these presents that Ransie Bilbro and his wife, Ariela Bilbro, this day personally appeared before me and promises that hereinafter they will neither love, honor, nor obey each other, neither for better nor worse, being of sound mind and body, and accept summons for divorce according to the peace and dignity of the State. Herein fail not, so help you God. Benaja Widdup, justice of the peace in and for the county of Piedmont, State of Tennessee."

The Justice was about to hand one of the documents to Ransie. The voice of Ariela delayed the transfer. Both men looked at her. Their dull masculinity was confronted by something sudden and unexpected in the woman.

"Judge, don't you give him that air paper yit. 'Tain't all settled, nohow. I got to have my rights first. I got to have my ali-money. 'Tain't no kind of a way to do fur a man to divo'ce his wife 'thout her havin' a cent fur to do with. I'm a-layin' off to be a-goin' up to brother Ed's up on Hogback Mount'in. I'm bound fur to hev a pa'r of shoes and some snuff and things besides. Ef Rance kin affo'd a divo'ce, let him pay me ali-money."

Ransie Bilbro was stricken to dumb perplexity. There had been no previous hint of alimony. Women were always bringing up startling and unlooked-for issues.

Justice Benaja Widdup felt that the point demanded judicial decision. The authorities were also silent on the subject of alimony. But the woman's feet were bare. The trail to Hogback Mountain was steep and flinty.

"Ariela Bilbro," he asked, in official tones, "how much did you 'low would be good and sufficient ali-money in the case befo' the co't."

"I 'lowed," she answered, "fur the shoes and all, to say five dollars. That ain't much fur ali-money, but I reckon that'll git me to up brother Ed's."

"The amount," said the Justice, "air not onreasonable. Ransie Bilbro, you air ordered by the co't to pay the plaintiff the sum of five dollars befo' the decree of divo'ce air issued."

"I hain't no mo' money," breathed Ransie, heavily. "I done paid you all I had."

"Otherwise," said the Justice, looking severely over his spectacles, "you air in contempt of co't."

"I reckon if you gimme till to-morrow," pleaded the husband, "I mout be able to rake or scrape it up somewhars. I never looked for to be a-payin' no alimoney."

"The case air adjourned," said Benaja Widdup, "till to-morrow, when you-all will present yo'selves and obey the order of the co't. Followin' of which the decrees of divo'ce will be delivered." He sat down in the door and began to loosen a shoestring.

"We mout as well go down to Uncle Ziah's," decided Ransie, "and spend the night." He climbed into the cart on one side, and Ariela climbed in on the other. Obeying the flap of his rope, the little red bull slowly came around on a tack, and the cart crawled away in the nimbus arising from its wheels.

Justice-of-the-peace Benaja Widdup smoked his elder-stem pipe. Late in the afternoon he got his weekly paper, and read it until the twilight dimmed its lines. Then he lit the tallow candle on his table, and read until the moon rose, marking the time for supper. He lived in the double log cabin on the slope near the girdled poplar. Going home to supper he crossed a little branch darkened by a laurel thicket. The dark figure of a man stepped from the laurels and pointed a rifle at his breast. His hat was pulled down low, and something covered most of his face.

"I want yo' money," said the figure, "'thout any talk. I'm gettin' nervous, and my finger's a-wabblin' on this here trigger."

"I've only got f-f-five dollars," said the Justice, producing it from his vest pocket.

"Roll it up," came the order, "and stick it in the end of this here gun-bar'l."

The bill was crisp and new. Even fingers that were clumsy and trembling found little difficulty in making a spill of it and inserting it (this with less ease) into the muzzle of the rifle.

"Now I reckon you kin be goin' along," said the robber.

The Justice lingered not on his way.

The next day came the little red bull, drawing the cart to the office door. Justice Benaja Widdup had his shoes on, for he was expecting the visit. In his presence Ransie Bilbro handed to his wife a five-dollar bill. The official's eye sharply viewed it. It seemed to curl up as though it had been rolled and inserted into the end of a gun-barrel. But the Justice refrained from comment. It is true that other bills might be inclined to curl. He handed each one a decree of divorce. Each stood awkwardly silent, slowly folding the guarantee of freedom. The woman cast a shy glance full of constraint at Ransie.

"I reckon you'll be goin' back up to the cabin," she said, "along 'ith the bull-cart. There's bread in the tin box settin' on the shelf. I put the bacon in the b'ilin'-pot to keep the hounds from gittin' it. Don't forget to wind the clock to-night."

"You air a-goin' to your brother Ed's?" asked Ransie, with fine unconcern.

"I was 'lowin' to get along up thar afore night. I ain't sayin' as they'll pester theyselves any to make me welcome, but I hain't nowhar else fur to go. It's a right smart ways, and I reckon I better be goin'. I'll be a-sayin' good-bye, Ranse – that is, if you keer fur to say so."

"I don't know as anybody's a hound dog," said Ransie, in a martyr's voice, "fur to not want to say good-bye – 'less you air so anxious to git away that you don't want me to say it."

Ariela was silent. She folded the five-dollar bill and her decree carefully, and placed them in the bosom of her dress. Benaja Widdup watched the money disappear with mournful eyes behind his spectacles.

And then with his next words he achieved rank (as his thoughts ran) with either the great crowd of the world's sympathizers or the little crowd of its great financiers.

"Be kind o' lonesome in the old cabin to-night, Ranse," he said.

Ransie Bilbro stared out at the Cumberlands, clear blue now in the sunlight. He did not look at Ariela.

"I 'low it might be lonesome," he said; "but when folks gits mad and wants a divo'ce, you can't make folks stay."

"There's others wanted a divo'ce," said Ariela, speaking to the wooden stool. "Besides, nobody don't want nobody to stay."

"Nobody never said they didn't."

"Nobody never said they did. I reckon I better start on now to brother Ed's."

"Nobody can't wind that old clock."

"Want me to go back along 'ith you in the cart and wind it fur you, Ranse?"

The mountaineer's countenance was proof against emotion. But he reached out a big hand and enclosed Ariela's thin brown one. Her soul peeped out once through her impassive face, hallowing it.

"Them hounds shan't pester you no more," said Ransie. "I reckon I been mean and low down. You wind that clock, Ariela."

"My heart hit's in that cabin, Ranse," she whispered, "along 'ith you. I ai'nt a-goin' to git mad no more. Le's be startin', Ranse, so's we kin git home by sundown." Justice-of-the-peace Benaja Widdup interposed as they started for the door, forgetting his presence.

"In the name of the State of Tennessee," he said, "I forbid you-all to be a-defyin' of its laws and statutes. This co't is mo' than willin' and full of joy to see the clouds of discord and misunderstandin' rollin' away from two lovin' hearts, but it air the duty of the co't to p'eserve the morals and integrity of the State. The co't reminds you that you air no longer man and wife, but air divo'ced by regular decree, and as such air not entitled to the benefits and 'purtenances of the mattermonal estate."

Ariela caught Ransie's arm. Did those words mean that she must lose him now when they had just learned the lesson of life?

"But the co't air prepared," went on the Justice, "fur to remove the disabilities set up by the decree of divo'ce. The co't air on hand to perform the solemn ceremony of marri'ge, thus fixin' things up and enablin' the parties in the case to resume the honor'ble and elevatin' state of mattermony which they desires. The fee fur performin' said ceremony will be, in this case, to wit, five dollars."

Ariela caught the gleam of promise in his words. Swiftly her hand went to her bosom. Freely as an alighting dove the bill fluttered to the Justice's table. Her sallow cheek colored as she stood hand in hand with Ransie and listened to the reuniting words.

Ransie helped her into the cart, and climbed in beside her. The little red bull turned once more, and they set out, hand-clasped, for the mountains.

Justice-of-the-peace Benaja Widdup sat in his door and took off his shoes. Once again he fingered the bill tucked down in his vest pocket. Once again he smoked his elder-stem pipe. Once again the speckled hen swaggered down the main street of the "settlement," cackling foolishly.

TICTOCQ: THE GREAT FRENCH DETECTIVE, IN AUSTIN

A Successful Political Intrigue

CHAPTER I

IT IS NOT generally known that Tictocq, the famous French detective, was in Austin [Texas] last week. He registered at the Avenue Hotel under an assumed name, and his quiet and reserved manners singled him out at once for one not to be singled out.

No one knows why he came to Austin, but to one or two he vouchsafed the information that his mission was an important one from the French Government.

One report is that the French Minister of State has discovered an old statute among the laws of the empire, resulting from a treaty between the Emperor Charlemagne and Governor Roberts which expressly provides for the north gate of the Capital grounds being kept open, but this is merely a conjecture.

Last Wednesday afternoon a well-dressed gentleman knocked at the door of Tictocq's room in the hotel.

The detective opened the door.

"Monsieur Tictocq, I believe," said the gentleman.

"You will see on the register that I sign my name Q. X. Jones," said Tictocq, "and gentlemen would understand that I wish to be known as such. If you do not like being referred to as no gentleman, I will give you satisfaction any time after July 1st, and fight Steve O'Donnell, John McDonald, and Ignatius Donnelly in the meantime if you desire."

"I do not mind it in the least," said the gentleman. "In fact, I am accustomed to it. I am Chairman of the Democratic Executive Committee, Platform No. 2, and I have a friend in trouble. I knew you were Tictocq from your resemblance to yourself."

"Entrez vous," said the detective.

The gentleman entered and was handed a chair.

"I am a man of few words," said Tictocq. "I will help your friend if possible. Our countries are great friends. We have given you Lafayette and French fried potatoes. You have given us California champagne and – taken back Ward McAllister. State your case."

"I will be very brief," said the visitor. "In room No. 76 in this hotel is stopping a prominent Populist Candidate. He is alone. Last night someone stole his socks. They cannot be found. If they are not recovered, his party will attribute their loss to the Democracy. They will make great capital of the burglary, although I am sure it was not a political move at all. The socks must be recovered. You are the only man that can do it." Tictocq bowed.

"Am I to have carte blanche to question every person connected with the hotel?"

"The proprietor has already been spoken to. Everything and everybody is at your service." Tictocq consulted his watch.

"Come to this room tomorrow afternoon at 6 o'clock with the landlord, the Populist Candidate, and any other witnesses elected from both parties, and I will return the socks."

"Bien, Monsieur; schlafen sic wohl."

"Au revoir."

The Chairman of the Democratic Executive Committee, Platform No. 2, bowed courteously and withdrew.

* * *

Tictocq sent for the bell boy.

"Did you go to room 76 last night?"

"Yes, sir."

"Who was there?"

"An old hayseed what come on the 7:25."

"What did he want?"

"The bouncer."

"What for?"

"To put the light out."

"Did you take anything while in the room?"

"No, he didn't ask me."

"What is your name?"

"Jim"

"You can go."

CHAPTER II

The drawing-rooms of one of the most magnificent private residences in Austin are a blaze of lights. Carriages line the streets in front, and from gate to doorway is spread a velvet carpet, on which the delicate feet of the guests may tread. The occasion is the entrée into society of one of the fairest buds in the City of the Violet Crown. The rooms are filled with the culture, the beauty, the youth and fashion of society. Austin society is acknowledged to be the wittiest, the most select, and the highest bred to be found southwest of Kansas City.

Mrs. Rutabaga St. Vitus, the hostess, is accustomed to draw around her a circle of talent, and beauty, rarely equaled anywhere. Her evenings come nearer approaching the dignity of a salon than any occasion, except, perhaps, a Tony Faust and Marguerite reception at the Iron Front. Miss St. Vitus, whose advent into society's maze was heralded by such an auspicious display of hospitality, is a slender brunette, with large, lustrous eyes, a winning smile, and a charming ingénue manner. She wears a china silk, cut princesse, with diamond ornaments, and a couple of towels inserted in the back to conceal prominence of shoulder blades. She is chatting easily and naturally on a plush covered tête-à-tête with Harold St. Clair, the agent for a Minneapolis pants company. Her friend and schoolmate, Elsie Hicks, who married three drummers in one day, a week or two before, and won a wager of two dozen bottles of Budweiser from the handsome and talented young hack-driver, Bum Smithers, is promenading in and out the low French windows with Ethelbert Windup, the popular young candidate for hide inspector, whose name is familiar to every one who reads police court reports.

Somewhere, concealed by shrubbery, a band is playing, and during the pauses in conversation, onions can be smelt frying in the kitchen. Happy laughter rings out from ruby lips, handsome faces grow tender as they bend over white necks and drooping heads, timid eyes convey things that lips dare not speak, and beneath silken bodice and broadcloth, hearts beat time to the sweet notes of "Love's Young Dream."

"And where have you been for some time past, you recreant cavalier?" say Miss St. Vitus to Harold St. Clair. "Have you been worshipping at another shrine? Are you recreant to your whilom friends? Speak, Sir Knight, and defend yourself."

"Oh, come off," says Harold, in his deep, musical baritone. "I've been having a devil of a time fitting pants on a lot of bow-legged jays from the cotton-patch. Got knobs on their legs, some of 'em big as gourds, and all expect a fit. Did you every try to measure a bow-legged – I mean – can't you imagine what a jam-swizzled time I have getting pants to fit 'em? Business dull too, nobody wants 'em over three dollars."

"You witty boy," says Miss St. Vitus. "Just as full on bon mots and clever sayings as ever. What do you take now?"

"Oh, beer."

"Give me your arm and let's go into the drawing-room and draw a cork. I'm chewing a little cotton myself."

Arm in arm, the handsome couple pass across the room, the cynosure of all eyes. Luderic Hetherington, the rising and gifted night watchman at the Lone Star slaughter house, and Mabel Grubb, the daughter of the millionaire owner of the Humped-Back Camel Saloon, are standing under the oleanders as they go by.

"She is very beautiful," says Luderic.

"Rats," says Mabel.

A keen observer would have noted all this time the figure of a solitary man who seemed to avoid company but by adroit changing of his position, and perfectly cool and self-possessed manner, avoiding drawing any especial attention to himself.

The lion of the evening is Herr Professor Ludwig von Bum, the pianist. He had been found drinking beer in a saloon on East Pecan Street by Colonel St. Vitus about a week before, and according the Austin custom in such cases, was invited home by the colonel, and the next day accepted into society, with large music classes at his service. Professor von Bum is playing the lovely symphony in G minor from Beethoven's "Songs Without Music." The grand chords fill the room with exquisite harmony. He plays the extremely difficult passages in the obbligato home run in a masterly manner, and when he finishes with that grand te deum with arpeggios on the side, there is that complete hush in the room that is dearer to the artist's heart than the loudest applause. The professor looks around. The room is empty. Empty with the exception of Tictocq, the great French detective, who springs from behind a mass of tropical plants to his side. The professor rises in alarm.

"Hush," says Tictocq. "Make no noise at all. You have already made enough." Footsteps are heard outside.

"Be quick," says Tictocq. "Give me those socks. There is not a moment to spare."

"Vas sagst du?"

"Ah, he confesses," says Tictocq. "No socks will do but those you carried off from the Populist Candidate's room."

The company is returning, no longer hearing the music. Tictocq hesitates not. He seizes the professor, throws him upon the floor, tears off his shoes and socks, and escapes with the latter through the open window into the garden.

CHAPTER III

Tictocq's room in the Avenue Hotel. A knock is heard at the door. Tictocq opens it and looks at his watch.

"Ah," he says, "it is just six. Entrez, Messieurs." The messieurs entrez. There are seven of them; the Populist Candidate who is there by invitation, not knowing for what purpose; the Chairman of the Democratic Executive Committee, Platform No. 2; the hotel proprietor; and three or four Democrats and Populists, as near as could be found out.

"I don't know," begins the Populist Candidate, "what in the h –"

"Excuse me," say Tictocq, firmly. "You will oblige me by keeping silent until I make my report. I have been employed in this case, and I have unraveled it. For the honor of France I request that I be heard with attention."

"Certainly," says the Chairman, "we will be pleased to listen."

Tictocq stands in the center of the room. The electric light burns brightly above him. He seems the incarnation of alertness, vigor, cleverness, and cunning. The company seat themselves in chairs along the wall.

"When informed of the robbery," begins Tictocq, "I first questioned the bell boy. He knew nothing. I went to the police headquarters. They knew nothing.

"I invited one of them to the bar to drink. He said there used to be a little boy in the Tenth Ward who stole things and kept them for recovery by the police, but failed to be at the place agreed upon for arrest one time, and had been sent to jail.

"I then begin to think. I reasoned. No man, said I, would carry a Populist's socks in his pocket without wrapping them up. He would not want to do so in the hotel. He would want a paper. Where would be get one? At the Statesman office, of course. I went there. A young man with his hair combed down on his forehead sat behind the desk. I knew he was writing society items, for a young lady's slipper, a piece of cake, a fan, a half emptied bottle of cocktail, a bunch of roses, and a police whistle lay on the desk before him.

"'Can you tell me if a man purchased a paper here in the last three months?' I said.

"'Yes,' he replied, 'we sold one last night.'

"'Can you describe the man?'

"'Accurately. He had blue whiskers, a wart between his shoulder blades, a touch of colic, and an occupation tax on his breath.'

"'Which way did he go?'

"'Out.'

"I then went –"

"Wait a minute," said the Populist Candidate, rising. "I don't see why in the h –"

"Once more I must beg that you will be silent," said Tictocq, rather sharply. "You should not interrupt me in the midst of my report."

"I made one false arrest," continued Tictocq. "I was passing two finely dressed gentlemen on the street, when one of them remarked that he had 'stole his socks.' I handcuffed him and dragged him into a lighted store, when his companion explained to me that he was somewhat intoxicated and his tongue was not entirely manageable. He had been speaking of some business transaction, and what he intended to say was that he had 'sold his stocks.'

"I then released him.

"An hour afterward I passed a saloon, and saw this Professor von Bum drinking beer at a table. I knew him in Paris. I said 'here is my man.' He worshipped Wagner, lived on limburger cheese, beer, and credit, and would have stolen anybody's socks. I shadowed him to the reception at Colonel St. Vitus's, and in an opportune moment I seized him and tore the socks from his feet. There they are." With a dramatic gesture, Tictocq threw a pair of dingy socks upon the table, folded his arms, and threw back his head. With a loud cry of rage, the Populist Candidate sprang once more to his feet.

"God darn it! I WILL say what I want to. I –"

The other two Populists in the room gazed at him coldly and sternly.

"Is this tale true?" they demanded of the Candidate.

"No, by gosh, it ain't!" he replied, pointing a trembling finger at the Democratic Chairman. "There stands the man who has concocted the whole scheme. It is an infernal, unfair political trick to lose votes for our party. How far has this thing gone?" he added, turning savagely to the detective.

"All the newspapers have my written report on the matter, and the Statesman will have it in plate matter next week," said Tictocq, complacently.

"All is lost!" said the Populists, turning toward the door.

"For God's sake, my friends." pleaded the Candidate, following them. "Listen to me. I swear before high heaven that I never wore a pair of socks in my life. It is all a devilish campaign lie." The Populists turn their backs.

"The damage is already done," they said. "The people have heard the story. You have yet time to withdraw decently before the race." All left the room except Tictocq and the Democrats.

"Let's all go down and open a bottle of fizz on the Finance Committee," said the Chairman of the Executive Committee, Platform No. 2.

To Him Who Waits

THE HERMIT OF the Hudson was hustling about his cave with unusual animation.

The cave was on or in the top of a little spur of the Catskills that had strayed down to the river's edge, and, not having a ferry ticket, had to stop there. The bijou mountains were densely wooded and were infested by ferocious squirrels and woodpeckers that forever menaced the summer transients. Like a badly sewn strip of white braid, a macadamized road ran between the green skirt of the hills and the foamy lace of the river's edge. A dim path wound from the comfortable road up a rocky height to the hermit's cave. One mile upstream was the Viewpoint Inn, to which summer folk from the city came; leaving cool, electric-fanned apartments that they might be driven about in burning sunshine, shrieking, in gasoline launches, by spindle-legged Modreds bearing the blankest of shields.

Train your lorgnette upon the hermit and let your eye receive the personal touch that shall endear you to the hero.

A man of forty, judging him fairly, with long hair curling at the ends, dramatic eyes, and a forked brown beard like those that were imposed upon the West some years ago by self-appointed "divine healers" who succeeded the grasshopper crop. His outward vesture appeared to be kind of gunny-sacking cut and made into a garment that would have made the fortune of a London tailor. His long, well-shaped fingers, delicate nose, and poise of manner raised him high above the class of hermits who fear water and bury money in oyster-cans in their caves in spots indicated by rude crosses chipped in the stone wall above.

The hermit's home was not altogether a cave. The cave was an addition to the hermitage, which was a rude hut made of poles daubed with clay and covered with the best quality of rust-proof zinc roofing.

In the house proper there were stone slabs for seats, a rustic bookcase made of unplaned poplar planks, and a table formed of a wooden slab laid across two upright pieces of granite – something between the furniture of a Druid temple and that of a Broadway beefsteak dungeon. Hung against the walls were skins of wild animals purchased in the vicinity of Eighth Street and University Place, New York.

The rear of the cabin merged into the cave. There the hermit cooked his meals on a rude stone hearth. With infinite patience and an old axe he had chopped natural shelves in the rocky walls. On them stood his stores of flour, bacon, lard, talcum-powder, kerosene, baking-powder, soda-mint tablets, pepper, salt, and Olivo-Cremo Emulsion for chaps and roughness of the hands and face.

The hermit had hermited there for ten years. He was an asset of the Viewpoint Inn. To its guests he was second in interest only to the Mysterious Echo in the Haunted Glen. And the Lover's Leap beat him only a few inches, flat-footed. He was known far (but not very wide, on account of the topography) as a scholar of brilliant intellect who had forsworn the world because he had been jilted in a love affair. Every Saturday night the Viewpoint Inn sent to him surreptitiously a basket of provisions. He never left the immediate outskirts of his hermitage. Guests of the inn who visited him said his store of knowledge, wit, and scintillating philosophy were simply wonderful, you know.

That summer the Viewpoint Inn was crowded with guests. So, on Saturday nights, there were extra cans of tomatoes, and sirloin steak, instead of "rounds," in the hermit's basket.

Now you have the material allegations in the case. So, make way for Romance.

Evidently the hermit expected a visitor. He carefully combed his long hair and parted his apostolic beard. When the ninety-eight-cent alarm-clock on a stone shelf announced the hour of five he picked up his gunny-sacking skirts, brushed them carefully, gathered an oaken staff, and strolled slowly into the thick woods that surrounded the hermitage.

He had not long to wait. Up the faint pathway, slippery with its carpet of pine-needles, toiled Beatrix, youngest and fairest of the famous Trenholme sisters. She was all in blue from hat to canvas pumps, varying in tint from the shade of the tinkle of a bluebell at daybreak on a spring Saturday to the deep hue of a Monday morning at nine when the washer-woman has failed to show up.

Beatrix dug her cerulean parasol deep into the pine-needles and sighed. The hermit, on the q. t., removed a grass burr from the ankle of one sandalled foot with the big toe of his other one.

She blued – and almost starched and ironed him – with her cobalt eyes.

"It must be so nice," she said in little, tremulous gasps, "to be a hermit, and have ladies climb mountains to talk to you."

The hermit folded his arms and leaned against a tree. Beatrix, with a sigh, settled down upon the mat of pine-needles like a bluebird upon her nest. The hermit followed suit; drawing his feet rather awkwardly under his gunny-sacking.

"It must be nice to be a mountain," said he, with ponderous lightness, "and have angels in blue climb up you instead of flying over you."

"Mamma had neuralgia," said Beatrix, "and went to bed, or I couldn't have come. It's dreadfully hot at that horrid old inn. But we hadn't the money to go anywhere else this summer."

"Last night," said the hermit, "I climbed to the top of that big rock above us. I could see the lights of the inn and hear a strain or two of the music when the wind was right. I imagined you moving gracefully in the arms of others to the dreamy music of the waltz amid the fragrance of flowers. Think how lonely I must have been!"

The youngest, handsomest, and poorest of the famous Trenholme sisters sighed.

"You haven't quite hit it," she said, plaintively. "I was moving gracefully at the arms of another. Mamma had one of her periodical attacks of rheumatism in both elbows and shoulders, and I had to rub them for an hour with that horrid old liniment. I hope you didn't think that smelled like flowers. You know, there were some West Point boys and a yachtload of young men from the city at last evening's weekly dance. I've known mamma to sit by an open window for three hours with one-half of her registering 85 degrees and the other half frostbitten, and never sneeze once. But just let a bunch of ineligibles come around where I am, and she'll begin to swell at the knuckles and shriek with pain. And I have to take her to her room and rub her arms. To see mamma dressed you'd be surprised to know the number of square inches of surface there are to her arms. I think it must be delightful to be a hermit. That – cassock – gabardine, isn't it? – that you wear is so becoming. Do you make it – or them – of course you must have changes – yourself? And what a blessed relief it must be to wear sandals instead of shoes! Think how we must suffer – no matter how small I buy my shoes they always pinch my toes. Oh, why can't there be lady hermits, too!"

The beautifulest and most adolescent Trenholme sister extended two slender blue ankles that ended in two enormous blue-silk bows that almost concealed two fairy Oxfords, also of one of the forty-seven shades of blue. The hermit, as if impelled by a kind of reflex-telepathic action, drew his bare toes farther beneath his gunny-sacking.

"I have heard about the romance of your life," said Miss Trenholme, softly. "They have it printed on the back of the menu card at the inn. Was she very beautiful and charming?"

"On the bills of fare!" muttered the hermit; "but what do I care for the world's babble? Yes, she was of the highest and grandest type. Then," he continued, "then I thought the world could never contain another equal to her. So I forsook it and repaired to this mountain fastness to spend the remainder of my life alone – to devote and dedicate my remaining years to her memory."

"It's grand," said Miss Trenholme, "absolutely grand. I think a hermit's life is the ideal one. No bill-collectors calling, no dressing for dinner – how I'd like to be one! But there's no such luck for me. If I don't marry this season I honestly believe mamma will force me into settlement work or trimming hats. It isn't because I'm getting old or ugly; but we haven't enough money left to butt in at any of the swell places any more. And I don't want to marry – unless it's somebody I like. That's why I'd like to be a hermit. Hermits don't ever marry, do they?"

"Hundreds of 'em," said the hermit, "when they've found the right one."

"But they're hermits," said the youngest and beautifulest, "because they've lost the right one, aren't they?"

"Because they think they have," answered the recluse, fatuously. "Wisdom comes to one in a mountain cave as well as to one in the world of 'swells,' as I believe they are called in the argot."

"When one of the 'swells' brings it to them," said Miss Trenholme. "And my folks are swells. That's the trouble. But there are so many swells at the seashore in the summer-time that we hardly amount to more than ripples. So we've had to put all our money into river and harbor appropriations. We were all girls, you know. There were four of us. I'm the only surviving one. The others have been married off. All to money. Mamma is so proud of my sisters. They send her the loveliest pen-wipers and art calendars every Christmas. I'm the only one on the market now. I'm forbidden to look at any one who hasn't money."

"But –" began the hermit.

"But, oh," said the beautifulest "of course hermits have great pots of gold and doubloons buried somewhere near three great oak-trees. They all have."

"I have not," said the hermit, regretfully.

"I'm so sorry," said Miss Trenholme. "I always thought they had. I think I must go now."

Oh, beyond question, she was the beautifulest.

"Fair lady –" began the hermit.

"I am Beatrix Trenholme – some call me Trix," she said. "You must come to the inn to see me."

"I haven't been a stone's throw from my cave in ten years," said the hermit.

"You must come to see me there," she repeated. "Any evening except Thursday."

The hermit smiled weakly.

"Good-bye," she said, gathering the folds of her pale-blue skirt. "I shall expect you. But not on Thursday evening, remember."

What an interest it would give to the future menu cards of the Viewpoint Inn to have these printed lines added to them: "Only once during the more than ten years of his lonely existence did the mountain hermit leave his famous cave. That was when he was irresistibly drawn to the inn by the fascinations of Miss Beatrix Trenholme, youngest and most beautiful of the celebrated Trenholme sisters, whose brilliant marriage to –"

Aye, to whom?

The hermit walked back to the hermitage. At the door stood Bob Binkley, his old friend and companion of the days before he had renounced the world – Bob, himself, arrayed like the orchids of the greenhouse in the summer man's polychromatic garb – Bob, the millionaire, with his fat, firm, smooth, shrewd face, his diamond rings, sparkling fob-chain, and pleated bosom. He was two years older than the hermit, and looked five years younger.

"You're Hamp Ellison, in spite of those whiskers and that going-away bathrobe," he shouted. "I read about you on the bill of fare at the inn. They've run your biography in between the cheese and 'Not Responsible for Coats and Umbrellas.' What 'd you do it for, Hamp? And ten years, too – geewhilikins!"

"You're just the same," said the hermit. "Come in and sit down. Sit on that limestone rock over there; it's softer than the granite."

"I can't understand it, old man," said Binkley. "I can see how you could give up a woman for ten years, but not ten years for a woman. Of course I know why you did it. Everybody does. Edith Carr. She jilted four or five besides you. But you were the only one who took to a hole in the ground. The others had recourse to whiskey, the Klondike, politics, and that similia similibus cure. But, say – Hamp, Edith Carr was just about the finest woman in the world – high-toned and proud and noble, and playing her ideals to win at all kinds of odds. She certainly was a crackerjack."

"After I renounced the world," said the hermit, "I never heard of her again."

"She married me," said Binkley.

The hermit leaned against the wooden walls of his ante-cave and wriggled his toes.

"I know how you feel about it," said Binkley. "What else could she do? There were her four sisters and her mother and old man Carr – you remember how he put all the money he had into dirigible balloons? Well, everything was coming down and nothing going up with 'em, as you might say. Well, I know Edith as well as you do – although I married her. I was worth a million then, but I've run it up since to between five and six. It wasn't me she wanted as much as – well, it was about like this. She had that bunch on her hands, and they had to be taken care of. Edith married me two months after you did the ground-squirrel act. I thought she liked me, too, at the time."

"And now?" inquired the recluse.

"We're better friends than ever now. She got a divorce from me two years ago. Just incompatibility. I didn't put in any defence. Well, well, well, Hamp, this is certainly a funny dugout you've built here. But you always were a hero of fiction. Seems like you'd have been the very one to strike Edith's fancy. Maybe you did – but it's the bank – roll that catches 'em, my boy – your caves and whiskers won't do it. Honestly, Hamp, don't you think you've been a darned fool?"

The hermit smiled behind his tangled beard. He was and always had been so superior to the crude and mercenary Binkley that even his vulgarities could not anger him. Moreover, his studies and meditations in his retreat had raised him far above the little vanities of the world. His little mountain-side had been almost an Olympus, over the edge of which he saw, smiling, the bolts hurled in the valleys of man below. Had his ten years of renunciation, of thought, of devotion to an ideal, of living scorn of a sordid world, been in vain? Up from the world had come to him the youngest and beautifulest – fairer than

Edith – one and three-seventh times lovelier than the seven-years-served Rachel. So the hermit smiled in his beard.

When Binkley had relieved the hermitage from the blot of his presence and the first faint star showed above the pines, the hermit got the can of baking-powder from his cupboard. He still smiled behind his beard.

There was a slight rustle in the doorway. There stood Edith Carr, with all the added beauty and stateliness and noble bearing that ten years had brought her.

She was never one to chatter. She looked at the hermit with her large, thinking, dark eyes. The hermit stood still, surprised into a pose as motionless as her own. Only his subconscious sense of the fitness of things caused him to turn the baking-powder can slowly in his hands until its red label was hidden against his bosom.

"I am stopping at the inn," said Edith, in low but clear tones. "I heard of you there. I told myself that I must see you. I want to ask your forgiveness. I sold my happiness for money. There were others to be provided for – but that does not excuse me. I just wanted to see you and ask your forgiveness. You have lived here ten years, they tell me, cherishing my memory! I was blind, Hampton. I could not see then that all the money in the world cannot weigh in the scales against a faithful heart. If – but it is too late now, of course."

Her assertion was a question clothed as best it could be in a loving woman's pride. But through the thin disguise the hermit saw easily that his lady had come back to him – if he chose. He had won a golden crown – if it pleased him to take it. The reward of his decade of faithfulness was ready for his hand – if he desired to stretch it forth.

For the space of one minute the old enchantment shone upon him with a reflected radiance. And then by turns he felt the manly sensations of indignation at having been discarded, and of repugnance at having been – as it were – sought again. And last of all – how strange that it should have come at last! – the pale-blue vision of the beautifulest of the Trenholme sisters illuminated his mind's eye and left him without a waver.

"It is too late," he said, in deep tones, pressing the baking-powder can against his heart.

Once she turned after she had gone slowly twenty yards down the path. The hermit had begun to twist the lid off his can, but he hid it again under his sacking robe. He could see her great eyes shining sadly through the twilight; but he stood inflexible in the doorway of his shack and made no sign.

Just as the moon rose on Thursday evening the hermit was seized by the world-madness.

Up from the inn, fainter than the horns of elf-land, came now and then a few bars of music played by the casino band. The Hudson was broadened by the night into an illimitable sea – those lights, dimly seen on its opposite shore, were not beacons for prosaic trolley-lines, but low-set stars millions of miles away. The waters in front of the inn were gay with fireflies – or were they motor-boats, smelling of gasoline and oil? Once the hermit had known these things and had sported with Amaryllis in the shade of the red-and-white-striped awnings. But for ten years he had turned a heedless ear to these far-off echoes of a frivolous world. But to-night there was something wrong.

The casino band was playing a waltz – a waltz. What a fool he had been to tear deliberately ten years of his life from the calendar of existence for one who had given him up for the false joys that wealth – "tum ti tum ti tum ti" – how did that waltz go? But those years had not been sacrificed – had they not brought him the star and pearl of all the world, the youngest and beautifulest of –

"But do not come on Thursday evening," she had insisted. Perhaps by now she would be moving slowly and gracefully to the strains of that waltz, held closely by West-Pointers or city commuters, while he, who had read in her eyes things that had recompensed him for ten lost years of life, moped like some wild animal in its mountain den. Why should –.

"Damn it," said the hermit, suddenly, "I'll do it!"

He threw down his Marcus Aurelius and threw off his gunny-sack toga. he dragged a dust-covered trunk from a corner of the cave, and with difficulty wrenched open its lid.

Candles he had in plenty, and the cave was soon aglow. Clothes – ten years old in cut – scissors, razors, hats, shoes, all his discarded attire and belongings, were dragged ruthlessly from their renunciatory rest and strewn about in painful disorder.

A pair of scissors soon reduced his beard sufficiently for the dulled razors to perform approximately their office. Cutting his own hair was beyond the hermit's skill. So he only combed and brushed it backward as smoothly as he could. Charity forbids us to consider the heartburnings and exertions of one so long removed from haberdashery and society.

At the last the hermit went to an inner corner of his cave and began to dig in the soft earth with a long iron spoon. Out of the cavity he thus made he drew a tin can, and out of the can three thousand dollars in bills, tightly rolled and wrapped in oiled silk. He was a real hermit, as this may assure you.

You may take a brief look at him as he hastens down the little mountain-side. A long, wrinkled black frock-coat reached to his calves. White duck trousers, unacquainted with the tailor's goose, a pink shirt, white standing collar with brilliant blue butterfly tie, and buttoned congress gaiters. But think, sir and madam – ten years! From beneath a narrow-brimmed straw hat with a striped band flowed his hair. Seeing him, with all your shrewdness you could not have guessed him. You would have said that he played Hamlet – or the tuba – or pinochle – you would never have laid your hand on your heart and said: "He is a hermit who lived ten years in a cave for love of one lady – to win another."

The dancing pavilion extended above the waters of the river. Gay lanterns and frosted electric globes shed a soft glamor within it. A hundred ladies and gentlemen from the inn and summer cottages flitted in and about it. To the left of the dusty roadway down which the hermit had tramped were the inn and grill-room. Something seemed to be on there, too. The windows were brilliantly lighted, and music was playing – music different from the two-steps and waltzes of the casino band.

A negro man wearing a white jacket came through the iron gate, with its immense granite posts and wrought-iron lamp-holders.

"What is going on here to-night?" asked the hermit.

"Well, sah," said the servitor, "dey is having de reg'lar Thursday-evenin' dance in de casino. And in de grill-room dere's a beefsteak dinner, sah."

The hermit glanced up at the inn on the hillside whence burst suddenly a triumphant strain of splendid harmony.

"And up there," said he, "they are playing Mendelssohn – what is going on up there?"

"Up in de inn," said the dusky one, "dey is a weddin' goin' on. Mr. Binkley, a mighty rich man, am marryin' Miss Trenholme, sah – de young lady who am quite de belle of de place, sah."